# *The Wolf l* 
# *Fate*
## *The Royals Of Presley Acres:*
## *Book 2*

### Roxie Ray
### © 2023
### **Disclaimer**

This is a work of fiction. Names, places, characters, and events are all fictitious for the reader's pleasure. Any similarities to real people, places, events, living or dead are all coincidental.

**This book contains sexually explicit content that is intended for ADULTS ONLY (+18).**

# Contents

# Chapter 1 - Ty

I stood next to my sleek black car, eyes glued to the glowing screen of my phone, oblivious to the world around me.

*Dead people can't tell tales. Keep that in mind, Alpha.*

Fucking Castro. Before I could throw the phone in anger at the bastard's words, movement from the house ahead caught my attention. A uniformed police officer emerged from the entrance, his footsteps thumping on the sidewalk as he steadily approached.

He gracefully ducked under the tape. "Alpha Keller, sir?" he inquired, a hint of authority in his voice.

The scorching sun beat down on the back of my neck as I listened to the police officer attempt to update me on the situation. Behind him, a black gurney was being carried from the house, a black body bag strapped to it, and the paramedics wheeled it to the waiting ambulance.

It seemed like time slowed as I tracked its path. The bitter taste of betrayal filled my mouth. It had been her all along. I'd never had such a strong desire to be proven wrong. It was difficult to accept that someone from my own pack could commit such a heinous act, but I knew Nico wasn't wrong. He'd shown me the emails from Castro. She'd been the traitor all along, and Castro had tied up the loose string. Dead men, or women in this case, told no tales.

Cecily Banks. She'd been right under our fucking noses the whole time. I'd known she'd a nasty side to her, a jealous streak a mile wide. That jealous, nasty streak had only worsened after I matched with Liza, but I never would've imagined that Cecily would join forces with the likes of Castro. My mind moved through the scenarios that had confused us, like when Liza had been photographed outside the farmer's market. With Castro in hiding, we'd come to the obvious conclusion that he had someone inside Presley Acres working for him. Never in my wildest dreams would I have believed Cecily to be the culprit.

My damn mind was reeling over the whole fucking ordeal.

I tried to focus on what the officer was saying to me, but the cacophony of thoughts raging in my head drowned him out. If Cecily had been Castro's mole, who had killed her? Would Castro have risked coming into town to tie up loose ends, or did he have someone else on speed dial ready to do his dirty work? Who could it be? Now that Cecily's betrayal had been uncovered, no one in the pack was above suspicion.

I was so lost in thought that I hadn't noticed Officer Hayes, a young shifter who worked for the local police, join us.

He reached forward to shake my hand. "Alpha Keller, once we've finished gathering evidence, you'll be free to begin your search of the residence." His words snapped me back to reality, making me realize how little attention I'd been paying. With everything going on, I couldn't afford to be distracted. I had to stay alert.

I nodded in understanding. As the alpha, I had the right to conduct my own investigation because Cecily was part of my pack. A conniving, traitorous bitch, but still technically under my charge. She might not have done right by me and my mate, but I'd fulfill my obligation to her.

I offered him a strained smile. "Thanks, Hayes."

My phone rang, and when I checked the screen, Dad's name popped up. "Excuse me." I held up a finger and moved away to answer the call. "Dad, what's up?"

"Ty, what the hell is going on? Nico just told me he discovered emails and texts between Cecily and Castro. That they're pretty incriminating." Dad's voice was laced with anger and concern. "Now I'm hearing Cecily's dead. Possibly murdered. Is she truly... gone?" He was quiet for a brief moment, then cleared his throat. "Any sightings of Castro?"

I stared at the asphalt and rubbed the tight muscles in my neck. "It's true, and the texts and emails aren't the worst of it. It looks like Cecily was working for Castro. No sightings of him in person that I've heard of, but from what we can gather, she was the one that left his scavenger hunt clues, took photos of Liza, essentially doing his dirty work for him here in town." I bit those last words out, pissed at myself for having not seen what seemed obvious now.

"Son of a..." he muttered under his breath. "I'm on my way."

"Thanks, Dad. See you soon." I ended the call and stepped back to the officer, who was waiting quietly. "My father is on his way and will join me shortly."

He nodded. "Very well, Alpha Keller. We'll let you know when we're finished in the house."

"Thank you." I smiled weakly.

I stood, leaning against my car, sunglasses on, and watched as the police traipsed in and out of Cecily's house. Some chatted casually, others spoke into their radios or wrote on their notepads. As I observed the activity, it became clear that there was a distinct lack of anything substantial for the police to find. I found myself impatient to gain entry to conduct my own search.

Finally, Hayes approached me again. I removed my sunglasses. "Hayes, how did you get on?"

"Alpha Keller." His frustration rolled off him. "To be honest, sir, it would be easier to tell you what we haven't found. Her phone isn't in the residence. No fibers. No latent prints, bodily fluids, or hairs apart from Ms. Banks's own." He glanced over at the house before returning his gaze to mine. "Maybe once the autopsy is complete, we'll have something, but for the moment, that's all I can tell you. We've concluded our investigation, so I can pass the property off to you."

I shook his hand. "Thank you. If I come across anything, I'll let you know."

I watched as he strolled to his vehicle. The sound of doors slamming shut echoed through the empty street, followed by the low rumble of engines when the police cruisers pulled away. As the last cars vanished, the neighbors emerged and stared at the crime scene, clustering into small groups. They whispered to each other in low murmurs beyond my range of hearing. Every so often, they'd cast looks in my direction.

I waited until Dad showed up before going inside the house. When he eventually arrived and got out of his car, his face was a portrait of barely contained fury. He glanced at the yellow tape surrounding Cecily's house and shook his head. "This is not a good look for the pack, Ty."

"Tell me about it." I gestured toward the neighbors who had stopped talking and were now looking at us. I could only imagine what they were assuming had happened that would require the pack alpha and the retired alpha, and how fast wild rumors would travel through Presley Acres. "Let's go inside and see what we can find."

We entered the house, which was a testament to Cecily's taste for luxury. The floors, made of polished marble, shone under our feet, and expensive artwork adorned the walls. The appearance of the place was misleading. It was so innocuous, it was hard to believe a traitor had lived here, but I couldn't deny the incriminating evidence.

"I'm assuming you've already seen the exchanges Nico found?" Dad asked as we methodically searched through drawers and closets.

"I saw them." I scanned the contents of a dresser drawer I'd spilled open. "The police mentioned that they didn't find Cecily's phone. We should look for it. She was never off that thing."

"Agreed." Dad continued to search, his movements methodical and precise.

Despite our best efforts, we came up empty-handed. Frustration gnawed at my insides like a hungry beast. Just as we were about to give up, I vaguely remembered the police mentioning the housekeeper, Mrs. Griffiths. My instincts told me that speaking to her was crucial.

"The police said Cecily's housekeeper was the one who found her. We need to talk with her." Hopefully, she hadn't gone far after the cops had questioned her.

Dad nodded in agreement, and we went to the backyard to the guest house. On our approach, I could see movement behind the curtains.

I knocked on the door. At first, I wasn't sure whoever was inside would answer, so I knocked again, louder. Eventually, a middle-aged woman with a trembling lower lip—I assumed she was the housekeeper—answered the door. Recognition flashed in her eyes as she caught sight of her alpha. I could tell she was shaken by the day's events. Who wouldn't be on edge after finding their employer dead?

"Alpha Keller, Beta Keller," she greeted us, her voice quivering. "I have shared all the information I have with the police."

As her eyes darted between the two of us, I sensed her pulse quicken to a subtle staccato beat. She was lying, or at least holding back from telling the full truth.

"Please, Mrs. Griffiths." I rested my hand briefly on her shoulder and looked directly into her eyes to convey the urgency in my voice. "We need you to be honest with us if we want to find out what happened to Cecily. You have to tell us everything, so we can catch her killer. I understand you're trying to protect your employer, your friend, but by doing so, you are also protecting her killer. Did you notice anything out of the ordinary? Not just today but in recent weeks? Anything you share will help." And then to emphasize, "We need to make sure there are no secrets, not if we want to learn the truth."

The woman looked nervous, and she hesitated for a moment, but she finally spoke. "Cecily received deliveries every week."

I raised an eyebrow. "What kind of deliveries?"

Her eyes darted between us. "The kind you'd expect someone to get from an admirer: exotic flowers, candy, expensive perfume. The packages were always accompanied by a note, though I never read them."

"Who were the packages from?" Dad crossed his arms, and I held my breath, hoping she could tell us exactly what we needed to hear.

"I have no clue. There was no return address on the boxes, and Cecily never talked about them... at least not to me. I did find it strange that she did not express excitement or happiness over the lavish gifts, and instead always appeared annoyed."

"Did she receive a package today?" I narrowed my eyes at the housekeeper, paying close attention to her physical responses. If she lied or withheld information, I'd pick up on it.

"Today wasn't any different." The housekeeper stood, clearly uneasy, her fingers fidgeting with a crumpled tissue. "Cecily received a box of bonbons this morning, and as usual, whatever was in the note upset her, but it didn't stop her eating the entire box while grumbling about men being frightened of commitment, and that they're worthless pieces of shit. But then she started getting sick. She vomited several times, and when I tried to call for help, she stopped me and insisted she was fine."

"Go on," I said, hoping she'd divulge whatever she hadn't told the police.

"But she wasn't fine," the housekeeper said, tears streaming down her cheeks. "She went to lie down, and I heard choking sounds coming from her room. I rushed in and found her convulsing on the bed. Her face was pale, her lips blue. I knew it wasn't good. That's when I called nine-one-one."

Cold fury settled within me. I suspected the autopsy would reveal the cause of Cecily's death, and I had a strong hunch it was the bonbons. Castro had killed her, poisoned her as a warning to our pack. I would have bet my life on it. It calmed one of my fears. Castro had managed this on his own, albeit from a distance. I wasn't looking for another snake in the pack.

I grabbed Dad's arm and pulled him to the side, out of earshot of the housekeeper. "Castro killed Cecily. There's no doubt in my mind. The candy was poisoned."

Dad nodded in agreement. "That sounds like something Castro would do, the sick fuck."

I returned my attention to the housekeeper. "Thank you for telling us. For your honesty."

"Actually." She paused, her breath hitching as she reached into her pocket and pulled out a phone. "This is Cecily's. I used it to call nine-one-one. I put it in my pocket after I called. Then, with everything that happened, I forgot about it until the police asked. I felt uneasy about giving it to them. Cecily always had such a tight grip on her private life, so I wanted to avoid getting in trouble for giving something away I shouldn't have. Working for her was challenging. She wasn't an easy employer. She instilled a healthy level of fear in me and held my job over my head most days. I didn't want to cross her, even in death. But you're right, Alpha, there should be no secrets."

"Thank you." I took the phone from her trembling hands. "You've helped us immensely."

She nodded, tears flowing down her cheeks.

"Your loyalty does you credit. You've done a great service to us today." My gaze softened, concern furrowing my brow. Even though we had much bigger fish to fry, with a little prompting, the woman had proven to be loyal to the pack. "Do you need anything? Anything at all?"

"No, Alpha. I'll be okay." Despite the slight waver in her voice, she forced a small grin.

With a last nod to the housekeeper, Dad and I left the guest house. Her loyalty had been both humbling and sobering in equal measure. I made a mental note to have a pack member check in on the poor woman. It wouldn't hurt to ask around, see if anyone was looking to employ someone with her experience. It was the least we could do.

As we walked back to our vehicles, I thought about what to do with Cecily's phone. I'd have to hand it over to the police, but I'd rather it was sanitized before it got to them. Without an informant to do the work for me, I'd have to improvise. I wasn't tech savvy enough to remove all traces of communication between Cecily and Castro without obliterating everything on the device. Thankfully, I knew who could do it. My business partner, Bryce Fulton, worked closely with the IT department at Keller Industries, knew what he was doing, and I could trust him.

"Dad, before we head to visit with her parents, I need to swing by the house. We can have a look through Cecily's phone there. I'm going to message Bryce to come over and delete the exchanges with Castro before we hand it over to the police. I don't want them involved."

Dad gave me that look that told me he wasn't pleased. "Haven't you got an informant who can do that? I thought Nico left you with a list of potential candidates?"

I was a grown man, but just one look from my father, and I felt like a teenager all over again. "I know. I just haven't had time to go through the list and schedule interviews. There don't seem to be enough hours in the day anymore. Castro's had us running from pillar to post."

"You need to get that sorted, son. An alpha needs an informant to keep the pack running smoothly." He sighed in resignation. "Come on, let's move."

Back in my car, with Cecily's phone safely stored in my glove compartment, I glanced at the rearview mirror. My father was tailing me closely. My mind raced with thoughts on how to do damage control before rumors started flying. No doubt, word had already gotten out that Cecily had been found dead in her home, but I couldn't let the pack think it was murder. Not that I wanted to deceive them—we had already told the world about Castro—but I didn't want them living in fear over it.

As I drove, my grip on the steering wheel tightened, the leather creaking. I knew what I had to do, and it fucking sucked. This wasn't just about preserving the pack's peace of mind, it was also about honoring Cecily's memory as best I could, despite her betrayal.

I wasn't sure both were possible.

Once we pulled up at the estate, Dad and I went into my office. Together, we examined Cecily's phone.

We unlocked the phone on the first try; her password being her birthday. Among the many messages and emails, we found the same incriminating exchanges Nico had discovered, confirming Cecily had been working with Castro. It was undeniable. She was a traitor.

Staring at the damning evidence, I decided not to share the truth with Cecily's parents. At least not yet. I dropped the phone into my desk drawer and shot Bryce a text.

*Cecily's phone in top left drawer of my desk. Delete exchanges between her and Castro, make it natural, need to hand it to the police.*

Before I'd even made it to the front door, my phone beeped. As I went down the steps to the car, I checked it, and sure enough, Bryce had responded.

*No worries. On my way.*

Dad and I took my car to Cecily's parents' house. A knot formed in my stomach as I thought about what lay ahead. The police would have delivered the devastating news of their daughter's death already, but as alpha, it was my duty to pay my respects and honor the dead. Traitor or not.

"Are you ready?" Dad looked at me with concern once we got out of the car. As we made our way to the door, he clapped me on the back. "This is just part of the job, son. Not saying it ever gets easier, but I'm certain you'll find the right words."

"Ready as I'll ever be." I steeled myself for the difficult conversation ahead.

A housekeeper led us into the living room, her eyes red-rimmed from crying, confirming the police had already visited. As we stepped into the sitting room, I was immediately struck by the sight of Cecily's parents. Her mother sat straight-backed in a chair, her face pale and streaked with tears. Cecily's father stood beside her, his powerful frame shaking and struggling to contain his emotions.

It was a portrait of devastation, and one that twisted my insides like a vise. The couple's world had been torn apart, their daughter's life and their hopes and dreams for her future taken away in one fell swoop. As their only child, they'd placed Cecily on a pedestal and given her the best of everything. Sure, that meant she'd been spoiled rotten, and I couldn't stand being around the woman, but she was still their daughter, and her life had been abruptly cut short by Castro.

"Mr. and Mrs. Banks," I began. "I'm so sorry for your loss."

Her mother looked up at me, her eyes filled with such raw pain that it took all my strength to hold her gaze. "You were always so good to her, Ty," she whispered, her voice trembling. "Cecily loved you so much. We always hoped... we thought maybe one day you two would—"

"Tina," her husband interrupted gently, placing a comforting arm around her shoulders. "Now's not the time."

"I'm sorry," she choked out, dabbing at her eyes with a tissue. "It's just... she's gone, and I can't believe it. I don't understand why anyone would want to hurt her. She was such a good girl."

I could feel the weight of the damning evidence in my pocket as I clenched my fists to help maintain my composure. Telling them the truth would only bring more hurt and upset. How could I tell them their daughter had betrayed the pack and ultimately brought about her own death? They'd been through enough.

"We'll find answers." My promise to her was surprisingly steady, despite the anxiety roiling inside me. "You have my word." I offered what comfort I could, though I imagined Mrs. Banks was only forcing pleasantries. After all, she'd made it clear I'd been expected to choose Cecily as my mate. I would not apologize for choosing fate, for choosing Liza. Mrs. Banks's bitterness was evident in her glares. We made our excuses and left, eager to escape the uncomfortable situation.

Mr. Banks saw us out. "Thank you, Alpha." Behind the pain in his eyes, I saw the gratitude. "Your visit and kind words mean more than you're aware. I'm sorry about Tina. Please, she means no offense. She's taking the news hard."

"None taken, sir. If we can help, let us know." With a final nod, Dad and I took our leave, both weighed down by the information we'd left unsaid.

On our way back to the car, I asked the question I couldn't push out of my mind. "Did we do the right thing?" I didn't want to sound like a pussy who couldn't look after the affairs of his own pack, but this was a sensitive issue that needed to be handled with care.

Dad clenched his fists. "There's no simple answer, Ty. But sometimes, protecting our pack members means shielding them from the darkest truths."

We left the grieving parents and headed back to the estate. Thank fuck I had a techie on my side. Bryce would scrub the emails and messages between Cecily and Castro off her phone and the cloud, but leave the rest behind so the police wouldn't get suspicious if I handed over a completely empty phone. We'd done enough by putting Liza's history with Castro out there.

This wasn't a human issue, and I didn't want the cops digging too deeply into pack business.

I found Bryce in my office, his feet propped on my desk. I leaned against the doorframe, waiting for him to become aware of my presence, but he was too engrossed in whatever was on his laptop screen. He'd moved mine across the desk to make room for his own.

"Quite comfortable, are we?" I finally asked.

"Jesus, Ty, what the fuck? Thought you were a wolf, not a cat. Seriously, man, don't sneak up on me like that." He opened his briefcase and tossed Cecily's phone at me. "Here, oh mighty leader, cleaned and ready for the police."

"Thanks for doing this. Until I get a new informant in place, I'm kind of stuck. I don't want to go running back to Nico unless I have no other option." I lifted the phone and shook it. "You have any problems with it?"

Standing, Bryce shook his head. "No, it wasn't too difficult. She wasn't security conscious, so there were no other passcodes or anything to get in my way. Did as you asked and just cleared off the conversations between her and Castro." He looked up as he packed his computer and paperwork into his briefcase, eyes blazing with fury. "How did her parents take finding out their darling daughter was nothing more than a two-faced, scheming b—"

"Enough, Bryce." I held up my hand. "I'm not enamored by her actions, either, but she's dead. Whatever her parents are, they are grieving the loss of their daughter." I sighed. "I'd better go if I want to get this into the hands of the detective tonight. See you later?"

Before he could say anything else, I turned and went back the way I'd come.

\*\*\*

"Here." I handed the phone over to the lead investigator in charge of Cecily's case. "This belonged to Cecily. We, er, found it at her house." I didn't mention the incriminating information I'd ensured couldn't be found or traced. Nor did I dwell on the fact that this piece of plastic and metal had felt like a ticking time bomb.

"Thank you, Alpha Keller." The lead investigator nodded and took the phone from me. "We'll examine it thoroughly and be in touch if we find anything pertinent to the case."

I winced internally, knowing they wouldn't find shit. At least I didn't have to worry about humans getting involved. I didn't have time to deal with their interference.

Before leaving the police station, I pulled out my phone and dialed the coroner. It rang twice before someone answered.

"Coroner's office," a gruff voice said.

"Good evening." I tried not to sound too urgent. "This is Alpha Tyson Keller. I need to speak with the coroner regarding Cecily Jameson's case."

"Of course, Alpha Keller. Please hold," the voice said, putting me on hold.

The seconds dragged on for what felt like eternity until the line clicked and the coroner answered. "Alpha Keller, this is the coroner, Eleanor Bailey. How can I help you?"

"Good evening, Ms. Bailey. You've just received the body of one of my pack members, Cecily Banks. Listen, can I ask you please test for any toxic substances? We've been given information to suggest she may have been poisoned. Also, could you ensure I have the autopsy report first as it's vital to the pack's investigation?"

"Understood, Alpha Keller." Her tone was sympathetic and professional. "Thank you for the information. I'll ensure you're contacted as soon as the report is ready."

"Thank you. I appreciate your cooperation." With that, I ended the call and got in my car, anxious to get home to Liza and fill her in on the situation.

As soon as I walked through the door, I spotted Liza and my parents waiting in the parlor, worry etched on their faces.

"What happened?" Liza asked, searching my eyes for answers.

"Where do I even begin?" I slumped onto the loveseat next to her and recounted everything, from the housekeeper's story of the mysterious gifts Cecily received to the missing phone. Liza's shock was palpable, her eyes widening with each revelation.

"Castro did this, didn't he?" The fear in Liza's words was unmistakable.

Mother, who'd been listening closely, said, "If it was Castro, we shouldn't tell the pack. It will only cause more panic, which is the very last thing we need."

I nodded. "I agree. We need to keep this information to ourselves for now."

"Are you sure that's the best course of action?" Liza bit her lip. "Won't people suspect something is amiss?"

"Maybe," I said, rubbing the back of my neck. "But right now, it's the lesser of two evils. I don't want the pack living in fear. We need to figure out a way to spin this so the pack doesn't lose their shit."

"I'm really not sure that's the best route." Liza shifted in her seat. "I think it's better to be honest.

The more lies we try to hide, the worse it will be. Yes, Cecily is dead, and that's devastating, but she was working with our enemy. We have to tell the pack the truth."

My father sighed, nodding in agreement. "Your mate has a point, Ty. Nico showed us the proof, and there's no denying Cecily was Castro's foot soldier. She set up the scavenger hunts and is just as guilty in all this as Castro. Cecily was a traitor, and as much as it hurts to admit, she paid the ultimate price with her life."

Mom nodded. "We don't want to paint her as a horrible person, especially since her family will still remain in the pack, so we have to keep some peace between our members. But Liza's right. There are consequences for our actions and, unfortunately, Cecily's death was a result of her own terrible choices."

With our decision made, I retreated to my office to work on the speech I would deliver to the pack about the truth of Cecily's demise. It wouldn't be easy to tell them the truth, but I would have to do it. I had no choice.

My fingers rested on the keyboard while I tried to decide how best to start the solemn speech. After an hour of typing and deleting, copying and pasting, I sat back and sighed. "Damn it." I stood and paced the floor, taking a sip of water, then loosened my tie and unbuttoned my collar.

Once I was refocused, my fingers flew across the keyboard as I chose my words carefully, striving to strike a balance between honesty and reassurance. There was no need for more fear and uncertainty.

Liza entered the office, her presence a warm comfort in the midst of my turmoil. Her eyes were soft with understanding as she crossed the room and perched herself on my lap, wrapping her arms around me.

"First week as alpha and we're dealing with this crap." I rested my forehead against hers. "It's been one fucking issue after another. Hopefully, I can write a speech that keeps our pack united. I don't want our people going bat-shit crazy with fear that Castro will murder them like he did Cecily."

Liza craned her neck to look at the screen. "Is it okay if I read what you have so far?"

I nodded, watching as her eyes scanned the screen, trying to gauge her reaction, and feeling surprisingly nervous about what my mate would think of the words I'd written.

A thoughtful expression crossed her face, and she turned to me. "It's good, Ty. Honest but compassionate. The pack needs to know the truth, but they also need to know we have the strength to deal with it."

"Thanks," I said with relief. Liza's approval meant I must've struck the right tone. We couldn't change the past or bring Cecily back, but we could learn from her mistakes and ensure that our pack remained united in the face of adversity.

I looked into her eyes, thankful for her unwavering support. "Thank you, Liza. Your faith in me means more than you'll ever know."

"Of course." She lowered her head and kissed me gently. "This is horrible, but we'll get through this and anything else thrown our way."

I hoped she was right, but all I could think about was Castro kicking our asses at every turn and laughing as he watched us scramble.

# Chapter 2 - Liza

"Son of a bitch." I shoved my finger into my mouth, tasting the metallic tang of blood after slicing my finger on the edge of a printed recipe sheet. There's normal pain and then there's papercut pain. It made me think of the saying *death by a thousand papercuts*. The sharp, searing sting could easily be an effective form of torture.

I sat back and looked around at the new furniture that had been delivered a few days ago. The ergonomic seat I'd bought cost more than all the furniture I'd ever owned combined, but Ty insisted I get the best of the best. I didn't like to be wasteful, but he'd argued it would be better to buy quality furniture that would last rather than cheap stuff that would need to be replaced. Who was I to argue?

Now that Ty was alpha, his parents had moved to a smaller cottage on the Keller Estate, and we'd moved into the big house. The decision to convert one of the guest rooms so I could work from home hadn't been difficult. It would save on travel on the days I didn't have to report to the main office.

I sat at the walnut desk that overlooked the rambling backyard. I wanted to review the list of potential fall recipes I'd been working on. Pumpkin risotto with sage, a hearty beef stew infused with red wine, and an apple pecan tart were just a few of the dishes that made my mouth water at the mere thought. There was something about the shift in the air each season that put me in the mood to create new dishes that reflected the weather. Making comfort food was my favorite season, so of course, I'd have to test each recipe, sometimes multiple times. I hoped Ty wouldn't mind putting on a few pounds since I planned on cooking up a storm.

As the alpha's mate, my role within the pack had changed, and so too must my career. It wouldn't be acceptable for the alpha's wife to be seen working for pack members. I'd no longer be able to work as a private chef in other people's kitchens. Now that I held a position of power, I had a whole new set of responsibilities I needed to take care of.

Cooking had always been my passion, and the idea of giving up the business I'd worked so hard to establish didn't sit right with me. My catering company would continue to operate, though I would have more of a behind-the-scenes role rather than being directly involved.

I'd devised a plan in a way that meant I'd be able to continue doing what I loved. The kitchen in my new home—it felt surreal to call the Keller Estate home—was as spacious and well-equipped as any commercial kitchen. I'd cook from here, preparing meals that would then be delivered to my clients.

As much as my life had changed since becoming Ty's mate, including the rise in my standing within the pack, I had to maintain some semblance of stability from my old life. I wouldn't feel comfortable just sitting back idly twiddling my thumbs—that was out of the question—but I wouldn't let go of my favorite hobby, either.

This way, I'd have the best of both worlds. I'd be Liza, mate to the pack alpha, as well as Liza, chef and small businessowner.

With this plan in mind, I turned my attention from the recipes to type up an ad for an assistant chef and driver. The requirements included culinary experience, a valid driver's license, and the ability to adapt to the ever-changing demands of our clientele. My company didn't just serve typical middle-class families. As my place in society had risen, so had the status of my clients. Whoever I hired needed to provide a five-star experience because, frankly, that's what my customers expected, no matter their standing in the pack.

I read through the job description one last time, a satisfied smile tugging at the corners of my lips. After posting it on a local social media page, I sent out emails to my clients, informing them about the new arrangements. My delivery service would come at no cost to them, as I'd been the one who altered the dynamics of our relationship. Those who understood would hopefully appreciate my efforts to continue providing them with delicious meals. Those who didn't? Well, that was fine, too. If my inbox was anything to go by, there would be plenty of people who'd happily take their place.

After I hit send on the last email, I leaned back in my chair, reveling in the satisfaction of having taken control of my career. Cooking was my lifeblood, and I wouldn't let being the alpha's mate strip that away from me.

A gentle knock at the door pulled me from my thoughts. "Working hard?" Ty asked with a playful grin as he peeked through the doorway.

"Always." I gestured for him to come over, then I showed him the new menu items I'd been working on, and he leaned in so close, his breath tickled my ear. Ty's eyes sparkled with excitement, and he pretended to wipe drool from his mouth.

I laughed.

"Can't wait to try that pumpkin risotto." He pointed at the recipe on the screen. "It sounds amazing."

"Thanks, babe." I beamed. As Ty massaged my shoulders, I closed my eyes and allowed myself to enjoy the intimacy. It had been an intense forty-eight hours since we'd been informed of Cecily's death, and we'd both been on edge trying to balance our pack and business responsibilities.

"So, how was your day?" I was curious to know how the pack had responded to the news of Cecily's death.

He sank into the chair next to me with a deep sigh, and I felt the comforting warmth of his presence. "As we expected, Cecily's death has made its rounds in the pack. Rumors are flying all over the place. Her parents are devastated, which is understandable. I've been holding off on telling them about her connection with Castro, but I really don't see how I can put it off much longer."

"Wow." I shook my head as I imagined Mr. and Mrs. Banks learning that their precious Cecily was a traitor. I knew I shouldn't think ill of the dead, but Cecily deserved every nasty thought I had. "That's not going to be an easy conversation. I certainly don't envy you."

"It's going to be horrible but necessary," Ty said, resting his hand on my thigh. "It would be better if I told them privately, rather than them finding out through someone else, or reading it online. Common decency aside, if that happened, it would cause a much larger problem. Her parents are already upset about me choosing you over Cecily. They'd lose their shit if they didn't learn the truth before the rest of the pack."

"Good point. You're probably right." Their reactions worried me, but that conversation was unavoidable. Part of me wished we could sweep it all under the rug and pretend everything was fine, but that wasn't an option. "At least we haven't heard anything from Castro since they found Cecily's body," I pointed out, trying to focus on the positive.

"True." Ty nodded. "It's been one less thing to think about. I'm certain it's just a matter of time before he makes another move... especially now that we're officially mated. That will have pissed him off."

My heart raced as I thought about the possible repercussions. Ty, sensing my fear, rubbed his thumb in small circles against my thigh, trying to reassure me with his touch.

The shrill ring of Ty's phone sliced through the silence, making us both jump. Ty glanced at me. Fear twisted in my stomach, tightening my chest, and I held my breath. Was it Castro calling? Had he installed some kind of listening device? Was it possible he had some way of eavesdropping on our intimate conversations within the estate? Surely not.

Ty must have sensed my apprehension, because his hand was strong and firm on my thigh as he answered the phone and put it on speaker.

"Alpha Keller," a kind female voice greeted him. "This is Eleanor Bailey. I'm calling to discuss the results of Cecily's autopsy."

Ty's eyebrow arched, and he got to his feet. "Yes, go ahead."

"A routine postmortem doesn't routinely test for poison. With the information you provided, we discovered a lethal dose of arsenic, likely ingested. I suspect it was concealed in something Cecily had eaten. Possibly some form of confectionary, as we found undigested chocolate present alongside traces of the poison in her digestive system." She paused, giving Ty a moment to absorb the information. "It's a cruel method, Alpha, but effective."

Ty grimaced. "What a horrible way to die."

"I'll have a copy of my report sent directly to you. Please get in touch if you have any further questions."

"Thank you," Ty responded solemnly before ending the call. He turned to me. "With this information from the coroner, Nico's discovery of Castro's emails and texts, and the housekeeper's account of the mysterious treats Cecily had been receiving... it isn't hard to put two and two together." His jaw set into a tight square. "It's time to talk to Cecily's parents. They deserve to know the truth, even though it'll destroy them."

"Are you sure it's a good idea right now?" I hated questioning Ty, but after Cecily's shock death, their grief might still be too fresh.

"It's now or never." Ty stood. "I'll have to make a public statement now that I have the coroner's report. The coroner will need to give it to the police. It's only a matter of time before it's leaked. If I hold off on telling everyone, then they'll hear about it through the grapevine, and you know it won't take long for the gossip to spread round town that she didn't die of natural causes. There'll be backlash from the council and from the pack. I'm new to the role of alpha, Liza. It won't be a good look if it appears I've lost control this early."

He was right. As the alpha, he had to maintain control. There would never be a right time to tell the Bankses that not only had their daughter been murdered, but that she'd been working with Castro. She'd been a traitor to the pack. There had been no love lost between Cecily and me. She'd seen me as an obstacle standing in the way of what she believed to be her rightful position in the pack. Her parents deserved dignity. Their daughter's sins were not theirs to bear.

Sitting there, I finally realized the full impact of everything that had happened in the past few weeks. Castro's threats, not knowing who, if anyone, to trust, discovering Cecily's treachery, her murder, and now the constant unease that seemed to hang over our lives like a dark cloud as we waited for the next inevitable attack. It was all too much to bear.

My mind began racing with uncertainty. I needed something familiar, something grounding to remind me of who and where I came from. I needed my parents.

"I should go see my mom and dad." I stood and stretched, my back popping in all the right places. "Good luck with Cecily's parents. And please be careful."

Ty put his arms around me and held me close. I breathed in the faint smell of his cologne. "Don't forget to take Jamie and Robin."

I didn't want someone following me around all the time, but the situation with Castro was serious. I couldn't ignore the potential danger. Leaning back, I looked up at Ty, searching his face for any sign of doubt or hesitation. He met my gaze with steely determination, his jaw set, and his eyes locked on mine.

"Ty, I'm only going to my parents. Do I really need to take minders with me? I'm going to be in town. There will be plenty of people around."

"Liza, we've been over this. Castro will strike again. We're just waiting for it to happen. If he had Cecily working for him, it's possible he has others." The last words came out as a growl. "You need to take them with you. I need to be sure you're safe."

His words made me soften. It would take a bit of getting used to having two men following my every move. "All right."

He pulled me back into his arms. "Thank you," he said, his voice muffled in my hair.

I gave him a quick kiss on the cheek and watched as he headed upstairs to gather his thoughts in his office.

Driving through town, I only half-focused on navigating the familiar streets. My security detail, following close on my tail, was yet another symbol of my new rank. I refused to be chauffeured about, though. I was more than capable of driving to the office or my parents' home.

As I got closer to the center of town, I noticed a peculiar buzz in the air. It seemed busier than usual. A long line of people snaked out the door of the local diner. The parking lot was full, forcing other cars to park haphazardly along the side of the road, filling every available space. It wasn't exactly cause for panic, but it struck me as odd. Had I forgotten some special holiday or event?

At a red light, I pulled out my phone and checked the calendar to see if there had been a celebration I'd forgotten about, or a seasonal event downtown. There was nothing marked for today's date.

"What the hell?"

I watched as a large group of people, all strangers, crossed in front of me from one side of the street to the other. Some of them wore crimson T-shirts with an Alabama team name emblazoned across the front. Who were these people and why had they chosen to visit the small town of Presley Acres, Texas?

My mind whirled, trying to find an explanation for the increased activity. However, nothing came to me, so I decided to push my unease aside for the time being and focus on visiting my parents. The light turned green, and I ventured on. Glancing at my dashboard, I realized I'd arrive around dinner time. My parents never got upset about me showing up unannounced, but I hated interrupting their meal.

I decided I'd let my parents finish their meal in peace. I'd been meaning to swing by my office to pick up some blank recipe cards, and this seemed like the perfect time to do so. Although I typed my recipes for my personal files, if my clients asked for them, I gifted them with a handwritten copy. Yes, it was more time consuming, but it was a personal touch, and a more authentic way of passing the recipe on from my kitchen to theirs. I only had a few cards left at the estate and didn't see any reason to purchase more when I had a supply at the office.

No matter how much money I had at my disposal, it felt disrespectful to the pack, to the environment to be wasteful, so I tried to do my part. Not that a few recipe cards would save even one tree, but I'd always felt a connection to the earth and nature as a whole. Maybe it was my personality, or perhaps it had something to do with me being an omega. Either way, I wanted to be respectful of what I'd been given.

It took me a minute to open the stiff door to my office, but once I did, I stepped into a dusty, stale room that needed some care. I hadn't been in here in quite some time. Weeks of neglect had made the once-tidy space seem completely abandoned. The office at home would be great for doing the paperwork without having to drive into town, but I didn't want to sell the building. I needed to have a physical location where I could meet prospective clients and suppliers. Ty and I both agreed that it wasn't a great idea to have strangers traipsing in and out of the house. It also helped to have an address in town where all my extra supplies could be delivered.

I pulled out my phone and made a note to ask the estate staff if they could recommend a commercial cleaning service. A few months ago, I would have hired someone without a second thought. Now, though, because I was the alpha's mate, I had to be mindful of the people I conducted business with. Any potential contractor or employee would have to be questioned exhaustively, and would need to undergo an extensive background check. Gods, I hated all the extra steps I had to take now.

I sat down at my old metal desk and rummaged through the drawers. Man, the chair was really uncomfortable. I couldn't help but compare it to my new ergonomic chair and beautiful desk.

"Shit." I slammed another drawer shut as I struggled to find the elusive recipe cards. Minutes dragged on without any luck, and my frustration grew with each passing second. I started to doubt whether I even had a stack here. I must have used them already.

Just as I was about to give up, a sudden flash caught my eye. Looking up, I noticed two people standing outside the front window, their phones pressed against the glass, aimed at me. It seemed like they were snapping pictures, but that made no sense. They wore baseball caps and sunglasses, almost like they didn't want to be recognized. An uneasy feeling crept into my gut. Something about the situation didn't sit right.

My security detail, who'd been stationed outside the office, sprang into action without me having to ask. They approached the people at the window, their expressions stern and intimidating. After exchanging a few terse words, it looked like the guards persuaded the people to stop photographing me and move along. I had no clue what they'd said to them, but I was fully aware that they didn't fuck around with potential threats to the alpha or his mate.

While I appreciated their efficiency, that nagging sense of unease lingered. I had half a mind to chase them down and ask what the hell their problem was, but Jamie and Robin wouldn't have any of that. They'd tackle me to the ground if I tried to approach a potential threat, and I wasn't in the mood to get grass stains on my jeans.

Pushing my concerns aside for the moment, I gave up on my quest for the missing recipe cards and quickly used my phone to order more online—the wonders of modern technology—then headed outside to let my entourage know I was heading to my parents' house.

Robin remained close to the door while Jamie had moved over to the opposite side of the road, watching to make sure the photographers didn't return. Both shifters were tall. Robin had dark hair and a swarthy look about him. His golden eyes scanned the area with a predatory gaze, always on the lookout for any potential danger. His companion Jamie had a lighter complexion, with sandy blond hair that seemed to catch the sunlight. He stood in what seemed to be their preferred position with his arms crossed over his chest, but his expression was more relaxed and casual. Despite their differences in appearance, both men gave off an undeniable sense of strength and confidence. It was clear that they were not to be messed with.

"Robin."

He turned his gaze to me. "Yes?" He had a deep voice. I felt intimidated, and they were there to help me.

"What did the people at the window want?"

He looked across at Jamie, who shrugged. "Sorry, didn't ask, just made them delete the photos they took and got them to leave."

Still none the wiser but with a gnawing sense of unease in my gut, I let both men know my plans, locked up the office, and continued on to my parents' house, determined to enjoy a brief reprieve from the mounting stress.

When I arrived at their house, I was surprised to find the door unlocked. I walked right. The door should have been locked. Even if they were home, the door should be locked. Since Castro had come on the scene and made our shared history known as well as his deep displeasure about Ty and me, we'd all had to increase our security—my parents included.

My stomach clenched.

This could be a trap. I could walk into the kitchen and find Castro holding them at gunpoint. Luckily, before I turned tail and ran to get Robin and Jamie, I found my parents sitting down to dinner, their expressions lighting up when they caught sight of me.

"Hey, sweetheart. I didn't know you were coming to visit today." Mom pushed her chair back and rushed over to envelop me in a warm hug. "It's been too long," she chastised gently, her eyes twinkling with affection.

"Mom, why the hell is the door unlocked? You are fully aware that Castro is still at large, right?" I crossed my arms, making her pull away from me.

She waved her hand in the air and scoffed. "Liza, Ty talked us into having guards stationed outside twenty-four hours a day. He allowed them to remain in their vehicle and not have them literally standing at the door. Why in the world would I bother locking the door? That's a little overkill, don't you think?"

"Overkill?" I hung my head and covered my face with my hands. "Mom, listen to me. Castro isn't someone you can be too cautious about. Trust me when I say that he is ruthless. Please, for the love of all the gods, lock your damn door."

Mom cocked her head to the side and placed her hands on her hips. "Fine. If it means that much to you, I'll do it."

"Hey, kiddo." Dad dabbed at his mouth with a napkin, then came over to me. "How have you been holding up?"

"I can't complain too much... other than Mom leaving the bloody door unlocked for all the world's criminals to enter as they please."

Dad laughed and guided me into the dining room. Despite my side trip to the office, I'd arrived in the middle of their dinner. Their warm reception, though, had me smiling and momentarily forgetting my worries, including the unlocked door.

"Have a seat, Liza, and I'll grab you some dinner." Mom moved quickly to the kitchen, then returned with a plate full of pork chops, salad, and freshly baked dinner rolls.

My stomach growled, reminding me that I hadn't eaten in several hours. The extra adrenaline from the creepers who'd photographed me had probably lowered my blood sugar levels, because I dug in ferociously, as if I hadn't eaten in days.

Dad raised an eyebrow. "Do they not feed you at the Keller Estate?" He chuckled at his terrible joke.

As we enjoyed the delicious meal, I filled them in on my plans for the catering company. "You guys know how much I love to cook. I hadn't given too much thought to how my career path might change once Ty and I were mated, but I can't just drive around to people's houses, taking charge of their kitchens, preparing meals for their families."

"Why not?" Mom eyed me over her glass of water. "If it's what you enjoy, your security detail can follow you anywhere. Right?"

"Well, that's true. It's just not that easy now. I'm the alpha's mate. My responsibilities are to the pack. I can't spend my days dealing with suppliers, speaking with potential clients, cooking, and serving them." I grinned. "Luckily, I've figured out a solution. I'll keep doing what I love but from the privacy of the estate's kitchen. I've already carved out time each day on my calendar to cook. Plus, I'm going to hire an assistant chef. I'm hoping to find someone new and right out of culinary school. That way, I can teach them my way of doing things, and share my recipes with them."

My father nodded in approval. "Sounds like you've put a great deal of thought into it and found a compromise that suits your new position as Ty's mate. What does he think about you cooking meals out of the estate's kitchen?"

I smiled, remembering Ty's excitement over my new fall menu. "He's very supportive. Plus, he'll get to try new recipes all the time, so I doubt he'll ever complain."

Before I could delve further into the conversation, the earlier events at my office nagged at me. "Have either of you noticed anything strange going on in town?" I asked, my tone turning serious. "People lurking around or taking pictures when they shouldn't be?"

My parents exchanged glances before shaking their heads. "Can't say that we have," Mom said, her brow furrowing with concern. "Why? What happened?"

I recounted the incident at the office of the two people who had been taking photos of me without my consent. Though they agreed it was odd, neither seemed overly alarmed.

"Maybe they were just tourists," Dad suggested, trying to ease my worry.

"Perhaps," I mused, although I remained unconvinced.

Presley Acres wasn't exactly a tourist hotspot. Like one of those annoying tunes that gets stuck in your head, I couldn't quite shake it. I promised myself I'd talk to Ty about it. Even if it was nothing, it was better to err on the side of caution, especially with Castro still lurking in the shadows.

# Chapter 3 - Ty

The late morning sun cast a warm glow over the trees lining the road as we drove to Cecily's parents' house. As fall arrived, and the days shortened, the trees began to change colors. There were still some green leaves defiantly clinging to the branches, but they were now mixed with the rich tones of reds, browns, and yellows—one of nature's beauties I didn't often take time to appreciate.

Right now, I'd have given anything to stop and just enjoy the crisp fall evening air, maybe even shift, let my wolf run and play in the fallen leaves. Tempting as it was, alpha duties demanded my full attention, and I needed to talk to the Bankses before someone else told them the truth about their daughter's death.

Liza had offered to come with me for support. When she'd first suggested it, I'd hesitated. I was afraid that bringing Liza along would inflame the situation. Mr. and Mrs. Banks had been very disappointed that I hadn't chosen Cecily as my mate. The news I had to deliver would only deepen their sorrow. But I had to agree with her after she'd pointed out, quite firmly, that as the alpha's mate, it'd be expected of her to accompany me in such situations.

I stole a quick glance at Liza, her platinum blonde hair catching on the sunlight. She was so fucking beautiful. I recalled how she'd looked when she'd got into the car, the way her tight jeans molded to every curve of her ass, the simple blue shirt that clung to her every curve emphasizing her eyes. Her strength was breathtaking. Even after everything she had endured, she had become my mate with such grace. I wanted to reach over and show her my appreciation, but then I remembered we weren't alone in the car.

My father sat behind us, his presence not only a cold shower to my fantasies about Liza and her jeans, but a reminder that this wasn't a simple visit for pleasantries. My grip tightened on the steering wheel.

"Relax, Ty." He must've picked up on my anxiety. "Remember, I'm here to help soften the blow."

I nodded, appreciating his attempt to calm my nerves. His experience as a seasoned alpha would lend some stability amidst the unanswered questions that swirled around Cecily's death. This was no ordinary visit. It was a task that required finesse, empathy, and an unshakable resolve.

My dad had called me yesterday before I left to meet with the Bankses and convinced me to wait until he could come with me this evening. He'd been Cecily's parents' alpha for decades and thought his presence might make it easier for them to accept the truth.

I tried to shake it off, but the feeling of dread settled in my chest like a heavy stone. If I weren't driving, I'd have cracked my knuckles—a nervous tell I'd outgrown as a teenager. With all the stress it had made an unwelcome reappearance. It was only my second week as alpha, and I was about to deliver the most horrific news to already-grieving parents. The news would be difficult enough to hear if I was just telling them she'd been murdered, but I had to tell them the horrible truth that their daughter had chosen to align herself with an enemy of our pack.

It wasn't the most favorable part of being alpha, but it came with the position. There was no way around it, no way to delegate to anyone else. I would be expected to handle these types of situations. Pack members died all the time, and it was my duty as alpha to pay respects to the dead and show my support for the living.

There had been murders before, but thankfully, they were few. This time was different, though. The factors swirling around Cecily's death were unprecedented. We'd never had a shifter turn on the pack in such a way. No one had actively worked against the pack with an enemy the way Cecily had.

My biggest fear was their reaction. How would a parent react when told their child, their only child, was a traitor? I'd already seen their grief firsthand when I'd visited them the day she died. Would they be angry at Cecily? Would they be angry at me? As the pack's alpha, shouldn't I have realized what was happening sooner and prevented her actions—her murder? Or would they be more concerned with how the other pack members would take the news and if it might affect their status within the pack? An ugly thought, but not an unrealistic one.

The Bankses had always been concerned about status. They'd always given Cecily everything she wanted. Yes, she was spoiled and had an ugly side to her, but I imagined her parents had only wanted the best for her. They'd had high hopes for Cecily, which included marrying me, pushing us together at every opportunity, and dropping not so subtle hints. I was confident Cecily never loved me; she liked the idea of being the alpha's mate, the status it would give her. She'd have gotten over her supposed heartache at "losing" me, and she'd have met someone. Mr. and Mrs. Banks could've been planning a wedding for.

Instead, because of Cecily's choices, they were planning her funeral.

There was no way to imagine the pain of losing a child. No parent should have to go through that trauma, and no parent deserved that trauma to be worsened by the words I was about to deliver. Cecily was a traitor.

"Hey." Liza reached over the center console to grasp my hand. Her touch was a balm to my nerves, even if only for a brief moment. "You've got this. Remember, you're their alpha, and you're taking time out of your busy schedule to have a one-on-one meeting with them. I'm sure there are other alphas out there who wouldn't give a second thought to the parents of someone who'd turned their back on their pack. They'll see your kindness, even if what you tell them shatters their world."

I smiled weakly at her. That was one of the many reasons I loved her deeply. She always knew what to say to calm me down. I wasn't sure her presence and comforting words would have the same effect on Cecily's parents, though. The more I considered the consequences, the more I worried that bringing her with me might not have been the best idea. Would they see it as me rubbing salt into their already painful wounds?

I couldn't reply. There was nothing to say. I just thanked the gods they'd blessed me with such a wonderful, caring woman to share my life with. I tried to focus on the task at hand instead of dwelling on the countless potential outcomes. My only option was to tell them the truth, provide evidence, and let them react in whatever damn way they would. It was out of my control.

Liza pushed a strand of hair behind her ear and grinned sheepishly. "Since they're mourning, I thought about baking them something to bring with us, but considering their daughter was just murdered with poisoned candy, I thought better of it."

I nodded, fighting the upward curve of my lips.

From the backseat, Dad barked out a laugh. "Good call, Liza."

When we pulled up to the Banks family home—
well, it was more like a damn mansion—I tried to
remember exactly what I'd planned on saying last
night. I was up until the early hours of the morning,
pacing my office floor, working on the speech I'd have
to give to the pack, and practicing how I'd deliver the
news to Cecily's family.

"Ready?" Liza asked. She'd removed her seatbelt
and turned slightly in her seat, blue eyes searching
mine.

"Let's get this over with." I squeezed her hand one
last time and gathered myself. Then, as if we'd
rehearsed it, the three of us stepped out of the SUV as
one.

The housekeeper waited patiently at the door. Her
expression was somber but less tearful than it had
been at my last visit. She gestured for us to follow her,
our footsteps echoing in the grand hallway as she led
us through the impeccably decorated home into the
same sitting room. The grandeur of the Banks family
home was hard to ignore—a testament to their
affluence and high status within the pack.

"Please have a seat," the housekeeper murmured
before retreating and closing the door behind her,

leaving us with Tina and Robert Banks, who were seated on a plush sofa across from us. Grief marred their faces, their eyes red-rimmed.

"Mr. and Mrs. Banks." Dad's deep and booming voice seemed to fill the room. "It's good to see you both again, though I wish it was under different circumstances."

"Thank you for visiting us." Tina avoided eye contact with Dad as she fiddled with the hem of her skirt nervously. She was clearly on edge and had to be wondering what necessitated a visit by the retired alpha, as well as myself, the current alpha.

"Of course." Dad's tone was gentle yet authoritative. "I know the police informed you yesterday that Cecily had been murdered. We have new information we wanted to share with you before Ty makes an official statement to the public."

He turned to me, giving me a brief nod of encouragement.

Without hesitating, I forced myself to speak the words that would shake the foundation of the Banks's home. "I'm sorry this isn't going to be easy to hear, but we've discovered evidence that Cecily was working with Castro, the fugitive still at large. We believe he's the one who sent the poison-laced bonbons that killed her."

Tina gasped and covered her mouth. Robert jumped up, anger flashing in his eyes. "Preposterous! Why would you come into our home after our daughter has just died and make these accusations?" He scoffed, his voice laced with bitterness. "You think your so-called evidence could justify tarnishing our daughter's memory? You have no right! Our daughter is gone, and nothing can bring her back! Your allegations only serve to add to our misery. You're no alpha, you're just a jumped-up nobody."

*Well, shit, that went well.*

I clenched my jaw, ignoring the sarcastic voice in my head. Luckily, I'd come prepared. I opened the folder I'd brought—the one that was filled with printed pages containing the damning text messages and emails between Cecily and Castro—and handed it over to her parents.

Robert sat back down next to his wife, and the air grew heavy as they scanned the damning pages, their expressions shifting from disbelief to shock.

The pages shook in Tina's trembling hands as tears streamed down her face. "Wh-what is this?" she stammered.

Robert tightened his grip on the paper.

"This is the evidence we've uncovered during the current course of our investigation. Unfortunately, the evidence is irrefutable," I said softly. "Cecily was working with Castro. While we don't have any answers yet about why she did this, we're still investigating."

Tina sobbed and collapsed against her husband, who wrapped an arm around her protectively.

I had always heard about the stages of grief, how some days were spent in deep sadness while others were filled with anger and resentment. I never imagined I'd witness all stages in the course of five minutes. Like a switch was flipped, their sadness turned to denial, turned to fury.

"This is all your fault," Tina hissed, pointing a shaking finger at Liza. "If it wasn't for you and your fucking omega powers, none of this would have happened. By marrying Ty, you put yourself in the spotlight and drew Castro to our town like a moth to a flame. Shame on you."

"Mrs. Banks, please," Liza implored, her hands outstretched.

"Liza lured Castro to Presley Acres," Tina spat. "And poor Cecily got caught in the crosshairs. She is... *was* an extremely intelligent woman. She'd never willingly choose evil over good."

Robert's face turned a deep shade of red, his voice shaking with rage. "Cecily loved you. She waited for you for years. She was so heartbroken when you cast her aside to mate with this... this... mongrel. Castro used her. She probably welcomed attention from another man, making her blind to Castro's intentions." His breath hitched. "My poor baby girl."

I clenched my fists, struggling to keep my temper in check. This was exactly what I'd feared when Liza insisted to come with me. Beside me, I felt her tense up, but outwardly she gave no reaction and remained silent.

"How dare you do this to Cecily? First you steal her mate, now you trash her reputation. I won't let this happen!" Robert roared as his face contorted with rage.

My alpha instincts kicked in the moment he lunged toward Liza. With lightning-fast reflexes, I stepped in front of her, blocking him from reaching her. Our eyes locked, and for a moment, all I saw was the burning anger in his gaze. But then, something shifted, a flicker of recognition. Who I was, perhaps? His place in the pack?

I showed leniency, understanding that his grief had pushed him to the edge, and stopped myself from doing something I'd regret.

"Enough!" I growled, asserting my dominance. My eyes were locked onto Robert's, conveying my authority. Although it sucked having to put a grieving father in his place, I had to remind him who was in charge.

Liza sat back on the couch, dazed at Robert's near-attack. She was shaken but maintained her composure admirably. I hated that Liza had been put into such a position when she had volunteered to come and support me, and had put her issues with Cecily aside to offer her condolences. The way she handled herself in such a high-stress situation impressed and awed me.

"Listen to me." My alpha had risen to the surface, making my tone low and dangerous as I narrowed my gaze on Robert. "I understand you're grieving, but if you ever attack my mate again, the consequences will be severe. I won't tolerate the same mistake twice, nor will I hesitate to put you in your place."

Anger burned in Robert's eyes as he stared at me, his chest heaving with ragged breaths. I feared he wouldn't back down, but after a tense moment, he lowered his head in submission. I released him, allowing him to slump back down on the sofa beside a sobbing Tina.

I returned to my seat next to Liza. "Consider this a warning for any future actions. Under no circumstances will I allow anyone to attack my mate. We are here to provide you with support, not to serve as targets for your anger."

Liza straightened, her gaze steady as she spoke to Cecily's parents. "I cannot begin to understand your grief, but I do understand your need to place blame on someone. The person we need to be pointing our fingers at, the real enemy, is Castro. He's the one behind all the suffering and heartache."

My chest swelled at her words. Even in the face of a grieving father's wrath, in the midst of a highly stressful situation, she'd stayed calm and collected. Her wisdom and grace shone through. She truly was the alpha's mate and continued to prove to me she'd be able to handle anything thrown at her.

I'd never wanted her more.

"Why? I don't understand. Why would Cecily do this?" Robert's voice shook with equal measures of anger and sadness. "Why did this play out like it did, ending in our daughter's murder? It just doesn't make any sense."

The anguish etched on his face showed me a broken man, genuinely distressed over the loss of his daughter. At that moment, I decided I'd made my point. He was grieving and had acted out of pain. It was obvious from his reaction that he had received the message loud and clear, and I doubted he would go up against his alpha in any way in the future.

"Like Ty said, we're still trying to piece everything together," Dad said. "But we thought it was important for you to know as soon as possible, so you were aware before the rest of the pack."

"Thank you." Tina sniffled and wiped her tears away. "We just can't believe our sweet girl would ever get involved with someone like that."

"People are capable of things we never expect," Liza added gently, her empathy for them emanating from her. "The heart can lead us down paths we never would've chosen for ourselves."

"Indeed," I said, remembering my own tumultuous journey to Liza. "Our priority is to find Castro and bring him to justice for all his transgressions."

"Tell us," Tina asked in a small, shaky voice, "what sort of relationship did Cecily and Castro have?"

"I'm not entirely sure," I said. "I know they went on at least one date when he was posing as Stone Black, but beyond that... I promise you, though, we won't leave any stone unturned. We will continue our investigation until we've got all the answers."

In the end, Cecily's parents accepted the truth, albeit reluctantly. Robert apologized for his outburst and thanked us for our understanding and patience. I wouldn't condemn him for his actions—not when he was struggling to come to terms with his daughter's death and betrayal—but I'd not forget about them, either.

As we left their home and climbed back into the SUV, I heaved out a sigh, feeling as though a weight had been lifted from my shoulders.

Dad clapped me on the back, pride shining in his eyes. "Both of you handled that situation well. I know it wasn't easy, but I couldn't be any prouder of you. Both of you. It was difficult for everyone involved, but you did right by them. We needed to be honest."

"Thanks, Dad."

"Speaking of handling things... you still need to choose an informant."

"Nico left me with a few of his recommendations. I have interviews lined up this afternoon." I glanced at Liza. "And I would really appreciate it if you would sit in on them with me."

"You would?" Her eyes widened in surprise. "Are you sure you want me there and not your dad?"

"Absolutely." I gave her hand a squeeze. "We both understand the importance of trust when it comes to choosing an informant. After the shit we've been through, I need to know that you trust them, too. Whoever we choose will be working for us both, possibly for a long time. Nico was with Dad for decades."

Liza beamed, visibly touched. "Thank you for including me."

"Of course," I murmured, leaning over to press a soft kiss to her forehead. "We're in this together."

The journey home was a quiet one, each of us lost in our own thoughts. Once I stopped the car in front of the estate, I turned to Liza. "I'm going up to my office to talk with Dad about what to look for in an informant. Could you check with the chef about arranging some kind of refreshments for our guests?"

"I have a better idea. I have a new cookie recipe I've been wanting to try." She glanced at her watch. "How much time do I have?"

"The first interview is in two hours."

Liza nodded and gave me a quick peck on the lips. "Perfect. I'll bring a tray of cookies to the office as soon as they're ready."

I watched her exit the car and go into the house, finding it hard to take my eyes off her fine ass. Just as I was about to catcall after her, I remembered my dad's presence and thought better of it.

We walked to the office. "Okay." I took a seat behind the desk as Dad pulled up a chair across from me. I still couldn't get used to us being on opposite sides of the executive desk. "So, what qualities should I be looking for in an informant, besides them being a sneaky motherfucker like Nico?"

"Yeah, he sure knew how to sneak up on the enemy and errant teenagers." He leaned back in his chair and gave a deep laugh. "You will want someone who is loyal, first and foremost. Someone who has the pack's best interests at heart."

I nodded. "Right."

"Trust is essential," he continued. "You have to believe that they'll be honest with you, even when it's difficult or news they know you won't want to hear."

"Like Nico was with you?" I couldn't keep the snark out of my tone. My father's informant had kept certain secrets from him about the Wylde pack.

"Exactly," Dad confirmed, surprising me with his honesty. "I was hurt when I found out he'd kept things from me, but it wasn't done out of malice. Nico was not just my informant, he was also my friend, and that made him so much better in his role. He always tried to make decisions that would benefit the pack and make me look good as alpha. You want someone who'll be comfortable making split-second decisions that are most beneficial for the pack."

"Friendship," I mused. "That's important, too, then."

"Yes." Dad held up a finger. "Just realize that the friendship part takes time. Whoever you hire will have to earn your trust, but after all the years Nico and I worked side by side, it was inevitable that our friendship would grow strong. Remember, Ty, this person will be your eyes and ears within the pack. They need to be observant and discreet. The last thing you want is an informant who's running his mouth around town."

"Discreet," I repeated, making a mental note.

"You'll also need to gauge their experience in the field. Ask them about past missions or assignments they've completed, successes and failures they've had. You'll want someone who's honest about their mistakes but can show they learned from them."

"Okay, I can do that." I cracked a walnut using one of the wedding gifts Liza and I had received. I'd never considered myself a nut guy but often found myself popping pecans or walnuts in my mouth when I was deep in thought. Better than chewing my lip to shreds. "Any other nuggets of knowledge, oh wise one?"

Dad rolled his eyes. "You should consider their motivations. Why do they want to be your informant? What are they hoping to gain from this position?

What are their expectations? Make sure their goals align with yours and the pack's. Lastly, you want someone who can think quickly on their feet, and not just quickly but creatively—someone who can think outside the box. Situations can change instantaneously, and your informant needs to be adaptable. Just look at how much shit has gone down in the past few weeks. Not just anyone could handle the physical and mental requirements of the job."

"Adaptable," I echoed, filing the information away. "Got it."

"Good," Dad said, and there was the pride in his eyes again. "Remember to trust your instincts when you're conducting these interviews. Nico's suggestions are likely all top-tier candidates, but you need to find the right informant for you and Liza. Trust is vital."

"Thanks, Dad." It was true. The right informant could make or break a pack's success, and I couldn't afford to make any mistakes during the hiring process.

"No pressure, though," Dad added with a wry smile.

I let out a dry chuckle at his attempt to ease the tension.

No pressure? What a fucking joke.

# Chapter 4 - Liza

After checking on the mixer, I scooted to the left and twisted the knob on one of the fancy ovens to preheat it for the cookies. The kitchen was a dream to work in. I'd worked in a lot of private kitchens in Presley Acres, but my new home base was better appointed than any of them, and better equipped, even, than some commercial kitchens.

I'd spent longer than I'd planned mixing the ingredients, but I had some time, so it was the perfect opportunity to try a new recipe I hoped to include in the fall menu. The base for the cookies was the same as any other sugar cookie, but I added cinnamon, cranberries, and a hint of orange zest for an extra kick.

The mixer stopped just as the chef walked into the kitchen. "What are you preparing today, Mrs. Keller?"

My immediate reaction to being called Mrs. Keller was to cringe, but I tried to mask my discomfort by standing up tall and composed. To me, that was Ty's mother's name, not mine. My new name was another one of the many things I still needed to get used to, including having my own personal chef. Before marrying Ty, others had hired me to be their personal chef, so the whole thing was fucking odd.

"I'm trying out a cookie recipe. Want me to save a few for you?"

"Absolutely. It smells delicious in here; my mouth's watering. Is there anything I can do to help?"

"Nah." I waved him off. "I'm in my element, Chef. You can leave me be."

I loved being in the kitchen. Some people used meditation to soothe their frayed nerves. I cooked. After the morning I'd had, I needed to release my pent-up energy.

He smiled and walked away, giving me my privacy to cook uninterrupted in the expansive kitchen. There were multiple pantries and more cabinets than I could count. Hell, it had taken me twenty minutes just to find the cooling racks.

While I rolled the dough into individual balls, I thought about Cecily's parents. Their reaction hadn't been a huge surprise. I'd fully expected the backlash, to be blamed in some way. What I hadn't anticipated was Mr. Banks lunging at me. The sudden, explosive movement coupled with the predatory look in his eyes had terrified me, I had to admit, and I wasn't sure how I'd summoned the strength to play it cool. Perhaps having Ty by my side had worked with our bond and given me some sort of subconscious sense of safety. One thing I was sure of? If Ty had been a millisecond slower in his reaction, Mr. Banks would've mauled me to death. The whole meeting, witnessing their grief and anguish, had been a horrific experience.

I glanced at the oven clock and saw that it was a quarter past one. I picked up the pace, quickly shoving the baking sheets into the oven. Ty had asked me to sit in on his interviews, and I wasn't about to be late. There were days when I found it difficult to envision myself as the alpha's mate. Today, though, I was standing by Ty's side while he delivered crucial information to pack members and interviewed potential employees who would hold our safety in their hands.

As soon as the cookies were cooled enough to be consumed, I hurried to Ty's office on the second floor. The door was open, so I took a moment to just take in my husband. He struck an imposing figure sitting behind what had been his father's desk. His dark hair was tousled from running his fingers through it as he sat at his desk, deep in concentration.

"Knock, knock. Do you have time for a cookie?"

He perked up and smiled, sending my heart fluttering. My mate was so damn handsome, it was hard for me to keep my hands off of him during the day. I tried to remind myself that he had important matters to attend to, though I would've much preferred he tended to me and my constant aching need for him.

"My schedule always allows for something sweet, but since I can't have you right now, a cookie will have to suffice." Ty took a cookie from the platter, then made a move to swipe another with his other hand.

Laughing, I pulled the plate out of his reach. "Tut, tut, Ty. Don't be so greedy. These aren't all for you. They are for our interviewees."

He grabbed my free hand and pulled me in for a tender, lingering kiss. "These smell delicious. Thank you for whipping them up."

I feigned outrage at his words. "I wouldn't quite call it whipping up. It's a science, meticulously choosing ingredients, balancing the flavors, and carefully baking them at the right temperature for the perfect amount of time."

"Eh, you say poe-tay-to, I say puh-tah-to." Ty shrugged, then laughed before he took a bite, moaning in approval.

I took a few minutes to set everything up, then glanced around the room, satisfied with my handiwork. The aroma of fresh baking filled the air, and a pitcher of cold water and glasses sat invitingly on the table next to the plate of cookies. Normally, I would have left such tasks to the staff, but Ty had asked me to be part of these meetings, and I wanted to add my own personal touch. A vase of bright flowers from the garden adorned the center of the table, providing a splash of color against the otherwise serious-looking office.

A member of the staff knocked on the door, and Ty stepped out, poking his head into the room a few minutes later. His gray eyes focused on me intently. "The first guy's here for the interview."

Unsure of what was expected of me beyond observing, I decided I'd treat it like I would an interview for my own business. I might not be the one asking the questions, but I could take notes on each candidate so Ty and I could consult after.

I retrieved a notepad and pen from the drawer and settled onto a chair at the side of the desk. "Okay, I'm ready. Bring him on in."

Moments later, a tall, skinny shifter entered, and Ty gestured for him to take a seat. The man introduced himself as Orlando, and an involuntary shudder ran down my back. I recalled how Nico had been terrifying, but something about this guy was downright creepy. His speech held no inflection. His monotone words flowed almost robotically from his blank-eyed face. I kept watching to see if he'd blink, and if it'd be like those aliens in the movies with his eyelids sweeping horizontally rather than vertically? I wondered if he had a soul, or if he might be some weird life form... perhaps even a reptilian shifter. My lips twitched as I suppressed a giggle, and I had to lower my head, letting my hair fall in a curtain over it to hide my reaction while Ty began asking Orlando questions.

"Thank you for coming in." Ty's face was expressionless, no doubt wanting to stay neutral toward the candidates. "Why do you want to be an informant?"

Orlando shifted nervously in his seat, and I wondered if he truly understood the implications of the job. "I've been looking for work for a long time and figured this would be as good a job as any."

I bit my tongue to avoid interrupting Ty's interview. This guy was a fucking joke. He didn't have the first clue what would be expected of him, hadn't even taken the time to find out the bare minimum the job would require. Ty should just put an end to the whole charade. Ty's expression glazed over as he cracked his knuckles. If I had to guess, he had already discounted Orlando as a potential employee.

"Orlando," Ty said evenly. "I understand you come highly recommended by Nico. What is your connection to him? Have you worked with him on security detail somewhere?"

"Nico is my uncle," Orlando said.

I sighed inwardly. There it was, the real reason Nico had recommended Orlando as a potential informant. He'd seen it as an opportunity to help out a member of his family. Nico went down a notch in my estimation. He, of all people, knew what the job entailed and what kind of person would be required. Why would he waste our time like this?

Ty thanked Orlando for coming in for the interview and escorted him from the office, leaving the man with a confused expression, no doubt puzzled by the abrupt end of the interview. Had he expected to be hired purely because his uncle had recommended him? Once the door closed behind them, I sat back and exhaled loudly. What a dumbass. The vibes were all wrong. My notepad remained blank, and there would be no conferring, no need for me to provide any feedback. Orlando was out of the running.

As I sat there, still feeling uneasy after the first interview, I wondered how the next few would go. If Orlando was the caliber of potential informants from Nico, I had no great expectations for the rest of them. I glanced at the clock. We'd ended the initial interview far quicker than expected. We had an hour before the next candidate arrived.

Ty returned to the office and went to his desk, picking up another cookie on the way. I stretched and moaned, shifting positions on the seat. My bones were tight. It had been a while since I'd shifted, and with everything that had happened over the last few days, I craved the freedom of a run and some fresh air.

"Hey, do you think I have enough time for a quick run?"

Ty looked up from his notes. "Sure, shouldn't be a problem. Just be fast, and don't lose track of time. I want your feedback on the candidates." He eyed me with concern. "You seem tense. Would you like me to join you?"

I waved him off. "I'm fine. I just need to stretch and get some air. Besides, you need to stay here in case your next interviewee shows up early. You wouldn't want to keep a potential employee with the amazing dynamic personality of Orlando waiting, now, would you?"

Ty rolled his eyes. "Yeah, that guy was a joke. How Nico thought Orlan*Doh* would be a good fit... Hopefully, the next ones will be better. They have to be, statistically speaking, right?"

"Right." I kissed the top of his head. "I'll let you get back to it. See you in about forty-five minutes."

Taking advantage of some of the last warm, sunny days before the weather really changed, I dashed into the forest on the estate grounds, stripping my clothes off and shifting in one smooth motion.

As I moved into a clearing, I relished the warmth of the sun on my fur, and the vibrant colors of the subtly changing leaves surrounding me. The energy of the moon was absent during these daylight hours, which made it a wholly different experience. I didn't often shift in the day, but the sights and sounds of the forest provided their own unique stimulation.

Sunlight filtered through the trees, painting patches of warmth amid the shadows as I sprinted through the woods, my paws pounding against the soft earth. The rustling leaves created a natural symphony that accompanied the rhythm of my strides. Piles of leaves were scattered around, marking the onset of fall in the forest. The air was alive with the scent of pine and damp earth, an invigorating blend that gave me the energy I'd require to make it through the rest of the interviews.

The gentle sounds of birdsong reached my ears, their melodies harmonizing and bringing me a peace I hadn't realized I needed so badly. The wind whispered secrets through the leaves as my keen senses picked up the faint traces of rabbit trails and squirrel paths. I watched as the small creatures scurried to hide from me, tempting me to give chase. I refrained, wanting to avoid the thrill of the chase and losing my sense of time—and the need for a shower before returning to Ty's office. A cookie would tide me over until dinner. I'd kept a hidden stash in the kitchen in case Ty couldn't help himself and ate everything I'd left out in the office.

The earlier meeting with Cecily's parents had left an uncomfortable heaviness in my chest, a mixture of sympathy and tension that lingered within me. But as I ran, the thud of my paws acted like a soothing balm to my soul. With each stride, the tension slowly ebbed away, replaced by a liberation I needed more than anything. The colors of the forest blurred as I picked up speed, my body moving effortlessly through the terrain.

Suddenly, an unfamiliar sensation gave me pause. My ears perked, and I went on high alert. Fear threatened to overwhelm me as I discreetly scanned the area for any signs of danger. I scouted through the trees, trying to act normal so as not to alert anyone I was on to them, but the feeling vanished as quickly as it had come. I laughed at myself, chalking it up to paranoia. After all, the estate was secure, with high fences, security guards, and cameras everywhere. There was no safer place I could be.

On my way to the house, however, I couldn't shake the nagging feeling that someone had been watching me. I shifted back into my human form and hastily pulled on my clothes, checking my watch. I only had two minutes before the next interview.

I rushed into Ty's office, breathless from my run and the strange sensation that lingered. The next interviewee was already seated across from Ty, waiting for my arrival.

"Sorry I'm late," I panted, taking my seat on the side of the room, and studying our next candidate. Ty introduced him as Harlem, and his aloof demeanor immediately put me on edge. He gobbled down a handful of my cookies, acting like the entire tray had been baked especially for him.

*What the hell?*

"These are delicious." He spoke with his mouth open, bits of half-chewed cookie flying out of his mouth and landing on Ty's desk. "Does your chef make these here at the estate?"

"Er, no." Ty stared at the nastiness accumulating on his desk. "Liza, my mate, made them."

"You have an excellent mate. You're smart to keep her in the kitchen, Ty. It's getting harder to find a woman who wants to look after her mate the way they should."

My mouth dropped open. Antiquated, sexist moron.

As the interview progressed, it became abundantly clear that this was not Harlem's only condescending thought regarding women. "Women should know their place," Harlem stated between bites of my cookies.

My blood boiled. Regardless of being the alpha's mate, there was no way I could stay quiet while he spewed such disrespect. "And where exactly do you believe a woman's place is, Harlem?" I challenged, eyes narrowing to slits.

"Clearly not here, trying to act like they belong in positions of power," he said, sitting back with a smirk.

Ty gave me a worried glance, but I refused to back down. "It sounds like you're the one who doesn't understand where he belongs," I shot back, my voice cold and unwavering. It wasn't too long after that Ty showed him the way out.

Needless to say, Harlem was another definite no.

As soon as he returned to the office, Ty scowled. "Which age did that asshole come from?"

Both interviews had been draining and disheartening. After discussing the day's candidates, Ty and I agreed that Nico's recommendations were questionable, to say the least. What the hell had he been thinking when he'd given the list to Ty? Was he screwing with us?

Ty laughed when I said that, showing me that the men's credentials checked out on paper. "It's just their personalities that are questionable."

We still had one more interview to get through. I hoped against hope that this one would be better than the rest.

Harlem's binge meant my plate of cookies was now more a plate of cookie crumbs, so I hurried to the kitchen and grabbed the remaining dozen cookies I'd hidden, thinking I was keeping them from Ty, not an antiquated, sexist prick. Luckily, there were no kitchen staff in my way.

I was fuming over Harlem's asinine comments. Who the fuck did he think he was, waltzing into his alpha's office, insulting his mate, and disparaging all female shifters? I wasn't surprised he hadn't found a good little woman. Good luck to him.

Ty wasn't in his office when I returned, so I wiped his desk of cookie bits and Harlem spit, then rearranged the fresh cookies, all the while grumbling under my breath about Harlem's sexist comments. "What kind of person insults not only women in general, but the alpha's mate while interviewing for the position of informant? Who the hell, in this day and age, thinks a woman's place is in the kitchen? Damn fool."

As I used my angry energy to rearrange the flowers, a voice from the doorway caught my attention. "Personally, I think women are more capable than men in many areas," the newcomer began, his tone warm and sincere. "I don't believe a woman belongs in the kitchen, but some of the best chefs I know are women. Women thrive in the kitchen... or any other venture they choose to take on."

I turned to see Ty standing at the doorway with the man who'd spoken. Ty introduced me to Isaiah. He was roguishly attractive, with salt-and-pepper hair that hinted at his age being in the mid-to-late-forties, smoky gray eyes that stole my breath away, and beautiful earthy brown skin. For a split second, I considered snapping a photo to send to my best friend Sabrina but thought better of it. I'd describe him in detail when I called her later.

Isaiah's intelligence and wit were displayed throughout the interview, his devilish smile and quick answers keeping us engaged.

"Tell me about your career. What kind of experience do you have that would lend itself to this position?" Ty leaned forward. He was fully engaged in the interview, totally unlike the others.

"I worked closely with Nico for several years and have actually served as a source for him," Isaiah explained.

"What do you mean, 'a source'?" Ty scribbled a note in his folder.

"There have been times in the past when Nico didn't have enough security or enough manpower for specific missions within the Keller pack. At those times, I served as a sort of substitute, or temporary employee, until the job was done." Isaiah sat up straighter in the chair. "I can assure you, Alpha, I have the capabilities necessary to handle the job you're attempting to fill. My background and experience give me the upper hand because I know how to be discreet and get the job done. No questions asked."

He spoke confidently, but I wanted to test his mettle. "How would you handle a situation like we're currently in? We have an enemy on the run who used a pack member for his bidding, causing damage to the pack. When he was done using her as a pawn, he murdered her and hung it over Ty's head, treating it like a game with no regard for the life lost."

Isaiah crossed his legs and clasped his hands in his lap. He took his time to answer, carefully considering his words. "First, I would gather all available intel on this enemy's whereabouts and activities." His eyes were focused and determined as he explained his hypothetical process. "Next, I would work closely with your pack's security to devise an appropriate plan of action to find and apprehend him. As for the woman who did his bidding, her unfortunate fate should serve as a cautionary tale to the rest of the pack."

I admired the conviction in his voice. He approached the matter seriously and, despite being put on the spot, considered the situation, then offered a credible plan of action. It appeared Ty shared my sentiments because he nodded along with Isaiah's words.

"Regarding the message to the public," Isaiah continued. "It's important to be firm. Our pack will not tolerate such actions. We need to show strength and unity while also honoring the deceased woman's memory."

I found myself liking Isaiah more and more, and his calm demeanor and attitude reassured me. Ty's expression suggested he felt the same way. After a few more minutes of small talk, Ty rose from his chair. "Thank you for your time, Isaiah. We'll be in touch soon."

We waited until he left before looking at each other.

"Out of all the interviews today, I think Isaiah definitely stands out," I said.

Ty nodded in agreement. "We'll see after tomorrow's interviews."

But I could tell he already had a strong inclination toward Isaiah.

Later that night, standing on the balcony off our master suite, I gazed out at the woods. We'd been so busy lately, I hadn't really had an opportunity to speak to Ty about the strangers in town, or the people trying to get my photo through the window at my office. The unsettling feeling from my earlier run still lingered in the back of my mind, and I hadn't mentioned that to him, either. With the interviews going on, it had seemed unimportant.

When I turned to head back inside, a figure in the trees caught my attention. Fear locked up every muscle. I covered my mouth, wanting to scream out to Ty, but the person would flee if I did. Instead, I prayed that our bond as mates would allow him to sense my distress.

Almost instantly, Ty rushed into the room. "What's wrong? Are you hurt?"

"Someone's in the woods," I said, unable to tear my eyes away from the shadowy figure.

Ty moved quickly to my side, pushing me protectively behind him. But in those few seconds, the person vanished.

"I don't see anyone." Ty leaned over the balcony, straining to glimpse the shadowy figure.

Confused and frightened, I squinted and scanned the tree line. "I swear someone was lurking under the trees. There was someone there just now, and there was someone out there when I was running. I promise I'm not fucking crazy."

"Liza, I know you're not crazy. Of course you're not. Why didn't you tell me there was someone out there earlier?" He looked hurt that I hadn't told him.

"I'm sorry, Ty, I meant to, but with the interviews and everything else, we were both so busy. Then I started second-guessing myself, but when I saw someone out there..." I was starting to panic, so I took in a few steadying breaths.

Ty pulled out his phone and called his head security guard. "I need everyone on hand to search the woods. Liza saw someone watching her." He turned to face me and cupped my face. "If there's someone out there, they'll find them."

I nodded. I hoped they'd catch the person. But what if I had imagined it? What if the stress of anticipating Castro's next move was getting to me? I certainly hadn't gotten more than five or six hours of sleep each night, but could those factors really cause hallucinations? Plus, I was certain my wolf had sensed someone in broad daylight during my run. It couldn't all be coincidental.

While we waited, we sat on the bed and tried to watch a movie. He insisted it would take my mind off everything but it didn't. How could I chill and watch a movie when there was a creeper lurking in the shadows, waiting to do gods only knew what?

An hour later, the head of security knocked on the bedroom door. I pulled the blanket up to cover my chest since I'd chucked my bra across the room thirty minutes earlier. Ty padded to the door in his comfortable sweatpants. He'd ditched his suit before I'd released the girls.

"We've searched every inch of the woods, Alpha. My men didn't find any intruders or any unfamiliar scents. I'll put extra guards around the perimeter of the woods tonight."

Ty nodded and thanked the guard before crawling back into bed with me. "Maybe you're just stressed." He pulled me close in an attempt to comfort me. "Why don't you try to get some sleep? Everything will be okay."

I forced a smile and kissed him before burrowing down in the high-thread-count sheets and down comforter, hoping it would lull me to sleep. But as I lay in bed that night, my thoughts racing, I couldn't shake the feeling that something was amiss. I wasn't crazy. There had been someone in those woods watching me. The question now was, who were they, and what did they want?

# Chapter 5 - Ty

I stretched and repositioned the pillow under my head, turning to find Liza awake, sitting upright on the bed beside me. I wondered if she'd had any sleep at all. The dark circles marring her beautiful face told me she hadn't. Her bright blue eyes, usually full of life, held a haunted look.

"Hey," I said, pushing myself up into a sitting position. I brushed a stray lock of hair from her forehead. "You don't seem yourself this morning. Are you okay?"

Liza stared into nothingness as she slumped against the headboard. I wrapped an arm around her shoulders and pulled her close, pressing a kiss to her temple. She remained stiff in my embrace.

Worry gnawed at my gut. I'd never seen her like this, so withdrawn into herself. She'd always seemed so strong, filled with warmth and light. Even through the nightmares about the truth of the Wylde's pack destruction, she never allowed Castro's games to dim her spirit. Not even her worries about being an omega—a secret she'd held her entire life—had kept her down. Now, it felt as if her light was fading as darkness crept in, creating a void between us.

"Talk to me, Liza," I said. "What's going on in that beautiful head of yours?"

Her gaze was distant, as if she couldn't quite focus on the here and now. "I don't know."

"Would you like a massage?" I offered, hoping to ease some of the tension. All I received in response was a shrug. It pained me to see her this way, so unlike the vibrant, confident woman I knew and loved.

I wrapped both arms around her now, trying to offer comfort through my touch, but she remained distant, her body rigid against mine. My concern only deepened, and I wondered if she was obsessing over the shadowy figure she'd spotted in the woods behind our estate.

"Are you worried about what you saw in the woods?" I asked, my voice soft yet insistent.

"No, I'm fine," she blurted. Not only was her tone unconvincing, but I felt the spike of fear through our mating bond.

She'd been okay last night after our interview with Isaiah, upbeat even, until the moment she'd seen the shadowy figure in the woods. I believed she'd noticed something, but I couldn't ignore the chance that her encounter with the mysterious figure was nothing more than a stress-induced hallucination. The extent of her powers as an omega remained unknown to us, and I couldn't disregard the possibility that they'd somehow played a role in what she'd experienced.

But for now, my priority was to make sure Liza felt safe and cared for. I needed to find a way to get through to her, so I decided to take matters into my own hands and do something special for her. I wasn't great at big gestures, but I could make her breakfast. It was usually a task reserved for the staff or Liza herself when she was in the mood, but today I wanted to surprise her and show her how much I cared.

"Take your time in the shower," I suggested gently. "The hot water will help you relax."

She nodded slowly, a ghost of her usual smile crossing her lips as she slid out of bed and trudged to the bathroom.

I slipped out of bed, pulled on a T-shirt, and padded down to the kitchen, where I found the chef working away. "Good morning, Alpha, what can I get for you and Mrs. Keller this morning?"

"Morning, I'm going to make breakfast for Liza and me." Chef gave me a grin. He'd been with the Keller family as long as I could remember and knew my cooking skills were pretty basic, but he happily left me to it.

I searched through the pantries for inspiration. There were plenty of ingredients at my disposal, but I wanted something simple and comforting. Something I could make without burning anything. Eventually, I settled on a basic dish of scrambled eggs with cheese, cinnamon toast with honey butter, and bacon.

The sweet scent of cooking filled the kitchen as I whisked the eggs and melted a generous amount of sharp cheddar into the mixture. The sizzle of bacon accompanied the aroma of cinnamon toast crisping in the oven, a rich layer of honey butter melting over its golden surface.

As I cooked, my thoughts kept going back to Liza. I couldn't overlook the possibility that I was partially responsible for her stress. If I had taken care of Castro from the beginning, we wouldn't be dealing with all this shit or worrying about people lurking in the shadows.

Once the meal was ready, I carefully arranged it on a tray, along with a glass of fresh-squeezed orange juice and a small vase containing a delicate rose I'd snatched from one of the many floral displays throughout the house.

Carrying the tray upstairs, I found Liza emerging from the bathroom, her hair twisted up in a towel, and a delicate peach satin robe that fell just below her ass wrapped around her slender frame. A jolt of desire shot through me at the thought of what I knew was hidden beneath that robe, but I pushed it aside for now. There were more pressing matters at hand.

"Surprise." I lifted the tray slightly. "I made breakfast."

Her eyes lit up, a genuine smile spreading across her face for the first time that morning. "Ty, this is so sweet. Thank you."

I led her out to the terrace, where we had a wrought-iron table set out for us to eat. She looked at me. "I'm sorry for being such a Debbie Downer this morning."

"It's understandable," I said, waving off her apology. "We've all been under a lot of stress lately."

She took a bite of the eggs and let out a small moan of appreciation. "This is so good."

"Are you sure?" I joked, raising an eyebrow. "You don't have to pretend."

She laughed a genuine, beautiful laugh that gave me hope. "I'm not pretending. It really is fantastic."

While she finished her breakfast, her tension seemed to reduce somewhat, though not entirely. It was time for me to make good on my promise to help her relieve the rest of her stress. I stood up, moving behind her, and firmly began massaging her neck and shoulders. Her body relaxed into my touch. Slowly, I let my hands slide down the front of her robe, cupping her breasts in my palms.

She gasped, feigning scandal. "Ty! We can't do this on the terrace... anyone of the security team could see us."

But through our bond, I sensed her building excitement, and an idea sparked. I was convinced this thrill would take her mind off her worries. "That's exactly why I want to do it right here. Right now," I whispered into her ear, watching as her eyes went wide in surprise.

My fingers teased her nipples, grinning as they hardened under my touch. Liza leaned back against me, letting out a soft moan as I slid one hand down her stomach, inching closer to that heat between her legs.

"Ty..." she said, her hips instinctively moving against my touch. "The staff could see."

"Let them watch," I growled, unable to contain my desire any longer. I spun her chair around to face me. Our eyes locked, and our lips met in a hungry, passionate kiss.

Tongues intertwined as hands glided across skin. I slid my palms up and down her curves, feeling every inch of her skin beneath my fingers. Grasping her hips tightly, I lifted her and pressed her against the stone wall of the terrace. She gasped into my mouth, her legs encircling my waist, hands gripping my shoulders for balance as I supported her with one arm around the small of her back.

My other hand moved from her hips to between her legs, eagerly teasing the soft flesh there. She gasped into my mouth, pleasure coursing through us both, before leaning forward and biting gently on my lower lip. My grip around Liza tightened even more as we sank deeper into our embrace.

My cock grew harder by the second, my desire yearning to break free. With one swift movement, I whirled around and lay back on the patio table, letting Liza straddle me. Her robe had come off entirely at that point, exposing her beautiful figure in all its glory to the morning sun.

"Fuck, Liza. Your tits are a sight to behold."

She grinned and ran her hands over her breasts, stopping to tweak her nipples, her eyes never leaving mine. Her lips quirked with a devilish grin. "Do you like it when I touch myself?"

"Hell yes." I licked my lips as my dick became as hard as granite. "What else can you show me?"

Liza leaned back, one hand on my leg to support herself. Then, in slow motion, she sucked her finger, swirling her tongue around it before sliding it down her body and between her pussy lips. I watched in pure awe as she pushed her finger inside herself, then pulled it up and down over her clit, her eyes rolling back into her head. She groaned as her finger changed directions, encircling just the tip of the swollen flesh.

"You're going to give me a fucking heart attack, Liza." I pulled her down toward me, kissing her hard. My hands continued to caress every inch of her skin as I bit the delicate curve of her neck and shoulders. My breathing became heavier as her hot center rubbed against my clothed cock with each movement. She moved faster, building up a steady rhythm that left us both trembling with need..

Liza slid off me to stand and pointed to my pants. "Off. Now."

A sly grin spread across my face before I obliged her, removing my clothing in two seconds flat.

Liza licked her lips as she took in the sight of my body. A low growl escaped her when she took my engorged cock into her hands. I melted under her touch, her fingers teasing and arousing me in ways I never thought possible.

"Liza, this is about you," I said softly, her gaze still locked with mine. "You need the release more than I do."

My heart raced as I watched her pleasure me, all hints of modesty gone now. I wanted, *needed* to drive her fucking insane. Liza caught me staring at her pussy and smiled before standing and putting a foot onto the chair. She tilted her hips toward me in invitation, and without hesitation, I knelt before her and appreciated every inch of her body with my mouth.

I licked my way up from her thighs to the folds of skin between them, relishing her heat on my tongue. My fingers moved expertly alongside my tongue to heighten the sensation as I savored every part of her deliciousness. Her body quivered beneath me as I worked my mouth over her wetness until she shuddered against me in a powerful orgasm. Her hand found the back of my head, fingers running through my hair and holding my mouth against her heated core as she rode out her climax.

Once her body relaxed, I stood and kissed her, letting her taste herself on my lips and tongue. She locked her legs around my waist and pulled me close as her tongue played with mine. I couldn't stop myself from pressing my erection between her legs, stroking her clitoris with my tip. Her eyes rolled back into her head again as she moaned, though this time it was different. It was a moan of intense delight, of a woman who was ready to be fucked.

She nudged me back, and following her lead, I lay back on the table again, grabbing the edge of the table for support as Liza positioned herself above me. Slowly, she teased the tip of my cock against her seam, her body moving with anticipation.

I let out a low growl when Liza sank down onto me. Fully seated, she gasped as I stretched her to her limits. She rose, hips tilting as she slowly lowered herself down onto me once more, her nails digging into my shoulders as she worked her way down until my cock was buried deep inside her. I could barely contain my need for her as my body writhed, her soaking pussy completely devouring my dick.

"Oh, gods." Liza moaned and threw her head back, riding me like a fucking horse at the Kentucky Derby.

I grabbed her ass with both hands, squeezing and pushing her down harder, wanting every centimeter of my cock to be inside her.

Her inner walls were still spasming from her orgasm, and it took everything I had to hold back. "Fuck, you're so tight," I muttered, biting my lower lip. "And so damn wet."

"You make me that way," she said, her eyes half-lidded with pleasure. "I'm so thankful I married a guy who loves to eat pussy."

My breathing became heavy with pleasure as I neared my release. Liza's breathing became erratic as she moved faster against me, pushing us both over the edge together. She clamped down on me, and I tightened my grip on her ass. Liza screamed, leaving nothing to the imagination for those who might be working on the grounds of the estate below us.

In a moment of intense pleasure, we came completely undone as I spilled every drop of seed deep into her, my body twitching from waves of satisfaction.

The intensity of it all left us both trembling, riding a euphoric high.

She collapsed onto my chest afterward, our sweaty skin sticking together from the warmth of the sun.

"Ty," she moaned, breathless from our encounter. "I love you."

Eventually, our heartbeats slowed, and we untangled ourselves.

Liza pressed a tender kiss to my lips, her eyes filled with warmth and gratitude. "Thank you for this," she said, brushing her fingers through my hair. "I needed that."

"Anytime. It doesn't matter what I have going on, I will always stop whatever I am doing to fuck you, or eat your pussy, Liza. You have my guarantee." I winked at her. "So, what's your plan for today?"

We moved back into the bedroom. Liza sat at the dressing table and smoothed her white-blonde hair back into a ponytail. "I've got a lot to catch up on with work. I won't be able to be there for the remaining interviews, but after yesterday, I feel strongly that Isaiah is the man for the job. He answered all of your questions with ease and seems to have a fantastic résumé. I doubt you'll find anyone else of his caliber."

"No problem." I wanted her to take the time to focus on her own business and hoped it would keep her from stressing about Castro. "I agree with you about Isaiah. I think it's just a formality to interview the other guys at this point. You never know, maybe I'll get lucky and one of them will be better than Isaiah. I'll let you know how it goes."

Even though I'd already had my mind set on Isaiah, it was important to give the other candidates a fair chance. Plus, I figured it would be a bad look if the alpha canceled scheduled interviews.

With that, we went our separate ways. Liza dressed and retreated to her office to handle her business matters while I headed to my own office to conduct the interviews.

The first candidate was a tall, broad-shouldered man with an impressive résumé. However, throughout the entire interview, he refused to make eye contact with me. Instead, his eyes darted nervously around the room, as if searching for an escape route. While I appreciated his honesty regarding his anxiety in high-pressure situations, that didn't make him suitable for the job.

The second candidate was an eccentric middle-aged man with wild, curly hair, and a penchant for talking about his multiple cats. While he seemed passionate about feline companionship, he lacked the focus and discretion needed for the job. Plus, his insistence on showing me photos of each of his cats during the interview only solidified my decision.

Neither of them held a candle to Isaiah. With his intelligence, confidence, and charisma, he was undoubtedly the best choice for the role.

Once the interviews were over, I was completely convinced that I'd found my informant. I just needed to make it official.

Picking up my phone, I dialed Isaiah's number.

"Hello?" He tried to hide it, but I heard the anticipation in his voice.

"Isaiah, after careful consideration, I'd like to offer you the position of informant," I said, cutting straight to the point.

"Thank you, Alpha Keller. I won't let you down." His tone was filled with gratitude and determination.

"Your first assignment will be to investigate anyone in town who might have connections to Castro. I'll send over all the information we currently have on him. We need to stay one step ahead of him. We can't allow him to sink his hooks into another one of our pack members like he did Cecily."

"Understood, sir. I'll get started right away."

With that settled, I called Dad to my office. One of the perks of my parents living on the estate grounds was the ease with which I could get in touch with him for an impromptu meeting. When he retired and passed the mantle over to me, he'd said he was going to enjoy his time loafing around the new house, reading books he'd meant to read for years, but he jumped at the chance to discuss pack business whenever I called.

Fifteen minutes later, Dad sat across from me as I shared the good news. "I've settled on an informant."

His eyebrows shot up. "Already? That sure as hell was fast. This is a huge decision, Ty, and it will affect your time as alpha. Are you sure?"

"I'm positive. His name is Isaiah Culver. His experience is impressive and his answers to my questions were spot-on. I like him, Dad. I've already called to tell him he's hired and give him his first assignment." I handed Dad Isaiah's file so he could see for himself.

After a quick glance, Dad nodded. "I must say, he does sound like an excellent choice. He seems like a shifter who will serve you well."

"I think so, too. I trust him, and right now, that's what we need." I paused for a moment before bringing up the other matter weighing on my mind. "There's something else that's been bothering me. Last night, Liza saw, or at least thought she saw, someone lurking in the woods behind the estate, but security found no obvious sighting or scent. It doesn't sit right with me, especially since she's been so stressed lately."

"Have you considered that it might be her imagination playing tricks on her?" Dad asked gently.

Rage snapped at my blood, but I couldn't deny the same thing had gone through my mind that morning. "Of course, but I know Liza. She's not inclined to seeing things that aren't there. I'm going to do a scout of my own. I know these woods. It's been my playground since I can remember. I'll know if there is anything amiss."

"Okay, son. Let me know if you find anything suspicious."

I ventured into the woods near the estate, determined to uncover any signs of danger that may be lurking there. I shifted into my wolf form, where my senses would be heightened, and prowled through the forest, noting the familiar sights, sounds, and scents that surrounded me. My hearing was alive with the sounds of birdsong and the rustling of leaves beneath my feet. The scents of damp earth and lush foliage filled my nostrils. I was starting to think Dad was right. She'd been dealing with a lot right now, so maybe Liza's imagination had manifested a boogeyman. Everything seemed to be as it should...

Until I reached the spot where Liza had claimed to have seen the shadowy figure.

I spent a good bit of time rooting around, and there, intertwined in the undergrowth, I discovered a piece of fabric caught on one of the trees. After shifting back to my human form, I extracted the fabric and examined the scrap more closely, noting that it appeared to be from a blanket. Bringing the fabric to my nose, I inhaled deeply, detecting a faint but unmistakable scent. It was Liza's, though subtly different. The discovery left me both puzzled and alarmed.

I raced back to the house, my instincts screaming at me to check on her. I didn't want to alarm her—I'd only just soothed and relaxed her tense, worried body this morning. I almost thought better of it since I knew she was busy, but my concern for her wellbeing outweighed inconveniencing her. I found her where I'd expected her to be, safe in her office.

I stood at the door, listening to her voice as she spoke on the phone with her customers, expertly scheduling around their needs to ensure they would still receive their meals on time, reassuring them she would still provide a first-class service.

As proud as I was of her, my concern only grew. I gripped the fabric in my hands, wanting to ask her about it, but knowing how stressed she'd been made me hesitate.

Liza's voice brought me out of my tangled concerns. "Is everything okay?" I glanced up to find her looking at me, one hand over the mouthpiece of the phone.

"Uh, yeah," I stammered, quickly shoving the fabric into my jeans pocket. "I just wanted to see how you were doing and let you know I hired Isaiah."

"That's great news. I liked him, too." She looked at me, lips pursing and brows furrowing. "Are you sure that's all? You're worried about something,"

Shit. The mating bond. She'd obviously felt the spike of my concern. "Sorry, babe. I was just thinking about Isaiah's first job. I've asked him to check if anyone else in town has connections to Castro. It eats at me that I can't trust people I've known all my life."

Liza stared at me for a long moment. "It's horrible to think of anyone else double-crossing us like that. I hope he finds there's no one else." She gave me a tight smile. "If that's all..." She gestured at the phone and waved me away with a shooing motion. I breathed a silent sigh of relief.

I hated lying to her, but I didn't want to worry her any more than she already was. "Of course." I forced a grin and left her office, but as I walked to my office, the nagging feeling that something was amiss refused to leave me.

As I overlooked the speech I'd written for tonight's pack meeting, I found myself absently rubbing the fabric between my fingers, contemplating its significance. The scent, so similar to Liza's, haunted me. Cecily's betrayal and death were still fresh in my mind, and I couldn't shake the feeling that we were overlooking something crucial. I couldn't let my guard down, not when Liza's safety was at stake.

"Ty?" Liza said from the office door. She gave me an odd look when I whipped my hand out of my pocket like a child with his hand in the cookie jar. "I thought I'd help you get ready for the announcement about Cecily at tonight's pack meeting."

"Thanks." I hesitated before admitting I was nervous. "This is my first meeting as the new alpha, and I'm more than sure the topic won't be well-received."

"Everything will be fine," she reassured me, her steady gaze instilling confidence. "You're doing a great job, Ty."

"I know you looked at this the other night, but I've made some changes. Would you mind reading this over again?" I turned my computer screen toward her.

She scanned the contents, then looked at me over the screen. "I wouldn't change a thing. It's perfect."

Her approval meant more than anyone else's, and with renewed confidence, I prepared for the meeting that would test our resolve and push us to face the pack's reaction to Cecily's involvement with Castro.

Later that evening, I waited for Liza in the foyer. At the sound of footsteps on the stairs, I looked up. She was dressed impeccably, radiating elegance and grace. Her tailored white suit accentuated her slender frame, perfectly representing her Arctic wolf heritage, and the blue shirt she wore underneath brought out the color of those incredible eyes. When she smiled at me, my heart flip-flopped, reminding me of how incredibly fortunate I was to have Liza as my fated mate.

How the hell did I get so lucky?

"Are you ready?" I offered her my arm.

"Always." She smiled and looped her arm through mine.

Together, we made our way to the backyard, where hundreds of chairs and a stage with a podium and microphone had been set up. We ascended the steps to the stage together, all eyes on us, no doubt curious to hear what we had to say.

I stepped up to the podium, squinting against the spotlight. This was my first official address as alpha. A lot was expected of me, and I didn't want to fuck it up.

"Good evening," I began, clearing my throat nervously. "I'm sure many of you are wondering why I've called this special meeting. The truth is, we have some important matters to discuss." I paused for a moment to gather my thoughts. "As you all know, Cecily Banks was found deceased a few days ago in her home. I have reviewed the coroner's report, and after performing a thorough investigation, it has come to light that Cecily had been working with Castro."

Whispers and murmurs erupted from the crowd.

"Castro manipulated Cecily into doing his bidding, and when he no longer had a use for her, he poisoned her. It is imperative that we remain vigilant and united against this enemy who seeks to divide and conquer our pack."

The murmurs from the crowd grew louder, a cacophony of disbelief, anger, and confusion as they wondered why Cecily would work with someone like Castro. My gaze shifted to the back of the crowd where Mr. and Mrs. Banks stood, their shoulders slumped, eyes cast downward.

I held up my hands, trying to quiet the crowd. "At this time, we do not believe Cecily was working with anyone else within the pack. I don't want to turn this into a witch hunt against pack members. Our primary focus now should be on the fact that Castro is a threat and will stop at nothing to achieve his aims. He's cunning, manipulative, and ruthless. Please," I implored, turning my gaze onto each of the faces gathered as I spoke, "I urge any of you, if you are approached by him or suspect that someone may be working with him, come to me immediately. I ask for your trust in these challenging times."

A few raised their hands, wanting to voice their concerns regarding my investigation into Cecily, disbelief in her turning against her pack, though there were just as many who stood up pointing out how jealous she'd been when I chose Liza to be my mate, and how they were unsurprised by her treachery.

"Ty," came a voice that silenced the rest. Mrs. Reid, a high-ranking elderly pack member, stood up from her seat. "Don't you see the truth here? Cecily is not at fault. She was but a pawn. Liza brought all this trouble to our front door! It's her fault Castro turned and murdered one of our own. Liza is to blame."

I clenched my fists, anger boiling within me at the accusation against my mate. My protective instincts flared, and I was about to defend her when Liza stepped forward, her expression calm and determined.

"Let me handle this, Ty," Liza whispered before she took her place at the podium. Before I could say another word, she adjusted the microphone and addressed the pack.

# Chapter 6 - Liza

I stood before the angry and confused pack members, allowing them to see the outwardly calm and collected mate of their alpha. On the inside, though, I was a fucking bundle of nerves. My heart raced, but that didn't matter. I had to push through my anxiety. I locked my knees so no one would know I was trembling like a leaf. This was something I had to do. There was no way I could let Ty speak up for me, not this time. If I did, I would lose any respect the pack had for me. I was the queen of this castle now, and this was my opportunity to show them I was not only a dependable mate to their alpha, but also someone who wouldn't take shit from any of them.

"If I can have your attention." I stood, staring out at the crowd staring back at me and tried to find the courage to address their concerns. "I understand that there is much confusion and anger among you, and I want you all to know that I hear you."

My mind raced as I desperately searched for the perfect words. I wanted to strike a delicate balance between honesty and diplomacy. It was quite a challenge. I'd never actively sought Castro's attention, but his unwavering fixation on me had completely disrupted our once-harmonious pack, causing division and chaos. I had to remind myself that his actions were beyond my control. I just needed to find the right way to express this without shifting blame. What I sought was genuine understanding and resolution.

"Castro has caused all of us great pain. He aided in the murder of my family, my pack, and, though I've been blessed—adopted into a wonderful family, accepted by you all into the Keller pack—the wound still cuts deep within me." I paused for a moment, my voice cracking slightly when I thought of my lost loved ones. "His obsession with me has nothing to do with who I am or what I have done. It's important for us all to remember that I am not the enemy here. Castro is the enemy."

Their eyes bored into me, searching for any hint of weakness or insincerity, but I stood tall and refused to back down. I kept my head up, willing them to hear the truth in my words. "I can't control another person's actions any more than any of you can. And though I understand your frustrations and the need to point fingers, the only one to blame is Castro."

I gathered my thoughts, looking into the eyes of my fellow pack members. The gravity of the situation was a heavy weight in the air as I reminded them of the impending danger. "It's common knowledge that Castro is a force to be reckoned with and a man with evil intentions. He has already proven he can turn one of our own against us without setting foot in town. Then once he had no more need for her, he callously killed her in a horrible, painful manner. Let us not allow him to succeed anymore. The strength of our pack's unity is of paramount importance at this critical moment. We need to rise above the chaos he has unleashed, stand shoulder to shoulder, and defend one another. Our collective resilience will be the shield against which Castro's evil cannot prevail."

The murmurs among the crowd seemed to die down a little, but I wasn't naïve. They were still skeptical. I couldn't blame them. If I struggled to believe that everything happening was because of one man's twisted obsession with me, how could I expect them to?

"Please," I implored. "Please try to understand that my only goal is the safety and wellbeing of our pack. I want nothing more than to stand beside Ty and help lead us all into a better future, but we can only do that if we stay united and focus on the real threat: Castro. He's a dangerous man, and we need to protect one another from him."

When I finished my speech, relief washed over me. I had spoken my truth, and now it was up to them to decide whether or not they would accept it. In their eyes, there was a multitude of emotions. Some still held on to their anger, while others seemed to be weighing my words carefully. My hands trembled from the rush of adrenaline, but I was convinced I had done the right thing by speaking up for myself.

"Thank you all for listening," I murmured, nodding at them before stepping back and allowing Ty to take center stage once more. I sensed his pride in me as he kissed my cheek, grabbing my hand and giving it a gentle squeeze. His support gave me strength.

"We have listened to your concerns, and we will continue to do everything in our power to keep this pack safe from harm." Ty's words were strong and commanding. "Now, let's move forward together and show Castro that he cannot break our bond."

The meeting dispersed, and I mingled with the pack, wanting to make sure they were seen and heard, but also to allow them to see I would not be cowed. It was strange being in a position of power when I was so used to staying under the radar, but I didn't want to let Ty down, or let the Keller family name down.

"Your speech was very brave," one of the younger pack members told me, her eyes full of admiration. "I don't think I'd ever be able to stand in front of all these people and speak as candidly as you did. I'm glad you're our alpha's mate."

"Thank you." My cheeks flushed with pride and a bit of embarrassment. "I just want what's best for all of us, and I hope that came across in my words."

I continued to make my way through the crowd, making myself available, answering questions when asked, and the tension in the air slowly dissipated. While not everyone was won over by my speech, many seemed more open to accepting me as their leader.

But that acceptance was short-lived when one of the elder pack members approached, red-faced and fists clenched at his sides. His eyes locked on mine, and he carried an air of violence like he intended to strike me and do physical harm. He stopped just inches from my face, his breath hot on my skin as he practically spat his words at me. "I'm not one who will be so easily swayed by your charms," he growled, disdain dripping from every word.

I held my hands up in a placating gesture. "I wasn't trying to charm anyone. I was just speaking the truth."

He scoffed, rolling his eyes. "You're nothing but an opportunist. Despite what you say, actions carry more weight than words in my book. No matter what you say, I'll never see you as the lady of this pack. You're just a little girl playing dress up, nothing more."

My stomach clenched, but I managed to keep my composure. It was a heavy blow to my ego, though I refused to let him see how much that had affected me. I wouldn't give him the damn satisfaction, fucking asshole.

I looked around, wondering if anyone else had overheard the elder's disparaging comments. He stood with his arms crossed, waiting for whatever response I might give him. I was positive he'd just take my words, twist them, and then regurgitate his nonsense back at me. How had Persephone dealt with this old geezer all those years?

As if summoned by my internal plea for help, Persephone appeared, gracefully crossing the room.

She wore a stunning emerald-green gown that clung to her curves, her dark hair cascading down her back in soft waves. She held her head high, exuding confidence and authority. I really did feel like a little girl playing dress up as she approached. I wasn't sure I'd ever pull off being the First Lady of the Keller pack the way Persephone did. She'd set the bench high.

Damn. The woman knew how to own a room. From the moment she entered with an air of confidence, her presence commanded attention. Not that I was jealous of Persephone, but observing her effortlessly captivate everyone around her was a reminder of the standards I aspired to meet. She inspired me to strive for greater self-assurance, which wouldn't be an easy goal to reach with backlash from elders and pack members alike.

"Excuse me," she said, her voice smooth as silk. "But I couldn't help overhear your concerns, Elder." She turned her gaze toward me, giving me a quick reassuring smile before turning her intense gaze back to the man. "However, must I remind you that questioning our alpha and offending his mate is not acceptable behavior?"

The elder's expression faltered, a flicker of uncertainty passing through his eyes, but he remained stubbornly silent, his lips a tight line. Persephone, sensing the tension, took my arm and guided me away from the disgruntled old man before he found his voice again to choke out a response that may escalate the situation further.

"Liza, let me give you some advice on how to deal with grumpy old people like him. My mother-in-law gave me the same advice when I married Dominic," she said as we walked toward the refreshments table. "Be polite, or they'll use it against you. Remind them of their importance—it plays into their ego. But most importantly, never let them have the last word or allow them to feel like they have the upper hand. They'll use it against you and simply walk all over you."

Before I had the time to question her further, another pack member hollered Persephone's name, interrupting our fleeting connection. She gave my cheek a gentle pat, her touch warm and comforting, letting me know everything was okay. The depth of her understanding shone from her eyes, instilling me with a sense of hope and courage.

"You're doing great, Liza," she said. Then I watched as Persephone joined one of the council members and his wife.

Glancing around the room, I realized I had no desire to speak to another soul. I needed a breather. Being in front of the pack like this was not something I was used to, especially since I'd always considered myself more of an introvert, happier to be in the background than upfront for all to see.

I stepped out into the cool, crisp air, taking a small winding path in one of the gardens that surrounded the house. I didn't go far, just far enough to breathe and clear my mind.

How had Persephone handled all of this with such poise and grace for so long without shattering under the pressure? It might do me some good to spend time with Persephone. I was sure she'd be happy to let me tap into her years of experience and wisdom and give me some pointers on how to approach being an alpha's mate.

The cool breeze caressed my face as I looked up at the moonlit sky, seeking solace in its calming presence.

A sudden shift in the air had goosebumps rising on my skin. My instincts were on high alert when I felt eyes on me again. I peered around the shadowy gardens. Night had hidden the gaps in the trees. The moon wasn't full anymore, so there wasn't enough light to banish the darkness of the woods. I didn't see anyone nearby. I was sure nobody had followed me out. Was it my imagination, or was something truly amiss?

I felt extremely vulnerable. I hadn't told anyone I was coming outside. After all our talk of Castro being our enemy and being careful to look out for one another, I'd stupidly left myself exposed. Just as I was turning to walk back inside, a voice I didn't recognize seemed to resonate directly in my mind. *"You'll know everything soon,"* it said, clear and unnervingly.

My heart pounded in my chest as my head whipped around, searching for the source of the voice. But there was no one here. I was completely alone.

Blood rushed through my veins. The overwhelming fear I experienced froze my chest and made it hard to breathe, but I fought against it, determined to maintain control. I couldn't let Ty sense this through our bond. There was no fucking way I'd let him see me like this, never mind tell him about what had happened here.

Despite my unwavering certainty about having seen a figure from our bedroom window the night before, I was fairly sure Ty thought I'd imagined it. If I told him I'd heard a strange voice in my head, he'd believe I'd gone batshit crazy, and I didn't want him to think he had made a mistake in choosing me as his mate, or that I was unable to handle my position as the lady of the pack.

I closed my eyes tightly, taking in some cleansing breaths before opening them again. It was just stress and lack of sleep that was causing my mind to play tricks. At least, that's what I kept telling myself. It was another matter entirely whether I believed in myself.

Although I returned inside and joined the remaining pack members, I couldn't shake the fear. Maybe I *was* losing touch on reality.

\*\*\*

When I woke up the next morning, Ty looked down at me with worried eyes. "You all right?"

Hesitating for a moment, I took a deep breath and mustered a smile that I hoped passed for genuine. "I'm fine." Deep down, however, I was far from it. My emotions threatened to overwhelm me, as if the world itself was closing in on me.

The guilt over not telling Ty nagged at my conscience. He had enough to be worried about with Castro and the pack, so I pushed the events of the previous night in the garden to one side, determined to soldier through the day.

Today marked the first day of launching the next chapter in my catering business, but I was completely out of it. The incidents of the previous evening weighed heavily on my mind, and I hadn't slept a wink. As I trudged along the corridor to my home office, I caught sight of my reflection in a hallway mirror and winced. No wonder Ty hadn't looked completely reassured. I looked like shit. No amount of eye cream or concealer would hide the dark circles under my eyes.

Sabrina arrived soon after I'd made my way downstairs to the office. It was bright and early, which wasn't exactly her favorite part of the day. She was a true night owl and slept in most mornings.

One of the house staff led her to my office. Sabrina walked in, rubbing her eyes with her index fingers, yawning loudly.

"Good morning, sunshine. I didn't realize you went anywhere before noon." I grinned as Sabrina cracked a smile.

"Seriously, though, thanks for showing up so early to help me get everything ready," I said. "And for offering to deliver the meals until I find a permanent driver."

"Of course," Sabrina said enthusiastically. "Anything for my favorite chef and lady of the pack. Doesn't hurt to be on the good side of the alpha's mate." She winked at me playfully, and I rolled my eyes.

We took my menu cards down to the kitchen and set about cooking the meals. While we carried out our tasks, Sabrina and I chatted about everything from pack gossip to the latest fall recipes we were excited to try. The laughter that bubbled up between us was a welcome distraction from the anxieties that had been plaguing me since I'd spotted that shadowy figure in the woods.

"Seriously, though," Sabrina said as she poured batter into a cake pan. "This kitchen is like something out of a dream. It's got to be the biggest and nicest one any of us have ever seen."

"I know. I still pinch myself every morning. It's hard to believe I get to work here every day." I lowered my voice slightly. "I think some of the house staff find it odd that I work in the kitchen. They're always really polite, but it's weird hearing people addressing me as Mrs. Keller." I choked back a giggle. "When I first heard it, I was looking for Persephone before I realized they were speaking to me."

"Ah, the perks of being mated to the alpha," Sabrina teased, nudging me playfully. "Also, you're not old, Mrs. Keller. You're just an old married woman." Her tone turned serious. "Jokes aside, Liza, you're a strong, confident woman. I can't tell you how much I admire you. You've never let anything hold you back. That's why you deserve this kitchen and that man of yours. You deserve all of this and more. You've worked so hard to get to where you are with your business and your place beside Ty. I'm really proud of you." She smiled at me warmly before turning back to the oven.

"Is it hot in here or just me?" I fanned myself and winked at Sabrina. "You're making me blush. Thanks, Sabrina. Your words mean a lot to me. Trust me, I really needed to hear them."

Sabrina raised an eyebrow. "Don't tell me you're concerned about your speech last night. You absolutely nailed it."

I hesitated, almost telling her about everything that happened—the shadow figure in the trees, the voice in my head—but thought better of it. The last thing I needed was Ty and my best friend thinking I'd lost my marbles. "No, I think the speech went over as well as it could have. Most of the feedback was positive."

"I still can't believe it all. I mean, Cecily betraying the pack and then getting poisoned? It sounds like the plot from a fucking soap opera." Sabrina laughed as she wiped her hands on a dish towel. "Honestly, though, I can't believe she'd do something like that. I always knew she was a bitch but damn."

"Yeah, it was a shocker for everyone." I really didn't want to talk through Cecily's actions all over again, so I shifted the conversation to something more positive. "I may have some good news, though."

Sabrina stopped in her tracks and turned to face me expectantly. "Ty hired a new informant. Isaiah. He's working on finding out the details of Castro and Cecily's relationship and how it came about that she helped him. We're waiting for his first report."

"Wow, things are moving fast, huh? I guess the new alpha doesn't waste any time getting down to business and hiring his staff." Sabrina paused, then gestured to the large stove. "On a lighter note, can we talk some more about this kitchen? It's gorgeous."

I laughed, glancing around at the state-of-the-art appliances and gleaming countertops. "I know, right? It takes me forever and a day to find cooking utensils and ingredients. Maybe I should come up with some sort of cataloging method, like the Dewey Decimal System they use in the libraries."

Sabrina, with an exasperated expression, rolled her eyes and swiftly grabbed the dish towel that lay nearby. Without hesitation, she playfully tossed it in my direction, aiming directly at my face. As the towel sailed through the air, she laughed and mockingly yelled, "Nerd alert!"

"Okay, okay." I giggled. "Back to work before Ty sends someone down here to check on us."

We finished preparing and boxing up my new fall menu items, chatting and laughing together as we worked. The camaraderie between us helped lift my spirits, pushing the crap that happened last night to the back of my mind.

As we loaded up the car, Bryce and Isaiah pulled up to the estate at the same time. Isaiah got out of his car first. I turned slightly so I could watch Sabrina's expression as she took in his appearance. I felt slightly smug at her reaction. She thought he was just as fine as I'd believed she might. I could practically see the hearts flying around her head. It was almost comical.

"Who's that?" Sabrina asked, not bothering to hide her interest.

"Isaiah," I explained, watching as he approached us with a friendly smile.

Isaiah looked Sabrina over but didn't address her. Instead, he turned to face me. "Liza, I have some information to report to Ty, so I'll head inside."

"Thank you, Isaiah." I smiled and gave a thumbs up, which, in hindsight, was super lame and probably didn't earn me any cool points with the new informant. "I'll be up to join you in Ty's office shortly."

With a gentle smile, he acknowledged my gratitude before directing a subtle nod toward Sabrina. If he had noticed my dumb thumbs up or Sabrina's attempts to undress him with her eyes, he didn't let on.

Bryce, who had been staring after Isaiah, now turned his attention to me with a perplexed look on his face. He squinted, his brow furrowing, clearly taken aback by Isaiah's sudden departure. "Who the hell was that?" Bryce asked with equal parts confusion and curiosity.

"Isaiah is our new informant. Ty just hired him this week."

Bryce scowled, clearly not too happy about Ty's choice in an overtly handsome man for his new employee. It was possible his displeasure came from Ty not informing him he'd hired his new informant, but I hadn't been the only one watching Sabrina. I had a hunch his sour mood had more to do with the way she'd been openly lusting after Isaiah.

# Chapter 7 - Ty

I walked into my office, greeted by heavy, cloying tension. It was fucking palpable. While I carried out quick introductions, Bryce glared at Isaiah with such intensity that it made me uncomfortable. Isaiah seemed unfazed by it, though. I found it strange that Bryce was reacting so strongly to someone he had never met, but I chose not to dwell on it. There were more important things to focus on, such as Isaiah's report.

"Isaiah." I extended my hand to him. "Please tell me you have some news."

"Yes, sir. I managed to find the information you wanted."

"Great." I picked up my phone. "Let me just shoot Liza a quick message to come and join us. We can discuss everything together."

Isaiah shook his head at the mention of Liza, then hesitated for what seemed like an eternity. It appeared the knowledge he'd acquired weighed heavily on him. I watched as some internal debate played out in his eyes before he finally responded. "With due respect, Alpha, given the gravity of what I've uncovered, I would strongly advise you to listen to what I have to say first before sharing it with Mrs. Keller."

His words immediately put me on edge, the hair at the back of my neck rising. What the hell had he uncovered? Based on his reaction and the way he had suggested we hold off on having Liza join us, I suspected he had something heavy to discuss. Trusting his judgment, I put my phone down on my desk.

I remembered my manners and gestured for them both to sit down.

They settled into their seats, and Isaiah made a subtle gesture to the right where Bryce sat, which I took to mean, *did I want him to hear this report?* Bryce was my business partner and closest friend. Though guilt gnawed at me for excluding Liza, I trusted him implicitly and valued his input. I nodded at Isaiah, indicating he should go on.

Isaiah relayed everything he'd discovered, and I was admittedly impressed by the sheer amount of information he'd gathered in just one day—not even a full day at that.

"I extracted more of the conversation between Cecily and Castro. It goes further back than what Nico found. From their text messages, it's obvious they had some sort of romantic relationship during his time in Presley Acres, when he used the alias Stone," Isaiah said. "Reading between the lines, however, makes it clear that it never became physical. Castro, as Stone, led Cecily on up until the moment he supposedly died."

I raised an eyebrow. "Explain? Because most of the shit he convinced her to do happened after his alleged death."

"After his death, he went on messaging Cecily from untraceable numbers—most likely burner phones— telling her he'd had to go into hiding and spewing lies about Liza. He told her Liza had set him up because he didn't want to be romantically involved with her. But she'd continuously pursued him, insisting that he choose her as his partner. When he declined her proposal, she went with you to make him jealous."

I scoffed. "What a fucking joke." The sheer absurdity and ridiculousness of this situation was beyond belief. How could Cecily believe all that shit?

"When Cecily pushed back and questioned why he wouldn't publicly acknowledge their relationship, Castro led her to think he was protecting her, that Liza would be furious that Cecily had taken him from her and would go after her. As improbable as this all sounds to us, you've probably guess that Cecily accepted Castro's every word as truth." Isaiah crossed his legs, his expression remaining neutral. "I never had the pleasure of meeting Cecily, but it seems she might've been desperate for some male attention, and that led to her being willing to believe anything he told her."

I cracked my knuckles. "Cecily felt threatened by Liza because Liza is my fated mate. I can't tell you for how long Cecily's parents tried to push her on me. Every time we had a social event, I'd turn around and Cecily would be there. Comments were made at every pack meeting. It became almost scary how forceful they were over our potential mating and how it would improve their standing within the pack. So, Castro played right into her hands by making Cecily believe Liza wanted him."

Isaiah nodded thoughtfully, understanding flickering in his eyes. "That explains a lot," he said. "To her, Liza going after all of her men, one by one, eroded her ego. It was like Liza became the embodiment of her own worst fears, a constant reminder of her own insecurities possibly fed by her parents pushing her to better their place in society. And so, fueled by a burning desire to reclaim her self-worth, she vowed to get back at Liza to prove that she was not to be trifled with."

Damn. Talk about a woman scorned. "So, her immediate response was to plant a bomb in the clock tower to potentially kill innocent people? That doesn't seem plausible, even for someone as senseless as Cecily."

"Castro had her convinced that all of this had turned into some twisted game, that his and Liza's feud would end with no one hurt." Isaiah glanced at Bryce. "Cecily was so blinded by her rage and jealousy, she accepted everything Castro said without question. She saw the only means of getting revenge on Liza was to hurt her in return, regardless of who else might suffer along the way."

Bryce, who had been silent up until that point, suddenly interrupted. "It sounds like Castro had Cecily wrapped around his little finger. I bet he observed her for a while, then used her jealousy to his advantage, implying that she could get even with Liza by taking something she wanted. I've got to hand it to the guy... Castro's a fucking genius."

I let out an exasperated sigh and crossed my arms as I leaned back into my chair. That narcissistic psychopath didn't deserve any accolades. "Well, I wouldn't exactly categorize him as a genius, but there's no denying his uncanny ability to pinpoint and exploit someone's vulnerabilities."

"I'm of the opinion that Cecily had no knowledge of the bomb she planted in the clock tower being real," Isaiah said. "Perhaps she believed it to be a prank, some trick that would scare you and Liza. But kill you? No, I don't think Cecily wanted you dead. If she'd realized you'd have been harmed, I'm not sure she would have been so easy to sway. After all, she couldn't have you, and she certainly didn't approve of your relationship with Liza, so why not make you miserable along the way?"

I rolled my eyes, taken aback and finding it hard to understand how anyone in their right mind could be that clueless. I mean, seriously, how could she have not noticed all the twisted wiring snaking all across the room connecting it to the ominous-looking device? And that wasn't even the worst part. At the end of the wiring, there had been a bundle of fucking explosives.

"Are you positive Cecily wasn't just acting the innocent? After all, if she didn't know the bomb was real, she wouldn't be punished as harshly if she were to get caught."

"I'm not arguing with you, sir. It's hard to accept, but the emails and texts are genuine." Isaiah handed me a folder. I opened it and scanned the printouts. "There's more."

"What is this?"

"Routine deliveries made to Cecily," Isaiah said. "Some extravagant flowers, and imported chocolates."

I raised an eyebrow.

"I'm assuming you don't need an explanation for that."

I shook my head. Of course, I already understood the significance of the chocolates. He'd groomed her into expecting the sweet treats, so when he no longer needed her, the last delivery she'd received contained the arsenic-laced bonbons that ultimately ended her life. Despite her poor decisions and horrific attitude, Cecily didn't deserve to die that way.

"All right." I set the folder aside. "I don't understand why you feel this information was something that should be kept from Liza? She already knows all of this. I consider Liza to be my partner, my better half, and I want her to be involved in these types of briefings." I paused for a second, remembering the asshole candidate who'd belittled Liza, and followed on with misogynistic comments in the middle of his interview. Surely, Isaiah didn't think that as a woman, Liza had no place in these meetings? "Explain yourself, Isaiah."

"Unfortunately, there's more, and it's, well... shocking." Isaiah slid another folder he'd been holding across the desk in my direction. "Besides the text messages and deliveries, I also found something rather disturbing on Cecily's laptop." Isaiah's voice took on a more somber tone.

"How were you able to access her computer? Don't the police have it?"

I interpreted the stare he gave me as a signal to not ask questions, which he only confirmed when he answered, "I could tell you, but if I did, I'd have to kill you, but I'm not a fan of clichés, and I really don't want to threaten my new boss." He flashed a brief grin before quickly continuing, the smile fading. "It's probably best if you're in the dark, Alpha—culpable deniability and all. When I got possession of the laptop, it was completely out of juice. Once I charged it up, it appeared to have been mid-reboot when the battery died. I was able to override it and discovered it had been accessed remotely, where someone had been attempting to delete files. Fortunately for us, Cecily wasn't someone who kept her laptop charged all the time. So I could see exactly which files the person— who I assume is Castro—attempted to erase."

As I opened the folder, my mouth dropped open at the contents. Inside were countless candid images of Liza, some taken in broad daylight, captured with some type of high-powered lens while she appeared to be working in her client's home. Cecily had been watching Liza for quite some time, documenting her every move.

"Why would Cecily have all of these photos?" I asked, forcing my voice to remain steady.

"From the emails I found, it seemed that Castro encouraged her to take them as references for buyers." Isaiah's eyes darkened with concern. "It seems he's planning to sell Liza off, her status as an omega being the main selling point."

"Are you fucking serious?" Anger and fear coursed through me as I stood abruptly, sending one of the folders to the floor. "Buyers? What the fuck?"

"Ty, I know it sounds insane, but that's what I found." Isaiah remained composed, despite my visible anger. "Look, neither of us wants to accept that Castro would actually do something like this. The information you shared with me suggests he wants her for himself because of a promise made in their childhood, so I understand your disbelief. But we'd be fools if we don't consider the evidence in front of us. Especially if he's as furious at you and Liza for marrying and completing the mating bond as you suspect. What I'm about to say is conjecture based on my investigation. He still sees Liza as his possession, but as you've officially mated, he now sees her as sullied. So, selling her is possibly his way of causing maximum hurt to her and, as an added bonus, destroy you. If he has already started the process of advertising Liza, that won't stop just because Cecily is dead."

I clenched my fists as I stared at the photos of Liza. How many people had seen them? What did they have planned for her? My blood turned hot as lava at the thought of deviant shifters whacking off to her image, trying to imagine what it'd be like to fuck the omega. I'd seen firsthand what happened to the men who caught a whiff of Liza's pheromones. Those sickos would stop at nothing to own her, and they wouldn't treat her as the queen she is. They'd use her for their own nefarious purposes, and who the fuck knew what they'd do when they were finished with her.

"Okay, Isaiah. We'll look into this situation and see if there's anything in it," I said, trying to keep my voice steady. "But you made the right call. I don't want Liza knowing about this just yet. Not until we have more solid information." If this turned out just to be some sordid fantasy between Cecily and fucking Castro, then she didn't need to know. I tapped the folders in front of me. "Thanks, Isaiah. You've done some impressive work here."

"I'll let you know if I find out anything more."

I retrieved the folder I'd dropped on the floor and put all the documents into my desk drawer. A sudden thought occurred to me. "What did you do with the files on the laptop?" I didn't want to risk the police seeing these pictures, or seeing Castro's plans to sell Liza off like some sick bastards' ultimate sex toy or breeding mare and leaking it.

"I took the liberty of ensuring the images and any reference to them were removed and scrambled from Cecily's laptop, sir. Nothing we've discussed can be found on the machine."

His quick and detailed probe left me genuinely grateful. Based on his actions on this first mission alone, he'd proved to be dynamic with his investigation skills and thought processes. Also, his compassion regarding my mate's feelings left me very impressed with Isaiah, and extremely happy I'd hired him. I had a suspicion he was going to become as valuable an informant to me as Nico had been to my father.

With a nod, Isaiah stood.

As Isaiah made to leave, Liza and Sabrina walked through the office door. It gave me a front-row seat to the drama unfolding between Sabrina, Bryce, and Isaiah. Now I realized exactly why Bryce had his fucking boxers in a bunch. I watched in amusement as

Sabrina immediately got hearts in her eyes like a damn cartoon character when she spotted Isaiah.

I coughed into my hand, covering my mouth, and trying not to snicker at my best friend. Bryce's glare flicked between Sabrina as she batted her eyes at Isaiah, and Isaiah's indifferent stare. Oh, Sabrina wanted to jump Isaiah's bones, and the only thing that would make it more obvious was if she stripped naked and offered herself up on a platter. We all knew it, but notably Bryce.

"We have some leftovers in the kitchen if you'd like me to make you a plate to go. I bet you burn a lot of calories working out." Sabrina's eyes traveled down Isaiah's fit body, and I almost choked, especially when Bryce turned an odd shade of red.

Isaiah stared down at her, his face blank. "No, thank you." He shot Liza a small smile and a nod before he walked away, with Sabrina staring after him like a fucking cat in heat.

I locked eyes with Liza, and we shared a knowing look. My eyes darted between Sabrina and Bryce, and Liza nodded discreetly. It took everything for us to hide our laughter. The levity was required to chase away the images of the pictures Isaiah had put in my head of Liza being sold like a piece of meat.

Sabrina turned to Liza. "Right, pretty lady, I am off to have a cold shower after that fine example and then make my deliveries. Best not to upset the mate to the alpha. I've heard she can be a real bitch." She and Liza laughed, and my heart swelled. It was good to see Liza looking happy and relaxed.

Bryce surprised me by saying, "I'll see you down to your car, Sabrina. I forgot something in my car." Sabrina gave Liza a quick hug and told her she'd let her know when the deliveries were complete, then left, giving no sign she'd heard Bryce, but he scuttled off behind her, anyway.

Liza and I waited till we heard them reach the stairs, then we both burst out laughing. "Well, that's going to be interesting to watch play out," Liza said.

She moved to the side of my desk and put her arm around my shoulders, teasing the fine hairs at the nape of my neck. Her touch made it hard to concentrate and sent all my blood rushing straight to my cock, until it immediately deflated when Liza asked. "So, what was Isaiah doing here? Did he find out anything more about Castro and Cecily?"

I couldn't tell her everything—not yet. Instead, I smiled and squeezed her hand. "Isaiah did a fantastic job of uncovering additional text messages and emails between Cecily and Castro. It turns out Castro had convinced Cecily that you wanted to be with him. Can you believe it?"

Liza looked physically ill at the notion. "Why in the hell would Cecily think that?"

"She believed what she wanted to believe. After all, we knew Cecily had already been jealous of you, wishing she could've been my chosen mate."

Liza rolled her eyes. "Don't remind me."

"Castro even made her think the bomb was all just a game meant to scare us." I left out the part about the photos and what they implied. I wanted to protect her from any unnecessary worry until we knew for sure it was something to be concerned about. I hoped like fuck that decision wouldn't come back to bite me in the ass.

"Wow, that's... a lot to take in," Liza said softly, chewing on the inside of her cheek. "But I'm glad you guys are looking into it. We certainly don't want anyone in the pack falling prey to Castro's manipulation again. If he can influence the richest bachelorette in Presley Acres, who else could he twist around his little finger to do his bidding?"

"Exactly. Isaiah's getting right back to it, seeing what more he can uncover," I assured her, hoping she wouldn't pick up on the fact that I was holding back information. My intention was to protect her from any unnecessary worry until we knew for sure whether there was something to be concerned about.

After Liza left the office, and before I lost myself in work, I pulled the file Isaiah had given me out of the drawer and sifted through the photos. The pictures took my breath away, not just because of how beautiful Liza appeared in the candid shots—and she was fucking gorgeous—but because of the fear. What if Castro actually attempted to sell Liza off? My stomach twisted into knots at the thought. Would he sell her, then kidnap her to take her to the highest bidder, or try to take her first? I would do everything in my power to ensure that didn't happen.

Bryce returned and found me staring at the images. "Ty, you've got to stop obsessing till we know more."

I looked up at him. He was right, I knew it, but he didn't have the first clue of the fear that was coursing through my system. It wasn't his fault. He'd know one day maybe, if he ever stopped bouncing from woman to woman, what it meant to love someone, but I hoped to fuck he never had to live through the torment Castro was putting me and my mate through.

"So, what exactly did you leave in the car?" I looked pointedly at his empty hands.

He stuttered, "Th-thought I left a file for this afternoon's meeting, but I remembered it was in your drawer."

I didn't push him about his reaction to Sabrina's infatuation with Isaiah. We had too much work to catch up on.

We worked until the late afternoon, making good progress. However, he was interrupted when he was called in to attend a meeting with a transport manager at one of the depots. The rest of the day seemed to drag on. I had a video conference with my team at Keller Enterprises about a drop-ship facility we were considering investing in. I completed the paperwork, then called in.

"Good afternoon, gentlemen. What's the latest on the new facility?"

"Good afternoon, Mr. Keller." Jason, one of my assistants, typically took control of the conference calls so we didn't talk over one another. "Based on the correspondence that they sent to me before the meeting, it looks like we're waiting for the information from the survey company."

"What exactly do we need to know?" I tapped my pen on the desk and stared out the window. I couldn't concentrate on anything other than those damn pictures of Liza.

"I'm going to refer that question to Randy, since he met with the surveying crew while they were on site. Randy, can you fill Mr. Keller in on the details they are looking for, please?"

Randy, one of the newest members of my team, nervously came into frame. "The survey crew assured me they'd have all the details by the end of the week. It's not so much the size of the lot that's holding us up, sir. We need to determine if there's enough space between our potential building site and the warehouse on the property next door. City ordinances require a specific amount of space between commercial buildings to allow for things like parking spaces and to be up to fire code."

"Thanks, Randy. I'm fully aware of the ordinances. Let me know when you get that information from the surveying company." With one eye on the computer screen displaying the call, an alert to a new email on the other screen caught my attention.

*Good afternoon, Mr. Keller.*

*After reviewing the sale package regarding your factory located at 223 Poplar Street, it is our company's intention to move forward with the process of purchasing the building.*

*We look forward to hearing from you and hope to set up an informational meeting at your earliest convenience.*

*Regards*

*Russell and Sons, LLC*

I interrupted the meeting. "Does anyone know anything about the old factory on Poplar Street being on the market?"

They all shook their heads. No one seemed to have a clue.

"I've just received a noted interest through from a company..." I read aloud, scanning through the email again. "Russell and Sons, LLC. Has anyone heard of them before?"

Silence met my question, giving me all the answers I needed. I would have to dig into this mysterious company myself. After bookmarking the email to revisit later, I finished discussing the new drop facility and ended the call, then took some time to research Russell and Sons. Unfortunately, they didn't seem very active online, which only made me more suspicious. Why would they want a small manufacturing plant?

A few minutes later, my phone rang. It was Tim, my financial analyst.

"Ty, I apologize for not mentioning the sale of the Poplar Street factory on the conference call," he began, his voice filled with regret. "I meant to bring it up with you before, but you've been busy with the pack and your lovely new bride. I'd been reviewing the figures, and it wasn't performing as well as we'd hoped, so I put it on the market a few weeks ago. There hasn't been any interest in it at all, but now with this offer from Russell and Sons, as your financial advisor, it would be remiss of me not to tell you to take the offer seriously. You should set up a meeting and try like hell to offload it."

"Thanks for telling me, Tim, but why am I just finding out about one of our businesses being on the market now? Once again, you've gone above my head and left me out of the loop, which is completely unacceptable." I didn't hide my ire. This guy was like the sound of fucking nails down a chalkboard. He should've said something earlier on the call, but he really should've included me in a decision to list an asset. "I'll look into it more. In the meantime, as the CEO of Keller Enterprises, *it would be remiss of me not to tell you to recognize your position* and keep me abreast of any and all business dealings."

I ended the call before he could say anything.

I spent a few more hours researching Russell and Sons but didn't find much of anything. Annoyed and feeling like I'd hit a dead end, I decided to call it a night. I looked at my watch and discovered I'd worked far later than I'd intended.

I walked up to our room to find Liza already asleep in our bed. As I got changed, my thoughts kept circling back to the photos of her and the horrifying possibility of her being sold off. The thought of my sweet Liza being auctioned off to the highest bidder like some kind of commodity filled me with an unparalleled rage. I needed to find answers, and fast.

Once I slipped into bed as quietly as I could, I watched Liza toss and turn in her sleep, moaning softly. My heart ached for her. She'd been so restless lately. As much as I hated it, I knew it was best not to put any more burdens on her.

# Chapter 8 - Liza

The dream began like a soft watercolor, hues blending together as a scene from my early childhood took shape. I looked to be about three or four years old, and the world seemed so much bigger, brighter, and full of possibilities. The grass was cool beneath my small feet, tickling my toes as I ran across the lawn. Sunlight filtered through the trees, dappling my pale blonde hair with golden spots.

Beside me, a little boy giggled as we played together. Although his features were strikingly similar—that same blonde hair and bright blue eyes that could pierce your soul—I knew for sure it wasn't Castro. We were playing tag, our laughter echoing through the air as we chased each other in circles.

"Can't catch me," he teased, sticking his tongue out playfully while darting around a tree.

I giggled, the innocent sound bubbling up from deep within my belly, and chased him as fast as my little legs would carry me.

Somehow, even in my dream, I knew this to be an actual memory. I recognized the pure joy that only comes with the innocence of childhood.

"Watch me!" I called out, my youthful confidence shining through. My chest tightened with excitement as I closed the distance between us, my small hand reaching out to touch his shoulder.

Just as I was about to tag him, he whirled around and scooped me into his arms, spinning us both around in a dizzying whirlwind of laughter and sunlight. I squealed in delight, the feeling of weightlessness thrilling me to my core.

"Gotcha," he declared triumphantly as he set me back on the ground, a mischievous grin plastered across his face.

I laughed, the warmth of our friendship radiating through me like sunshine.

"Aw, you win." I was panting slightly. "I get you next."

"Deal." He nodded solemnly, extending his pinky finger toward me in a childish gesture of agreement. I hooked my own pinky around his, sealing our pact with an air of importance that only children can truly understand.

"Pinky promise?" I asked, my eyes wide and searching as I sought reassurance in his gaze.

"Promise." The conviction in his voice solidified our bond. We stood there for a moment, simply basking in the joy of each other's company, before collapsing onto the grass in another fit of giggles.

We lay side by side, our fingers intertwined and our breaths mingling in the warm summer air. I was at peace in the dream—something I hadn't experienced in a very long time. It was a fleeting moment, a snapshot of innocence captured within the confines of a dream, but it was beautiful, and real, and it belonged to me.

Slowly, the colors faded, the edges of the dream blurring as reality called me back from the depths of slumber. The bright sunlight dimmed to the soft gray light of morning filtering through the curtains of the master suite. Laughter echoed one final time before dissipating into silence, leaving only the faintest trace of memory in its wake.

I blinked, disoriented and confused as the remnants of the dream clung to the edges of my consciousness. Who was that boy? Why had he appeared in my dreams now, after all these years? I tried to hold on to the memory, to grasp at the fading strands of emotion and connection, but it all slipped through my fingers like sand, lost to the reality of waking up as an adult. Not just any adult, but one who heard voices in her head and saw figures no one else could see.

I stared up at the ceiling, grappling with the strange sense of longing that tugged at my melancholy heart. I sighed. Yet another mystery for which I had no answers. That dream, that moment of pure happiness, had been a gift, and a glimpse into a past I could never reclaim.

"You okay?" Ty's voice broke through my thoughts, and I turned my head to see him watching me intently, concern etched into the lines of his face. Guilt coiled like a snake in my insides. Yet another morning I'd woken to see worry across my mate's handsome features.

"Fine," I said, smoothing away the worry lines on his forehead with my fingers. I forced a smile and pushed the lingering echoes of the dream to the back of my mind. "Just a weird dream, that's all."

"Want to talk about it?" Ty offered gently as he brushed a stray strand of hair from my face.

I hesitated, then shook my head. I didn't want to delve into the memories just yet. "Not right now," I said softly. "Maybe later."

"Okay." Ty pressed a soft kiss to my forehead, his love and support a warm embrace. "Whenever you're ready."

I headed to the bathroom to begin my morning routine, pushing thoughts of the dream aside. I stared at the bags under my eyes, a testament to my disturbed night. Groaning, I turned on the faucet and splashed cold water onto my face, hoping the shock of it would wash away the lingering fatigue.

Next up was brushing my teeth, and the rhythmic motion had a soothing effect on my jangled nerves. After rinsing my mouth, I began working through the tangles in my hair, wincing as I encountered several particularly stubborn knots. More proof—as if I needed it—of my restless sleep.

I heard Ty take a call from the bedroom, his voice suddenly low and serious. He'd put it on speaker, allowing me to catch snippets of a male voice. It belonged to the security guard stationed at the front gate of the estate. When I heard the word "problem", my stomach churned. As if we needed any more issues.

"Stay there," Ty instructed firmly before hanging up, worry darkening his features. "Liza, can you come out here?"

Abandoning my hairbrush mid-stroke, I rushed to join him, anxiety coiling in my gut like a snake poised to strike. "What's going on?" I tried not to sound too overly concerned, but after everything that had happened recently, my nerves were on the damn edge.

"There's an issue at the front gate," he said grimly. "The gate guard on duty said something about a crowd of people trying to get in."

"Who are they? What do they want?" My mind raced with possibilities, each more unnerving than the last.

"I don't know, but we'll figure it out." Ty's jaw clenched, steely resolve flashing in his eyes. "Let's go down to the security office and see what's happening."

We got dressed and hurried to the security office down in the estate's basement, adrenaline pumping through our veins as we prepared to confront the unknown threat. The room was a hive of activity.

Security guards huddled around monitors displaying live feeds of various angles around the estate.

"Look at this," one of them said, pointing to a screen that showed a throng of people gathered outside the front gate. "I have no idea who these people are or what they want."

"Neither do I," Ty muttered, his face tight. "But they're getting restless, and we need to get to the bottom of this as fast as we can."

While we tried to make sense of the situation, my thoughts drifted back to the dream that had haunted me just hours earlier. The lost happiness, the innocence of childhood... it all seemed so far away now—far away from this ensnaring, ever-growing web of danger and uncertainty.

"All right." Ty snapped me out of my spiraling thoughts. "Let's figure out a plan to deal with this crowd, and find out why they're here. We can't let them storm our property."

My pulse ratcheted when Ty's phone rang again, the shrill sound cutting through the tension like a knife. He put the call on speakerphone. "Okay, Isaiah, I've put you on speaker so Liza can hear you, too."

"Good morning, Alpha Keller, Mrs. Keller," Isaiah said. "I'm imagining right about now you're wondering what the hell's going on around the estate? I think I might have some answers for you about that crowd outside your gate."

"You'd be right. Wanna fill us in?" Ty said, his eyes locked on the monitor, showing the sea of unfamiliar faces.

"They're there for Liza," Isaiah explained. "People from all over the country are trying to catch a glimpse of her. They're fascinated by the idea of an omega, and they want to see it with their own eyes."

I flinched at being referred to as an "it". Although my kind were rare, I refused to be treated like an artifact on display in a fucking museum. The thought of being the center of attention and having strangers gawking at me made my skin crawl. It felt so unnerving, I couldn't help but feel a sense of panic.

"But I made the announcement weeks ago! When I wasn't mobbed immediately after, I just figured people didn't care," I said in a high-pitched voice that did not sound like my own.

"Seems they only really started believing it now," Isaiah said.

"Fuck," Ty muttered. "How bad is it, Isaiah?"

"Bad enough that every Airbnb and all the hotels are fully booked. There's not a room available in a hundred-mile vicinity." Isaiah sighed into the phone. "I wish I had better news for you, but I'm afraid this isn't going away anytime soon."

I listened with one ear as Ty finished up the call, a sinking feeling settling in my stomach. This was bad. All these people were here because of me. Then I remembered the incident at my office the other day—two strangers taking photos of me through the window.

Shit. I'd forgotten to tell Ty. Would he be pissed that I hadn't told him until now? Did I really have to ask myself that question? Of course he would be.

"Hey, Ty. Something like this happened to me the other afternoon." His eyes widened. "I know I should've told you sooner, and I meant to, but I guess it just slipped my mind."

The muscles in Ty's jaw contracted. He was more than a little annoyed. "What exactly happened? Are you telling me a group of strangers bombarded you?"

I shook my head. "No, nothing like that. When I went to my parents' place the other day, I noticed the town was busier than normal. It seemed a little odd, and I thought I'd maybe missed a date in the calendar or something." I tried for levity, but Ty wasn't in the mood. I was only delaying the inevitable. "So, anyway. I went to the office, and while I was in there, a couple of people outside came up to the windows. It looked like they were trying to get photos of me with their phones. Jamie and Robin kept me safe, saw them off. That's all."

"That's all?" Ty lowered his voice. "You should've told me, Liza. For that matter, your fucking security detail should've reported the incident. I'll have to speak to Isaiah about it."

"I thought it was a strange fluke. Just some teenagers doing weird teenage shit. I suppose it makes sense now. Look, I know I should've said something sooner," I said, feeling a spasm of guilt. "But I've had a lot on my mind lately."

Not that I could tell him exactly what had been on my mind—or would that be in my mind, imaginary people, and voices? I know in my heart they were real. Ty already knew about the figure I'd seen in the trees, but the thought of telling him about what happened in the garden... Something else I hadn't told him.

"I understand," Ty said, but I heard the irritation in his voice. "We can't let stuff like this fall between the cracks again. I get it's not been easy, Liza, but this is your safety we're talking about. You're my top priority."

Frustration and confusion consumed me. By some weird twist of fate, I'd been born an omega—something that people thought was a mythical beast, like a unicorn—and now I was at the center of a media circus that threatened to spiral out of control. I'd wanted to get in front of the rumors when I'd made the announcement, but I hadn't known I was digging my own grave.

"Look, let's just focus on getting these people off our property," Ty said. "We don't know what they're capable of, or what their true intentions are. We need to handle this carefully."

Just as I was about to say something, Persephone's high-pitched voice reverberated through the house. My in-laws had arrived. Dominic's demanding tone cut through the air like a knife as he stormed into the room. "What the fuck is going on out there, Tyson? Who are all those people?"

"Have a look at this." Ty gestured for his parents to come over and examine the screen. Lowering his voice, he explained the situation, "Apparently, they're all here to catch a glimpse of the first known omega. Isaiah said there isn't a hotel room to be had for miles, but it's not just strangers. I recognize people from the pack out there. People who've known Liza for years."

Persephone gasped and covered her mouth with her hand. "Oh my gods." The shock in her voice mirrored the disbelief still coursing through me.

"Can you believe it?" I tried for sarcasm, but fear laced my words. The whole thing was like a twisted nightmare. The thought of others wanting to see me when I'd walked amongst them as a regular, middle-class member of the pack only a few months prior was mind-boggling.

As we continued to watch the crowd, my phone rang. The caller ID showed it was my parents. Gods, I hadn't even given them a single thought. Were they in danger?

"Hey, Mom, Dad. Are you okay?"

"Liza." My dad's voice trembled, which immediately put me in fight-or-flight mode. "There are people outside our house wanting to see you.

They're chanting the word omega, and they are not responding to the security guards. We don't know what to do."

My stomach clenched. Panic bubbled up inside me, but I forced myself to keep it together for their sake. "It's okay, Dad. Just stay inside and keep the doors locked. We'll get them off your property as soon as possible."

"Okay, sweetheart, stay safe," Mom said, then added, "Please be careful."

"Of course, Mom. Love you both." My hands shook so hard, I struggled to press the end button on my phone screen.

"I've called the police. They're on their way to your parents' place now," Ty said as he put down his phone. He must've overheard my conversation. "Our team will take care of the people at the gates."

"Thank you," I said, trying to find comfort in his words, but the situation was far from resolved, and I wasn't convinced the people could be taken care of— as Ty had put it. They wanted to see an omega. Just how far were they prepared to go in order to see one?

We huddled together, discussing plans to disperse the crowd. My frustration threatened to boil over.

How dare they demand to see me? Whatever happened to respecting someone's privacy? Especially the alpha's mate?

"Look," I blurted, pointing to the screen. I chewed nervously on my lower lip as everyone watched some of the people trying to climb the gate. Their desperation was evident in their frantic movements and determined expressions.

"Can you believe this?" I asked shrilly. "They're actually climbing the gate just to get a glimpse of me. Should I just go down there so they can see me? Would that help? If they see me, maybe they'll go away?" Even as the words tumbled out of my mouth, I knew it was a stupid fucking idea, but desperation and fear were leading me now.

"Absolutely not," Ty said, his eyes never leaving the screen. Persephone and Dominic both agreed it would be too risky for me to approach the mob.

Even the security guard seemed compelled to weigh in. "I don't want to butt in, Mrs. Keller, but going down to the gate is a terrible idea. We can't be sure that everyone's intentions are pure. Someone in that crowd could be there to hurt you."

They were right, but the thought of all those people putting themselves in danger just to see me sent bile rising up my throat. What had my life become?

I slapped my hands to my mouth as a few people toppled from the top of the gate. One fell headfirst onto the ground, pulling another person with them. The entire ordeal lasted a split-second, but they seemed to move in slow-motion as I watched. Shocked screams from the crowd traveled all the way to the estate. It didn't stop more people from attempting to scale the fence.

I swallowed hard, trying to keep myself from vomiting.

Ty pulled my frozen body out of the security room and away from the monitors. We all retreated to the movie room, seeking refuge from the chaos outside in the soundproof room. But as we turned on the enormous screen to watch something, anything to take our minds off the sights from the estate's security monitors, the news came on. There would be no escaping the world's obsession with the first omega born in centuries.

"Seeing the omega would be like seeing a real-life entity. Like Big Foot, or an alien or something," one woman gushed during an interview, her eyes wide with excitement. She went on to share the tales of omegas and their supposed supernatural powers, stories that were quickly becoming all too familiar. "An omega's powers are so much stronger than that of a normal shifter. Their powers are supernatural. They're like a super shifters or something."

"Omegas can cure diseases, like the most incurable of diseases, with just a single drop of their blood," another one added eagerly. "And they say that omegas also have the powers of an alpha, that they can actually be stronger than an alpha."

Yet another came on. "Omegas were known to have the strength of the gods. I want to see her powers for myself."

I scoffed at the screen. Did they actually believe the bullshit they were spouting? What would they want from me? Instead of cooking, I should have bottled my miracle cure Omega blood? The absurdity of it all was too much to bear.

"Enough," I muttered, pacing the room. "Turn it off, please. Some of them are not just here to see me. They want to see me to perform some type of damn miracle, to prove I truly am an omega. I'm not some performing animal in a circus, and I sure as hell won't dance simply because people want me to."

"Of course not." Ty lowered his head and made eye contact with me as he rubbed my arms. "You absolutely don't owe anyone anything."

"Listen," Dominic said, breaking into my thoughts. "We need to get these people out of town soon. Fanatics can get crazy, and we don't want you or anyone close to you in danger."

"How do you propose we do that?" Persephone crossed her arms and leaned back in her chair. "These people are hyper-focused on Liza. Even if we run these ones out of town, more will follow."

"Well, maybe we can distract them," I suggested. "If they're so fixated on me performing some type of miracle, why don't we give them something else to watch? We could create a spectacle or something, I'm sure there are plenty of entertaining things that would keep their attention away from me."

"Maybe." Ty frowned. "But a distraction would only work for a short amount of time. You heard what Isaiah said. News of an actual omega has traveled all across the country. Mother's right. More will come."

"Is your new informant formulating a plan? That's what you hired him for, so make sure he's doing his job. This shouldn't be on your shoulders, Ty." Dominic narrowed his gaze at his son. "Decide what you can do to keep Liza safe and then work with your men to come up with a long-term solution."

"Right now, Liza is on lockdown," Ty said, his jaw ticking.

My frustration reached its peak, and rage burned through every cell of my body. I hadn't had an outburst since Ty and I mated, but this was too much. I wanted nothing more than to be the mate to the alpha that everyone expected, and that everyone deserved. I wanted to run my catering company and create delicious food people wanted to eat. Now, through no fault of my own, I was being punished, put on lockdown yet again, to keep me safe. It wasn't fair. I felt like a child being punished for being born.

Having the freedom to come and go as I pleased was important to me. I needed my space and couldn't be cooped up here no matter how big the estate was. The intense pain in my head blurred my vision, and I struggled to maintain my focus.

I shut my eyes as the ringing in my ears got so loud I couldn't hear myself think. When I finally opened them, I looked around the room at the shocked and scared faces of my in-laws. Were my powers stronger than I realized?

Even Ty took a step away from me, his head cocked to the side and a curious expression on his face. He finally moved closer and took my hand, squatting down slightly until he was at my eye-level.

Placing my hand on his chest, he took in a slow, deep breath. "Liza, breathe in with me." I did. "Good. Now let it all out slowly." Beneath his hand, I felt the strong, steady beat of his heart.

It took several rounds of calm, steady breathing, but eventually, my vision returned to its normal state.

"I promise the lockdown is only temporary until Isaiah and I can figure out how to handle this situation swiftly and safely. I need you safe and sound, not being trampled over by psychotic extremists. The last thing I need is for more people getting hurt on our property and turning around to sue us."

I nodded. I understood, I did, but that didn't take away from the overwhelming reality of it all. As the adrenaline rush subsided, my body slumped, and my shoulders drooped in exhaustion.

Dominic stepped forward, his expression mirroring Ty's, full of curiosity. "Your aura, Liza... I've never seen anything like it on a female shifter before. When you were angry just now, it resembled that of an alpha. Maybe there's more to your abilities than we know." He studied me carefully.

I didn't like the way he was looking at me, and I certainly wasn't a fan of the attention I'd garnered simply because I'd come clean about my true identity. Now, the entire world wanted to study me under a microscope.

As if I needed more crazy added to my plate.

# Chapter 9 - Ty

The scintillating scent of perfectly cooked filet mignon permeated the air when Liza and I sat down to eat in the main dining room of the estate. The chef had prepared a feast with all the trimmings. My mouth watered in anticipation as a member of the house staff placed the final platters of food on the dining table. I couldn't wait to dig into the succulent meal.

Originally, I'd planned to take Liza to the steakhouse in town, but with the tourists swarming every inch of Presley Acres, that wasn't feasible. Taking her out would cause a riot. One word to the house manager was all it took. He assured me he'd speak with the chef and have him create a fantastic meal for the two of us, but he'd gone the extra mile and decorated the dining room with candles. Soft music played in the background. Truly, he'd outdone himself.

The staff vanished into their quarters, leaving the two of us alone. The amazing smell was just a prelude to the outstanding flavors. As a chef for other people, I knew she didn't have time for more than a quick snack or leftovers, so having something as incredible as this... I hoped it would be a treat for her.

Liza seemed to enjoy the food but was unusually quiet. I glanced at her, taking in her thoughtful expression. Her silence made sense after the day we'd had. Hell, I wasn't even sure how to start a conversation that wasn't focused on the dumbasses who'd attempted to climb our gate and had fallen on their damn heads. It was honestly one of the wildest things I'd ever seen. I'd been to a few concerts in my time and had seen my share of teenagers losing it for the latest pop idol, but this was supposed to be the estate of the alpha, not the home to a fucking rock legend.

I could only imagine what was going on in Liza's head. Apart from the tourists trying to catch a glimpse of the rare omega, their very presence in town had reminded us all just how much attention Liza would continue to attract. I reminded myself that no one had seen an omega. They'd been fairytales when I was a kid, like Goldilocks and the Three Bears. Folklore.

Yet in all her beautiful glory, the omega was my mate. With all the new people in town, we'd taken on extra security, but I was feeling helpless about keeping her safe. I hated this sense of being incapable. I want to be the one to look after my mate, but because of her biology and a fucking psycho forcing her to out herself, I'd been required to hire others to do what was my job. If I was feeling powerless, I hated to think how Liza felt.

As if that wasn't enough, Dad's comment earlier after Liza's panic attack about being put in lockdown gnawed at my thoughts. The idea of Liza being stronger as an alpha seemed impossible, and yet I couldn't quite dismiss it.

I'd seen Liza losing her shit before we'd mated, and it wasn't a pretty sight. Her strength was shocking, but was it more than a flare of anger? What if she possessed powers we couldn't even begin to understand? We knew so little about omegas and their potential, we'd resorted to cobbling together bits of stories and legends, none of them fact.

The meal had been a quiet affair, both of us lost in our own thoughts about the day, but neither wanting to discuss it. Liza suddenly put down her fork, and I braced myself for a long conversation and more pushback on the lockdown. Instead, she looked at me wearily. "I think I'm going to take a long, hot bath and read a bit before bed." She stood from the table.

I nodded. "You deserve to relax after everything that's happened today. I need to make a few phone calls. I'll be up in a bit."

"Don't stay up too late. You could do with an early night, too." She gave me a small smile before leaving the room. "Thank the chef for me. Dinner was fantastic."

I remained at the table and spooned some of the decadent dark chocolate and cherry gateau into my mouth. As soon as I was sure Liza was out of earshot, I pulled out my phone and dialed Dad's number.

He answered immediately. "Ty, what can I do for you? Everything okay?" His deep voice rumbled through the speaker.

"Yes, everything's fine. Well, as fine as it can be with a fucking mob outside the gates." I shifted in my seat and lowered my voice. "Listen, I've been thinking about what you said earlier when you mentioned how Liza's powers could possibly be as strong as an alpha's." I hesitated. "I know well enough not to believe everything I hear, Dad, but that woman on the news, the one who said an omega is as powerful as an alpha... When Liza first showed signs of anger, like the display this afternoon, before we mated, I thought I sensed an alpha's energy. I dismissed it at the time since I knew she was an omega, and put it down to that, but now I'm wondering if there's more to it." I sighed, rubbing my hand over my face. "What if it's possible for omegas to have alpha traits?"

I could practically hear the furrowing of Dad's brow over the phone. "It's an interesting question. I'd never heard of that particular tale until the news interview, but then again, there are so many stories about omegas that have been lost or exaggerated over time. It's difficult to know what's true and what's not, especially since the people who would have possibly seen an omega with their own eyes and would know the truth of Liza's powers have been dead and gone for years now. As far as I'm aware, nothing was ever written. Everything we know is all hearsay. And, as we all know, stories can be exaggerated the more they're told."

"True. Do you think I should be worried, though?" I asked, concern for Liza tightening my chest.

"Only time will tell. You'll have to keep a close eye on her, Tyson. We can't know what she's capable of, and any information falling into the wrong hands could put her in even more danger. I know I don't have to say it, but just be there for Liza. If this is troubling us, imagine what she's going through. Watch what you say to people, be cautious, and pay extra attention."

"Thanks, Dad." I was grateful for his guidance. Even though we were all in uncharted waters, at least I knew I could rely on my father. He had several decades of alpha experience under his belt, and his advice was priceless.

I ended the call. My mind raced with theories of Liza and her potential powers. If her powers could match or even exceed mine, would the dynamic between us change? Liza was so much more than my mate. I considered her to be my partner in all things and trusted her completely. I'd hate it if our powers interfered with that dynamic. But I figured as long as we worked it through together, we'd be fine. With all the obstacles we'd overcome to get this far, we'd be more than fine.

I cracked my knuckles and stared out the window. Every time Liza experienced one of her rage episodes, it seemed to get more and more out of control. It got more difficult to reason with her each time. We hadn't been mated then, so I hadn't been alpha and hadn't thought of it in terms of the leader of the pack. But now that I was the alpha, I had to consider if her abilities could be a liability to the pack. What if she continued to draw crowds, making it near impossible for us to even leave the estate? It made us vulnerable. These strangers didn't just want a glimpse of the omega, they wanted a fucking piece of her. I rubbed my forehead, trying to stave off the headache starting to bloom. There was too much to consider.

A staff member knocked and appeared in the open doorway. "Sir, Isaiah is here to see you."

I nodded. "Let him in. I'll meet with him here."

A few moments later, Isaiah entered the dining room, an apologetic expression on his face. "Sorry to bother you so late, Alpha, but I have an update on Castro. I figured you'd want to hear anything as I found it. I've made extensive inquiries into the underground, specifically related to trafficking. Fortunately, I have contacts, and I created algorithms for the dark web using key search words. I also used reverse image searching with the pictures of Liza I found on Cecily's laptop. So far, I've found nothing. I can tell you with utmost confidence that there are no signs of any dealings in the underground related to trafficking, so it seems he was most probably bluffing about selling Liza."

Relief crashed into me like a tsunami. I let out a long breath. One less thing to worry about. Out of all the pressing matters, Liza being kidnapped and sold to the highest bidder was the one that had kept me up at night.

"Thank you, Isaiah," I said, hoping my tone conveyed my gratitude. "Please continue to dig, and keep your ear close to the ground. Castro is a sneaky motherfucker, and there's no way he'd just give up. I really wouldn't put it past him to have some trick up his sleeve we might not see coming."

Isaiah nodded and left the room, leaving me alone with my thoughts once more.

The quiet of the room was broken when my phone pinged, pulling me from my speculations on Castro. It was an email from Ted.

*Good evening, Ty. Just a quick reminder to look into the deal with the LLC.*

I cursed under my breath. The matter had completely slipped my mind. I had been focused more on Liza's potential alpha-like powers and how they might affect the pack, all the out-of-town visitors willing to do anything and everything to get a glimpse of the omega. Earlier in the evening, someone had had the gall to attempt to bribe one of my security team. Fortunately for Liza and me—not so fortunate for the members of the public—my team was honest and well-paid, so they weren't swayed by money or sex.

Determined to rectify my earlier business oversight, I headed upstairs to my office and typed Russell and Sons LLC in the search engine of my laptop.

I done a cursory searched when I'd received the offer and hadn't found an awful lot, but I'd only searched Russell and Sons. Apparently, adding the LLC made all the difference. The first result listed a man named Mason Russell as the owner of the company. A deeper dive told me the original owner had died two years ago. How the fuck did a dead man make business deals from the grave? Did he float up to the nearest psychic and ask them to type offers up on his behalf? Something didn't pass my bullshit test, something most assuredly was off, and it wasn't the filet mignon, so I decided I'd report the company for potential fraud and emailed Tim, letting him know what I'd found.

Still a nagging in my gut, an intuition that had never let me down, persisted that there was more to the story. Why was this company interested in purchasing a building from Keller Enterprises? My curiosity getting the best of me, I sent an email to the address provided on the buyout offer, hoping for a response. If someone was trying to fuck with me, I wanted to know who and why.

*To Whom It May Concern,*

*Thank you for contacting Keller Enterprises. We appreciate your interest in our property. In order to move forward, we require additional information regarding your company and manufacturing processes.*

*I've been unsuccessful in finding this information in my research. Kindly respond with all pertinent information and any details you're willing to provide on your company's product line.*

*Thank you,*

*Tyson Keller*

The night wore on as I responded to several more emails. Exhaustion crept up on me, and I finally called it a night after I found myself nodding off in front of the computer and waking to a screen full of letter Cs.

I made my way to the bedroom, tiptoeing in and closing the door with a quiet snick so as not to wake Liza.

Once my eyes adjusted to the dark, I quickly noticed Liza's absence from the room. A soft breeze drifted through the open balcony doors, and I followed it outside, finding her gazing at the moonlit sky, her eyes unfocused.

"What's on your mind?" I didn't like her quiet demeanor.

She was focused on something in the distance. "I wish I was born normal," she said.

I pulled her close, laughing softly. "You are perfectly normal, Liza."

She shot me a disbelieving look, causing me to chuckle again.

"Normal is boring. Don't you think?"

Liza's lips curved into a slight smile. "I could use some boring in my life right now. Sabrina called earlier to update me on the circus in town. She said people are making signs with my face on them, bedazzling them with glitter and all types of decorations." Liza raised her head to meet my gaze. "They're even marching on the streets, chanting and demanding to see the omega."

I hugged her again and pulled her close, not knowing what to say. We had to get to the bottom of this. I didn't know how much longer Liza could handle all this stress, and I was scared to find out how her omega wolf would respond if she was pushed much further. The estate was supposed to be a refuge for Liza, a place she where she could be comfortable and at ease. Today had torn that security from her, and had turned the estate into her prison.

Liza buried her face in my chest. "I don't like this, Ty. I'm not fucking normal. I'm far from it."

I wished I could take away her pain and fear. "I know you're dealing with a lot right now, but I want you to understand how valuable you are to me. I don't give a shit if you're a human, a shifter, a fucking omega, or something else entirely. I will always love and support you no matter what."

Liza looked up at me, tears brimming her eyes, but she managed the ghost of a smile. She wrapped her arms around my neck as if she was afraid I might vanish. The raw pain that radiated from her broke my heart. I hoped she believed I would do anything to protect her because I absolutely would.

That night, Liza tossed and turned in bed again, her restless dreams keeping her from finding peace. At one point, I propped myself up on my arm and watched her. What troubled thoughts haunted her sleep? Finally, I succumbed to my exhaustion and somehow slept soundly, even with Liza's limbs swatting my back.

The next morning, a phone call jerked me awake. Cursing under my breath, I answered it quickly, hoping not to disturb Liza.

Bryce's voice greeted me, but something was off. He sounded tense. "Hey, Ty. I got an email late last night. Maximus Langston is requesting a meeting with you."

That brute of an alpha only cared about power and stature, and he thought he was a king among wolves. "What the hell does he want with me?"

"Apparently, he has a business proposal for you. I'll forward the email to you. Let me know how you want to handle it."

I scanned through the proposal that Bryce sent over and scowled. As much as I wanted the whole meeting proposal to be an obvious waste of my time, it appeared legitimate. Maximus was looking for backers in a business venture. Though I didn't trust the guy further than I could throw him, I was intrigued and interested to hear what he had up his sleeve. With something between a sigh and a groan, I texted Bryce to set up the meeting.

Setting my phone down on the nightstand, I turned to see Liza looking at me.

Smiling, I pulled her close. "Good morning, beautiful. How about the two of us spend the day together? What would you like to do?"

Liza pursed her lips. "I'd love to go for a run with you, just the two of us."

"That's an excellent idea," I said. "Being out in the forest will help us get our mind off things." I pulled her to her feet and led her to the bathroom. "How about a shower first?" I winked at her and turned the hot water on full blast.

Liza stripped out of her pajamas. I turned my back, not wanting to attack her, even though I wanted nothing more than to press her into the tiled wall of the shower and have my way with her. If that was something she wanted to initiate, fine. Otherwise, I would be her support person throughout the day, lending an ear when she wanted to talk, or a dick if she wanted to fuck.

While Liza showered, I brushed my teeth and pulled on some jeans and a T-shirt. I had no meetings scheduled for the morning. Plus, we were about to shift, and I preferred to take a shower after the exertion of running several miles in the dirt.

When she was ready, Liza took my hand, and we went down to the kitchen.

Chef greeted us with a smile. "Good morning, Alpha, Mrs. Keller. It's such a beautiful morning. Would you like to take your breakfast out on the back patio?"

Liza returned his smile. "That's a great idea, Chef. Thank you."

Within a few minutes, we were feasting on French toast, crispy bacon, and freshly squeezed orange juice as we looked out over the wooded acreage just beyond the backyard. When I was done eating, I sent a quick text to the head of security.

*How are the crowds at the front gate today? Any better?*

The reply came within thirty seconds. *About the same, Alpha. The team is keeping them back from the property, but they're still lining the streets, hoping to get a glimpse of Mrs. Keller. I would strongly advise that you and she remain on the property today.*

I put my phone away and smiled at Liza.

She took a sip of orange juice. "Everything okay?"

"Yes, everything's fine." I didn't want to upset her by bringing up the fanatics again. She was fully aware of their presence. Discussing it wouldn't make any difference. "Ready for that run?"

Liza nodded and stood, taking my hand, and leading the way down the path to the clearing in the woods. We stripped down and shifted. Liza's white fur glistened in the dappled fall sunlight, and it mesmerized me. She was gorgeous. Her wolf stood with such grace and strength.

I shook off my thoughts and quickly nipped at her paws in a playful manner, urging her to run with me. We raced through the woods, our adrenaline pushing us forward. The forest seemed to breathe new life into Liza. As we ran, her playful demeanor returned, and she darted around my wolf with a lightness that made my heart swell. The vibrant scents and sounds of the forest enveloped us, creating an atmosphere of calm and freedom from the turmoil just beyond the estate's gated walls.

Suddenly, Liza stopped, her attention drawn to an injured bird on the forest floor. The poor creature flopped on its stomach, trying to fly, but one of its wings was crushed.

I watched Liza closely, curious about what she would do. Would she cry and allow a tear to heal the bird like she had the rabbit?

Gently, she licked the bird's wound. The bird went still, completely motionless. Was it playing dead from fright? Then the small creature hopped to its feet and took flight. The sight was nothing short of amazing. I had witnessed Liza's healing abilities before, but I was still left in awe. My mate was miraculous.

Liza glanced up at me briefly before running back toward the estate. I followed, my mind reeling. How had she healed the bird? Had a tear fallen from her eye without me seeing it?

When we shifted back into our human forms, I stared at her expectantly.

Liza smirked. "What? Why are you looking at me like that?"

"How does the healing work?" I cleared my throat as heat crept up my neck. "I mean, you don't have to tell me, but it's absolutely fascinating."

She shrugged. "I thought it was through my tears. That was how I healed my brother and then the rabbit in the woods. When I was staring at the injured bird, my instincts kicked in, and I found myself curious to know if my saliva would work, too. I suppose it's just something in my DNA that does the trick."

A chilling realization settled in my gut. The rumors about Liza's blood having healing properties might very well be true. If they were, it meant she was in far more danger than I had initially thought. People who were seriously ill tended to be desperate and had nothing to lose. And desperate people with nothing to lose would do anything, especially if they thought it meant they'd live. I understood those people, to a point—they just wanted to live—but there would be assholes who'd see it as a way to benefit themselves financially, and they would do anything to get their hands on her blood. No matter which way we looked at it, my mate was at risk, and it was up to me to ensure that never happened.

# Chapter 10 - Liza

I was lost in the depths of my dreams. The little boy's laughter echoed through the air. The dream was more vivid than any other I'd had before. The whole atmosphere seemed to be pulsating with life. We were both young. Again, I couldn't have been more than three years old, yet there was a familiarity that tugged at my heart.

We were tucked away within an elaborate pillow fort, our own secret hideout. The walls were constructed from what seemed like a hundred pillows, stacked high, and teetering precariously. Stuffed animals served as guards, keeping watch over the entrance, their button eyes glinting in the dim light. Twinkling fairy lights hung overhead, casting soft shadows across the room, bathing everything in a warm, golden glow.

As I looked around, taking in every detail, the blond-haired boy grinned at me. There was something about him—something that filled me with warmth and affection. I searched through the recesses of my memories, but I simply couldn't place him. Even so, I couldn't help but feel drawn to him, connected in some inexplicable way.

"Come on, let's explore," he said excitedly, crawling deeper into the fort. I followed closely behind, entranced by the positive energy radiating from him.

We navigated our way through the labyrinth of cushions and blankets, giggling as we discovered hidden treasures: an old toy, a forgotten book, a half-eaten cookie. It seemed like we could spend an eternity nestled within our fortress, hidden from the outside world.

A voice from downstairs interrupted our play time, pulling us out of our adventure. "Time for tea, you two."

The boy glanced toward the entrance, then back at me, a mischievous grin on his lips. "Five more minutes?" he pleaded, a twinkle in his eye.

I covered my mouth and giggled, watching as the boy raised his eyebrows expectantly.

"All right, five more minutes."

The entire interaction and location was magical, but as much as I tried to hold on to that moment, the dream slipped through my fingers like water, leaving me with nothing but fragments and echoes of what had been.

I woke with a start, my heart pounding, sweat drenching my nightclothes, plastering my hair to my forehead. As I gasped for breath, I felt wetness on my cheek. I'd been crying. With mounting frustration, I tried to grasp onto the fleeting memory of the boy's face. What had he looked like? Blond hair that was almost white, and blue eyes. Beyond those two features, the details were already slipping away into the murky depths of my subconscious.

I needed to understand why this boy was haunting my dreams. I glanced over at Ty, who was sleeping soundly beside me. Not wanting to disturb him, I tiptoed across the room to my desk, pulling open the bottom drawer and retrieving the packet tucked in the back.

As I ran my fingers over the worn folder, memories of the Wylde pack—the pack I had been born into—surfaced, and tears spilled from my eyes again. The pack I was now part of had brutally murdered my pack, my family. Thoughts of the lives lost, those who never got a chance to live out their full potential, haunted me every day.

With shaky hands, I pulled out the pack registrar and began scanning the list of names, searching for any clue that might reveal the identity of the mysterious boy. My gaze flicked over the names, lingering on boys born around the same time as me. Could one of them be the boy from my dreams? And if so, what did that mean?

Then I remembered. Some families had moved away before the pack's destruction, fleeing Castro's intense bullying tactics. Even at a young age, he'd been a terror. What if they were still out there, hiding under assumed names and keeping their true identities a secret?

"What are you doing up?" Ty's sleepy voice interrupted my thoughts.

I looked over to see him rubbing his eyes, the clock on the nightstand casting its digital glow across his face.

"Three in the morning? Really, Liza?" he mumbled as he sat up. "You've barely slept. What are you looking at?"

I hesitated, then remembered his plea not to keep things from him again. Yes, this wasn't about my safety, but Ty was my mate, my partner. I'd told him the other morning I'd had a dream, so he probably already had an inkling that my odd dreams had returned.

I stood from the desk, carrying the packet with me, and took a seat next to Ty on the bed. "I've been having a recurring dream about a little boy who looks a lot like Castro."

He gaped at me, the slightest mention of Castro setting him on alert.

"It's not Castro," I reassured him when alarm flashed in his eyes. "This boy is different. Kind, playful... I can't explain it, but I know these are more than just dreams."

Ty leaned back against the headboard and rubbed a hand over his face. "Well, we both know your dreams about your past haven't exactly been just dreams."

I nodded. "They've always been memories I've repressed, and this time it's about a boy I can't quite place. Honestly, I'm not sure why I'm dreaming about him. I wish I could remember who he was and why we were allowed to play together so much. I'm not much more than three, maybe four years old in my dreams.

Either way, the dreams about him are becoming a regular occurrence."

Ty grabbed his side and feigned injury. "Do you play-wrestle by any chance? That might explain why I wake up with bruised ribs each morning."

"Oh, please." I chuckled and swatted at him. "You could always sleep on the couch if it bothers you."

"Never." Ty pulled me close and kissed me gently. "So, what are we going to do about these dreams?"

I held up the packet. "I want to find the surviving kids from the Wylde pack. Several families moved away to avoid Castro. They have to still be out there somewhere."

Ty regarded me thoughtfully, the smile fading from his face as he considered my words. He took the packet from me, flipping through the pages. "If others got away from Castro, we should do everything we can to find them. Those families were extremely lucky to get out when they did."

The mood in the room quickly turned somber. Neither of us spoke, but I knew we were both thinking about the slaughter of my pack.

Ty pulled me close again, brushing his lips tenderly over my forehead. "Consider it done. Now, can we get some more sleep?"

"Of course. I'll be right back." My throat was dry from all the crying, so I drank some water in bathroom and glanced at the mirror. My reflection showed a weary woman with wild hair who needed sleep more than anything else. I looked like I'd aged a decade. With a sigh, I crawled back into bed, my mind buzzing with possibilities and questions.

Who was the boy from my dreams? Were there other survivors from my pack out there, hiding from Castro's wrath? The answers seemed just out of reach, like fragments of a puzzle scattered across time.

It took a while for my brain to settle down. I didn't think I'd sleep, and I prepared to wait for the sun. Surprisingly, when the dreaded alarm clock went off, I woke up. I'd fallen back into a dreamless slumber and gotten a few more hours of sleep, after all.

"Ugh, do I have to?" I groaned as I reluctantly threw off the covers. Today would be more than a little busy. I had four interviews for an assistant chef and driver scheduled. Hopefully, they wouldn't be put off by the crowds at the gate. I dragged myself out of bed, trying to shake off the lingering tendrils of sleep that clung to my body. At least I didn't have to drive across town for the interviews.

Given the omega insanity currently taking over Presley Acres, Ty didn't think it was safe for me to go into the office in town. Instead, we'd decided to hold the interviews at the estate, where we had more control over security and were in a position to screen candidates at the gate before they were allowed inside. We couldn't be too careful these days.

The hot water soothed my aching neck. I must've slept weird because it hurt to turn my head to the left. The scent of coconut clung to the steam as I lathered up with a new organic shampoo I'd purchased at the farmer's market before it was overrun with crazy tourists. Working the shampoo into my scalp, I focused on my goal for the day. I'd chosen candidates with some experience who were also looking to grow and learn. I loved my career, and I'd always wanted to teach others the ropes. My busy schedule hadn't allowed that, so I looked at the new hires as living out part of that dream of having my own apprentice.

After drying my hair, I put on some lip gloss and mascara, then dressed in something casually professional. My stomach growled. You'd think as a chef I wouldn't need reminding that food was a priority.

"Time to find sustenance," I muttered to myself, making my way to the kitchen. To my delight, there was a pastry tray waiting on the counter. The chef must have left it for me. I grabbed a bagel and coffee, grateful for small mercies and kitchen staff.

"Okay. Interviews. Let's do this," I said, psyching myself up as I carried my breakfast into my new office.

Two quick knocks rapped at the door.

"Come in," I called, taking a small bite of my bagel slathered with cream cheese.

"Your first interviewee has arrived, ma'am," the staff member informed me.

Nodding for her to lead them in, I pulled out my notebook and got ready to meet Alex.

"Hi there. Good morning. I'm Liza,. You must be Alex Strand. Sorry for the gate gestapo. I'm afraid it's a necessary evil at the moment." I extended my hand, offering a warm smile. "Tell me about your experience and what led you to apply for this cooking position."

Alex blinked rapidly. "I guess you could say I'd like to try something different, though everything I put my mind to turns to gold, so to speak."

Wow. Okay, that was different. "Sounds like you have a firm grasp on your skills. Why don't you tell me about some of the jobs you've had in the past and ways you could have improved yourself... maybe a challenge you faced that pushed you outside your comfort zone?"

Alex scoffed. "Honestly, nothing has been a challenge for me up to this point. I slay any situation that's thrown at me. That's why I get bored easily. At least this position, working at the alpha's estate, would be interesting."

"I see." I pretended to make a note in my notepad while I gathered my thoughts. Alex's résumé had been promising, but his know-it-all attitude clashed with my laid-back approach. We wouldn't be able to work cohesively, and that's what I needed. I was already fairly certain I would not be hiring him.

As I posed a few more questions, it became abundantly clear that our personalities would collide instead of harmonizing. I quickly brought the interview to an end.

"Thanks for coming in, Mr. Strand. Best of luck in your future endeavors." I stood and gestured toward the door. He didn't move, just sat there with an unnerving smile spread across his face.

"One of the staff will escort you to the front door," I said firmly, trying not to let my unease show.

Still, Alex remained seated.

"Here's the thing, Liza," he began, leaning back in his chair, resting his hands behind his head, and crossing his leg. "I'm not here for a job. Sorry. Well, not sorry. I couldn't give a fuck about being an assistant chef. I faked my résumé, used my friends as references, and landed this interview. Pretty genius, huh? I live locally and heard through the shifters that you were the mystical omega. I'm only here because I wanted to see if you're as magical as everyone seems to think."

"Excuse me?" I exclaimed. What on earth would possess someone to go to all of that trouble? "I think you've seen everything you're going to, Alex." My voice was like ice. "I think you need to leave. Now."

"Wait," he protested, standing up abruptly, and I jerked back. "I want to witness a miracle. That's all.

Just one little miracle." His eyes became dazed, and a sinking feeling settled in the pit of my stomach.

There was a security guard right outside door, but it did nothing to quell the fear that threatened to overwhelm me. This situation was spiraling out of control, fast.

I opened my mouth to call for a guard, but Alex reached for a box cutter that had been left on my desk when my extra office supplies had been unpacked.

"No!" I screamed in horror as Alex grabbed the box cutter. His hand moved quickly to his wrist. Oh my fuck, he was going to cut himself.

My cry alerted the guard outside, who burst into the room just in time. He disarmed Alex, the box cutter clattering on the floor, and pinned Alex there with it.

"Are you okay, ma'am?" the guard asked, panting slightly.

"Y-yeah, I'm fine. Thank you," I stammered, my body shaking. Sitting back down, I tried to regain some semblance of composure.

"Is everything all right in here? I heard Liza scream. What the fuck happened?" Ty suddenly appeared in the doorway. No doubt he'd heard the commotion from upstairs in his office.

"Sir, this man tried to harm himself with a box cutter, but I managed to stop him." The guard continued to restrain Alex, who still seemed dazed.

He had to be on something. I wanted him out of my fucking house.

I took a shaky breath and held up Alex's résumé. "He faked all of this just to get into a room with me. He said he'd heard from some local shifters that I'm the mystical omega and wanted to witness me performing a miracle." I put a hand over my eyes. "I can't imagine what would've happened if security hadn't intervened."

Ty knelt next to me, worry blazing from his blue eyes. "I don't think you should hold any more interviews with non-pack members, Liza. At least our people can be trusted. Give me your list, and I'll cancel the rest of your interviews today."

"Maybe you're right," I said, still processing everything that had just occurred. But before we could discuss it further, a timid voice interrupted from the doorway.

"Excuse me? Is this a bad time?" A young redhead stood there, clearly out of place amidst the chaos. "I'm here to interview for the assistant chef position."

My instinct was to send the girl away, but I hated not giving her a chance after she'd gone through the whole process, including the screening at the front gate. Not that it had stopped the illustrious Mr. Strand.

"Come on in." I refused to let Alex's actions ruin the rest of my day. "Have a seat." I pointed to the chair across from me as security escorted Alex from the room.

"I'll be right outside if you need anything." Ty kissed me on the forehead, and I turned my attention to the redhead.

I flipped through my notes, suddenly flustered. "I'm sorry, can you remind me of your name?"

The girl smiled. "I'm Rosalie."

Right. The twenty-one-year-old cook. I remembered being impressed with her résumé, but now I couldn't help wondering if she'd also doctored her work history.

"Nice to meet you, Rosalie. Why don't you tell me a little about yourself?"

Rosalie grinned and giggled before clapping her hand over her mouth. I was immediately drawn to her bubbly personality. "I live here in Presley Acres and, honestly, I've been a big fan of yours ever since you catered an event at my aunt's house a few years ago. Your chicken pancetta is to die for." She waved her hand in the air. "Sorry, I'm already way off track. Uhm... I've been working as a cook at the Italian place on the edge of town. Maybe you've heard of it? Bella Cucina?"

"Yes, I've eaten there a few times. The pasta is handmade, right?"

Rosalie nodded. "Yeah. It's a tedious process, but you can't beat the flavor."

We talked for half an hour, and Rosalie impressed me with every passing minute. She was certainly a breath of fresh air after the ordeal with Alex.

"All right, Rosalie. Let's put your skills to the test." A challenge would determine if she was as talented as she claimed to be.

"You want me to cook for you? Right now?" Rosalie shifted in her seat, her cheeks flaming.

"If that's okay with you."

"Of course. I'd be happy to." Rosalie stood and pointed toward the door. "Would you mind if I grab my cooking tools, Mrs. Keller? They're in the car."

A girl that traveled with her supplies? Be still my beating heart. "Absolutely. I'll let the staff know that I've asked you to meet me in the kitchen. They'll take you through. Oh, and Rosalie? Please call me Liza."

It was just as well that I'd let Ty cancel the rest of my interviews. Over the next hour and a half, I watched in awe and approval as Rosalie moved seamlessly from one station in the kitchen to the next. To my delight, she whipped up a delicious dish that showcased her culinary prowess. In fact, it was so good that I decided to offer her the job on the spot. Ty wanted me to hire a pack member, but I had a good feeling about Rosalie.

"Rosalie, once we clear your background check, I want you to be my assistant chef," I announced, grinning at the shock on her face. "I'll send over a contract for you to look over, but I think you're perfect for this position."

"Thank you so much, Mrs.—uh, Liza. Wow, I can't believe this is happening." She giggled and went in to hug me but thought better of it and extended her hand instead. "I promise I'll be the best assistant chef ever." Gratitude shone in her eyes. Something settled inside me, telling me I'd definitely made the right choice in hiring her.

A few minutes after Rosalie left, Ty found me in the kitchen. "Hey, babe. How are you holding up after everything?"

"Honestly, I'm still a bit shaken up over the fact that people are that fanatic over seeing an omega." I held up a finger. "No, not just seeing me. They want to witness my magical abilities. Or, as that ass put it, a miracle. The lengths he'd gone to just see me... It's fucking terrifying."

Ty leaned against the kitchen counter. "I agree. How did the interview go with the redhead?"

I grinned up at him. "Actually, it was fantastic. Rosalie met every requirement I had for the position and then some. I even had her cook a meal for me, and it was delicious. Here." I scooped up a bite of her food and shoved it into her mouth. "Isn't that fabulous?"

Ty raised his eyebrows. "Wow. That is pretty damn good. So, what's the next step? A second interview?"

"Actually, I already hired her. That is, of course, if her background check comes back clean." I glanced up at Ty, bracing for his reaction over not hiring a Keller pack member.

He shrugged. "Well, at least the interview process is over, and we won't be having strangers in our home... at least for now. We'll get some of the staff to do the deliveries. Do you feel like you can trust Rosalie, seeing as how she's not a member of the pack?" He crossed his arms. "I have to admit, having an outsider in our home worries me a little."

"I got a good feeling about her." I was ready to argue my choice, but Ty just nodded.

"I trust your judgment, babe. I'm happy you found someone so quickly. Oh, there's something else I wanted to tell you." Ty moved across the kitchen and lowered his voice. "I asked Isaiah to track down the surviving members of your pack."

My jaw dropped as Ty pulled me into his arms. It was happening. Maybe I'd meet the boy who had been haunting my dreams. At the very least, I could potentially meet people who looked like me.

Ty kissed the top of my head. "I hope you find some closure in all of this, because it seems like at every turn there's a fresh memory that haunts you. I know these latest memories aren't traumatizing, but I still can't help but feel terrible about the fact they trouble you at all. You haven't had a sound night of sleep in a very long time, and I feel so helpless."

I wrapped my arms around him and stood on my tiptoes to kiss his cheek. "Just remember that none of this is your fault. I've made peace with what happened to my pack, but I still need to fill in the empty spaces of my memories. I may have been young when everything happened, but there's clearly a lot I still need to know."

Ty was silent for a moment, then he whispered, "My only hope is that it all gives you peace in the end, because that's all I want for you, Liza."

Peace. That sounded lovely, yet so far out of reach.

# Chapter 11 - Ty

I stood in front of the mirror, adjusting my tie with practiced efficiency. The knot tightened to perfection, but as I straightened my collar, a nasty feeling settled in the pit of my stomach.

Gods, I hated suiting up like this, but it was all part of the game, whether it was meeting with potential clients and business partners, putting my best foot forward, or meeting with other alphas. My reflection stared back at me, the tailored suit hiding an unexplained hesitation beneath its crisp lines.

The unsettling feeling refused to leave. As an alpha, I knew all too well to trust my instincts. Something about this meeting with Maximus did not sit right with me. Unable to pinpoint the cause, I reached for my phone and dialed Isaiah's number.

"Alpha?" His voice carried a hint of surprise. "What's going on?"

"Isaiah, I need you to have your team ready while I'm meeting with Maximus. I've got a bad feeling." My words were clipped and precise. No time for beating around the bush.

"Sure thing, boss." Concern was evident in Isaiah's tone. "You think there might be trouble?"

"I don't know. It doesn't feel... violent, just off. I want backup, just in case."

"Got it. We'll be on standby, ready to step in if needed. You just need to give the signal."

Isaiah wasn't someone who dragged his feet, and I appreciated that characteristic in my informant. I was more than capable of handling things myself, but it never hurt to have backup. I'd made the right choice in giving him the position. No regrets.

I sighed, pocketing my phone, and stepping away from the mirror. The unease lingered, but I pushed it aside in order to concentrate on the task at hand. All the warnings in the world were useless if you weren't focused.

Grabbing my wallet and briefcase, I strode down the stairs, the polished wood gleaming beneath my feet. My footsteps echoed through the hallway. Our entire world was crashing down around us, but one thing was certain, our staff were fucking top notch. The estate was immaculate.

Bryce was waiting for me in the foyer, his attention glued to his phone. He glanced up as I approached, and surprise flickered across his face. "What the hell is going on with you?" He frowned, eyes flicking over my face.

"I've got a bad feeling about this meeting with Maximus." My voice came out a little lower and more intense than I intended. "I already don't trust the guy, but on top of that, something seems off."

Bryce went somber. "If it feels sketchy, we'll end the meeting immediately. Remember, Maximus is coming to our territory for this meeting. If he tries anything, he'll be declaring war, which isn't smart. Honestly, I doubt Maximus is that arrogant or stupid to pull any shit."

I nodded, gripping the handle of my briefcase tightly. "I know. But either way, I'm on edge."

"Let's just see how it plays out." The reassurance in his tone had me wondering if I was overthinking it all.

We climbed into Bryce's sleek black sports car, the warmth of the leather seats seeping through my suit. The engine purred to life, and Bryce pulled away from the house.

When he turned left out of the estate drive, I cast him a sidelong frown. "Why are you going this way? It's much quicker to turn to the right."

"I set up the meeting in town at the steakhouse. The staff blocked off the back room for the meeting, so we won't be interrupted by the blue hairs ordering their early-bird specials."

"Why not just meet at Keller Enterprises' main office?" My gaze was fixed on the passing scenery as we made our way into the downtown area.

Bryce tapped his fingers against the wheel to the beat of the rock song playing through the speakers. "I just thought it'd be smarter to meet on neutral ground. Give Maximus the benefit of the doubt. Maybe he genuinely wants to cut a good business deal with us."

"Right." It made sense, but meeting outside our office might make Maximus think he had the upper hand. Only time would tell. I just wish Bryce hadn't sprung it on me. I'd already pulled an employee up this week for pulling the same crap. Granted, a meeting place wasn't the same as selling a factory, but even so, Bryce was lucky he was my friend.

When we turned onto Main Street, I caught sight of Liza's office. A cluster of people had gathered outside the entrance.

"What the fuck is wrong with these people?" I muttered, my stomach tightening.

"Looks like they're camping out or something," Bryce observed. "Want me to pull over?"

"Yeah." I checked the time on the dashboard. We had a few minutes to spare. It would be enough for me to handle the situation.

As Bryce parked the car, I took a deep breath and tried to lower my blood pressure. The crowd casually chatted like they were sitting at a backyard barbecue, seemingly oblivious to their trespassing on private property.

Stepping out of the car, the tension made my skin tight as I approached the crowd strewn across the lawn in front of the office building. "Do you have business here?" I called out, trying to maintain some semblance of politeness. "From the looks of things, this business isn't open."

A woman, looking ludicrous in an enormous sun hat, looked up at me from her lawn chair, her lips curling into a coy smile that made me roll my eyes. "We're just waiting for someone."

I stifled a snort. Waiting? More like stalking. Who the fuck did this woman think she was? She looked like she was lounging at the beach.

Even though they were all loitering, I decided to give them a chance. "This is private property. You can't just hang around here."

One of the men in the crowd shifted his weight uneasily, recognizing me. He pointed and yelled out, "Holy shit! It's the omega's mate."

His words shocked me. Liza had always been referred to as *my* mate, and now I was hers. It was odd to be on the opposite side of things. Liza would get a kick out of that. A smirk tugged at the corner of my mouth as I tried not to laugh, but I kept my expression stern.

"All right." I held up my hand. "You have two choices: either leave on your own, or deal with the police. Your call."

The crowd grumbled like displeased children, their gazes darting between each other and me. Slowly, they began to disperse, casting wary glances over their shoulders as they slinked away. I overheard the beach lady calling me a hard ass.

*What a bitch.*

I stood my ground, arms crossed beneath my chest, keeping a watchful eye on every retreating figure. The streets cleared slowly, and even though I had somewhere to be, I refused to get back into Bryce's car until they were gone.

Once the last straggler disappeared around the corner, I allowed myself to breathe. Liza's office was safe... for now.

I returned to Bryce, who leaned against the car in the universal pose of relaxation, one leg crossed over the other and his arms over his chest, a shit-eating grin on his face. He glared over his sunglasses at me, clearly amused by my recent display. "Wanna stop anywhere else to chew a crowd out? Maybe the grocery store or the post office? I bet if we search hard enough, we'll find a Girl Scout troop trying to sell cookies in an undesignated area."

I shot him a look that was equal parts annoyance and amusement. "Shut the fuck up, Bryce."

"Okay, okay." Bryce chuckled and raised his hands in mock surrender.

As he started the engine, I took one last look at Liza's office building, wondering how the crowd would have responded if Liza had been inside. I doubted they would've just sat idly on the lawn, especially after seeing those fuckers climbing the gates at the estate. They may have seemed peaceful, but it would only have taken one of them to start a riot. I took my phone out and texted Isaiah, requesting he put a detail on the office building, even if she wasn't there.

"Ty?" Bryce's voice pulled me from my thoughts. "You okay, man?"

"Fine." My fingers tapped rhythmically against the door handle, betraying my unease.

The drive to the steakhouse was otherwise silent, save for the low hum of the engine and the occasional rumble of tires over uneven road. My gaze drifted past the world outside the window, buildings and faces blurring together as my mind continued to grapple with the uneasy feeling that haunted me. The meeting with Maximus loomed over me like an impending storm, its potential consequences impossible to predict. I could only hope that my instincts and our backup would get us through the meeting and whatever fresh hell awaited us.

We arrived at the steakhouse right on time. Good that we weren't late—one less thing Maximus could throw in my face.

"Ready?" Bryce parked the car near the door, his earlier teasing gone.

"Let's get this fucking over with."

The hefty wooden door creaked open when we stepped inside, and we were immediately assaulted by the unmistakable scent of Maximus. Dim lights cast shadows across the polished hardwood floor while the gentle clink of glasses and silverware met my ears.

I almost laughed at the pathetic attempt to assert dominance through scent. It was nothing compared to my own. My gaze swept across the room, finally settling on Maximus lounging in a booth like a mob boss, surrounded by his muscle.

As I approached, his face twisted into a scowl. He must have realized his scent had absolutely no effect on me. I could easily overshadow his, but it wasn't worth the waste of energy.

"Tyson." Maximus greeted us, flashing a smile that irked the fuck out of me. "Glad you could make it."

"Maximus." I acknowledged his existence but didn't bother to act happy.

"Shall we move this to the private room?" Bryce and I walked through while Maximus and his bootleg boys scurried to follow. I allowed Maximus to take a seat and then sat across from him as Bryce slid in beside me. The smugness radiating from Maximus made me want to punch him in his face. The man thought way too fucking much of himself.

"Let's talk business." Maximus leaned back in his seat. "As you may have heard, I've been making some deals lately, and they've been quite successful. Most have been online ventures, but I'm ready to move to a brick-and-mortar establishment."

I arched an eyebrow. "Success is relative, Maximus. The Keller empire's deals are on a much larger scale than yours."

"Ah, but we all have to start somewhere." Maximus smirked, doing nothing to hide his arrogance.

I hated these cock swinging contests, but they were a necessary part of business, especially with the likes of him.

"True, but if you're trying to impress me, you'll need to do better than that," I stated flatly.

"Fine, let's get down to it, then." Irritation flickered across his face before he regained his composure. "I'm sure you're aware of my latest venture."

"Not at all." I crossed my arms and leaned back. "Why don't you fill me in on the details?"

"Of course." A predatory grin spread across his face, and I braced for whatever asinine idea he'd concocted. "You see, I've been working on a project that has the potential to make us all very, very rich."

"Go on." My interest piqued, despite my better judgment.

"Imagine a luxurious hotel and casino, catering to the elite of our society," Maximus began, attempting badly to paint a picture with his words. "A place where people can indulge their every whim and desire, all under one roof. And we, my friend, will be the ones reaping the profits."

"Sounds ambitious." I couldn't shake the feeling that something was off about this whole thing. "But what makes you think you can pull something off on such a large scale? You said yourself that most of your dealings have been online."

"Because I know people, Tyson." Maximus's voice dripped with confidence. "And I know what they want. With your backing, there's no way this can fail."

There it was. He needed my backing, my money, my influence, and my power to get his idea off the ground. Why did he think I was the person to partner with? He should have been speaking with Hiram. After all, his expertise was casinos. For fuck's sake, the guy literally lived in one of his casinos in a penthouse on the top floor.

"Have you considered reaching out to Hiram for investment?" I raised my eyebrows, curious to hear his answer. "He's made quite a name for himself with his casinos. I'd think someone serious about that type of business would seek out the one person in Texas who's made bank in that sector."

"Absolutely not," Maximus said sharply, his smug demeanor faltering for a moment. "He's my competition, and I have no intention of sharing my success with him."

"Interesting." Maximus was far from being a businessman. His response to my questions showed he was trying to play in the big leagues when he was clearly only suited for softball. "Hiram may be known for bending the rules, but he's undeniably successful. If this is your operation of choice, you should reach out to him." I paused, studying Maximus's reaction. "Or are you afraid you can't control him?"

"Control has nothing to do with it," Maximus snapped, his eyes narrowing. "This is my business venture, and I'll choose my partners as I see fit."

"Fair enough," I said. Hiram respected me. He might not have the best bedside manner, but he was fully aware of the situation with Castro, and I considered him a current ally. I had absolutely no intention of going into competition against him. It simply wasn't a smart business move.

"Listen, Maximus." My tone was measured and deliberate. "Let me give you some friendly investment advice. If you want to make this work, you need to be willing to collaborate with those who can bring value to your project, even if that means setting aside your ego. Hiram may be your competition, but he could also be the key to your success."

"Perhaps," Maximus muttered, clearly displeased by my suggestion. "But I don't need Hiram. I've got other potential investors lined up."

"Of course you do." I smirked. The guy was bluffing. "But remember, you came to me for a reason. You saw something in my empire that you wanted for yourself. Don't let pride stand in the way of your success."

Maximus scowled at me, but the defiance in his eyes couldn't mask the unease that simmered beneath the surface. It was clear that he recognized the truth in my words, even if he didn't want to admit it.

"Look." I leaned forward and fixed Maximus with a level stare. "If you agree to bring Hiram onboard, then I'll consider investing. Your business could be lucrative with the proper funding and backing, but as it stands now, it seems like you're looking for me to be the largest shareholder. I don't mind that, as long as I know I'll get my investment back. In its current state, I don't feel comfortable investing that sort of money."

Maximus's eyes narrowed, his jaw clenching. "You're making a mistake, Ty."

I held his gaze, unflinching. "I've been doing this since I was a teenager, Maximus. I know business better than most people. I've made countless deals for my family, and I can tell a bad one within minutes. As I stated, as it stands, this is not a good deal."

Before he could respond, a waitress entered the room, her presence providing a brief reprieve from the tension. "Would you gentlemen like to order?"

Maximus seethed, his fury apparent even as he ignored her existence.

I gave her an apologetic smile. "We don't need anything, thank you."

She scurried away from the simmering animosity between Maximus and me.

"Really?" Maximus spat, glaring at me. "You insult me and then act like nothing's happened?"

"Insult you?" I raised an eyebrow. "As a businessman, you should be grateful when someone offers you free advice. Usually, I charge a consultation fee. I'm suggesting that you weigh the pros and cons to see if it's worth it to forge an alliance with someone who could benefit your business in the long run."

"Free advice?" He scoffed, shaking his head. "More like sabotage. You're afraid I'll show you up, and that I'll take away your position as a respected businessman. I see right through your fucking façade, Tyson Keller."

"Is that what you think? That I'm trying to sabotage your plans? No, Maximus. I'm trying to prevent you from making a colossal mistake. If you're unwilling to work with others, even those you perceive as rivals, then your business will never reach its full potential."

He clenched his fists, his nostrils flaring as he fought to contain his anger. "You have no idea what you're talking about, Ty."

"Maybe not. But when it comes to business, I've yet to be proven wrong."

"Whatever," he muttered. "Just... get out of here. I'll call you if I decide to take your 'advice'."

"Sounds like a plan." I rose from my seat, more than eager to get the hell out of there. One more second with Maximus, and I couldn't trust myself not to punch him square in his arrogant face. I gave him one last measured look, my dominance settling over him like an oppressive fog.

As I turned to leave, Maximus reclined in his seat, a sinister glint in his eyes. "You know, Keller, a real businessman would sell that little mate of yours to the highest bidder, considering what she is." The corners of his mouth curved into a cruel smile. "I'm sure Liza would fetch a pretty penny. More than enough to cover all my business endeavors, don't you think?"

A primal growl rumbled in my chest, every muscle in my body tensing as I prepared to launch at him. Bryce, sensing the danger, jumped to his feet and grabbed my shoulders, his grip like iron as he struggled to hold me back.

"Ty, don't," he warned, his voice strained with effort. "This isn't worth it."

Maximus's scent filled the air, a nauseating mixture of arrogance and fear. His beta moved to shield him, but the guy was nearly buckling under the weight of my dominance.

"Listen to me, you pathetic excuse for an alpha," I spat. "If you ever mention Liza's name again, if you even think about coming near her, I won't hesitate to tear your head from your body. That's not a threat, Maximus. It's a promise."

"Come on, Keller." Maximus sneered, attempting to maintain his bravado in front of his goons, despite the trembling of his hands. "There's no need to get so worked up. We're all friends here, aren't we?"

"Friends?" I scoffed, the word tasting like poison on my tongue. "You've mistaken me for someone who tolerates cowards and opportunists. Good luck with your venture, Maximus."

I shrugged off Bryce's grip, my gaze never leaving Maximus as I seethed with barely suppressed fury. The dim lighting of the restaurant seemed to flicker in his terrified eyes. He understood the gravity of what he had just done. "I mean it. One wrong move, Maximus, and you're dead." I growled, throwing one more warning glance at him before turning on my heel and stalking toward the exit.

"Ty, wait up!" Bryce hurried to catch up with me. The heavy door slammed shut behind us, sealing off the stench of Maximus's presence. Cold night air enveloped us, but it did nothing to cool the heat raging through my veins.

"Keep an eye on that bastard." My voice strained with the effort of keeping my anger in check. "I want to know his every fucking move."

"Already on it." Bryce pulled out his phone. "I'll call Isaiah right now." I picked up on the concern in his voice, but I didn't have the energy to reassure him. All I wanted was to be home with Liza, to wrap her in my arms and shield her from the predators that seemed to be closing in from all sides.

As we walked to the car, my hands trembled with the force of my rage. I needed to fucking punch something. Each mile back to the estate was like an eternity, the thought of Liza alone and vulnerable gnawing at me like a ravenous beast. My mind raced with dark thoughts that I tried to push away, but they were all-consuming, causing my wolf to pace with anxiety and a longing to protect his mate.

"Maximus won't get anywhere near her," Bryce said, breaking the tense silence between us. "You know that, right?"

We couldn't get home fast enough. All I wanted was to be close to Liza, to protect her from the likes of Maximus and anyone else who would dare threaten to take her.

# Chapter 12 - Liza

The soft glow of my computer screen illuminated the dimly lit office as I diligently worked on invoices, my fingers flying across the keyboard. The monotonous task was almost a welcome distraction from the constant action surrounding me during the day and the vivid dreams I had every night.

A ping alerted me to a new email. Rosalie's background check..

"Please, please be good news," I muttered to myself as I scanned the email with bated breath.

Rosalie's background check was all clear, and her references checked out perfectly. Unable to contain my excitement, I clapped my hands together and squealed like a giddy schoolgirl. Rosalie would make an excellent assistant chef. Her talent in the kitchen and hardworking nature were undeniable, and her cheery disposition would brighten up the workplace after a long day of cooking.

"Finally, some good news." After having a maniac in my office attempt to slice open his wrist just days prior, it was nice to have confirmation that Rosalie was exactly who she said she was, and that my judgment wasn't completely off. I didn't have to worry about her being some omega fanatic who'd lied her way into my home in hopes of witnessing a miracle.

I grabbed my phone, eager to share the news with Rosalie. As I dialed her number, my leg jumped with anticipation. I couldn't wait to have her by my side as not only an assistant chef but also a student—someone I could pour my time and energy into.

"Hey, Liza!" Rosalie's voice chirped through the phone, bursting with enthusiasm, which wasn't surprising in the least. "What's up?"

"Rosalie, I have some good news. Your background check came back perfect, and your references were glowing. You're officially hired as my assistant chef!" I blurted, unable to contain my excitement any longer.

"Seriously? Oh my gods, Liza, thank you so much," she squealed, her voice bubbling over with joy. "I promise you won't regret this. I am going to work so hard for you."

"I have no doubt about that. Your passion and skill in the kitchen are just what I've been searching for." My statement was filled with pride. "I'll email you soon with an official start date and time. I'd love to get you set up to start working this week. Will that work for you?"

"Sounds perfect. I'll keep an eye out for the email. Thanks again, Liza. You have my word that I will perform my hardest for you."

I smiled, already thinking of the incredible dishes we'd create together. "Take care, Rosalie."

After we said our goodbyes, I leaned back in my chair, my chest swelling with happiness. This was a new chapter not only for me and my company, but also for Rosalie. Together, we would take Presley Acres by storm, one delicious dish at a time.

I was feeling energized, and the sound of the printer whirring to life was a sign of productivity. Some days, it seemed I just chased my tail in circles between pack duties, meetings, and keeping my business afloat. But today, everything had clicked into place for once.

As the printer spat out Rosalie's paperwork, there was an odd shift in the atmosphere. I cocked my head to the side, trying to make sense of it. The scent was subtle, barely discernible, but unmistakable, nonetheless. Ty was home, and something was very wrong.

His footsteps drew nearer, and if I'd had any doubts before, I had none now. Fury rolled off him in large, fast waves. I heard a pause in his steps, and that fury in the air lessened a bit, as if he were trying to stifle it the closer he came to my office, but it was still palpable beneath the surface. My heart thudded as my instincts screamed that trouble was brewing.

"Hey, babe." Ty forced a smile as he stepped into my office, but his eyes betrayed him. The rage simmering within those familiar depths put me on alert.

"Ty, what happened?" My voice wavered slightly. "Are you okay?"

"Nothing happened." He dismissed me and tried to pretend like everything was perfectly fine, though his words were blatantly hollow.

"Come on, Ty. You can't hide your emotions from me. I know you too well. I'm your mate." I raised an eyebrow, calling him on his bullshit.

He raked a hand through his hair. "I had a meeting with a guy named Maximus, an alpha from a non-allied pack. The arrogant bastard comes to me with some business scheme, thinks I should throw money at his ridiculous casino idea, but refuses to contact Hiram for advice."

Ty obviously didn't like this Maximus guy, but I never would've expected a simple business meeting to make him that angry, especially when the guy obviously had a dumb proposal. Typically, Ty would have just shrugged it off and moved on.

"A sucky meeting didn't make you this furious. Are you sure that's all that happened?"

He hesitated, averting his gaze. Bingo. Ty was definitely keeping something from me.

"Ty, we've been through this before. Secrets have come between us in the past, and I don't want that to happen again." I stood and made my way across the room. "Why can't you confide in me?"

"Liza, telling you everything about the meeting won't make a damn difference." Ty was defensive but finally making eye contact with me again. "I'm not keeping secrets to be secretive, it's just something you don't need to know."

What the hell was this? His explanation wasn't good enough for me. Had we taken two steps backward in our relationship after everything we'd been through? I crossed my arms and narrowed my eyes. "Maybe it's not a big deal to you, but you're obviously upset, which makes me worried and uncomfortable. Why won't you tell me? I don't see what the big fucking deal is."

"Because it's not important!" Anger flared in his eyes. "Knowing every detail of the meeting won't affect us or our life. It was just an arrogant man trying to piss me off. Why do you have to push so much?"

"Because I care, Ty," I whispered, trying to keep the hurt out of my voice. "You say we're partners, but when I want to help, you push me away."

"Sometimes, Liza"—he gritted his teeth, his hands clenched into fists at his sides—"you need to learn when to leave well enough alone."

"Gods, you have such fucking double standards. You want me to tell you everything about my feelings, even if it has nothing to do with you. Then you tell me you're not being secretive, that it's not anything I need to know. Isn't that the meaning of the fucking word secretive?"

Ty's face reddened, and he took a step back toward the door, like he needed to physically separate himself from me. His muscles tensed, and his jaw clenched, his eyes darkening.

"Damn it, Liza. You really need to learn when to leave shit alone."

His outburst surprised me, hurt me. He'd never spoken to me like that. Quite the opposite, in fact. Ty always treated me with respect, and I swallowed past the lump forming in my throat.

Nodding, I managed a tight-lipped smile. "Fine, Ty. I won't ask again."

I grabbed my purse and keys, storming past him without another word. The sound of my heels clicking on the hardwood floor punctuated my exit, and I left Ty standing there in the empty office, his expression a mixture of anger and regret.

As I made my way through the house, I decided that visiting my parents would be the perfect distraction from whatever had crawled up Ty's ass. I announced my plans to the guards stationed near the entrance.

"I want to go to my parents' house." I placed a hand on my hip, expecting instant compliance.

They exchanged hesitant glances. One of the guards nervously darted his eyes around as he stammered, "Uh, ma'am, we can't do that. We need to obtain permission from Alpha Ty first."

My blood boiled first at their hesitation, then at the inference that I couldn't leave the estate without Ty's permission. "Listen." I pointed at him, my voice dripping with sarcasm. "I am the lady of this pack, and I do not need my mate's approval to go see my own parents. So, if you don't mind, let my security detail know I am going to my parents and to meet me at the car with the fucking keys."

The guards fumbled over their words, their faces turning a lovely shade of beet red. "Of course, Mrs. Keller. We apologize for any inconvenience."

"Good." I pulled my purse up onto my shoulder and stormed past them and out the front door.

As they scrambled to follow my orders, I smirked at their flustered state. It wasn't often that I flexed my authority in such a manner, but it had been necessary this time, and it had felt damn good.

Robin and Jamie had, as instructed, collected the keys, then met me at the car. We were now driving through the downtown area toward my parents' house. I rested my head against the car window, attempting to absorb the town's energy.

What the hell? I'd been so focused on the goings-on within the estate's walls that I hadn't noticed the apparent shift within the fanatics who'd come to town in the hopes of catching a glimpse of me. It hadn't taken long for their adoration to morph into loathing. As we passed my office, my breath caught in my throat. "Stop the car."

Angry red paint and venomous words smeared the front of the building. The word FRAUD had been painted over and over across it. A small crowd were gathered outside, waving around signs that also accused me of being a fraud. Hell no. They'd vandalized my office and gathered to spew their nastiness, and it was all directed at me.

Jamie, who was driving, hesitated.

"Jamie, stop the damn car. Now."

He reluctantly pulled over but didn't shut off the engine.

My thoughts raced as I took in the scene before me. Rage bubbled and boiled over as I flung open the door. Robin, who'd been sitting in the rear seat of the car beside me, called out, "Liza, don't! It's not safe. Please, get back inside."

I sent him a feral glare over my shoulder, the fire in my eyes daring him to try and stop me. The sudden fear in his gaze momentarily drew my attention away from the crowd as he whimpered and took a step back. What the fuck? Since when was Robin scared of me?

I was caught off guard for a moment and didn't see the tomato hurtling toward me. It splattered across my chest, the cold, slimy pulp oozing down my shirt.

"Fraud!" someone in the crowd shouted. "Fake bitch, sending the alpha down to hide your bullshit. You're nothing but a lying bitch!"

"Get back in the car, Liza." Robin tried to instruct me again, this time from afar, but I was deaf to his pleas. I was surrounded by a sea of hatred, and overwhelmed with a burning desire for revenge.

"Who the hell do you think you are?" I snarled, stalking toward the building. "You have no right to do this."

"Fake bitch!" another voice called.

The rage in my chest grew stronger, wilder, almost like it was taking on a life of its own. Their hateful shouts and taunts echoed around me, but their words barely registered. It was the sight of my office building, its windows smashed and graffiti covering the once-pristine walls, that turned my blood into fire. The subconscious voice in my head, the familiar one that had been growing stronger since I'd discovered the truth about my heritage, urged me to keep calm. But the rage was too powerful, too consuming, to be contained.

"You're nothing!" someone yelled, their voice dripping with disdain. "You don't deserve to be with an alpha. Bet you got Alpha Keller to believe you were an omega so he'd fuck you."

The ground beneath my feet trembled, a low rumble that matched the fury coursing through my veins.

My voice, once it emerged, was more wolf than human. A guttural growl that demanded submission. "Look at what you've done!" I snarled, stalking closer toward the mob. "This is my business, my life! You have no right to destroy it!"

The stench of fear permeated the air, thick and heavy, like a blanket smothering the crowd. People stepped back, their expressions shifting from anger to unease as they realized they might have pushed me too far.

"Liza, Liza!" Ty's sharp, commanding voice cut through the tension. He moved to stand between me and the crowd, his broad frame acting as a barrier against their hatred.

I couldn't figure out how Ty had managed to arrive on the scene so quickly, but there he was, standing between me and the hateful mob. His presence both infuriated and soothed me at the same time. My wolf yearned for vengeance, but I knew deep down that this wasn't the way.

"Please, Liza, listen to me," Ty said firmly, his hands on my shoulders, grounding me and forcing me to focus on him. "The police are on their way. They'll handle these people, but you need to calm down. For your own sake."

For a moment, his presence appeared to quell the storm within me, the rage receding like waves on a shore. But I looked beyond Ty at my office building, my place of work that I'd built from the ground up, and these people weren't happy because I hadn't come out and performed at their command like a fucking clapping seal. They thought they had the gods-given right to the destroy my property. It felt like the calm inside me Ty had begun to restore was too far gone. The damage had already been done, and it was too late. The power within me, wild and untamed, demanded to be released.

"Please, Liza," Ty begged, his eyes locked on mine, filled with unease. "You need to calm down. This isn't the way."

I heard his words, saw the concern in his gaze, knew the love in his touch. Together, it soothed me, a balm to my frayed nerves. Slowly, reluctantly, the anger began to ebb. In its place, bone-deep weariness settled like nothing I'd ever experienced. It left me hollow and cold.

"Fine." My voice was hoarse from the strain of holding back my wolf.

Even though I was still struggling with the simmering fury just beneath the surface, when I looked at Ty's worried face, there was a certain quality to his gaze that gave me pause. I closed my eyes and let out a deep sigh, focusing on regaining control of my emotions, feeling drained and disoriented as the anger slowly dissipated.

"Ty," I rasped. "What happened? How did you know where I was? How did you make it here so quickly?"

He shook his head. "I'll explain later. We need to get you out of here."

As we turned to walk away, the crowd murmured among themselves, their voices tinged with awe and fear. It seemed they had finally gotten a taste of the power they'd been so eager to condemn, and it had left them shaken to their core.

We walked toward Ty's car as the fanatics' shouts echoed around us, their tone shifting from anger to something more akin to reverence.

"Did you see that?" one of them exclaimed. "She made the ground shake. She truly is an omega."

"Her power is incredible," another person said in awe. "I've never seen anything like it. My placard floated right out of my hands. The stories were true."

I gritted my teeth, a bitter mix of validation and disgust churning in my gut. They'd witnessed a glimpse of my power and, suddenly, their hatred had been forgotten and transformed back into admiration. It was sickening, but at the same time, a part of me reveled in their newfound respect and their fear. Perhaps they'd think twice before hurling more insults or damn tomatoes my way.

"Focus only on me, Liza." Ty's fingers tightened around mine as he led me to his car. "Don't let them get to you."

Easier said than done. But for now, I had no choice but to push the feelings aside, trusting that Ty would help me make sense of the chaos by filling in the gaps I couldn't quite remember.

Once we were back at the estate, I barely had time to catch my breath before Ty turned to face me, his gray eyes a storm of concern and frustration. "What happened with the fanatics tonight was partially my fault. I'm so sorry. When I saw them lounging about outside your office on my way to the meeting with Maximus, I got pissed off and chased them away. If I'd left them alone, they wouldn't have turned on you like that, and you wouldn't have gotten angry."

"This wasn't your fault, Ty. We both knew they'd turn against me. It was only a matter of time. I wasn't giving them what they wanted. I have to share the blame. When I saw what they'd done to my office, I demanded that Jamie stop the car. They both tried to get me to listen, but I couldn't. I saw the destruction, and I was just so fucking angry."

Ty grabbed my hand, his much larger hand encapsulating mine. "Liza, you can't let yourself get angry like that in public anymore."

My hands trembled as I tried to steady myself against a nearby table. "This isn't my fault, Ty. Something is changing inside of me again, and I don't even know what happened out there. I remember seeing that my office building was trashed. Then Robin kept demanding I return to the car. Robin... Robin was frightened of me, Ty. Someone through the tomato and it splattered all over me, and I was so damned furious. Then you were there, in front of me. You still haven't told me how you arrived so quickly."

Ty looked at me like I had sprouted another head. "Liza, you were there for over thirty minutes. Jamie called me when you refused to get back in the car. I drove there as fast as I could. By the time I arrived, you were making things gravitate off the ground. Your eyes were focused straight ahead, and no matter how many times I yelled your name, you wouldn't snap out of it."

I stared at him in stunned silence. He had to be exaggerating, but the grave expression on his face made it abundantly clear that he wasn't. What the hell was happening to me?

Ty continued, his tone low and steady, as if trying to keep me grounded. "Even the picket signs were flung from the fanatics' hands. Jamie and Robin's guns flew from their holsters as well."

"Are you serious?" My voice wobbled, and I wrapped my arms around myself. "What's wrong with me?"

"I don't know. We'll figure it out. Maybe you should consider some anger management until we understand what's causing the changes in your magic."

"Anger management?" My eyebrows shot up in disbelief. "Do you really think that will make any difference?"

"It might," Ty said. "Doing something is better than not doing anything at all. You scared me, babe. I didn't think I could reach you to bring you back to me. What if it happens again..." He looked so worried, and his voice was near breaking. "What if I don't succeed in bringing you back next time? I never want to see you lose control like that again."

"Neither do I," I said. Uncertainty and fear clamped down on my mind. The thought of losing control of my magic and potentially hurting someone in the process terrified me.

"Promise me you'll try, Liza." Ty pleaded, his eyes searching mine for any sign of agreement.

"Fine. I promise. But we need to find out what's going on soon. Whatever this is, I feel as if I've got no control over it, and it's changing fast. I don't know how much longer I can handle it."

Ty pulled me into a tight embrace, his warmth enveloping me like a protective shield. "We will, Liza. We'll figure it out together. You realize I won't let anything happen to you in the process, right? I need you to trust that I have your best interests at heart."

I nodded. For now, that would have to be enough., but as I leaned into the safety of Ty's arms, I wondered if there was truly any way to protect myself and others from the growing darkness within me.

# Chapter 13 - Ty

My favorite time was always the early morning silence before the estate came to life with its hustle and bustle, when the day was full of possibilities. There were no landscapers using their noisy equipment outside in the gardens, no staff shuffling throughout the house performing their various duties.

I was on the balcony outside our bedroom. Last night's rain had amplified the forest's scent. My wolf itched to be out there. I considered waking Liza to see if she'd like to go for a run and enjoy everything the morning had to offer, but I stood for just a bit longer, gazing out at the grounds. It was so damn peaceful, which was exactly what we needed.

Peace.

My moment of Zen was rudely interrupted when my phone vibrated on the wrought-iron table, jarring me out of my thoughts. Rubbing my temples, I knew the tranquility of the day was gone. I dropped my gaze to the screen to see a text from Isaiah.

*Got info on Liza's pack members. Headed your way.*

I raised an eyebrow and typed out a reply. *Give us an hour.*

Last night had been chaotic, with Liza losing her temper and scaring the hell out of her so-called omega fans. She'd withdrawn into herself, her memories fragmented. Her face had been a canvas of emotions as she silently tried to make sense of the events that had unfolded. She'd listened in disbelief as I recounted everything. I'd witnessed her fear at her actions communicated through our bond.

She held onto me, tears streaming, shaking with sobs, telling me over and over again that she was sorry. I tried to reassure her, but she was terrified of losing control around people and not being able to protect herself around others.

Despite the late hour, we'd contacted Liza's doctor on his personal cell and asked if he knew anyone discreet who could provide help with her anger management. He'd given us a name, and I planned to reach out later today.

Before I could set my phone down, it buzzed again. This time, it was Bryce.

*Checked social media yet? Think you should.*

Shit. If Bryce was concerned, did I really want to open it? I didn't want to study the comments, but I forced myself to face the music. I opened my account and scrolled through posts about the incident outside Liza's office. As I read the comments, it took all my restraint not to crack my phone in my grip.

*"Omega loses her shit, cusses out strangers."*

*"Omega threatens innocent people, sends posters flying across the street using only her eyes."*

Thank the gods no one had captured what had really happened on camera. That would've been much more difficult to explain away. I groaned. Now we had to add damage control to our growing list of top priorities. I glanced at Liza, still peacefully asleep in our bed, her soft breaths stirring the strands of hair framing her face. She deserved better than this chaos.

"Good morning, gorgeous," I said, pressing a gentle kiss to Liza's forehead.

Liza stirred, her green eyes fluttering open. She stretched and yawned, sitting up abruptly as she sensed my urgency through our connection.

"Morning. What time is it?"

"Early," I said, keeping my voice soft. "But I got a text, and there's something we need to talk about."

She tensed. "What is it?"

"Last night's incident at your office has blown up on social media." I tried to keep my tone steady. "People are talking, posting... it's not good."

Liza grabbed her phone from the nightstand and scrolled through the posts, anger, fear, and worry flickering over her face.

I watched her closely, worried about how she'd react. Would she spiral out of control again?

To my relief, she just heaved out a sigh, slumped back, and tossed her phone on the bed.

"This is such bullshit," she muttered under her breath, then pushed herself out of bed. "I need to shower before I can deal with all this."

"Whatever you want." I squeezed her hand, trying to offer some comfort, though I wasn't sure how this whole mess would play out.

"Thanks." Liza gave a weak smile as she trudged to the bathroom.

I watched as she shook her long hair out the messy bun. It always shocked me how someone could look so fucking gorgeous when just waking up.

I couldn't stop myself from following her with my eyes, drawn to her exposed skin as she stripped off her clothes. I found myself staring at her breasts, my desire for her a burning need.

She caught my gaze and quirked an eyebrow playfully, her lips tugging into a sly smile. "Why are you still dressed? Come on."

Hell yes. I didn't need any more encouragement. I quickly shed my clothes and joined her in the large shower I'd helped design with intricate tile work and multiple shower heads. It was an oasis in the middle of the estate. A place to wash off the sins of the day. In this case, it was a place to fuck our worries away.

Liza had already lathered up her hair, so I turned on the rain showerhead next to her. Hot water cascaded down my body. I still needed to make up for my actions yesterday. Not being there for her, shouting at her. I couldn't blame her for wanting to get away.

"I'm so sorry for what you had to go through." My voice was barely audible above the sound of the running water. "I should have been there with you."

Liza turned to face me, and she looked so damn vulnerable that it broke my heart. "I'm scared, Ty."

Her admission caught me off guard. I lathered up a loofah and gently ran it over skin, doing my best to comfort her. "We'll get through this together." I might not have been able to promise what the outcome would be, but I was damn sure I'd be by her side through it all. I pressed a soft kiss to her lips.

"Thank you," Liza said against my mouth. "For everything."

The tension between us slowly dissipated as we continued washing each other. Despite the chaos surrounding us, we were a team and had agreed on the night of our mating ceremony to support one another, no matter what. And that was all that mattered.

I moved my hands to Liza's hips and tugged her closer, the warmth of our bodies radiating against each other. Our eyes locked as I guided us farther into the shower stream, the steam surrounding us like a protective barrier. I lowered my lips to hers again in a slow kiss, tasting her sweetness.

Liza responded eagerly. One rumor about the omega that I could confirm was this. Her hypersexuality was nirvana to my cock. Wrapping her arms around my neck and deepening the kiss, Liza moaned into my mouth as our tongues tangled in an erotic dance. My hands roamed over her slick body, fingertips running along her curves until I cupped her breasts. Another soft moan dragged from deep in her throat. My thumb brushed against her hardened nipples, and she moaned again, pressing herself against me, begging for more. I complied without hesitation as I trailed kisses round the shell of her ear, down the side of her jaw, down her neck, teasing my way to the sweet spot below her earlobe.

I moved down between Liza's breasts, placing gentle kisses on the soft, supple mounds. One of my hands slid down the side of her body, and Liza was quick to grab it and guide it farther down her hip. Eyes hooded with desire, she moved my hand lower until she held my fingers nestled between her legs.

She was already dripping wet, her soft folds responding to my every touch. With my free hand, I cupped her face and pulled her in for a scorching kiss, exploring her mouth thoroughly with my tongue. She clutched my neck, her body arching backward into the stream of water, her breasts thrusting forward, nipples hard against my chest.

She sighed into my mouth as I cupped her breasts, teasing her nipples with my thumbs.

"Your nipples couldn't be any harder."

Liza arched her back, and I lowered my mouth to nibble on the hard nub. She gasped, and the noise that left her mouth was like music to my ears. I dragged my mouth over to her other breast, delicately teasing the pink bud with the tip of my tongue.

My hands continued to roam her body, exploring every inch of her skin. My cock swelled as Liza's mouth found my ear and nipped gently at the lobe. Her hot breath made the hairs on my arms stand at attention.

Liza's hands traveled across my chest, pinching my own nipples as she journeyed down my stomach, stopping just enough to tease me and make me yearn for more. She moved her arms back around my head, running her fingers through my wet hair, then gliding down my back to my ass. Her nails pressed into my flesh as she squeezed my ass cheeks, and my cock hardened even more. She pressed up against me, grinding her core into my erection.

Her arousal was an intoxicating scent. I gave in to the urge to explore her wet pussy and feel the heat of her core. I slid my hand down her stomach and cupped her pussy, lightly stroking the seam of her lips with my fingers. Her breath hitched in her throat, and she moaned deeply, arching to push her pussy against my hand.

I loved how responsive she was, how she writhed against me, silently urging me to push my fingers between her folds. She wanted her release, but I wanted her desire to build until she thought she couldn't stand it anymore, then build it higher still. Slowly, I slid two my fingers inside her. She sighed, her breath hot against my neck.

My lips never left her skin, as I licked, flicked, and nibbled across her chest, before sucking a nipple into my mouth, my fingers working her pussy. I curled my fingers, eliciting a long moan that only encouraged me. My thumb moved rhythmically around the bundle of nerves, creating a pattern up around and down, then back to the top. I slid my fingers inside, my thumb never leaving her clit. Her hips jerked against me, her pussy clenching around my fingers. She ground against my hand, moaning my name as the muscles in her pussy quivered.

My free hand moved behind her body, cupping her ass, and I eased a third digit inside her, my fingers pumping in and out of her. In and out. In and out. Her pussy tightened around my fingers as she whimpered, her juices sliding down my hand. She was close. I pulled my fingers out to her entrance, stroking that sensitive opening.

Liza moaned and lost control as I pushed to stroke her inside. I increased my pace, my fingers moving in and out of her, my thumb lightly stroking her clit. She was so close to coming, except, I wasn't ready for her to come just yet. I didn't want her to stop, but I also needed to be inside her.

I pulled my fingers away, and Liza gaped at me. "No, please. Please don't stop. Fuck, Ty. I was so close."

I kissed her full lips, then moved lower to her neck, her stomach, and down to the soft patch of hair just above her womanhood. I admired her golden curls and placed a reverent kiss to them before moving a step back, my gaze trailing down her body.

"Fuck me," Liza pleaded, her fingers digging into my biceps. "Please."

I gave her a wicked smirk before lowering myself between her legs, cupping her ass. She squirmed and whimpered as I kissed her inner thighs, gently prodding her opening with my tongue. Her hands moved to the back of my head, caressing my hair as I teased her with my tongue.

"Yes, Ty. Yes. Gods, that feels so good."

Her hips jerked toward my mouth as I eased my tongue inside her. She moaned a deep, guttural sound, and I smiled against her sweet spot. I made sure to go slowly, my tongue grazing her swollen and sensitive bud as she continued to tremble. She tasted incredible, and as her juices slid across my tongue, my cock throbbed. I could eat her out for hours, but I wanted to be inside her. Reluctantly, I pulled my mouth away from her body.

Liza looked down at me, her eyes full of lust and uncertainty. "Why did you stop?"

I rose to my feet and kissed her so she could taste herself on me, her hands immediately finding their way to my lower back. I moaned as I kissed her, my cock brushing against her slick pussy. I loved the way she groaned and shuddered as I kissed her, heightening my desire for her.

"I need to be inside you." I raised an eyebrow, as if daring her to disagree with me. Eyes smoldering, she wrapped her arms around my neck and lifted her legs to encircle my waist. I grabbed her hips and gave a small thrust, sliding my erection inside her, her pussy tight around my cock. She groaned as I buried myself deep inside her warmth, pulling me in for a kiss.

I pumped in and out of her, her hot breath on my neck sending a shiver down my spine. She moaned loudly, her nails digging into my back, urging me to fuck her harder. And I did. I pumped into her, our hips moving in unison. The shower was filled with the sensual sounds of our bodies as I pushed harder and deeper into her.

I moved and pressed her body against the cold, stone tiles of the shower wall.

"Fuck, Liza. Your pussy is so tight."

"Ty, I'm so close," she whimpered. "Fuck me harder."

I planted firm kisses and soft bites on her neck, her ears, and her lips. Her hands moved to my hair, guiding my face up so her lips were on mine in a scorching kiss. "Please. I'm so close. I need to come."

"My pleasure."

I pulled out and thrust inside her again, driving myself deeper into her, her breasts pressing against my chest. She moaned as her orgasm came crashing down, her pussy tightening around me, her body shaking in ecstasy. Her orgasm pushed me over the edge as I buried myself inside her.

"Ty!" Liza's head fell back when she screamed my name. I erupted inside her, my cum spurting in glorious waves of ecstasy, filling her. She milked me dry, our combined juices sliding down my shaft.

My arms trembled as I held myself over her, her body quivering from the aftershock. I slid down the shower, holding onto her until I came to rest on the shower floor. After we caught our breath, we sat there trying to recover. I cupped my hand over her pulsating pussy, pressing on her clit, giving her every drop of pleasure she needed. It was the least I could do.

Something about fucking in the shower was rejuvenating. If every day started like that, I wouldn't have a care in the world.

As I pulled on a shirt, there was a knock at our bedroom door. A staff member poked her head in. "Sorry to disturb you, sir. Isaiah is here."

"Escort him to my office. We'll meet him there shortly."

Worry gnawed at me, eating away at the happiness that had sparked inside me. What had Isaiah found out about Liza's long-lost pack members? I silently prayed to the gods it was something positive. I didn't think I'd be able to bear to see Liza endure more bad news on top of everything else.

"Did you know Isaiah was coming?" Liza said from behind me, a towel wrapped around her body.

"He texted me earlier, saying he had information about your pack."

Her smile lit up her eyes. "I'm so excited. I hope he found the boy from my dreams. I couldn't imagine a better way to start the day, other than the blinding orgasm you just gave me."

I laughed and took her hand. "Touché."

We headed toward my office. The anticipation built with each step, and yet, a part of me dreaded what we might discover. It was almost like ripping a Band-Aid off. It hurt, but the wound might be healed. On the flip side, it might be fucking infected.

When we entered the office, still hand in hand, we found Isaiah sitting opposite my desk, his gaze intent on the folder in his hands. When he looked up to greet us, the atmosphere in the room shifted. The air grew thick with tension.

Liza and I sat, and I braced myself.

"Ty, Liza," Isaiah acknowledged, his voice somber before he slid the folder across the table. "I've found some information about the pack members you were looking for, but it wasn't easy."

Liza and I exchanged a glance, our emotions mingling between excitement and unease.

"What do you mean, exactly?" Liza bit her bottom lip anxiously. "Are they still alive?"

"Finding them was difficult because the parents of the children who left the pack clearly didn't want to be found." Isaiah's dark eyes filled with concern. "They had cut off all ties and left no trace of themselves."

I frowned, trying to make sense of the information.

Liza's grip tightened on my hand, her nails digging into my skin. "That's strange. They left because of Castro, didn't they?"

"That's my understanding, yes." Isaiah nodded and cocked his head to the side, no doubt wondering where Liza's train of thought was headed.

Liza shifted in her seat. "Do you think it's possible that the parents of these kids somehow knew back then that Castro would turn out to be as dangerous as he is now?"

I tried to imagine a child who was so fucking evil that multiple families in the pack wanted to be as far away from him as possible before he became an adult.

"I'm not sure what their motives were, but I can say for certain that the families cut off all ties with the Wylde pack when they left. There were no records of contact except one."

Liza raised an eyebrow. "Would you mind if I took a look at the file?"

"Of course." Isaiah handed her the folder, giving me a quick look that I couldn't quite interpret.

As Liza flipped through the pages, I kept my attention on her expression, trying to gauge her reaction. She shook her head slowly, her lips pursed. "None of them seem familiar," she said. "Their hair is wrong."

"Wrong, how?" My curiosity was piqued. How was it possible to know for certain that none of the adults in the photos were the boy from her dream?

"Even though I don't remember the boy's face clearly, his hair was as white as mine." Liza lifted a strand of her platinum hair for emphasis.

"Maybe they dyed their hair over the years." That explanation seemed logical to me, but Liza continued to shake her head.

"That's not all." Her hands gripped the folder tightly. "It's my gut telling me that none of these people are the boy from my dream." Her words hung heavily in the air, laden with frustration and disappointment.

"Trust your instincts," I said softly. "You've always had a strong connection to your gut."

Liza handed the folder back to Isaiah and stared straight ahead, lost in thought. Deep lines marred her forehead, and I could feel her worry about finding the mysterious child she had a strange connection to. It was odd for someone to try and find a person from their dreams, but not for Liza. She'd proven more than once that her dreams were fueled by her powers, and, like everything about them, we didn't understand, but they served as a guide in her waking hours.

Finally, she spoke up, her voice tinged with hope. "Hopefully, the people Isaiah tracked down might know who the boy from my dream was."

The early morning sunlight filtered through the blinds, casting a warm glow on Isaiah, who placed another folder on my desk. "There was only one record of contact between the pack members who left and Liza's old pack." He flipped through the folders until he came to a specific photo. He pointed at a woman, her features similar to Liza's. "Her name is Isabel Russell."

That last name gave me pause. It had to be a coincidence, because given the vastness of the world, what were the chances that Liza was associated with a company doing business with Keller Enterprises?

"According to my research, Liza's parents were the only record I found in relation to Isabel Russell." He held out a piece of paper, the ink stark against the white background. "This is a money wire transaction from Liza's father to Isabel's father for a hundred and twenty-five thousand dollars."

Liza and I gaped at the receipt.

"Why would my father send Isabel's father that much money?" Her face was a portrait of confusion. "Did my father owe money to this family?"

Isaiah's forehead creased, his broad shoulders moving slightly. "I looked but couldn't find a connection. Isabel's parents clearly weren't struggling financially. In fact, they seemed to be doing quite well for themselves."

I racked my brain for a logical explanation. Maybe there was a connection to the LLC who wanted to buy one of our manufacturing plants. "Is it possible it was some sort of silent business investment?"

"Possible, but there were no signs of any return investment." Isaiah put his hands into his pants pockets.

Suddenly, Liza jumped up from her seat, her eyes alight with urgency. She ran to the opposite side of my desk, grabbed my laptop, and opened it.

I moved to stand over her shoulder, watching as she typed furiously. "Are you looking for something in particular?"

"I'm checking the bank account my parents left for me." Liza opened the account and entered the login and password. "What if there are other payments out to the families who escaped? I haven't been paying much attention to it, since I haven't needed the money—" Liza stopped talking.

"Have you found anything unusual?" Isaiah asked, getting up to lean over the desk.

Liza's fingers paused on the screen, her breath hitching. "There's a transaction from a week ago, for ten-point-five million dollars." Her voice was barely above a whisper, disbelief etched across her face. "My parents already left me money... much more than I ever thought I'd see in my life. And now this."

"Where did it come from?" I tried to maintain a calm exterior despite the growing turmoil inside me.

"An LLC." Liza's gaze locked on the screen. "Russell and Son, LLC."

Shock coursed through me. It couldn't be the same Russell family I'd researched... the same ones wanting to do business with me.

Isaiah's fingers danced across the screen of his phone, his face tense as he delved into the information. "The business isn't registered under Isabel's father's name—Mason Russell—anymore. It's been changed recently to one Liam Russell."

Without hesitation, I pulled out my phone and shot a text to Tim.

*Any changes of ownership to that LLC over the past few days?*

I was certain that when I checked it out, the company had been registered under Mason Russell, but now it wasn't. The connection was too strong to be a mere coincidence.

"I'm more confused than ever." Liza shook her head in frustration. "Who the hell is Liam Russell?"

I could practically see the wheels turning in her head.

"Perhaps there's something in the security deposit box that might give us some answers." Liza turned in the office chair to face Isaiah, her face flushed. "I haven't given it much thought since Ty told me about it and the money my parents left for me. Honestly, I've never even gone to the bank to inquire about it." She shrugged. "Who knows? Maybe the answers are in that box."

"Perhaps," I said, my mind racing with possibilities. "We should check it out."

"None of this came up with my initial research. I had no idea the business account even existed," Isaiah said. "But now that I do, I'll look into it and let you both know what I can find out about Liam Russell."

"I wish we could figure out the connection here." Liza stood and crossed her arms, her eyes downcast. "I guess it was unrealistic of me to think we'd find the boy so easily."

"Leave it all to me." Isaiah shoved his phone into his back pocket. "I'll find out everything I can."

"Thank you, Isaiah." I clapped him on the shoulder. "We appreciate your help."

Liza retreated to her office to work on the menus for her next client, while I set about doing damage control with the press. The last thing I needed was for people to think Liza was some sort of supernatural freak. Luckily, there were still no videos about yesterday's incident, but it had made its way into the local news site, so pulling the stories was relatively easy after a few well-placed threats.

"Mr. Keller," the CEO of the local news station said nervously over the phone, "I assure you, we'll remove the story immediately. It won't happen again."

"See that it doesn't," I warned curtly. "If the story isn't retracted within the next ten minutes, you can kiss the endorsement from the Keller pack goodbye."

I almost laughed at the horror in the CEO's voice. He knew fucking well that if he didn't sit when I said sit, he'd no longer get first dibs on all interviews and live coverage of all pack press releases.

I proceeded to send an email to the owner of a local newspaper, threatening to pull all funding and send the publication into the ground where it was headed anyway, thanks to social media. My fingers flew across the keyboard, each keystroke fueled by instinct to protect Liza, and anger over the whole fucking predicament we'd found ourselves in.

"Your little paper will crumble," I said aloud as I typed, "and you'll be left with nothing but the ashes of your own ignorance."

Even though I'd squelched the local media stories, I couldn't stop the traction the story was gaining on social media.

I glanced at the thousands of comments and shares under the main thread. Fuck. This could get extremely crazy and out of hand real fast. The truth would very likely be twisted into something far worse than what had actually happened. Luckily for us, though, the more insane the story became, the less believable it would be in the eyes of the public.

My fingers hovered over the keyboard for a moment, considering how I could put an end to this before it spiraled even further out of control. A wicked grin spread across my face as an idea took hold.

I created an anonymous account and typed a ridiculously outlandish account of what had happened.

*I was there and saw the whole thing with the omega. She turned her head upward, and the gods descended from the heavens, assisting her in terrifying the bystanders and blowing objects through the air. Even the god of thunder himself assisted in making the ground quake.*

I leaned back in my chair, chuckling to myself at the absurdity of it. Sure enough, comments flooded in, many expressing doubt and disbelief at the story. More and more people called the whole incident a hoax, pointing out the lack of photographic evidence as just a sad attempt by omega-obsessed followers to get their fifteen minutes of fame.

Within thirty minutes, the story died a quick death, many dismissing the story as being fake. I closed my computer, satisfied that I'd quelled the rumors and protected Liza's reputation.

Unfortunately, there was still the matter of Russell and Sons LLC hanging over our heads. I tried to focus on other work matters while I anxiously waited for a response from that fucking asshole Tim.

# Chapter 14 - Liza

I wandered through the halls, staring at the artwork I'd observed too many times to count. I'd been stuck indoors for nearly a week because of the influx of tourists and the incident at my office, and I was going stir crazy. I really needed to get out of the house. As I passed an ornate tapestry, the reality of my confinement bore down on me.

I would have given anything to visit the ice cream shop. Hell, I would have settled for going out and going through the drive-thru.

Spinning on my heels, I headed down the hallway directly toward Ty's office. I knocked on the door, hoping I wasn't interrupting an important meeting.

"Come in." Ty's voice was muffled by the heavy wood. Upon entering, I found him bent over his desk, poring over some documents. Slowly, he pulled himself out of whatever he was reading, lifted his head, and focused on me, a smile spreading across his face. "Are you here for some lunchtime fun?" he asked, raising an eyebrow.

"Ty," I said, rolling my eyes and crossing my arms. "Ha, as much as I'd love that, I know the deadlines you're under." I paused, biting my lip. "I'm not here to distract you, but I need you to figure out a way for me to leave the estate. If I don't get out of here, I'm going to go crazy. Soon."

He gave me a strange smile. "Ah, babe, great minds think alike," he said cryptically before picking up his phone.

Curious, I took a step closer. "Who are you calling?"

"It's a surprise. You trust me, don't you? Just go get changed and pick out something comfortable. I'll take care of everything. Meet me at the front door in fifteen minutes."

Excitement bubbled in my chest as I practically skipped to our room. I wondered what the heck Ty had planned behind my back, but honestly, I didn't care as long as it got me out of here. Following his recommendation to dress casually, I opted for a comfortable pair of shorts and a loose-fitting T-shirt. I dressed in a hurry, applied a small amount of lip gloss, and added a touch of mascara. I put my hair up in a high ponytail, feeling the cool air on the back of my neck, then hurried downstairs to find Ty waiting for me at the door.

"You look gorgeous. Sure I can't convince you for that afternoon fuck?"

I laughed, bouncing on my toes. "Sorry, Ty, you promised me an outing, so I want the outing."

"Everything's been taken care of." He leaned in and pressed a tender kiss on my lips. "I pulled some strings and rented out Presley Acres Country Club for the morning. Sabrina will meet you there."

"Really?" I beamed at him, my heart swelling with gratitude. Would this man ever stop surprising me? Not only had he realized how much this forced lockdown was weighing on me, but he'd included my best friend, too.

"Yep, really," he repeated with a grin. "No other guests today. You won't have to worry about any omega fans, and there won't be anyone else at the place. It'll just be you, Sabrina, and the staff. You can unwind, take a dip, and indulge in delicious food and drinks, and there will be someone to drive you around the golf course, if that's what you want to do."

"Thank you." As I hugged him tightly, I thought of all the little things Ty did to make me feel special, and I felt my heart overflow with love and gratitude. What had I done to get so lucky to have such an amazing mate?

Jamie and Robin stood just outside the door and escorted me to one of the blacked-out SUVs. I turned to wave at Ty, who was watching me from the doorway.

When I entered the country club, I realized how eerie it was without its usual guests bustling through its halls, and memories of busy events as both a caterer and Ty's mate flooded my mind.

Sabrina stood in the middle of the ballroom, her vibrant blonde hair shining as brightly as ever, a frozen cocktail clutched in her hand.

I sighed sarcastically and shook my head. "What did we say about your day-drinking habit?"

Sabrina spun around with a wide grin, laughter bubbling out of her as she rushed at me. She wrapped her arms around my neck, careful not to spill a drop as she giggled. "This is the best surprise ever. It's a refreshing change from my usual routine of mindlessly snacking and binge-watching soap operas."

"Always happy to save you from boredom." I leaned in closer, inspecting her drink.

A waitress appeared beside us, offering me a drinks menu. My gaze flickered over to Sabrina's strawberry concoction before pointing at it. "I'll have what she's having."

"Excellent choice." The waitress nodded before disappearing to fetch my drink.

Sabrina tugged my hand, leading me to a plush couch nestled in the corner area of the bar. She plopped down, patting the cushion next to her for me to join. "So, spill it. What's been going on? I saw those social media posts about your angry outburst the other night. Are the rumors true?"

I waved my hand dismissively, hoping to make the whole situation sound less serious than it really was, if not for Sabrina's sake, then for my own. I still hadn't come to terms with my uncontrolled powers, so it was difficult to admit. "Ty's taking care of it. Hopefully, the chatter will stop soon. But, yes, it was... scary."

"Scary?" Sabrina echoed, her tone immediately changing from high energy to concern as she leaned closer. "What happened?"

"Ugh, it's hard to explain." I hesitated, searching for the right words. "My anger just... overtook me, and

I lost a whole section of time. I can't recall the specifics, but from what Ty's told me, it wasn't good."

Sabrina's eyebrows knitted together as she studied my face. "That sounds terrifying. Are you okay?"

"Mostly," I said with a heavy sigh. "It's just so lucky I didn't hurt anyone, but it sounds like I gave them a good scare. It happened so suddenly no one even thought to pull out their cameras to capture the moment, so Ty's managed to kill most of the stories. Still, some persistent people are hanging around. The hotel owners in town are doing all right out of it. Ty said they've put their prices up three times the normal rate." I laughed sardonically. "At least someone is benefiting from the situation."

I deflated, fear of the unknown resurfacing. "The magic within me is uncontrollable. It frightens me, it feels unsettling, and my nerves are on edge. I'm worried about what might happen next time."

"Next time?" Sabrina questioned, her eyes widening. "You think it could happen again?"

"Who knows?" I tried to keep my tone light, despite the unease coiling in my stomach. "But enough about me and my magical meltdowns. Let's focus on having fun today, okay?"

"Absolutely," Sabrina said, her infectious grin returning. "We're going to make the most of this day, Liza. No more worries, just good times, and plenty of laughter."

"Deal," I said with a smile, clinking my glass against hers.

"Cheers!"

Sabrina's worried gaze lingered on me, and I didn't blame her. I felt like a weird, magic-filled freak. But then, her eyes brightened, and she leaned forward with a conspiratorial grin.

"Hey, you need some fresh air, right? Why don't we play a round of golf to get your mind off things?"

I burst out laughing at the thought. "Do you remember the last time we played golf? We both sucked at it."

"True." Sabrina held up her second margarita with a sly grin. "But this time, we'll be drunk."

"Speak for yourself, lightweight." I rolled my eyes, but the smile that tugged at the corners of my mouth felt like the first genuine smile all week. Sabrina never failed to find a way to cheer me up, even in the strangest situations.

"Come on." Sabrina stood and pulled me from the couch. "We could use some fresh air, and who knows? Our golf skills might have magically improved since the last time."

"Miracles happen, I suppose." My laughter lightened my heart as we made our way outside, the sun casting a warm glow over the meticulously manicured golf course.

We enjoyed a few more cocktails, working our way down the menu, then when Sabrina deemed we were at peak drunkenness for a game of golf, we went over to the golf carts, where a staff member approached us with a polite smile. His gaze flickered between Sabrina's flushed cheeks and my own amused expression.

"Would either of you ladies like someone to drive you around in the golf cart?"

Sabrina waved her hand dismissively, her words slurring as she proclaimed, "Do you know who this is? This is the alpha's mate. We can take care of it ourselves." She snatched the keys from him.

"Are you sure, ma'am? Alpha Keller was quite strict with his instructions..."

I failed at stifling a laugh over Sabrina's exaggerated display of confidence. "Thanks for the offer, but I think we've got it from here." I took the keys from Sabrina's outstretched hand.

He nodded, still looking slightly concerned, before walking away.

"Ready for this?" I asked, settling into the driver's seat.

Sabrina clambered in beside me, gripping the side of the cart dramatically. "Born ready, darling." She grinned, tossing her hair over her shoulder.

As we weaved through the course, I marveled at the stunning landscape. Lush, manicured greens rolled and dipped, vibrant flower beds, and towering trees casting dappled shadows on the ground below. It was the perfect setting for an afternoon of amateur golfing.

"Okay, let's see if we can actually hit the ball this time." Sabrina squinted into the sunlight once we reached the first hole.

I smirked, feeling a surge of competitive energy. "Prepare to be amazed." I stepped up to the tee and positioned myself carefully. My hands gripped the club tightly, my knuckles turning white from the effort. I swung, willing the ball to soar gracefully through the air, only to watch it travel a mere few feet before plopping unceremoniously onto the grass.

"Ouch." Sabrina winced, her eyes full of mock sympathy. "That was... something."

"Your turn," I said, passing her the club and folding my arms across my chest. She took a moment to line up her shot, her tongue poking out from the corner of her mouth in concentration, her hips wiggling as she prepared to hit the ball.

While we continued our hilariously terrible attempts at golf, I somehow forgot all about my magical mishaps and the omega fanatics. For the first time in a long while, I could simply be Liza, laughing with my best friend, making the most of a beautiful day.

"Watch and learn, sweetheart," she teased at the next tee off, swinging with all her might. The ball flew farther than mine but veered wildly off course and landed somewhere in the bushes. We devolved into a fit of giggles.

"Whoa there, Tiger Woods," I teased, stepping back to give her some space. "You should've given that last margarita back to the barman."

"Ha!" She pointed at the ball. "I'm just as terrible as you are."

"Hey, at least we're consistently awful together." I grinned, linking my arm with hers as we walked toward our golf balls.

"True friendship right there." She nodded sagely, raising her margarita in a toast. "To sucking at golf and having fun anyway."

"Cheers to that." I clinked my almost empty glass against hers.

"Do you think we should take up mini golf instead?" I suggested, wiping tears from my eyes as we climbed back into the golf cart.

"We should stick to drinking margaritas." Sabrina raised her glass in another salute.

Later that evening, the hum of the SUV's engine almost lulled me to sleep as I watched the town's lights blur outside my window. My shoulders were stiff from golfing with Sabrina. I'd used muscles I hadn't used in years, but it was so worth it. My mind was clear, and I was re-energized, despite the fatigue weighing down my body. A day with Sabrina had been exactly what I needed.

An unexpected buzz in my purse jolted me out of my trance.

"Oh, I need to check this," I muttered, more to myself than to the security guard driving me home. Fishing out my phone, I stared at the screen, puzzled by the anonymous email address.

*Is the money enough? Do you need more to get away?*

Confusion and suspicion swirled within me like a storm. Get away from what? Who the fuck had sent this?

My gut twisted. The only money I'd received recently had been the mysterious deposit. That meant the unknown sender was likely none other than Liam Russell. But why would he think I needed to get away? And why now? A heavy unease settled in the pit of my stomach as I contemplated how to respond, or if I should even respond at all. My instincts told me there was more going on here than just a business transaction. Something about this felt personal.

"Damn it, Liam. Who the fuck are you, and what are you playing at?" I muttered to myself, my thumb hovering over the keyboard. It was tempting to fire off a snarky response, but caution held me back. Better to wait and discuss this with Ty first. He always seemed to have a clearer head when it came to these things.

Sighing, I slipped my phone back into my purse, letting the uncomfortable silence envelop me once more as the car sped toward home. Whatever that email meant, one thing was certain...

It had just added another damn layer of complexity to an already messy situation.

The memory of Ty's thoughtfulness and the lightness of the afternoon with Sabrina faded, and darkness and fear crept back in.

The moment we arrived at the estate, I spiraled into a loop of asking who and why, who and why. My anxiety spiked. My pulse quickened, and cold sweat prickled at my temples. I needed answers, and I hoped Ty could help me understand the cryptic email.

I didn't wait for the car door to be opened for me. I jumped out and dashed up the stairs two at a time, and ran through the house, my heart hammering in my chest. The door to Ty's office was slightly ajar, the sound of soft tapping of computer keys drifting into the hallway. Taking a deep breath to steady myself, I pushed the door open and strode into the room.

"Ty, you need to see this." I held up my phone with the email displayed.

He frowned as he scanned the screen, his eyes narrowing in concentration.

"Block the email." His extremely tense tone took me by surprise.

"Why?" I paused, searching Ty's face for some explanation. "Shouldn't I respond to it? Find out who they are?"

Ty fiddled with the collar on his shirt. "There's an LLC trying to purchase a manufacturing plant from Keller Enterprises. When I first received their offer, I did some digging. The owner was deceased, so it didn't add up. I asked for more information from them but haven't heard anything back. Then we discovered the same LLC deposited money into your account. Suffice to say, I think this Liam guy is connected to it all in some way. Something's off, Liza."

I blinked in shock. "What does that have to do with me?"

Ty shifted his gaze to the window and went quiet. I wondered if I'd completely lost him. He finally spoke up. "I can't help but feel like it's all somehow connected to your old pack. Maybe some of the Keller pack's skeletons aren't buried after all."

An uneasy feeling settled in my gut. "Do you think that Liam realized I was alive and decided to give me the money anonymously? Maybe he owed it to my parents." My mind swirled with possibilities. "Perhaps that's the reason behind the email. What if Liam thought I was broke and needed an escape?"

"Maybe." Ty leaned back in his chair, his expression darkening. "But we went public with our relationship. Everyone knows you're not hurting for money. Hell, Liza, you're the wealthiest woman in Texas between my family's wealth and the money your parents left you."

I chewed on my lip, mulling over his words. Ty was right. Everyone knew we were together now. My mind raced, trying to connect the dots. "If that's true, then this could be connected to what happened to the Wylde pack. It means Liam might know what happened in Heather Falls."

Ty shook his head. "That wouldn't be good for the pack. For us." Ty's jaw clenched, and I could see his mind working.

We sat in silence for a few moments until I glanced at my watch. "When do you want to go to the bank to look into the security deposit box?"

Just then, my phone rang, an unknown number flashing on the screen. My stomach twisted into knots as dread washed over me again. I looked across at Ty and showed him the screen.

"Answer it," Ty said, concern etched across his face. "Ignoring it might bring more trouble."

I hesitated for a moment before putting the call on speakerphone. "Hello?"

"Hello, my dear." Castro's voice oozed from the other end, making my skin crawl. It was as if he had been waiting for a new bomb to drop on me with the new information about Liam. "I see you're using some of your smarts, Liza dear, putting some of the puzzle pieces together. Well done." Castro gave a sarcastic, slow clap. "I have to ask... what triggered it? What made you look into Liam Russell?"

"Fuck." Of course Castro knew what we'd been focused on. The bastard was always two steps ahead of us.

Castro laughed. "Don't be mistaken, Liza. my silence doesn't mean I've given up on you, regardless of you being mated to Ty. I have absolutely no intention of just letting you go."

Ty snarled and glared at the phone with an intensity that scared me.

Castro continued to laugh. "I've been lying low since the truth about Cecily was revealed." He tutted with his tongue. "What a shame it was to kill poor Cecily, but she started questioning me, even when I asked her not to. How rude. Then I picked up on the fact that she'd been so damn sloppy, leaving little breadcrumbs all over the fucking place. I knew it wouldn't be long before you both figured out she was working for me."

Castro paused for a moment.

"Ty? I know you're there. I must commend you for your new lap dog. Isaiah is a very capable man and that, unfortunately, makes him dangerous." Castro sighed into the phone. "It's a shame I can't touch him. He knows people in high places. If I were to make a move against him... well, my game would be over far too quickly. So sad. I'll just have to make sure I'm smarter than Isaiah from now on."

I swallowed hard, my voice trembling. "Why are you calling, Castro? What do you want?"

"Ah, Liza." The unsettling tone in his voice made me sick to my stomach. "Isn't it obvious? I'm calling because of Liam Russell. You see, this isn't just about business. Liam knows things. Things that no one else does. The money he sent you wasn't for a business deal. It was because of his guilt."

"His guilt?" I asked, my knuckles aching as I clutched the phone like my life depended on it. "How do you know about any of this, Castro?"

He laughed, the sound chilling me to the bone. "Now, what fun would it be for me to just give you the answers, my dear? I would have told you everything had you chosen me, but instead, I'll leave you to figure it all out on your own. Just remember, once everything comes out, you'll realize I'm the only one who can help you."

"Help me?" I spat, anger rising within me. "All you've ever done is hurt and manipulate me."

"Ah, but that's where you're wrong," Castro said smugly. "You see, your parents had more secrets than you know, and I can't wait for you to see them for what they truly were. You'll need me then, Liza."

"Like hell I will," I muttered under my breath, wishing I could reach through the phone and strangle him.

"Time will tell, my dear."

Before I could say another word, Castro ended the call.

My hand shook as I lowered the phone, barely able to keep my grip on it. Ty's snarl echoed through the room, matching the turmoil inside me. I couldn't believe Castro had reared his ugly head again, just when we thought we were making progress in unraveling the mystery surrounding my family and the Wylde pack.

My entire body quaked, and I had to grip my phone with both hands to keep from dropping it. The aftershocks of Castro's call coursed through me, leaving me on edge and craving relief.

"Son of a bitch," Ty spat, his eyes blazing with fury as he paced the room. "We knew Castro would rear his ugly head again, but why now? Right when we start sniffing around Liam?"

"I don't know," I said, my voice wobbly. "But it can't be a coincidence. There has to be a connection."

Ty stopped pacing and crossed his arms, his jaw clenched tight. "Castro's been too quiet since he killed Cecily. I should've known he was planning something. He's just thrown another wrench into your life, Liza."

My hands became clammy. Castro's maniacal laughter still echoed through my mind. "But we won't let him win. We'll get to the bottom of this and find out the truth about my parents and the money from Liam. I have to know, Ty."

He nodded firmly. "We'll figure it all out together. Castro won't win this game."

As much as I wanted to believe that, I couldn't shake the nagging fear that Castro's words were just the beginning of an even darker chapter in our lives. My heart pounded like a jackhammer against my ribcage. I stood abruptly, feeling the walls closing in on me. "I need some fresh air."

Without waiting for a response, I strode onto the balcony. The cool night breeze caressed my skin, providing a temporary reprieve from the heat that threatened to suffocate me.

I closed my eyes, wishing I could shift and run free for days upon days, away from Castro's threats, my own anger, and all the fucking secrets.

But I couldn't escape. Not now. Not when there was so much at stake. A bitter laugh escaped my lips. Every step closer to the truth seemed to open up another bottomless pit of questions and fears.

"Damn you, Castro," I said, gripping the railing so hard my palms hurt. "Why can't you just leave us alone?"

"Because he's a manipulative bastard who thrives on chaos," Ty said, stepping out onto the balcony beside me. "And he won't rest until he gets what he wants."

"Which is me." The bitter taste of resentment coated my mouth as I stared out into the darkness. "He's never going to give up, is he?"

"Neither will we," Ty said, his hand covering mine on the railing. "Hey. I'm here, okay?"

I looked at him, saw the concern, the fear on his face, and felt a sudden rush of frustration. "What if I just... stop searching for answers? What if I let all this go?"

"Then, you'll never find closure." His voice was gentle, and I recognized he was treading lightly around me, probably worried I might cause an earthquake or some other fucked-up catastrophe.

"You'll always be wondering, and I know you'd be miserable if you gave up on filling in the gaps of your life."

"Maybe I'd rather be miserable than have everything I thought I knew torn apart," I said, fighting back the tears. But it was no use. The tears spilled over, pouring down my cheeks like a dam breaking under the weight of too much pain.

"Hey, hey," Ty said, pulling me into his arms. "We'll get through this, Liza. Castro is playing a game, but it's a game he won't win."

I clung to him, needing his strength, his reassurance. "How can you be so sure?"

"Because we're stronger together than he'll ever be." Ty cupped my face. "We'll find out everything and finally put a stop to him." He glanced at the time, hesitating for a moment before speaking again. "If you really don't want to go to the bank, we don't have to."

I bit my lip, considering. Yes, I was afraid of what I might find, but Ty was right. Without the truth, there could be no closure, and wasn't that what I wanted more than anything?

"Let's go." I wiped my soaking wet face. "I need to know the truth, no matter how painful it may be."

# Chapter 15 - Ty

The tension in the car was a lot fucking heavier than I liked. I stole a sideways glance at Liza to see her leg jumping up and down with nerves. I placed my hand on her thigh, giving her a gentle touch, hoping it would calm her restless energy.

She looked at me, her blue eyes filled with uncertainty over what she was about to do. We had called the bank ahead of time, informing them that Liza would be arriving soon to open the deposit box in her name. The associate had been thrilled to have us come in, no doubt curious about what had been hidden away for so long.

"Ty." There was hesitation in her voice. "I'm worried about what we might find in there. You know, after what Castro said about my parents having a lot of secrets." She grimaced, biting her nails nervously. "What if it's something... terrible?"

"Like what?" I was genuinely curious about what was going on in that wonderful head of hers, considering I'd only expected to find more money or, at the most extreme, documents that pertained to the Wylde pack.

"Like... teeth from the people they killed or something." Liza's voice was barely above a whisper as she shut her eyes tightly.

I immediately burst out laughing at the thought, but when I saw the seriousness on Liza's face, I quickly composed myself. Clearing my throat, I shook my head. "I highly doubt it's anything like that, Liza. Maybe you've been watching too much of that crazy murder mystery show you like."

We'd been sitting outside the bank, waiting till Liza wanted to go in. This had to be her decision. If she chose not to do it today, we'd go home, regroup, and come back another time. I was happy to wait for as long as it took.

She stared out the window, still troubled. "I just feel like whatever's in that box is going to complicate matters and send me into a tailspin."

"Hey," I said softly, gently turning her face toward mine. "Any good detective gathers all the available information before drawing conclusions. Don't you want to know everything there is to know about your parents? And what about the little boy in your dreams? Maybe the information in the box will point us in the right direction."

Liza's eyes searched mine, and when she found what she was looking for, she relaxed against the leather of the seat. "Thank you. Maybe I shouldn't always jump to the most fucked-up conclusion, but after everything, it's kind of my default."

I watched as she closed her eyes again, taking a moment to take a few deep breaths to steady herself, her chest rising and falling with each exhale. She was trying a breathing exercise we'd read about online when we'd searched for simple solutions to control anger. When she opened her eyes again, there was a glint of determination that hadn't been there before.

She unbuckled her seatbelt. "I've gathered my thoughts, at least the ones I could focus on long enough to tame. Let's go inside and face whatever's in that box. Here's hoping it doesn't involve severed limbs."

The chatty branch manager greeted us with a wide grin. "Ah, Mr. and Mrs. Keller. We've been expecting you. I must say, it's not every day that we have a deposit box like this one."

"Nice to meet you," Liza said politely, eyes darting around the bank. "What do you mean, like this one?"

"Oh." The manager seemed surprised. "The box has been in this bank for many years, and no one has opened it before. We've all been curious for a very long time."

I sized the manager up. He seemed like the typical bank manager, not threatening in any way.

"Glad we could bring some excitement to the bank today." I raised an eyebrow and glanced around, making sure there weren't other lurkers hoping to get a glimpse of the omega or her security box.

"Indeed, the anticipation has been quite intoxicating." His enthusiasm bordered on unsettling. "It's all anyone has been able to talk about since your call, Mr. Keller."

"Really?" My eyebrows shot up. What an odd thing for people to be so interested in. "Well, then, I suppose our presence here is the highlight of your day." I was being sarcastic, but the manager nodded and smiled from ear to ear.

The guy gave me the fucking creeps.

"Shall we get down to business, then?" The manager gestured for us to follow him down a narrow hallway.

"Lead the way." I placed a protective hand on the small of Liza's back as we followed him.

Once we entered the vault housing the security deposit boxes, my gaze fell upon the box placed conspicuously on a red cloth that had been draped over the table.

The manager gestured to it with a grand flourish. "Here it is! Please, take your time. No need to rush."

"Thank you," Liza said, her gaze fixed on the box.

The manager hovered near us, his eyes flickering between Liza and the box eagerly. His lingering presence grated on my nerves. What the hell was wrong with the guy? Did he seriously think he could stay in the room while Liza opened the box?

"Is there something else you need?" I shot him a death stare, hoping I wouldn't need to ramp up my threats to get my point across.

"No, no, of course not. I'll leave you two to it." He backed out and shut the door behind him.

"Finally." I turned to Liza, who was staring at the key she held with trembling fingers.

"You don't have to do this if you're not ready."

Her eyes met mine, her jaw set. "If I don't do it now, I'll never be ready. I could keep working myself into a frenzy and talk myself out of it, but that's not the path I want to take. I don't want uncertainty to render me completely paralyzed."

"All right." I swallowed hard. What if Liza's instincts about the contents of the box were correct? I sure as hell didn't want to see something gruesome, and I certainly didn't want Liza to be even more traumatized by her parents' past. Whatever was inside that box, we would face it together, even if it was a bag of teeth.

As I watched Liza put the key into the lock, my senses heightened. The air was thick with anticipation. Liza slowly lifted the lid, revealing a single envelope nestled on top of a stack of paperwork. She set the envelope aside and pulled out the documents.

"These are deposit slips and information for an offshore account." Her eyebrows lifted in surprise.

I shook my head, wondering just how much money Liza's parents had had. It was certainly more than Liza could spend in a lifetime. At least I could be certain she wasn't with me for my money. If anything, she was my sugar momma.

"I can't believe this is it," Liza said, her voice shaking slightly as she picked up the envelope again. "After Castro's call, I suppose I was expecting something... grander. Clearer cut and revealing."

"Sometimes the most important messages are hidden in plain sight." I couldn't ignore the protective instincts surging within me. If her parents left this note for Liza, it had to be something major.

We sat there for a few minutes as Liza absorbed what she was looking at. When she stood, I followed suit. "Are you ready to go?" I tried to gauge her emotions, but I couldn't quite get a read on them.

Liza nodded, gripping the envelope tightly. "I don't know what to do with all that damn money, so I'll just leave the rest of the paperwork here for now." At the doorway, she hesitated. "Maybe I should give it to charity."

"Maybe." We could talk about it more later, but I'd seen all those commas on the account information. It was a hell of a lot of money to simply just give away.

As soon as the door opened, the manager of the bank appeared. He was practically quivering with barely contained curiosity.

Fuck. Had he been standing outside the door the entire time? Did he not have a bank to manage, something better to do with his time? Security deposit boxes must've been his equivalent of crack.

"Thanks," Liza muttered as she stepped past the manager.

I eyed him closely when he stared at the envelope in Liza's hand. "So, what was in the box?" He tried to sound nonchalant, but his brow was dotted with sweat, and he shifted his weight from side to side.

Liza glanced at me, her eyes seeking reassurance.

He cleared his throat. "I know it's intrusive of me to ask, but that box has been the object of much speculation over the years." He laughed nervously. "We even have a running game where we place bets and come up with new theories every year at our Christmas party."

I tried not to roll my eyes. "Sounds like a blast." Bankers must have nothing fucking better to do.

Liza nodded at me, presumably letting me know she was fine sharing the disappointment of the box with this asshole. I watched his face.

"Just some account information and what I assume is a letter." She held up the envelope as evidence that the box had been a bust and definitely nothing to get so worked up over.

The manager's face fell. His eyes shifted between the two of us. I wasn't sure he believed us. "Oh. That's... kind of a let-down."

We walked out the door, and I couldn't help myself... I looked back over my shoulder and caught his eye. "Such a shame you wasted all that time trying to figure out the private property of one of your clients. What will you do at the Christmas party this year? Guess the balance?" I smirked and could almost see him shaking in his shoes. Served him right, the nosy fucker.

Liza squeezed my hand, a smile tugging at her lips, and we left.

As we drove away from the bank, Liza stared down at the envelope. I knew she wasn't ready to open it just yet, so I respected her wishes and focused on the road. When she was ready to talk about it, she would. One thing I'd learned about Liza during our time together was that she couldn't be forced. She did things at her own speed, and she'd never do something she wasn't ready to do.

"Since we're already in town," Liza said, breaking the silence. "I'd like to stop by my parents' graves. Is that okay with you?"

"Of course." This was the perfect time to show Liza what I'd done for her. I hoped I hadn't made a mistake. Maybe I should've waited and asked for her input. Oh well, it was too late now. All I could do was hope she'd like it.

The cemetery was quiet at that time of day, with only a few people visiting the dead. We pulled up near the gravesites, and as Liza stepped out of the car, she saw the surprise I'd prepared. Her parents' graves now bore new headstones with their real names engraved into the stone.

JOSEF WYLDE. PORTIA WYLDE.

"Ty..." she said, tears forming in her eyes. "You did this?"

I nodded, wrapping my arms around her as she sobbed into my chest. "Nobody deserves to be forgotten. Everyone should have their names. Your parents didn't deserve to be forgotten, and they sure as hell should have their true names on their memorial." When I'd ordered the headstones, I was trying to right a wrong, to commemorate a pack that

311

had been wiped out. I hadn't realized how important it was for her.

"Thank you." Liza slowly composed herself and pulled away, turning to examine the matching marble stones. She traced her finger across each name. As she wiped the tears from her cheeks, I took a step back, giving her some space to be alone with her parents.

Liza knelt by the graves, plucking a few weeds that had already sprouted near the headstones. She tucked her legs under her, talking softly. Though I couldn't hear what she was saying, I knew those moments were important to her, and I watched from a distance, guarding her as she reconnected with her lost past, sending my own message to the long-gone couple, promising I'd do everything I could to protect their daughter.

After a while, Liza rose and walked over to me, taking my hand in hers without a word.

"Ready to go home?" I asked gently.

She gave a quick nod.

Liza seemed to have found solace after visiting her parents' graves. She seemed more at peace, and I sensed a new calmness in her demeanor. Just as I went to shift the car into drive, she placed her hand on mine, stopping me.

"Wait." Her tear-filled eyes met mine. "I want to open the letter now."

"Are you sure?" I wanted to make certain she was ready for whatever the contents might reveal.

She gave a nod, her hands trembling as she reached into her bag to retrieve the envelope. She tucked her finger into the back flap of it and dragged her finger along, breaking the seal. As she unfolded the letter, she frowned and bit her lip. "Ty, look at this."

Puzzled, I took the letter from her. Of course, it wouldn't be simple. The letter was written in code. There were numbers and random words scattered throughout, some even in Russian Cyrillic. Without the cipher, it was impossible to decode. And the bizarre thing was that the letter was written from top to bottom, not left to right.

"Ugh, why do I feel like I'm living in a *James Bond* movie?" Liza banged her head against the seat, clearly frustrated. "We have to figure out riddles just to catch the bad guy, and now we have to decipher a code to understand my parents' message from beyond the grave. Fuck."

I laughed and leaned over to kiss her on the forehead. "Don't worry. I know a guy who might be able to help."

"As far as I'm concerned, those could just be random squiggles on a piece of paper. You're sure he'll be able to work it out? Can we take the letter to him now?" Liza glanced at her watch, and her eyes filled with hope. "Think he'd see you on such short notice?"

"Oh, yeah. Zephyr is used to my sporadic visits. Let's go."

I drove straight to Zephyr's computer repair shop. As we stepped out of the car, Liza raised an eyebrow and pointed to the strip mall. "This is where your genius works? I expected something a little more ominous, like a hollowed-out cave in the side of a rocky cliff."

I chuckled and took her hand. "Zephyr doesn't want people to know about his superpowers."

"And what, exactly, are his powers?" Liza giggled. "According to the sign, all he does is repair computers."

"Oh, my dear, he does so much more than that. Zephyr is a fucking genius. He can break through firewalls, hack any electronic communication you can think of, and I'm fairly certain he can decipher this letter."

Said genius was at the front desk, talking to a mom and her pre-teen son, who was having issues with his gaming console.

"Mom, I swear I didn't do anything," the boy pleaded, looking desperate. "One minute it was working fine, and the next... it just froze."

"Did you try turning it off and on again?" Zephyr asked, trying to keep a straight face.

"Of course," the boy said, rolling his eyes with all the attitude of childhood. "I'm not an amateur."

Zephyr glanced up and caught sight of us, his eyes widening in surprise. He quickly turned back to his customers, stopped teasing the kid, and assured them he'd diagnose the problem and call them by the end of business the next day. Once they'd left, Zephyr approached us, curiosity radiating off him.

"Ty, what's wrong now?" he asked, clearly concerned. He turned to Liza. "I'm assuming this is the Mrs.?"

I nodded. "Zephyr, this is Liza. Liza, Zephyr."

"Nice to meet you." Zephyr extended his hand to Liza. "So, what can I do for you two?"

Liza handed Zephyr the coded letter. "This is a letter my parents left for me in a security deposit box. I don't know what it says, but Ty seems to think you can figure it out."

Zephyr whistled as he scanned the letter, his eyes darting between us and the mysterious note.

"Wow, this is definitely an interesting code." He ran his fingers over the strange characters. "I'll do my best to decipher it."

"Please, make it your top priority." I pulled my phone from my back pocket and sent him a hefty advance to his bank account to motivate him. It was crucial we got this figured out swiftly.

Zephyr's own device made a notification sound. When he checked it, he gave me a crooked smile and saluted me. "Thanks, boss. It's officially number one on my to-do list. I'll call you as soon as I break the code."

When we left the shop, Liza seemed troubled. "Do you really think Zephyr can figure it out?"

"Trust me." I squeezed her hand. "If Zephyr can't crack this code, no one can."

# Chapter 16 - Liza

Rosalie and I, with our aprons tied around our waists, chopped vegetables, the rhythmic smack of the knives against the cutting the only sound in the kitchen. Miscellaneous utensils were strewn across every surface of the kitchen. Her petite frame moved with ease and precision at her station, slicing through red bell peppers so quickly and perfectly that I stopped to admire her handiwork. The fragrant aroma of caramelizing onions wafted through the air, mingling with the heady scent of garlic and rosemary. I was in my happy place, and it seemed Rosalie was as well.

"Did you hear about that new restaurant opening up downtown?" Her demeanor was light and airy, and I appreciated a conversation that didn't involve omegas or fucking psychopaths.

"Only about a million times." I rolled my eyes. "I swear, everyone I've spoken to has been talking about it non-stop. It's not like Presley Acres is short on restaurants."

"True." Rosalie moved to the sink, rinsing a colander of mushrooms in cold water. "Maybe they're just desperate for something new and different."

The damn tourists were certainly looking for something new and different, except it wasn't a fucking restaurant. They wanted a glimpse of me and my so-called miraculous powers. Perhaps a new place to eat would pull their unwanted attention from me, but I very much doubted it.

We shared a knowing smile, our hands never ceasing in their work. As much as I enjoyed our small talk, part of me was glad to be as busy as I was. The bustling kitchen provided a distraction. With Isaiah's silence regarding Liam, and Zephyr giving us no news on the letter, my mind had been a whirlwind of worry and frustration. My focus now lay on the task at hand, each chop and sizzle pulling me further away from my anxieties.

"Boo!" Sabrina burst through the door with wide eyes and her hands over her head, causing both Rosalie and me to jump in surprise. She howled with laughter as she took in our shocked expressions. "A little jumpy, are we?"

"For fuck's sake, Sabrina." I clutched my chest dramatically. "You nearly gave me a heart attack."

"Sorry, sorry." She giggled and waved her hand dismissively. "Weren't you expecting me?"

"Of course." I glanced at my watch and smiled sheepishly—I'd lost track of time. "I got caught up in everything. Rosalie and I are making good progress. Speaking of which, I don't think you two have officially met." I gestured between them. "Rosalie, this is Sabrina, my best friend and partner in crime. Sabrina, meet Rosalie, my amazing new assistant chef."

"Nice to meet you, Sabrina," Rosalie said warmly. "I've heard so many great things about you."

"Aw, shucks." Sabrina slung her hair over one shoulder. "Don't believe everything you hear. I am far better than the stories if I do say so myself."

As they exchanged pleasantries, I stepped back to observe their interactions. Watching them put the finishing touches on a few dishes, one would think they'd been friends for years. They were immediately two peas in a pod, their laughter and easy conversation giving the atmosphere a sense of calm.

I had an idea Rosalie and Sabrina would get on, but it was nice to see I was right. I didn't want to toot my own horn, but damn it... toot-toot. Rosalie was such a fantastic choice for my assistant and student, and I was overjoyed that she slotted in so effortlessly.

"Okay, ladies." I clapped my hands together, drawing their attention. "Let's get this show on the road, shall we?"

They each dived right into their tasks, the kitchen, once again, alive with the sounds of culinary creation. I found myself completely content knowing that, despite the uncertainties looming overhead, my business was poised for greatness. My clients had remained with me despite the changes my marriage and the lockdown had caused. I'd been forced to turn away a new customer just that week. Even with the extra hands, there was no way I'd have been able to fulfill her order. The woman took my rejection with good grace and asked if I'd keep her on my cancellation list. She'd had a meal at one of my regular clients and had been blown away with my four-mushroom risotto.

The unmistakable sound of Ty and Bryce's laughter seeped into the kitchen seconds before they entered, the enticing scent drawing them in like moths to a flame. I turned toward them, wiping my hands on my apron. "Hey, guys. I set some food aside for you in the warming drawer. If you're not hungry, I can always give the meals to the security guards."

"No way." Ty laughed. "This is perfect timing. My stomach was about to eat itself." Ty smacked his lips as he approached the warming drawer. Bryce followed suit, though his gaze lingered on Sabrina for a second longer than necessary.

Sabrina glowered at Bryce. "It's a good thing shifters can't catch STDs," she quipped, her eyes narrowing at him. "If they did, your dick would have rotted off by now."

Rosalie and I choked on air, our eyes widening at the blunt, unsolicited statement. The only sound in the kitchen was the pots boiling on the hob as Bryce squared his shoulders and met Sabrina's glare head-on.

"Jealous much?" he shot back, a cruel smirk twisting his lips. "I just got bored with you, sweetheart. Perhaps if you could hold a real conversation and had more to offer than just your looks and a tumble between the sheets, you'd be able to keep a man's attention. Without that, you're kind of boring."

Sabrina visibly jolted as if he'd slapped her across the face.

My blood ignited, and my anger rose within me like a tidal wave. There was no way in hell I'd just stand there and listen to him insult my best friend. She was more than able to fight her own battles, but I still had to speak up. "Choose your words carefully when speaking to her," I warned, my tone stone cold.

Bryce froze, mouth open in confusion. A moment later, Ty was standing in front of me, gripping my face in his hands, his gray eyes staring right into the depths of my soul. His touch brought me back from the edge as I used the breathing techniques and tried to calm myself.

"Shit, I'm so sorry," I muttered, shaking my head, looking back up at Ty. He was staring at me as if he'd seen a ghost.

"Are you okay?" There was something different in his tone, but I couldn't identify it.

"I just... I lost control for a second." My cheeks burned with embarrassment. "Sorry, everyone. I know my anger can affect those around me if I don't keep a handle on it."

I glanced around Ty to apologize to Bryce, but he was backed against the wall, looking utterly terrified.

Rosalie's eyes were wide with shock, her gaze darting between me and Bryce. "Whoa," she said under her breath, unable to mask her surprise.

"We need to go, Liza." Ty's eyes never left me. He was determined to remove me from everyone's stares, but why?

"I can't just walk out. I'm busy. Ty, what's going on?" I asked, my voice trembling with confusion and fear. Had I done something without realizing it?

"Just get your shoes on." He led me out into the dining room. "I'll explain later." He turned back into the kitchen. "Sabrina, can you and Rosalie finish up Liza's orders and get them delivered?"

I hesitated, glancing back at the tense faces of Sabrina, Rosalie, and Bryce, who still looked shaken.

"Sure, no worries." The tension in Sabrina's voice was unmistakable. What had I done?

Swallowing hard, I nodded and quickly changed from my safety clogs into my shoes before Ty led me to his car.

As we drove in silence, my mind worked overtime. What had happened? Why had Bryce looked like I'd transformed into a demon in front of him? I curled my hands into fists, nails digging half-moons into my palms as I tried to make sense of it all.

"Where are we going?" I finally managed to ask, barely above a whisper.

"Remember the specialist your doctor mentioned?" Ty said, his grip on the steering wheel tightening. "I sent her a message and got a last-minute appointment. We're going there. We can't risk your anger flaring up like that again."

"What do you mean?"

"Your anger... it's... different," he explained, keeping his eyes on the road ahead. "You basically tried to force Bryce to submit to you, Liza. One more little push, and he might have actually done it."

The air left my lungs in a rush. Was that even possible? I didn't know anyone had the ability to force their influence over other shifters like that. Despair settled heavily in my stomach, nauseating me.

"Is that... is that why everyone was so scared?" I said, tears pricking at the corners of my eyes.

"I'm afraid so." Ty's jaw was set firmly. "But we'll figure this out. Whatever's going on, we'll get to the bottom of it."

I groaned and buried my face in my hands, a thousand questions racing through my mind. What was happening to me? How much worse could this possibly get? And what would it mean for my relationships? How would I face my friends again? If I didn't get control of this anger, I'd never leave the house again.

"Ty." My voice was muffled by my hands, but I couldn't bring myself to uncover my face. "What if I can't control it? What if this doctor can't help me?"

"Then, we'll find another solution. Together."

Ty's support was a lifeline, pulling me back from the brink of despair. It wasn't hard to imagine that most mates wouldn't be as determined as Ty. How many would just throw up their hands and say *fuck it*? Another wave of terror crashed over me as I imagined myself having an anger flare directed at Ty, and him deciding I was too much trouble, then choosing to leave me.

The thought terrified me.

We pulled up at the address, and a woman wearing a pair of black pants, a red shirt, and a white physician's coat stood by the door, awaiting our arrival. "I'm Anna Anderson." Her warm smile was directed at me. "I'm Jim's sister. Doctor Anderson," she explained at my puzzled look. "When you spoke to him and asked for someone with my skills, he thought we would work well together. Jim gave me some background information, and Ty has briefed me on the current situation. I assure you, Liza, you have my utmost discretion." I sensed an air of professionalism and kindness, which immediately put me at ease.

She turned to Ty, her gaze firm. "I'm sorry, but you won't be allowed in the room during our session."

Ty frowned, and I thought he'd argue, but Anna lifted an eyebrow in a gesture so like his, it nearly made me smile.

"I'm not pushing you out to be cruel, Mr. Keller. Hearing Liza's unfiltered thoughts is crucial, so I need to speak with her directly. I'll make sure you know what you need to do to help her," Anna assured him. "Just give me some time alone to chat with her. You can wait in the room down the corridor on the left."

"All right. I'll be right outside if you need me." His eyes, filled with such love and concern, met mine.

I nodded in response.

Anna led me into her office, and I took a moment to gather myself. I hadn't had a moment to myself since the kitchen, and I needed to understand my own thoughts before I could share anything with her. So I stood there, silently observing the room, trying to take it all in. The walls were adorned with abstract paintings that seemed to evoke emotions rather than clear images. They reminded me of a modern version of those old inkblot tests. Sunlight filtered through sheer curtains, casting a soft glow on the various plants placed around the space. Opposite the large mahogany desk stood a bookcase filled with leather-bound volumes, some well-worn from use.

Anna gestured toward the seating options. "Please, take a seat."

There was a hammock chair hanging in one corner, a typical psychiatrist's leather sofa against the wall, and a pair of regular armchairs. I opted for the chair, hoping I'd be more grounded in a chair than suspended or lying down.

"So, you've been having some anger flares?" Her gaze was piercing, yet it held a certain warmth that made me feel safe. I liked that she was direct and didn't waste any time.

I nodded, my gaze drawn to the framed degrees displayed proudly above her head.

"Would you care to share what has happened?"

I chewed on the inside of my cheek, then let out a sigh. "When I get angry, something comes over me. I assume it's my omega powers, but it's almost like I blackout. When I come back to myself, I'm overwhelmed by the horror of what I have done."

"Such as?" Anna probed.

"Making the ground shake, levitating objects, or forcing someone to submit completely to me." I shuddered as I remembered the terrified expression on Bryce's face.

"Interesting." Anna took in the information with an air of calm that helped to soothe my nerves. "That must be frightening and confusing."

"Definitely," I said. Though I felt vulnerable, I was relieved to share my burden with someone who seemed to understand.

Anna's pen glided across the notepad, her eyes never leaving mine. The kindness in her smile radiated warmth. I was strangely at ease in her presence, which wasn't something I'd experienced around people lately. Sabrina was having to speak to any new clients in person, I'd lucked out with Rosalie, and having her with me in the kitchen was great, but after the nightmare interview, I'd shied away from most people, fearing they all had an agenda. Yet, right from the offset, Anna Anderson seemed to be someone I could trust, and that alone was comforting.

Anna set the notebook aside. "Let's discuss your triggers and ways you can safely manage them."

I mulled that over as I searched for the source of my outbursts. "My main triggers appear to be anger and stress. There's been a lot of that in my life lately."

Anna nodded sympathetically. "I can imagine it must be very hard on you. What have you been doing up to now when you're overwhelmed?"

I was embarrassed to admit that Ty and I had searched the internet. "We found some breathing and visualization techniques on a webpage. When I get the feeling that I'm about to have a meltdown or get angry, I close my eyes. I imagine the anger is black air, and calm is pink air. When I inhale, I imagine the air is clean pink, and when I exhale I visualize that blackness of the anger leaving my body. The first few exhales are very black, then it's a muddy mix of both till I'm only breathing the clean pink air." I looked up, expecting her to judge me for using the internet, or reprimand me for using therapy ideas, but she nodded along.

"That's a tried-and-true technique, Liza. It's especially useful if you can recognize the emotions before they erupt into the symptoms you've described. Absolutely carry on with it if it works for you, but it's only one tool in the toolbox. Every tool is used for something different. You wouldn't use a hammer on a screw, you know? It's essential to have many tools to use for every situation. Have you ever considered herbal medicine for your nerves?"

I shifted in my seat, and a small, nervous laugh escaped from my lips. "Well, I don't knock anyone for their recreational uses, but it's a no for me."

She chuckled. "There are teas that may help with your nerves and mellow you out. They're one hundred-percent safe if you choose to use them." Anna paused before continuing, "For now, I want you to practice restraint. When you become aware of the triggers, try to redirect your thoughts away from what's making you angry. Try using 'see, hear, touch'."

I gave her a quizzical look. "What's that?"

"So, if you start to feel your anxiety rising, I want you to find three things you can see, hear, and touch. For example, I can *see* the books on the bookshelf. I can *hear* your voice in the room, and I can *touch* the pen in my hand. It doesn't have to be said out loud, it can be internal. We're trying to find a way to move your focus away from your triggers. You can use that in combination with your breathing and visualization."

Easier said than done, but it was a start. I nodded, willing to give it a try.

"Now," Anna said as she stood. "Let's bring your mate in before he wears a hole in the floor of my waiting room."

I was surprised to find myself laughing along with her.

She opened the door, signaling at Ty to enter. He strode into the room, his gaze flickering between us with curiosity and concern.

"Ty, you may come in now." Anna gestured toward the seat next to me. "As Liza's mate, I want you to pay close attention to her stressors and do your best to keep them to a minimum. Too much stress could result in something far worse than making things float."

Hearing her describe items floating was so bizarre. How did my life get to this point?

"Thanks for seeing us so quickly, Anna." Ty reached out and shook the woman's hand.

Anna smiled. "It all worked out well. I had a cancellation. After speaking with Liza, I'm reassured that the methods we discussed today will be helpful. If we all work together, Liza will most definitely see an improvement in her anger flares. If you need me urgently, you know how to reach me, but I'd like to see you again in two weeks, Liza."

I glanced at the calendar on my phone. "I can manage eleven a.m.?"

She nodded, and we both made notes in our respective diaries.

"Thank you, Anna." I forced myself not to shed the tears that threatened to spill onto my cheeks. Today had already been emotional enough without me crying yet again. "I'll talk with you soon."

With that, Ty and I left the room and made our way back to his car, our steps in sync as we navigated the narrow hallway.

Once we were settled into the car, it was obvious that something was off. Ty stared straight ahead as he gripped the wheel, but he didn't start the ignition. My heart ached as I studied his clenched jaw and the tense muscles in his shoulders. Was this it? Had he finally reached the breaking point and wanted to end our marriage?

"Ty, what are you thinking about?" My fingers brushed against his forearm.

He let out a heavy sigh, his eyes not leaving the windshield. "I feel guilty."

"Guilty? Why?"

"I wish I'd helped you move through your anger flares without them advancing as far as they have." He lay is his head against the steering wheel as if that could conceal the regret in his voice.

Shit. Like I wasn't already carrying enough guilt. None of this was his fault, and I needed him to know that. "Ty, it's not your fault. You've been nothing but an incredible support to me. You hear me, Ty Keller? This. Is. Not. Your. Fault." I punctuated each word with a tap of my finger on his arm.

He turned to look at me, his gaze softening.

"It's just the cards we've been dealt, and we'll handle all of this the best we can. I don't expect you to be glued to my side every second of every day. You're the alpha of our pack, and you have a lot of people depending on you." I lowered my gaze. "Now that I've met with Anna, I'm feeling more hopeful that I can get a handle on my emotions."

The shrill ringing of Ty's phone shattered the moment. I huffed. What now? Couldn't we have one drama-free moment. But Ty showed me the tiny screen. It was Zephyr. Ty put the call on speaker so we'd both hear what the tech wizard had to say.

"Hey, Zephyr. What's up?" Ty's tone was cautious. No doubt he was just as anxious as I was to hear what Zephyr had determined about the code.

"I've deciphered the letter."

# Chapter 17 - Ty

We drove to Zephyr's office in apprehensive silence, and the horrified look on Bryce's face popped into my head. In all the years I'd known him, I'd never seen him look so helpless and scared. I had no power to predict the future, but I was certain if I'd flashed one damn second ahead of time, Liza would've had Bryce under her complete control. If I hadn't stepped in front of Liza, shielding Bryce from her line of sight, she would've completely overtaken him.

I glanced over at her, and there was no missing the stress on her taut face.

*Great job keeping that stress you'd literally just promised Anna you'd keep to a minimum, Ty.*

She gazed out at the passing scenery with blank eyes. I wanted so badly to ease her worries, but that would have to wait until we done with Zephyr. The gods knew we needed some good news from the letter her parents had left her.

Liza said nothing as we drove, which left me alone with my thoughts. If she couldn't gain control over her anger, what would that mean for us? Our pack?

There was a lot more to omegas than any of us realized. Honestly, I'd never seen an alpha force another pack member into submission. The whole fucking scene had been like something out of a horror movie. I needed my father's advice on what to do next, but I also had to find a way to help lessen Liza's mental load.

"How you holding up, babe?" I asked Liza, though it was a stupid fucking question. She didn't give any sign she'd heard me, her gaze never leaving the passing landscape.

I silently prayed to the gods that Zephyr would have something positive for us. Anticipation gnawed at me, but I stayed focused on the road, doing my best to keep my emotions in check. At least one of us needed to remain level-headed.

"Almost there, Liza," I said, my voice steady despite the storm of emotions roiling inside me. She nodded wordlessly.

We finally pulled up to Zephyr's small shop and practically raced to the door. Zephyr was slumped over the front counter, his hair disheveled and heavy bags under his eyes.

"You look like hell," I commented, earning a weak smile from him.

"Thanks for the words of affirmation." Zephyr cleared his throat. "Not gonna lie, it took a lot to crack this one. First, I had to translate everything from Russian, and even then, the sentences didn't make any sense. Then I added in the numbers, and I was more than a little fucking perplexed."

Zephyr sighed deeply, running a hand through his unkempt hair. "But I finally managed to figure it out." He handed a piece of paper to Liza, and I read it over her shoulder. My throat tightened as I scanned the words, trying to understand the message from beyond the grave.

*Dearest Liza,*

*If you are reading this letter, we are so sorry that it came to this. It means that we left this world before we were able to tell you everything. First, know that we love you more than you'll ever know, our precious princess. Unfortunately, we made some bad dealings. Liza, we realize now we weren't the best role models, and for that, we are truly sorry. By now, you must know that you are an omega. There is so much complexity to what you're going to be someday, and we hope you'll find this letter before it's too late. There is someone who knows everything and can help you. Your brother Liam will explain everything to you. We are so sorry for the decisions we made because those decisions were what took us from you so soon.*

*All of our love,*

*Mom and Dad*

At the bottom was a phone number.

"Are you serious?" Liza stared at the letter. "I have a *brother*?" Shock rang loud and clear through her voice.

I reached for her hand, twining our fingers together, silently reminding her to keep her stress levels down. To keep her anger at a minimum.

Zephyr broke the silence that had fallen over us. "I took the liberty of checking the phone line, and it's still active."

"No shit?" I couldn't hide my disbelief.

The letter shook violently in Liza's hands, and her breath hitched in her throat.

"Liam sent me the money... but now we can definitely say that Liam is my *brother*." Her voice faltered on the last word, and I sensed the mixture of relief and fear warring within her.

My mind raced to connect the dots. Liam's name wasn't on the pack's register, which was odd enough, but to compound matters, he was making moves to buy out pieces of my company. Why? What was his end game? As much as I wanted to protect Liza, I needed to understand the bigger picture here, and right now, that remained frustratingly out of reach.

"Zephyr, thanks for your work, man." I pulled out my wallet and handed him a wad of cash. "None of what you learned today leaves this room."

He laughed, pocketing the money with a grin. "Ty, you pay me entirely too well for me to ever betray you. Besides," he added, his tone losing teasing quality. "You know how far back we go. I would never do something like that to you."

He was right. We could trust him.

I patted Zephyr on the shoulder before guiding Liza toward the door. We had to find Liam, and soon. Every moment that passed only heightened the urgency to figure out what was going on. And above all else, I needed to keep Liza safe.

Stepping out into the cool, early evening air, Liza crumpled the letter in her hand, her knuckles white from the pressure. All it took was one glance in her direction for me to understand the storm of emotions brewing inside her: anger, sadness, fear. They raced between our bond, and she made no effort to hide them. It was enough to make my own heart ache.

"Hey," I said gently, guiding her toward my car. "We'll figure this out together. You're not alone, remember that. I promise."

I pulled out my phone and texted my dad, asking him to come to the estate as soon as possible. There were too many questions left unanswered, and his guidance was sorely needed. As I hit send and pulled out of the parking lot, Liza stared numbly out the window.

"Talk to me," I said. I wanted her to open up, but she remained silent, her eyes glistening with unshed tears.

After a few long moments, she finally spoke so softly I barely heard her. "When will all this be over, Ty? When will all the secrets end?"

"I don't know, but no matter what happens, I'll be by your side. You're not alone in this, even if you think you are."

"Thank you." But the smile she gave me didn't reach her eyes. It was obvious she was hurting, but she wasn't going to let the revelations break her. And neither would I.

If Liam truly was Liza's brother, what did he want from us? Why was he trying to reach out to her so surreptitiously, insinuating she needed help to escape? And who the ever-loving fuck did he think he was making moves on parts of my business? And why now?

The car hummed as I turned onto the long, winding driveway leading to the estate. The moon cast eerie shadows on the darkened landscape, reflecting the shitty mood we were both in.

Dad was waiting outside. He hadn't responded to my text, so I was relieved to see him. Maybe with his insight he'd shed some light on everything.

Dad greeted us, as usual, with his deep and authoritative voice. You could take the alpha out of the man, but not the man out of the alpha. Like Isaiah, I despised clichés, but it seemed fitting. We followed him up the stairs and into my office in silence, where the door clicked shut behind me.

"Did you know?" I whispered, unable to wait a second longer. "Did you know Liza's parents had a son?"

Dad's eyes widened, his shock mirroring my own. "No." He held up his hands in defense and shook his head. "I swear, Ty, I had no idea." His gaze shifted to Liza, a flicker of empathy passing between them. "Give me the rundown. What the hell's going on?" Dad crossed his arms and took a seat, the lines on his face deepening with concern.

I cracked my knuckles and inhaled sharply. "Long story short, we found out today that a man named Liam Russell is not only Liza's long-lost brother but also the owner of Russell and Sons LLC. They reached out a couple of weeks ago with a request to buy one of our manufacturing plants. It's a lot to swallow."

Dad leaned forward, his elbows resting on his knees. "You should've called me sooner," he said, frustration lacing his words. "That's a fucking lot for you two to handle while settling into your role as alpha."

"Tell me about it," I muttered, running a hand through my hair. "Unfortunately, that's not the only new development."

Dad gave a questioning look. "Oh?"

I glanced at my exhausted mate. "She's had a hard day. It started with her omega powers taking over again. This time, she was pissed at Bryce and tried to make him submit to her. It was one of the scariest confrontations I've ever witnessed."

"What exactly happened?" Dad looked at Liza, and she lowered her head.

"Liza doesn't remember. All she knows is that she was pissed at Bryce. But... her eyes were glowing red, and she shifted partially. Her powers took over the room. The lights flickered, the kitchen cabinets and appliances shook, and I swear to the gods, I saw her feet come up off the floor."

"Holy shit."

Dad stood up and paced the room, the way I'd seen him do a thousand times when this was his office. His footsteps echoed through the quiet space. Suddenly, he stopped and turned his attention to Liza, studying her closely. "How are you feeling about all this, Liza?

Out of everything you've just shared, my biggest concern is the alpha traits you exhibited earlier."

"Overwhelmed," she admitted, shifting uncomfortably under Dad's scrutiny. I couldn't blame her. It was a lot for anyone to handle, and she was doing it and still trying to keep her day-to-day as normal as possible. She was so much stronger than she realized. "I don't know what's happening to me, and, quite frankly, I'm scared out of my fucking mind. I could be in serious danger. I've already had one outburst in public, and people are discussing my powers. What if they try to come after me because of it?" She paused and glanced toward the office door. "Plus, my new employee, Rosalie, witnessed the thing today. I don't think she'd say anything, but she's young and might be easily influenced into discussing her time working for the mythical omega."

My fists clenched at the thought of Maximus. Though his threats had been veiled at our previous meeting, he would undoubtedly use Liza to further his own ambitions if he caught wind of her alpha-like powers. There were too many like him—men who would prey upon her to use her powers to sustain their own.

"We need to talk to Rosalie," Dad interrupted my thoughts, his eyes hardening with resolve. "She's the only loose cannon right now."

Liza glanced at her watch. "Rosalie and Sabrina should still be working in the kitchens for another half hour before they leave to deliver the food for tonight's function." She pulled out her phone and dialed Rosalie, requesting her presence in my office. Minutes later, the petite redhead appeared in the doorway.

"Please, have a seat." Dad gestured to an empty chair. Rosalie hesitantly sat next to Liza, her eyes flicking between us.

Dad smiled kindly at her. "Rosalie, I'm sorry to call you up here like a kid to a meeting with the principal. You're not in any trouble, I swear. In fact, Liza has spoken highly of you. I really need to ask you a few questions, and I'm hoping you'll be honest with us all. We need to know your thoughts about what happened earlier in the kitchen today with Liza."

She glanced at Liza before answering, a hint of determination in her eyes. "I know what people in town are saying about Liza being magic, but I don't care about any of that. Liza took a chance on me giving me this job. I wouldn't tell a soul about anything I saw. I know I haven't worked for Liza long, but she feels more like my friend than my boss, and I would never betray her like that."

I watched her closely, sensing the honesty in her words. My instincts told me she could be trusted, but it never hurt to remind people of the consequences of betrayal. "If you were to betray us, you'd be considered a traitor to the alpha of our pack and punished accordingly."

Rosalie's eyes widened slightly, and she nodded her understanding. "I promise, I won't tell anyone."

Good. One less issue to deal with, yet so many fucking questions left unanswered.

"Thanks, Rosalie. Can you and Sabrina finish up and take the food to the venue? Everything is set up, and Sabrina knows what to do. For what it's worth, you feel more like a friend to me, too," Liza said with a small smile.

Once she left, Liza stood up and stretched. "I'm exhausted. It's been a day and a half. I think I'll go take a hot bath."

"Great idea." I stood to follow her, but Dad shot me the same look I used to get when I was a kid sneaking a cookie from the kitchen.

Right. No pussy.

As soon as the door closed behind Liza, Dad turned to face me. "Ty, we've got some work to do. We need to find out more about this Liam Russell and his business dealings."

I nodded in agreement and projected my laptop screen onto the flat screen against the wall. We scoured the internet for hours, but none of the information added up. Russell and Sons was a distribution center, dealing with third-party selling, like online auction sites.

"Sure, he might need a bigger facility for holding products," I mused aloud, "but why would he want that factory?"

The company Liam wanted to purchase from us had been a pet project years ago when kids were obsessed with fidget toys. Keller Enterprises had purchased a small building where we'd manufactured our own versions of the toys and enjoyed moderate success. As noted by Tim, the sales were still satisfactory but nowhere near their previous levels. We were willing to part ways with the company to shore up our bottom line for investors.

"I can't imagine Liam wants the building to keep making fidget toys. They're a dime a dozen now. There's no future in them."

"Look at this," I muttered as Dad and I continued digging into Liam's past. "Liam's first business was a cosmetic brand that did fairly well." He sold it and branched out into other ventures that have also been successful, making him a fortune.

Dad leaned in; his brow furrowed in concentration. "So, he's got a history of building up businesses and making a damn killing from them. But it's still not answering the question. Why our factory?"

"Exactly," I growled. "None of this makes sense."

"Maybe there's more to it than just what's on the surface," Dad suggested. "Maybe there's a reason we can't see yet."

"Let's call Tim," I decided, pulling out my phone and putting it on speaker. "He might have some insight."

"Ty, what's up?"

"Tell me, Tim," I began, rubbing my temples. "What do you make of Russell and Sons LLC? We're going over their business dealings, and something doesn't add up."

"Ah, yes. I noticed that, too. I've looked into it," Tim said. "It's strange how certain transactions they engage in don't match the family's wealth. It suggests the potential for shady dealings happening behind closed doors."

"Shady dealings?" I echoed, my gut twisting with unease. "Keep me posted, Tim." I hung up without saying goodbye.

Was there a possibility of Liza's parents being involved in those dealings? There was that wire transaction from their account. But why pay them? For what? Something fishy was going on, and I planned to find out exactly what it was.

# Chapter 18 - Liza

The moon hung low in the sky, casting an ethereal glow on the forest floor. Suffocated by the secrets and chaos that had taken over my life, I'd needed to leave the house. So, I shifted into my wolf form and sprinted through the trees, relishing the release as my muscles stretched and contracted with every leap and bound.

Ty watched me leave the house, but he hadn't followed me. Our mating bond ensured that he'd always know when to give me space. But now, as I sat under the canopy of leaves, staring up at the serene beauty of the night and alone with my thoughts, I didn't want to be alone anymore. I wanted Ty to join me more than anything.

As if I'd summoned him through our bond, Ty appeared from the shadows, walking toward me with a soft smile on his face. He hadn't shifted, but I knew he'd been watching me from afar, keeping an eye on me without intruding on my solitude. He sat down next to me under the tree, his warmth a comforting contrast against the cool evening air. I leaned into him.

"Thought you might be ready for some company," Ty said gently, his deep voice resonating through my bones.

I huffed in response, amazed at how well he'd learned to read my mind in such a short amount of time. Slowly, I lay down, so my head rested in his lap, the tension in my body dissipating as he instinctively reached out and scratched at my fur.

*Always know just what I need, don't you?* My eyes closed as a wave of contentment washed over me.

Ty's fingers worked through my thick coat, finding all the right spots that made me sigh with pleasure. His hands were large and strong, the hands of a true alpha, yet they moved with a tender touch I'd come to crave. There was an almost reverent quality in the way he caressed me, as though I was something precious and fragile. But we both knew I was anything but fragile.

"Your brothers would probably kill me if they could see us now," Ty mused, restrained laughter coating his words.

I snorted at the thought of Mason and Michael's overprotective tendencies. Despite their wildly unique personalities—one an outgoing jock, the other a quiet intellectual—they were united in their fierce love for me, their little sister. Ty and I were mates now, so it wasn't the same as them busting into the basement while I attempted to make out with a high school flame.

No, this was something entirely different. This was a love I'd only ever dreamed of—one that, despite a shit load of trials, was proving to stand the test of more than just time. His love for me never wavered, even though we struggled to comprehend my Omega tendencies.

"I spoke to Bryce earlier." Ty's fingers worked through my dense fur as he interrupted my thoughts. "I told him the stuff he said to Sabrina was inappropriate. He's agreed to apologize to her."

With so much chaos and confusion after Sabrina's altercation with Bryce, there hadn't been an opportunity to ask her about what happened. The venom in their words told me there was more to the situation than just two people sniping at each other. And now my curiosity piqued. Tilting my head upward to catch Ty's gaze, I growled inquisitively.

"Ah, you're wondering what happened between them?" he asked, a knowing glint in his eyes. "Bryce told me they went on a date. He said it went really well, and he was keen to see her again, but Sabrina has been... indecisive, to put it mildly. She was giving him mixed signals. One moment she wanted him, the next she was cold and distant."

My ears perked at this information. As much as I hated to admit it, that sounded just like my best friend. Sabrina might appear to be fickle, but she had the ability to fall hard and fast. If I had to guess, she had strong feelings for Bryce, but he had a reputation for being the biggest Playboy in town. She'd be afraid to admit it to him... and herself.

"Apparently, Bryce got fed up with it and told her he wouldn't see her again until she figured things out. Then Sabrina saw him on a date with another woman, and, well..." Ty trailed off, his fingers never ceasing their gentle exploration of my coat.

A growl built in my chest. Yes, Sabrina could be flighty, but that didn't excuse what Bryce had said to her.

Ty seemed to read my thoughts because his voice took on a more serious tone. "I told Bryce it wasn't okay, what he said to her. Sure, Sabrina may have taken a jab at him first, but he went too far. He knows he crossed a line."

A soft huff escaped me, signaling my agreement, and Ty chuckled, his warm breath stirring the fur on top of my head. His hands continued their calming journey across my body, each touch a testament to our unbreakable bond.

I knew Ty wanted to ask me what was on my mind, but I appreciated him for not doing so. An intense wave of exhaustion washed over me. I was so drained, I couldn't find the words to express how I was feeling. My life had become an intense game of whack-a-mole. Whenever I got a handle on one thing, something else would come crashing down.

Forcing myself to leave the comfort of Ty's warm lap, I shifted back into human form. I stole a glance at Ty and caught him staring at me as if he'd never seen me naked before. I managed a faint smile and lay down on my back in the soft blades of grass, using Ty's lap as a pillow once again. He looked down at me, that ever-present concern in his eyes, and all I could do was stare up at him. There was nothing more to say.

The moonlight illuminated his chiseled features, and I stopped to marvel at his beauty. "You know, I should be over this by now," I said. "But you're still the most beautiful man I've ever seen."

His laughter rumbled deep in his chest, his tender caress on my cheek sending shivers through my body. "You're the only person who can call me that and get away with it."

I laughed with him, surprised to discover that I still had a place of joy inside. But then the reality of our situation settled over me again, and I sobered. "Gods, I wish all the secrets and danger would just end. I always figured once I found my mate, we'd settle down and live a quiet life together. This is the complete fucking opposite."

He searched my eyes. "I can't promise you that there's an end in sight, Liza. I can't promise you won't face any more challenges, but I can commit to be by your side every step of the way."

He paused, considering something before continuing. "Perhaps something familiar would help you feel better, apart from my lap." He winked. "I was thinking we could go visit your parents."

Relief flooded through me. The warmth of family, even if just for a little while, sounded wonderful.

Ty and I went inside to get dressed, with our fingers interlaced as we walked up the steps. A warmth spread through my chest at the thought of spending more time with him. Ty released my hand and turned to face me.

"Hey, I have an idea," he said, grinning. "Since renting out the country club for you and Sabrina went so well, why don't we do that again and invite our closest friends and family? Of course, that includes Bryce and Sabrina."

I blinked in surprise. "That sounds like fun. But is it okay to rent out the entire country club again?"

"We might not manage the entire club at short notice, but definitely the private function suite, and we can take extra security with us. I can't see it being a problem." Ty chuckled. "You seem to forget that you're married to the alpha now. They'll gladly take my money and cater to us for the evening. Feel like dressing up?"

"Are you kidding? I have a new dress I've been dying to wear!"

"Perfect." Ty planted a kiss on my forehead. He pulled me to my feet, and I pulled on the robe I'd worn to come down to the woods to shift. My heart rate slowed, and I was more settled with Ty beside me. For the first time in a really long while, I felt complete and content.

He knew how much I was struggling with the revelations from my parents' letter. I didn't even want to think about it. I knew I needed to get a handle on my powers, but that would mean reaching out to Liam Russell, my *brother*. It was strange to think that I had a brother out there. We were both on edge, waiting for Castro to make his next move. He was there waiting. Ty had sensed my need for normality. I never knew what to expect from him. He always found creative and heartwarming ways to show his love. But this...

This exceeded my expectations. A night with family and friends—no omega, no mystery powers, or long-lost relatives. Ty was giving me a night of freedom where we could ignore everything weighing us down and focus on ourselves.

While Ty called the country club, I stepped into the shower, the warm water soothing my tense muscles. I let all the shit drain away and enjoyed the gift Ty was giving me.

Dressing up and spending an evening with family and friends felt so *normal* that it made my heart swell. I pulled out the dress: a deep red number with a plunging neckline and thigh-high slit. It was daring, but I felt like being bold.

"Time to go all out," I said to myself, applying makeup with precision, accentuating my eyes and lips. I curled my hair, letting it cascade over my shoulders. And then, just because I could, I painted my nails a matching crimson.

"Damn, I clean up nicely." I smirked at my reflection.

Ty entered the room just as he hung up the phone. His gaze met mine in the mirror, then he gave a low, appreciative whistle. He clutched his chest jokingly. "Damn, Liza. Give me a heads-up next time."

I tossed my hair over my shoulder and did a little twirl. "So, you approve."

"I more than approve." Ty grabbed my hand and ran it down the front of his pants, where his massive cock threatened to break through his zipper.

I fanned my face. "Oh, my. Mr. Keller. I don't think there's time for that."

Ty let out a low growl. "Fine. But you'd better keep one eye open, Mrs. Keller. I'm liable to snatch you up and have my way with you in a broom closet."

I playfully slapped his arm. "Are we good to go?"

"Everything's arranged at the country club, and I've texted everyone. The club agreed to lay out a buffet for us. They're going to staff the bar, but I've had the staff vetted so we don't have any surprises, and even a DJ if we want music."

My eyebrow arched as I turned to face him. "You don't think it had anything to do with the exorbitant amount of money you offered them, do you?"

Ty laughed, his eyes dancing with amusement. "I'd never do that, now, would I?"

We arrived at the country club and made our way to the bar. After Ty, both of our dads, Bryce, and even my brothers decided to play a round of golf, I found myself drinking champagne with my mom, Sabrina, and Persephone. My red dress immediately caught their attention.

"Liza, you look absolutely stunning," Sabrina gushed.

"Thank you," I said with a grin, getting up from my stool and doing a spin to show off the dress. "I figured, why not go all out for once?"

"You might have given me a heads-up that you were going to pull out all the stops tonight." She glanced down at her black jumpsuit with disgust.

"Are you kidding me?" I rolled my eyes. "You can wear a potato sack and look sexy as hell. Shut the fuck up."

"Would it make you feel better if I did a twirl, just to show there's no animosity between our outfits?" Sabrina didn't wait for an answer before standing and twirling, her hands dramatically raised over her head.

We all laughed at her, and I reveled at the carefree atmosphere. The guards were hidden from view, but I could feel their presence. Their watchful eyes allowed me to truly relax and to pretend, for one evening, that there was nothing to worry about without any lingering concerns.

We chatted about everything under the sun, carefully avoiding any mention of the tumultuous events that were plaguing my life.

"Another round of mimosas?" Mom raised her empty glass with a playful smile.

"Absolutely." I signaled for the bartender. As he filled our glasses, I watched Bryce walking past Sabrina, not even sparing her a glance. The tension between them was palpable throughout the evening, but they avoided going at it again. I didn't need a repeat of what happened in the kitchen. I never wanted to scare Bryce like that again.

Persephone leaned in closer, whispering conspiratorially, "So, Liza, how long do you think it'll take before Sabrina and Bryce finally admit their feelings for each other?"

"Your guess is as good as mine," I said with a smirk. "But knowing those two, it'll probably involve a lot of drama and stubbornness. I don't think it'll happen any time soon."

"Ugh, tell me about it." My mom, who'd been eavesdropping, rolled her eyes. "It's like watching a cheesy soap opera unfolding in real life."

We laughed, enjoying the lighthearted banter as we sipped our drinks.

When the night came to an end, I found myself looking over my shoulder, trying to assess the amount of stress in my body. Without realizing it, I'd curled my hands into fists at my side, anxiety taking hold of me once again. As much as I just wanted to enjoy my time with loved ones, I kept waiting for something to go wrong.

The night had been so carefree and fun, surely something terrible was about to happen. That's how my life worked, right? One minute, things are going fantastically well, the next minute I'm turning into a fucking rage monster that blacks out and levitates off the ground.

To my surprise, the air was quiet and still. I felt relieved that everything had remained peaceful. Saying our goodbyes, I hugged each woman tightly. I held Sabrina a few seconds longer.

She pulled back at arm's length and studied my face. "Are you okay?"

"I'm great. Couldn't be better." I forced a smile.

"I don't believe you for one damn second." Sabrina rolled her eyes and pulled me into another hug. "Enjoy the rest of your night with Ty. Stop allowing your worries about the future to affect the present."

I pulled away and squeezed her hands. "You're right. I'll try."

Ty and I lingered at the club after everyone else had left, waving from the front doors as they drove away. He slipped his hand into mine and led me back into the main ballroom. I glanced around the empty room. All the glasses and plates had been cleared away. We stood in the middle of the dance floor, and my heart damn near jumped out of my chest when he shouted, "Hit it!"

The lights in the room dimmed, and the soft strains of romantic music filled the air as Ty pulled me close, his hands resting gently on my waist.

As we swayed to the music, my heart overflowed with love for this incredible man. I gazed up at him through hooded eyes, and my lips curved into a sultry smile. "Ty, did you plan all this?"

He pulled me even closer, his breath warm against my ear as he whispered, "I've been waiting all night to have you alone on this dance floor."

I closed my eyes and rested my head on his chest, inhaling his scent, melting into his warm embrace. It was as if every worry seemed to vanish at that moment.

"Did you enjoy your night?"

"More than you know." I smiled up at him. "I really needed this."

"I know you're under a lot of pressure." He spoke with such sincerity, his gray eyes filled with compassion and understanding. "I know I've said this before, but I will continue to repeat myself until you have complete faith in what I'm saying. You're not alone, Liza. I'm with you always, whatever comes our way. We'll face it together."

# Chapter 19 - Ty

The heavy, uncomfortable silence nearly suffocated me as Liza, Dad, Isaiah, and Bryce gathered in my office. It had been several days since Zephyr had deciphered the letter, and Liza was now ready to make the call to her brother.

Excitement shone in her wide eyes, the iridescent blue reflecting in the soft glow of the sun through the office windows.

I took her hand in mine as I sat next to her at my desk. "Are you ready? There's no pressure. If you're not, no one is pushing you. I just want you to know you can stop at any time."

She stared at the letter her parents had left for her. "I'm not going to lie, I'm scared, but I'm also really excited to speak to my brother... I have so many questions." She sat silent for a moment, then she squeezed my hand. "Make the call, Ty."

I grabbed the phone and dialed the number listed at the bottom of the coded letter from Liza's parents. We'd agreed beforehand to have the call on loudspeaker just in case this was some ruse that might place Liza in danger.

In my mind, I'd imagined this, Liam sitting by the phone all these years, hoping to hear from a sister he assumed to be dead that he'd grab the phone up after only one ring, excited to be reunited. But instead, a woman's hesitant tone greeted us.

"Hello?"

"Good afternoon. This is Alpha Keller speaking. May I ask who's on the line?" I kept my tone light and friendly.

There was a brief moment of hesitation before the woman said, "Isabel Russell."

"Isabel." She certainly wasn't who we were looking for. "I'm trying to reach Liam. Is he available?"

"Um, I'm sorry. We haven't seen or heard from Liam in almost ten years." Her voice quivered slightly.

My eyebrows furrowed at this revelation. In the letter Liza's parents had written that she should phone this number to speak to Liam, and that he'd answer her questions. If he'd left ten years before, why not take the number with him? Why keep the number live but not keep it with you?

Liza's shocked expression matched my own. She wiped a tear tracking down her cheek. It felt like we'd come one step forward and taken two back.

Considering the money recently sent to Liza, and that anonymous email, supposedly from Liam, we'd thought it meant he wanted some form of contact with his sister.

And if he was attempting to buy one of my factories out, he must be alive and well. Or someone was using his name. But why? There were too many questions that required answers. I needed to approach the situation cautiously, hoping to pull more information from Isabel.

As if reading my thoughts, Isaiah caught my eyes and made a subtle motion with his hands, urging me to continue pressing for answers. I obliged, leaning a little closer to the phone.

"Isabel, when exactly was the last time you saw Liam?"

"Right after our father died." Her words were heavy with emotion. "Liam got the majority of shares in my dad's company, and then he just... disappeared."

"Can you tell me how you and Liam are connected?" Hoping not to upset Isabel, I continued to press on with the questions, praying to the gods I wouldn't push her too far that she hung up. Liza needed answers.

She hesitated.

"Isabel, like I said earlier, I'm the alpha of the Keller pack. The questions I'm asking are related to a very important pack matter. Your cooperation would be greatly appreciated." I hated playing the alpha card but hoped that reminding her of my position would give her the nudge she needed.

After a long pause, she finally said, "Liam is my half-brother."

Confusion rippled through the room like a stone thrown into still waters. My gaze fell upon Liza, whose hands were on either side of her face, her eyes wide and searching. For the first time during the call, she spoke up, her voice trembling with emotion.

"Explain, please," she said, desperation lacing her words.

Liza pulled her chair closer to me, leaning forward on the table, her eyes locked onto the phone as if she could see Isabel's face through the speaker. "Isabel, my name is Liza Keller. Liza Wylde. I think Liam is my brother."

Isabel gasped. "Look, nobody else knows about this, but I've heard of you, Alpha Keller. I trust you'll keep this to yourself?"

Liza was nodding along furiously, her eyes silently pleading with me.

"Yes, of course, Ms. Russell. You have my word."

"When my parents lived in Heather Falls, my mom Heather had an affair with the alpha of the pack, Josef Wylde."

Oh shit, that was Liza's father. My stomach clenched at the revelation.

Isabel continued. She'd been holding on to this story for a long time, and now the words were tumbling out like a dam breaking apart. "That affair resulted in Liam's conception. My mom knew the pack would be scandalized if the truth came out, so she kept her pregnancy a secret from him. Everyone assumed my dad was the father."

The weight of this information settled over us, thick and suffocating. It was almost too much to comprehend.

Isabel continued. "When Liam was born, he was strong... much stronger than my father, who was a beta. Liam was most definitely an alpha, and as male betas can't conceive alphas..." Isabel laughed nervously. "I was ten when everything happened, but I remember it all as clear as day."

If I was in shock, I could only imagine how Liza felt. "Please continue, Isabel."

"Eventually, Steve confronted Josef Wylde, and the truth came out. They knew he couldn't publicly acknowledge Liam, so he agreed to provide for him financially. With each passing year, it became more apparent that Liam shared a strong resemblance to the alpha. My parents knew the secret wouldn't last long."

Slowly but surely, Liza's past was being revealed like a puzzle, with each fragment falling into place. The hurt and confusion on her face tugged at something deep within me, an instinctual urge to shield her from the pain.

"Because my father was a beta, Liam needed a mentor. As it was the alpha's responsibility to ensure Liam was raised to be a proper alpha, Josef started training him."

So, that's why Liam had been at the alpha's house, and that explained Liza's memories of them playing together. Her dreams had been memories of a brother who came in and out of her life, depending on when he trained with Josef, Liza's father.

Isabel cleared her throat. "In the beginning, Liam didn't know Alpha Wylde was his father, but he found out when he overheard my parents talking. He was extremely angry. He didn't understand why the alpha had disowned him. In the end, he asked Alpha Wylde why he didn't want him," Isabel said, her voice barely more than a whisper. "Josef Wylde sent us away. He gave my parents money to take care of Liam and ensure that we never went back."

"Why send them away? Was Wylde worried someone would find out about Liam?" I glanced at Liza to find her head resting in her hands.

"If I'm being honest with a more mature mindset, yes, that was probably part of the reason he sent us away, but there was more to it than that. The alpha and his mate Portia had a daughter. Liza." At the mention of her name, Liza looked at me. I could see she was concerned where this was going. "Portia allowed Liza and Liam to play together. Liam would see you when he went round for training, and you would play together while he was waiting for the alpha to begin his training.

"Alpha Wylde said we had to leave because of a boy named Castro. I remember him. He was a horrible kid—a real bully. He was insanely jealous of Liam and how close he was to you, Liza. Both my father and Alpha Wylde were concerned that Castro would come after Liam." Isabel paused, lost in the heaviness of her memories. "It was too much of a risk to stay."

A shadow crossed my mind as Isabel spoke of Castro and his jealousy over Liam's closeness to Liza. His dangerous obsession with her had made her father fear for Liam's safety. That was a fear I shared all too deeply.

I watched Liza's face, seeing the anguish and confusion that clouded her expressive eyes.

"Liam resented Josef Wylde but loved you deeply. He knew that causing trouble would only bring trouble to you, Liza, so he agreed to stay away. He swore he'd return one day when he could face his father and Castro and get to know his sister again. But then the massacre in Heather Falls happened. Liam was devastated. He thought Liza was dead."

The revelation seemed too heavy for Liza to bear any longer. A sob guttered out of her. She covered her mouth, trying to quiet herself, but her shoulders shook with the force of her emotions. I wrapped my arm around her, gently pulling her close as I tried to offer comfort. "Isabel, please continue."

"Okay," Isabel said hesitantly, taking a deep breath. "Liam focused on becoming a better alpha, using his pain and anger as fuel for his growth. He began working for my father, but as I mentioned, when he died, Liam just... disappeared. We know he's alive because of the money he sends to us every month." Isabel paused for a moment. "Liza, when I saw you on the news, I was shocked to learn that you were still alive. I knew Liam would want to know, so I tried getting in touch with him several times. I couldn't find him. You were all over the news, though, so I'm sure he knows by now."

Liza tensed, her sobs subsiding as she listened to Isabel's words.

"Thank you, Isabel," I said sincerely when she finished speaking. "Your honesty is greatly appreciated. If you hear from Liam, will you please let us know?"

"Of course, Alpha Keller," Isabel said as a goodbye.

I sighed, sinking back into my seat as Isaiah scribbled furiously in his notepad. He'd been taking notes throughout our call. So far, he hadn't found a single trace of Liam Russell connected to the Russell enterprise.

Isaiah looked up from his notes, meeting my gaze. "With this new information, I might be able to find Liam. I still can't make any promises, but I'm much more confident now. I'll be in touch soon." He grabbed his jacket and strode out of the office without another word.

I was learning Isaiah wasn't the most talkative person, but I had to hand it to the bastard, he didn't drag his ass. When he had an assignment, he dived in feet first.

Liza had been quiet up until that point, but suddenly she burst into hysterical laughter.

I stared at her with wide eyes before looking across the room at my father. We exchanged a bewildered glance before turning our attention back to her.

Liza's laughter quickly dissolved into a rant. "Of course, my father was a cheater. I mean, why the fuck not? He was already a mob boss, doing who the fuck knows what. What's the harm in adding a cheater to the damn mix?"

Her words hung heavily in the room. Her emotions were on a teetering point. I had to help her calm down. I knelt in front of her, my hands resting gently on her knees.

Tears streamed down her face. "I promise I'm not sad or mad. I'm just so damn frustrated. Did my parents ever stop to think about any of their actions and how they would affect their children?"

She wiped her eyes with the back of her hand.

I couldn't answer her, literally having nothing to contribute. Unfortunately, I never got to meet Liza's parents, but after hearing what Dad had told us, and now Isabel's account of Liza's father cheating, I found myself questioning their morals.

When Liza stood, I followed suit, studying her closely. Her tear-streaked face showed no signs of weakness, only determination. I didn't want to annoy her, but my instincts picked up the same scent I noticed when she had an angry flare in front of the loiterers at her office and when she was pissed at Bryce. The therapist wanted me to watch for signs and try to assist Liza in calming down, so that was exactly what I intended to do.

Liza turned on her heels and held up a hand. "Calm down, Ty. I'm not going to completely lose my shit, even though I honestly feel like it's warranted. If anything was going to make me blow up, this would have been it, right? You can take a step back. I promise, I'm okay."

I could see the truth in her eyes. She wasn't okay. She was as far fucking from it as you could get.

Clenching her hands into fists, Liza turned to face the door Isaiah had just walked out of. The fire in her eyes was unmistakable. "Isaiah needs to find my brother," she said, her voice unwavering. "I don't care what it takes."

With that, Liza stormed off down the hall. I watched as she stomped into our bedroom and slammed the door. The anger radiating from her exit was obvious. Dad rubbed his arms as he stared after her with wide eyes, and I could only nod in agreement. We'd both felt it, that wave of an alpha's essence growing stronger within her.

It was fucking scary.

With her safely in her room and away from others, I grabbed my keys from the desk.

"Where do you think you're going?" Dad stared at me in confusion.

"I'm going to the building Liam is trying to buy." It was on the other side of town, so the thought of bringing Liza along tugged at me. Maybe a change of scenery would help get her head into a more positive space. She obviously needed her space, though, and I didn't want to bother her.

I turned to Bryce, who had been quietly observing everything from a corner. He narrowed his eyes at me. "What are you looking at?"

"Come on. You're with me."

As we drove toward the warehouse, Bryce shot me a curious glance. "What exactly are you hoping to find out here?"

"I'm not sure," I said, the steering wheel squeaking under my grip. "I just want to understand why Liam is so interested in it. He could have purchased any building, anywhere, so why a factory that makes fidget toys? A factory that belongs to Keller Industries?"

The twenty-minute drive gave me some time to consider the connections between Liam, the Russell LLC, and my seemingly insignificant business. There had to be something more to it. Some hidden thing that connected Liam back to Liza.

We pulled into the empty parking lot and parked in front of the main entrance. The building was closed for the workday, but I had a master key.

"Let's see what we can find." Unlocking the door, we stepped inside. The factory floor was quiet and still, with rows of machinery standing dormant like silent sentinels. There was nothing particularly special about the place; just another production line churning out the latest trend. The metal framework stretched high above, supporting the ceiling and various ventilation systems. A few workstations were scattered throughout, each with their own set of tools and equipment.

"Doesn't look like anything special." Bryce echoed my thoughts.

"Let's check the office," I suggested, leading the way toward a small room at the far end of the factory floor. It was cramped, cluttered with paperwork and files. I sifted through them, searching for anything that might reveal why Liam was so interested in this place.

"Tim went through the financial statements, but maybe he missed something." My fingers danced over spreadsheets and invoices, looking for any hint of a financial anomaly, but there was no significant wealth to be gained by buying out this company. It was just another mediocre business in a sea of similar ventures.

"Nothing here," I muttered, frustration gnawing at me. Why did Liam want this place? What was he hiding?

Before Bryce could reply, a sudden noise from the factory floor tore through the silence, making us both jump. We exchanged a glance before racing out to investigate.

As we neared the source of the sound, the pungent smell of smoke hit us like a wall. One of the machines had caught a spark, and the small flame was greedily licking at its metal frame.

"What the fuck?" I scanned the factory floor, trying to come up with a plan of action. Panic surged through me as I grabbed a nearby fire extinguisher, Bryce doing the same.

Together, we aimed at the growing blaze and pulled the triggers. The cold spray shot out violently, smothering the flames and choking out their oxygen supply. Within moments, the fire was out, leaving only wisps of smoke in its wake.

Breathing heavily, I stood there with my hands on my hips. Gods, what would have happened if we hadn't been there? The entire factory could have burned to the ground.

"I don't understand what the hell just happened." I turned to Bryce. "How could the equipment spontaneously burst into flames when everything was turned off?"

Bryce rubbed his chin and looked around. "Wait. I've got an idea." He disappeared into one of the back rooms, returning a few minutes later with a triumphant look on his face. "The noise we heard earlier was a circuit breaking."

"Shit. How is that possible?" I frowned. I was meticulous about maintenance for all my companies. Our machinery was top tier. Nothing broke on a whim, and it sure as shit didn't catch fire out of damn thin air.

"Accidents happen," Bryce said. "Maybe maintenance missed that and one of the circuits was faulty."

"Maybe," I said reluctantly. "Sure, accidents happen, but something about this doesn't sit right with me. With everything going on with Liam, I wonder if it was done on purpose. What are the chances a fire would break out at the exact time we were here?" I locked eyes with Bryce, whose expression turned serious.

"I'm putting Isaiah on this. We need answers."

# Chapter 20 - Liza

The pungent aroma of freshly diced garlic and simmering beef swirled around me while I attempted to focus on the task at hand. My mind, however, was a chaotic tornado of revelations. My father's infidelity, a brother I never knew existed—it was all too much to process.

The sizzling pan hissed, mocking me, as if to say, *You're screwed, Liza Keller. No matter what you do or say, your parents' pasts will continue to haunt you until the end of fucking time.*

Touché, cast-iron skillet. Touché.

"Hey, Liza," Rosalie piped up, slicing through my thoughts like only a young, no-care-in-the-world person could, and in a sing-song voice, no less. "How long do we need to let the beef wellington bake?"

I blinked, forcing myself back to the present. "Erm, about twenty-five minutes, or until the pastry is golden brown." I shook my head, trying to clear away the haze. "Sorry for spacing out. You're doing great, by the way."

Rosalie stared at me, her blue eyes narrowing. "You've been out of it lately. Not to make you feel bad,

383

I've just noticed you don't quite seem yourself. Is everything okay?"

"Nothing I can't handle," I lied, forcing a smile. "But you know what? You can go for the day if you want. You deserve it. I'll pay you for a full day. It's my fault that I can't quite stay on task."

Before she could protest, I held up a finger. "Wait right here." I dashed out of the kitchen and into my office, grabbing the envelope containing Rosalie's first paycheck. It was a tangible reminder of the hard work she'd put in since joining my team.

I returned to find Rosalie stirring a pot of red wine reduction, her face flushed from the heat. "Here," I said, holding out the check. "You've been the perfect assistant, and I'm really looking forward to working with you more."

"Thanks, Liza." She accepted the envelope with a nod. "But I think I'll stick around. There's so much still to do. We haven't even started on the orders for the entrée for Mrs. Jacobson's party. I don't want you to be more overwhelmed than you already are."

"Rosalie, you're a good kid. I appreciate it." I was truly touched by her sense of loyalty and work ethic, and I wished more people had her internal moral compass.

While we continued to prepare the beef wellington, Rosalie's presence calmed me, like a soothing balm on my frayed nerves. Perhaps, despite all the chaos in my life, there was still hope for something beautiful to emerge from the wreckage.

Rosalie turned her attention back to the beef wellington, carefully brushing egg wash over the puff pastry. "You know," she began hesitantly. "I haven't talked about this very much before, but I was raised by my grandmother." She paused, the pastry brush hovering above the dish.

"Your parents weren't around?" I asked, intrigued by her sudden openness.

"Yeah. My... well, sperm donor, that's what I call him. I wouldn't give him the title of dad or father. No way does he deserve it. He didn't want anything to do with me. He was married and had an affair with my mom, who wasn't the best person, either. She couldn't handle being a single parent, so she took off." Rosalie's voice wavered, but she continued. "My grandmother stepped in and became my everything, my mom and dad. She was the one who made sure I did my homework, made it to basketball practice, and brushed my teeth before bed. I'm sure it wasn't something she expected in her older age, having to care for her granddaughter, but she did it without hesitation."

"Wow." I could somewhat sympathize with Rosalie's grandmother, since my adopted parents had taken me in and loved me as their own when my pack was killed. Of course, my parents had been in the prime of their lives, not retired.

"Anyway," Rosalie continued, giving me a small, sad smile. "When my grandmother passed away eighteen months ago, I moved away for a fresh start. Dominic let me stay here in town. That's partly why my loyalty to the pack runs so deep. My grandmother and I bonded over food, and that's where my love for cooking began."

"Speaking of which," I interrupted, eyeing the beef wellington. "Let me look at that."

Rosalie shifted her gaze back to the dish, expertly sealing the edges of the pastry.

"It's ready to bake. Great job." I smiled in approval as she slid the pan into the oven.

My phone buzzed, reminding me that it was time to check the loaf of cinnamon raisin bread we'd popped in the other oven. "Mm, this looks perfect." I carefully placed the loaf on the cooling tray on the granite countertop as Rosalie clapped her hands. "What do you think? Should we drizzle vanilla icing over the top once it cools?"

She nodded her head. "That'll be delicious. Honestly, if the general population of Presley Acres had a taste, we could build a separate business off the orders we'd receive on it alone."

I laughed. Maybe she was right, but that wasn't my goal. I simply wanted to add fall-inspired cuisine to my catering menu because I enjoyed using seasonal ingredients. It simply tasted better. Winter strawberries tasted bland. I hardly had time to keep up with my pared-down client list as it was, not to mention adding a side hustle.

Rosalie watched as I stuck a toothpick in the center of the bread and showed her how it came out clean.

"So, what made you love cooking? Or were you just born with oven mitts on?"

I thought back to my childhood in Presley Acres, growing up with my adoptive parents. A memory surfaced of me playing in the garden, creating my own recipes out of flower petals, dirt, and water. I smiled at the pleasant thought, one of the few I'd had in days. "I started baking as a means of escape. None of the kids in the neighborhood wanted to play with me because of my white hair and pale features, so I spent a lot of time by myself."

"Wow." Rosalie's eyes filled with empathy. "Kids can be so cruel."

I snorted. "You can say that again. Luckily, my mom introduced me to baking, and I loved it. But I also enjoyed making my own recipes out of random ingredients. She taught me to cook, and I discovered I had a natural talent." I smiled, realizing there was a connection to Rosalie I hadn't expected. "Cooking became my sanctuary, a way to escape from the world. And I guess the kitchen is still where I come to cope with life." I scoffed at the realization.

Rosalie nodded, understanding glimmering in her eyes. "I get that. There's something about creating a delicious meal from scratch that's just... therapeutic."

"Exactly," I said.

The two of us continued to work side by side, our shared love for cooking forging an unexpected bond between us.

While Rosalie focused her attention on the baking beef wellington, checking it every few minutes to ensure the crust didn't burn, I wondered about her own experiences with family.

"Rosalie," I began cautiously. "How do you feel knowing your father abandoned you?" I silently thought about how I hoped to maybe understand how my brother Liam had felt over the years.

She paused in her task, her hands stilling on the pastry. Then she sighed and looked me straight in the eye. "Honestly? As a kid, I didn't really feel much about it because I didn't know him, so I never felt the loss of my father." She wiped her hands on a towel. "But as I got older and learned who he was, there was a lot of resentment."

I nodded, listening intently as her eyes flickered with a hint of sadness.

"I have siblings out there who don't even know I exist. I don't even think the man who I share half my DNA with would even recognize me if he passed me on the street." Her breath caught in her throat, and she took a moment to control her emotions. "There have been times where I wanted to out him to everyone, but that wouldn't bring me any closure. I would hurt his family, and he'd just resent me."

Rosalie took a deep breath and let it out slowly. "So, I made peace with the fact that I was fatherless. It doesn't change who I am as a person. It just means I don't have a dad, and I'm okay with that because who would even want a father who didn't want them anyway? And bonus! It's one less birthday and holiday present I have to buy."

Her words hung in the air between us, heavy with truth and vulnerability. The raw emotion in her voice was pitiful. She had been through so much, yet she remained strong and dedicated to her passions.

"Rosalie," I said, reaching out to give her hand a gentle squeeze. "Thank you for sharing that with me. It means a lot."

A sudden noise from the oven made us both jump. The timer went off, signaling that the beef wellington was ready to come out.

"Whew," Rosalie said, forcing a smile as she pulled on oven mitts and carefully removed the dish from the oven. "Almost forgot about that."

I chuckled, welcoming the momentary distraction from the heavy conversation.

Rosalie's words haunted me for the rest of the day, gnawing at my thoughts like a persistent itch. Sitting at my computer, I pondered her declaration that she wouldn't want a father who didn't want her. Was that how Liam felt about our father? The question nagged at me until curiosity won out, and I decided to look up Isabel on social media.

I found her profile quickly. My hands trembled as I scanned through her photos, scrolling back as far as ten years ago. There were posts about vacationing in exotic locales, crystal-blue waters, and pristine white sands. There were other images showcasing mouthwatering dishes she'd eaten in some fancy restaurants I'd heard of, accompanied by tantalizing descriptions of their flavors. I even stumbled upon a painting she was proud of—a strikingly detailed depiction of a wolf lounging beneath the glow of a full moon.

And then I found it. A picture of Isabel from thirteen years ago, standing beside a young man. He looked to be in his early to mid-twenties, but the face and hair were unmistakable. It was the boy from my dreams, only older, more mature, and undeniably handsome. Lacking any photos of my parents, I relied on the flashes of memories to piece together their faces. Isobel was right. Liam definitely had our father's features. The resemblance was uncanny.

I printed the photo—the only one of him that Isabel had tagged in the image—and when I searched through Isabel's friends list, there was no trace of him. My investigation was cut short by a call from the security company, informing me that the alarms at my office in town had been triggered, and that police had already been dispatched. Fuck.

I quickly abandoned my home office, rushing downstairs as I tried calling Ty. He didn't answer. Glancing at my watch, I realized he was still out at a business meeting. Ty wouldn't be too thrilled about me going to the office alone, so I called my father.

"Hey, Dad," I said, trying to keep my voice steady. "The alarms at the office went off, and the police are on their way. Can you meet me there?"

"Of course, sweetheart," he said, and I heard the concern in his tone. "I'll be there as soon as possible."

"Thanks, Dad." With my security detail in tow, we headed into town and toward my office building.

I pulled up to my office, saddened by the graffiti still painted on in red daubs over the front of the building. My heart leapt into my throat when I spotted the police waiting for me by the front door. Taking a deep breath, I got out of the car and approached the policeman.

He smiled kindly before getting right down to business. "Seems like the door was picked, but the alarm went off when the code wasn't entered fast enough. Whoever it was left pretty quickly." He gestured toward the building. "Nothing appears to have been taken."

"Thank you," I said, relief washing over me. Deciding to do a quick walkthrough of my office, I cautiously stepped inside. As I walked through the space, I glanced from side to side, searching for anything that seemed out of place or missing. There had been plenty for the intruder to grab had they wanted something of value, so why the hell hadn't they? My gaze fell on the safe in the back corner, and I entered the code with shaky fingers. The door creaked open, revealing everything just as it should be. The police were right. It didn't seem like the intruder had taken anything thanks to the alarm.

I turned and headed toward the front of the office, scanning the room one last time. An envelope sat on my desk. It hadn't been there the last time I was here, and I couldn't recall Sabrina mentioning coming into the office. And apart from Ty, she was the only other person with a key. My gut told me that the envelope wasn't from her, but I hesitated about mentioning it to the police. Instead, I shoved it into my back pocket.

Just then, my father arrived.

I held up both hands and forced a smile. "Everything's fine, Dad. The alarm scared whoever it was off, and they didn't take anything."

He hugged me tightly, his eyes searching mine. "Are you sure?"

I nodded. "I'm going to have the lock replaced with a keypad so no one else can try to break in again."

While we talked, Ty arrived on the scene. He chatted briefly with the cops, but kept glancing over their shoulders at me as I spoke with my father. I was no stranger to that look in Ty's eyes. It was one he wore a lot lately. He was worried about me. After thanking the police for their quick response, he made his way over to my side and pulled me into a hug.

"You okay?" Ty asked, his concern for me seeping into my bones. He looked at me like he was expecting me to fucking wolf out, to completely obliterate every person within a half-mile radius of my office, while simultaneously forcing random objects to levitate off the ground.

Forcing a smile, I assured him that I was fine. I tried to crack a joke. "It's a good thing the alarm scared whoever it was off, or they would've left with a ton of printer paper and miscellaneous cooking supplies. Maybe they could've unearthed my lost recipe cards." I laughed at my own attempt at humor, but Ty didn't share in my amusement.

Clearing my throat, I acknowledged his concerns but couldn't help being a bit annoyed. "You can't expect the worst reaction out of me every time something goes awry, Ty. I'm keeping the therapist's recommendations in the front of my mind and trying not to allow my thoughts to go there. It freaked me out, but I'm okay, so stop looking at me like I'm some kind of freak."

Ty opened his mouth, perhaps to apologize or retort, but in the end, he just smiled weakly and put his arm around my shoulder, leading me away from the office.

He motioned for one of the security guards to drive my car back to the estate. "I'd prefer you ride with me so we can talk."

As we climbed into his sleek, black SUV, the tension between us became a heavy, static ball. The engine purred to life, and we started our journey back toward the estate.

"Did it look like anything was taken from your office?" Ty asked, his eyes never leaving the road as he navigated through the busy streets.

I exhaled deeply, the weight of the unopened envelope in my back pocket pressing against me. "No, they didn't take anything." I reached into my pocket to retrieve the envelope. "But they certainly left something."

The vehicle slowed to a stop at a red light, and Ty grabbed the envelope. He turned it over in his hands, examining the plain exterior. "It hasn't been opened," he commented, an eyebrow raised in curiosity. "Did you tell the cops about this?"

"Of course not. Lately, a lot of things have been revealed, and the police aren't aware of what your father used to dabble in. Mysterious notes like this usually come with more secrets."

Ty's chuckle held no humor, only a bitter acknowledgment of the painful truth. "You're right," he said, his grip on the steering wheel tightening as the light turned green. "I wonder what's in it, though."

I shook my head, staring out the passenger window at the blur of passing scenery. "Whatever it is, I'm fairly certain that nothing good is going to come of it."

# Chapter 21 - Ty

I clutched the envelope in one hand and the steering wheel in the other, feeling more than a little fucking annoyed. My thoughts kept drifting back to the meeting I had with the inspector earlier that day. He'd confirmed my worst suspicions. Someone had intentionally tampered with one of the machines at the warehouse. A cut cord had caused the machine to malfunction. The machine had been set to warm up far earlier than scheduled, which was a blatant and malicious act that could have cost lives.

"Ty, are you okay?" At some point, Liza had stopped staring out the window and had shifted her focus on me.

"Someone messed with one of the machines at our warehouse," I said, gritting my teeth. "And now I have HR and the manager investigating and questioning workers to find out who's responsible."

"Gods, that's awful. Why would someone do that? Do you think it was an employee?"

I shrugged. "I have no idea. I'm hoping the manager can make sense of it."

We pulled into the estate driveway and walked inside silently, no doubt both of us completely drained of our mental energy.

Just as we crossed the threshold into the house, my phone rang, slicing through the air like a blade. Glancing at the screen, I saw Tim's name flash before me. *Fuck me.* What fresh hell did he have in store for me now?

"Tim," I answered, my voice clipped. "What do you want?"

"Ty, I need you at the main office immediately," he demanded, and I clenched my jaw, annoyed by his entitled and commanding tone.

"Right now's not a good time, Tim. Surely whatever you're worried about can wait until tomorrow."

"I'm afraid not." Tim's heavy sigh distorted his voice over the phone. "It's urgent."

"I'm on my way." I hung up and handed Liza the envelope. "Don't open it until I get back," I instructed, pressing my lips to hers in a lingering kiss, my apology for being so absent lately.

Her mouth moved against mine, the heat of our connection making my wolf stir, but there wasn't time to indulge in the passion that brewed between us.

Pulling away, Liza looked into my eyes. "I know your world doesn't stop just because I've got things going on."

"Wrong," I corrected her, hoping I could make her see my fierce devotion to her. "You are my world, Liza, and I'd stop the Earth on its axis for you. Your problems are my problems, and we'll get through them together."

Reluctantly tearing myself from her embrace, I headed back out the door, steeling myself for whatever awaited me at the main office.

The moment I entered the building, the tension prickled the hairs on the back of my neck. Something was off, and I didn't like it one bit.

I strode into Tim's office, and my suspicion was confirmed when I saw Hiram lounging in one of the leather armchairs. My gut clenched. This situation was about to go from bad to worse.

"Tyson," Tim began, standing up in a huff. What the hell was his problem? "You should have informed me about the deal Maximus proposed. Why you didn't take it, I have no idea."

Tim's accusatory tone had me growling low in my throat, my wolf bristling beneath my skin. "I make certain business decisions without your advice, Tim. You do know that it's my business, right? That you work for me? I am perfectly capable of making decisions and making deals without you."

Before I could continue, Hiram cut in. "I heard about Maximus's little casino plan, Ty, and I wanted to thank you personally for not becoming my competition." His eyes flicked over to Tim, who shifted uncomfortably under his gaze. "A little birdie shared some interesting information with me. It seems Tim here tried reaching out to Maximus to continue negotiations, despite your decision to shut it down."

My anger flared, and I glared at Tim with barely controlled rage. "What the fuck's gotten into you, Tim? You know good and well that you don't make decisions about my businesses without my knowledge or consent. You need to remember your damn place." Tim opened his mouth to defend himself, but I cut him off, my patience wearing thin. "No. I warned you when you went over my head to sell one of my own damn factories. I'm done. I'll see you're paid till the end of the month. I think it's best if we part ways."

For a moment, I thought he'd argue, but he thought better of it. Gritting his teeth, he started clearing out his desk.

Realizing that Hiram was the reason I'd been called in, I turned to him. "Would you like to talk over a drink?"

Hiram agreed, and we left Tim's office, my irritation still simmering in my blood like one of Liza's pots on the stove.

As we walked to the parking lot, Hiram glanced over his shoulder. "Keep an eye on that one, Ty. He smells like a rat."

"Trust me, I plan to." I nodded, picking up my phone. I called security and asked them to ensure Tim left with nothing more than his own belongings, making it clear he was no longer welcome on the premises. My wolf strained beneath my skin at the betrayal.

We arrived at the bar—a dimly lit establishment with worn leather seats, and the faint aroma of cigar smoke lingering in the air. The bartender, an old, grizzled man with a thick beard, nodded in our direction as we took our seats. Hiram and I both ordered whiskey neat, and the amber liquid slid smoothly down my throat, the warmth doing little to quell the burning of my anger.

"Look, I'm grateful for what you did with Maximus. You could've just as easily agreed to fund his hell of a venture, leaving me scrambling in the dark to combat new competition." Hiram took a sip of his own drink. "And to show you my gratitude, I wanted to give you a heads-up about something."

"I'm listening." My fingers tightened around the glass. This didn't sound good.

"Let's just say... hypothetically speaking, of course, if there was such a thing as shifter trafficking, and hypothetically, your Liza's name might've come up." Hiram paused, watching my reaction carefully. "Maximus has been running his mouth, claiming he's witnessed things that prove Liza is... more than she seems. There's talk of getting proof."

My grip on the glass threatened to shatter it as my anger surged like wildfire. My wolf snarled within me, desperate to protect our mate. I fought to keep him under control, focusing on Hiram's words.

"Before you lose it, I want you to know that I stepped in," Hiram continued. "I told the underground communications that Maximus is full of shit and just looking for money to fund his failed business ventures. It seems the others believe me, but remember, Ty, it only takes one to believe Maximus. Keep a close eye on your omega and Maximus. He's working all angles, and I wouldn't put much past the fucker."

"Thank you, Hiram," I said through gritted teeth.

He smirked. "Told ya I'd make a good ally."

I forced a grin and slapped him on the back. "Yep, that you are."

We finished our drinks and parted ways, with me saying I had a few more things to handle before going home. Once I was back in my car, I immediately pulled out my phone to call Isaiah. There wasn't a moment to waste.

"Hello?" he answered.

"I'm sorry." I clenched my jaw, wishing I didn't have to ask my new employee for another favor.

"For what?"

"For putting more on your plate. I'm fully aware that you're already swamped, but something's come up." I paused and rubbed my temple. "I just had a meeting with Hiram. He's heard rumblings from the underground. Maximus is telling everyone about Liza's powers, and he's caught the attention of those who are interested in trafficking."

"Fuck." Isaiah was a man of few words, but he sure knew how to briefly summarize a situation.

"Fuck, indeed. I need you to look into this underground business Hiram mentioned. See if there's any truth to it."

"Of course. And don't apologize. This is what you hired me to do. Try not to worry, and I'll check in soon." Isaiah hung up first, presumably getting straight to work.

I sat there, gripping the steering wheel, seething with rage. The message I wanted to send Maximus was simple: if he came anywhere near Liza, there would be hell to pay.

The thought of Maximus even thinking about touching Liza was enough to ignite a fury so deep inside me I was afraid I'd explode.

"You're gonna pay, Maximus," I said. Making a snap decision, I turned my car toward his residence, an hour away.

As I approached Maximus's land, I marveled at the wide-open expanse. Presley Acres was more residential and commercial. Maximus's pack territory was much more rural. A locked gate greeted me—a symbol of his arrogance and false sense of security.

I snorted in derision. That damn thing wouldn't keep me out. Backing up, I revved the engine, feeling its power beneath me. With a surge of adrenaline, I accelerated forward and broke through the gate with ease.

I laughed maniacally. "Ready or not, Maximus, here I come."

When I arrived, I observed the immense structure that was Maximus's residence. The white house was solid and stood tall, giving off an imposing fortress-like appearance. The pristine windows and towering columns at the entrance were indications of the wealth and power exuded by every inch of the place, but they didn't intimidate me.

Ignoring any semblance of decency, I marched up to the door and banged on it with my fist. Not waiting for a response, I pushed it open, striding in like I owned the damn place. Wide-eyed staff stared back at me, one of them frantically speaking into a phone, most likely contacting security.

I held up my hands, smirking. "Nothing to worry about, ladies and gentlemen. I'm just here to visit my good ol' friend, Maximus."

At the mention of his name, Maximus appeared at the top of the staircase, looking down at me with utter confusion. His council members emerged from an office behind him, their expressions equally puzzled.

I stared up at him, my eyes blazing with anger. "I know, I know," I said nonchalantly. "You weren't expecting me. But you know what? I wasn't expecting you to make the stupid fucking mistake of trying to sell my mate."

"Ty, I don't know what you're talking about," Maximus stammered, but his wide-eyed gaze told a different story.

"Cut the bullshit," I warned. My wolf rose within me, urging me to protect Liza at any cost.

Maximus hesitated before slowly descending the stairs, his eyes locked onto mine, his fear flickering within their depths. He stopped a few steps above the main floor, his body tense as if he were afraid to come any closer.

"Ty, I have no idea what you're talking about," he repeated, but the tremble in his voice betrayed his words.

My anger boiled over, and I growled low in my throat. "Don't play dumb, Maximus. I've heard about what you've been up to. For your sake, I hope it's just rumors." Each word dripped with menace. I didn't give two shits if it offended him.

"Look—" Maximus tried to speak, but I cut him off with a sharp wave of my hand.

"Let me make myself clear," I warned, my voice deadly calm. "I have connections everywhere. There isn't a corner of this world where you could hide from me if I wanted to find you. You and everything you own would be mine in an instant."

He swallowed hard, sweat glistening on his brow. "Ty, I swear, I have no idea what you're talking about."

"Enough!" The thin thread that held my patience at bay snapped, and I allowed the rage of my alpha to pour forth, filling the room with its intoxicating scent, forcing obedience upon all those who dared to challenge me.

I stepped closer, pointing a finger directly at Maximus's face. "You do not want me as your enemy, Maximus," I snarled, my words laced with venom. I never thought myself capable of being vicious, but when it came to Liza, my mate, I would burn the whole damn world to the ground to keep her safe.

"Ty, please..." Maximus attempted to interject, but I spoke over him, making sure every word seared itself into his mind.

"Listen carefully. If I so much as hear a whisper about Liza being connected to any dirty dealings you're trying to make, I'll ensure you're licking the dirt off my boots just to earn a penny."

I allowed my wolf to let out an ear-piercing growl, its power reverberating through the room. Maximus's eyes widened in terror, and he stumbled backward onto the steps, his body trembling uncontrollably.

"Understood?" My expression was cold and unforgiving, not giving an ounce of room for Maximus to misinterpret my words.

He nodded, too afraid to utter a single word.

The staff members around me scattered like frightened mice, their eyes wide as they hurried to escape my alpha presence. Fear laced Maximus's voice as he continued to play dumb, assuring me I wouldn't hear anything else about Liza's involvement in his business.

"Ty, I promise you, I had no idea," he stammered.

My gaze swept over his councilors, who had backed themselves up against the wall, desperate to put as much distance between us as possible. Their faces were a mixture of shock and horror, clearly not accustomed to seeing their leader so thoroughly cowed. Bitter satisfaction welled up within me at the sight.

"Good," I growled, turning away from Maximus, and stomping toward the door. "I hope this little display has taught you a lesson."

As I stalked past the remaining staff members, their bodies stiffened, and they averted their eyes.

Maximus's council and staff would remember this day, and it would serve as a reminder of the consequences of crossing me. Adrenaline pulsed through my bloodstream, the protective instincts for my mate fueling my every move.

Embarrassing Maximus in front of his staff and council should do the trick. If it didn't... well, I'd have no qualms about tearing him apart, limb by limb.

"Remember, Maximus," I called over my shoulder as I walked out the door. "Liza is off-limits. Cross me again, and you'll regret being born."

With that, I slammed the door behind me, leaving him to contemplate the gravity of his actions. I reveled in the power I held over him. It was thrilling, invigorating, and it left me feeling more alive than ever before.

"Maximus," I said under my breath, my eyes narrowing. "You'd better pray this is the end of it."

The engine of my car roared to life after I climbed in, gripping the gear shift tightly. With one last look at Maximus's house, a cold resolve settled over me.

"Because if it's not, I'll bring your fucking world crashing down around you."

# Chapter 22 - Liza

Ty's side of the bed was still empty. My fingers traced the spine of the book I had attempted to read, but the words swam across the page, refusing to make sense. Anxiety gnawed at me like a damn jock itch. I rubbed my temples in a circular motion, which had zero effect on my mood. *Where the fuck was he?* The techniques Anna had given me didn't seem to be working. My peppermint tea sat forgotten on the bedside table. I was lying on the bed, repeating the same mantra repeatedly: *see* the curtains, *hear* the wind, *touch* the paper. It wasn't helping, neither were my visualizing and breathing exercises.

The door creaked open, and finally, Ty entered the room. I turned to face him as relief pulsed through my very being.

Before he could speak, I cut him off. "I'm too tired to worry about the letter tonight. Can we just deal with it in the morning?"

He nodded, his eyes shadowed with the same exhaustion that weighed on me. When he sat down on the bed next to me, I could practically feel the ache in his muscles, and the weariness seeping into his very bones. We'd been through a fucking lot. Maybe we could ignore it all for one night.

"Feels like we haven't spent much time together lately, and when we do, we're just putting one damn fire out after another," Ty said, apologetic. "Things have been crazy, and I know I've been neglecting my role as your mate." He pulled me close, his arms wrapping around me, offering warmth and protection. "Starting right now, I promise to be more attentive."

Ty grabbed my ass with an urgency I couldn't ignore. Of course, we were both tired, but a second wind of energy, of need, bolted through my body. His touch was all it took to ignite a desire deep within my core, overriding my anxiety.

Ty's lips met mine in a passionate kiss that took my breath away. His tongue flicked the tip of mine as he pulled me on top of him. He rolled back onto the bed so that I straddled him. "I thought you said you were tired?" He eyed me with a devilish grin. "I suppose I can muster up the energy… if you're up to it."

"Up to it?" Ty laughed and rolled me onto my back, his hips pressing hard into mine as he ran his hands up my silk nightgown. "Are you asking about me

413

personally, or my cock? Either way, we're both up to it."

He lowered his mouth, but this time, he went directly to my neck, knowing that tender spot under my ear made my nipples hard every time without fail.

I wriggled against him. "Oh, so you do have a sense of humor. I was beginning to worry."

He lifted his head long enough to reply with a husky voice. "I'm funny because I'm tired. I'm horny because you're so fucking hot."

I ran my hands over the broad expanse of his back, feeling the contours and muscles beneath his hot skin. When I reached his shoulder blades, I dug my nails in and pulled his chest against mine, grinding my hips against him. "Well, if you're tired, maybe we should put you to bed."

His eyes glimmered with arousal and mischief. "I don't think I could sleep, anyway. I think my cock would keep me awake."

"That could be a problem," I teased.

"Not for me." Ty turned me around on the bed so that I was on all fours.

I turned and started to get up, wanting to throw my gown off.

"Fuck, Liza, stay just like that." He moved my hair to the side and kissed down my neck to the firm swell of my ass. All I had on was a thong, making it easy for his hand to slide over my damp flesh as his lips pressed against the sensitive skin of my neck, sending a jolt of electricity down my body and straight to my pussy.

"Ohh," I moaned softly when his tongue traced a line from my neck to my lower back, and I could feel his lips curling into a grin. He knew damn well the effect he was having on my body. As his hand moved up my side, he pushed his other hand under me to touch that sweet spot between my thighs.

He slid his fingers between my legs, caressing my aching flesh over the lace thong. There was just enough fabric between my clit and his fingers to drive me crazy.

"How about we slip these off?" Before waiting for my response, Ty moved with expert ease to slip my thong down my legs and onto the floor. "There, that's better."

His hand found my outer lips and teased me with a gentle pressure. I shifted my hips, trying to move against his hand. He playfully moved his fingers away from where I wanted them. I waited, anticipating his next move, only to feel him slipping the fingers of his other hand back over my ass to where I needed him most.

I had to bite my lip to keep from moaning. My core pulsated with need, and I couldn't stand it anymore. I twisted my body around and pulled my gown up and over my head, tossing it onto the floor.

Ty stared at my breasts as my nipples squeezed into even tighter buds under his gaze. "Gods, help me." He dived straight for them, placing his face between my tits, and moaning as he caressed my nipples. My head fell back at the sensation of his tongue circling my left breast as he squeezed and kneaded them with both hands.

He pulled away long enough to strip.

I watched in anticipation, waiting for him to unleash his massive cock. It always took me by surprise, and this time was no different. It grew in front of me in all its veiny glory. My mouth watered as he climbed back onto the bed.

Ty reached for me, but I had another idea.

I pushed Ty back onto the bed, and he eyed me quizzically. "Stay right there." I twisted my body around until I straddled him, my ass pressing against his face.

He didn't hesitate, grabbing my ass cheeks and pulling my body down to his mouth. He found my swollen bud, lapping at it with the tip of his tongue. My inner thighs were soaked with my arousal as he sucked on my clit.

Not wanting him to miss out, I grabbed his massive cock with both hands and lowered my mouth over the head. The first taste of Ty's cock was always pure ecstasy, like water in a dessert. Blood rushed to my head as I swirled my tongue over the head. I wanted to make him feel as good as he made me feel.

He moaned into my pussy in response.

I circled my tongue around the shaft, then sucked on the head while I stroked with my hands. His cock hardened even more in my grasp. I loved the taste of him, and the fact that he was so completely in my control was an aphrodisiac that drove me crazy.

Ty's tongue probed deeper into my pussy, and I couldn't stop myself from pushing back against it. He was licking my pussy so fast the air was hitting my clit, sending waves of electricity through my body. I held his cock tightly in my hands and licked up and down the shaft, dragging my tongue over the soft skin. I teased the opening with the tip of my tongue as I caressed his balls. Ty moaned against me, sending vibrations across my clit as I sucked his shaft with a slow, firm pressure.

My breath caught in my throat as Ty shoved a few fingers deep into me.

His tongue swirled around my clit, forcing me to concentrate on his cock or I would have come instantly. I closed my eyes and took him deep into my throat, sucking hard with my lips as I pushed against his face.

He slid his fingers into my pussy again. Cool air hit my ass as he spread me open and licked my tight little asshole, creating an intense sensation that almost pushed me over the edge.

I sucked him harder. The sound of our slurping and sucking echoed in the room. I couldn't get enough of this. I wanted to touch every inch of his body, but before I could move, Ty shot up and grabbed me, turning me around.

I shrieked when he rolled me onto my back. The head of his cock pressed against my dripping pussy. I raised my head to kiss him, and he wrapped his hand around my neck, pressing me tightly.

He pushed himself into me with one long, forceful stroke as he lowered himself onto me, my breasts pressing against his chest.

The kiss we shared was electric, his tongue diving into my mouth, tasting my juices on his lips as his cock filled me. He pulled my legs up to his hips and plunged into me even deeper.

"Fuck yes." I moaned against his lips. I loved the feeling of his weight on me, pressing me down into the bed. My pussy walls were throbbing with an intense pleasure that sent tingles through every part of my body. Ty's hips slid against mine as he pounded into me at a steady, relentless pace. My nipples hardened against his chest, and I pushed my hips up to meet him with each stroke.

Ty's lips trailed from my mouth to my neck, sucking on my sensitive skin. His teeth raked against my neck as he pounded into me harder and faster.

I dug my nails into his back, needing the leverage to push myself against him.

I pulled my head back to look into those gray, stormy eyes. The corners of his mouth curled into a smile as he licked his lips. His chest was covered in sweat, and his skin glistened under the glow of the lamp on the nightstand. He raised my legs higher and pushed them out as far as they would go. I felt myself stretching to accommodate him. The restraints he placed on my legs kept me trapped beneath his body. I wanted to move, but he was too heavy to escape.

Ty's body was damp with perspiration, and the skin of his ass was tight and taut as he pushed hard into me. He lowered his head to my ear and said, "I'm going to come so hard inside you."

I moaned, raising my hips to meet him.

Ty grabbed my hands, pushed them up over my head, and held them there as he thrust deeper into me. He moved one of his hands down to my clit, stroking it in slow, sensual circles. The friction drove me crazy. My pussy throbbed around his cock.

Ty pushed his hands under my ass and lifted me off the bed. His mouth found my breasts, and the sensation of being lifted into the air, held by Ty's strong arms, while he suckled on my nipples, had my orgasm crashing over me violently, my pussy milking his cock.

He fucked me harder as my orgasm mounted deep within my body. I clung to his neck as I bit into his shoulder and scratched his back. I wanted him to fill every inch of me.

Ty thrust his hips up harder and deeper into me as he licked at my nipple, sending waves of pleasure through me. With my head thrown back, and my eyes closed, my body shook. The pressure built again quickly. There was no point in trying to fight it. An explosion was imminent. I just had to hang on tight.

I dug my nails harder into his back as the wave built to a crescendo. Ty's lips crashed against mine as he thrust into me wildly, sending the wave shooting through my body.

I came hard and fast, the walls of my pussy squeezing and pulsing around his cock. Ty's thrusts became more frantic as my orgasm triggered his. He grunted as the head of his cock swelled and pulsed inside of me, his cum filling me.

His body shuddered with the power of his orgasm. He collapsed on top of me, briefly resting his head on my chest as his breathing slowed. I ran my hands through his thick hair, loving the feel of his weight on me. When he rolled over, I rested my head on his chest, my body still pulsating with pleasure.

\*\*\*

Morning light streamed through the curtains, coaxing me from a deep sleep. I stretched lazily, glancing at the bedside clock. Almost ten in the morning, yet I had no desire to leave the sanctuary of our bed. A knock at the door startled me, and I hastily grabbed a housecoat, throwing it over my naked body before opening the door.

"Mr. Keller asked that you be served breakfast mid-morning, ma'am," the girl said, holding out a tray full of delicious treats. I thanked her, taking the tray and inhaling the scent of freshly brewed coffee, warm croissants, ripe berries, and fluffy scrambled eggs.

With a contented sigh, I climbed back into bed, grateful to have the day off work. I was exhausted and in dire need of some downtime. While I ate, my thoughts drifted to Ty and his promise to be home early to discuss the mysterious letter I'd found on my desk.

Truth be told, I wasn't eager to open it. Trouble seemed to follow me like a shadow. Was there another long-lost relative I didn't know about? Or maybe the envelope held information about yet another bank account left for me by my deceased parents. How much money did one person need?

My day passed in leisure, munching on chocolate-covered strawberries while binge-watching my favorite TV shows, painting my toenails a vibrant shade of purple, and scrolling through social media. All the while, the unopened letter sat on the bedroom dresser, taunting me.

The vibration of my phone against my leg startled me out of the trance I'd fallen into while painting my fingernails. Recognizing Sabrina's number on the screen, I tapped the speaker option.

"Hey, girl, what's up?" I carefully focused on applying the perfect coat of purple to each nail.

"Guess what? The tourists are finally leaving town." There was a hint of amusement in her voice. "Seems like they've given up on catching a glimpse of Liza the Magnificent and her miraculous powers."

I laughed, but inside, I was relieved. "Oh, thank the gods. It's about time they moved onto their next obsession."

"Right? You'd think they were hunting for Big Foot or something," Sabrina snickered.

"Or the Loch Ness Monster," I added with a smirk.

It was refreshing to joke about the whole ordeal. In reality, though, the last thing I needed was to be caught out in public again by my so-called admirers. We'd been lucky last time. I hated to imagine how my omega powers would react if I was pushed too far again.

"Anyway, just thought you'd want to know," Sabrina said, her tone returning to normal. "Have a great day off, chica."

"Thanks. You, too." I ended the call with a smile on my face, which was a nice change of pace.

Later, as I sat in my office scribbling down some favorite recipes on my new recipe cards, my phone rang again. Assuming it was Sabrina calling back—she had a habit of forgetting to tell me things—I picked up without checking the caller ID.

"Hey, Sabrina, what did you forget this..." My words died in my throat as an icy chill swept through me, the menacing tone on the other end of the line not belonging to my best friend.

"Ah, Liza, so good to hear your voice," Castro purred menacingly. "But I'm not Sabrina."

"Castro," I said, my heart pounding in my chest. "What do you want?"

"I have news to deliver, my dear." He spoke in a hiss, much like a snake, but I was intrigued by his words. By the time the call ended, I shook from adrenaline, sitting in my office chair and staring blankly out the window.

A fire ignited within me, a rage building that I couldn't control. Ty wasn't home yet, so discussing the matter with him wasn't an option. I needed to shift, to run, to escape the house that suddenly suffocated and oppressed me, but I didn't want to be alone.

The moment I pulled into my parents' driveway, their faces lit up with surprise and joy. They immediately stopped working in the front flower garden and headed in my direction. But as they approached the car, their expressions turned to concern.

"Sweetheart, what's wrong?" Dad asked, his eyes scanning me for any signs of distress.

"Can't I just visit my favorite people without there being something wrong?" I tried to deflect with a playful smirk, but I wasn't fooling anyone.

"Nice try, Liza." Mom folded her arms across her chest. "We know you too well."

I held my hands up, admitting defeat. It was true. As a teenager, I could never hide anything from them. They were like lie detectors when it came to me and my true feelings. "I just need to be surrounded by family right now."

Without hesitation, they encircled me in a loving embrace, and I melted into their arms, some of the oppressive weight falling from my shoulders. As we stood there, a thought crossed my mind. "Would you guys like to go for a run with me?"

A small smile tugged at Dad's lips. "Of course, sweetheart."

"Let me just grab one of your guards and then we'll shift." Mom walked to the blacked-out SUV that had followed me to their house.

It had been ages since I'd last run with just my parents. We all shifted, our clothes vanishing and our wolf forms taking over as we bounded through the woods; the wind whipping past us. For a moment, I actually felt free, as if I didn't have a care in the world.

Just as I let my guard down, focusing solely on the crisp fall air whipping through my fur, a voice invaded my thoughts, chilling me to the bone. *"You're stronger than you know, Liza. You're being stifled from your true potential. You need to set your wolf truly free."*

I held my breath as I tried to shake the voice away. Who was that? How were they inside my head? Panic coursed through me, and fear gripped my soul. I backtracked, running away from of my parents, trying to catch someone who might be lurking behind a tree, but there was no one there.

I returned to my parents' house, nerves frayed and on edge. Ty was waiting for me, his gray eyes lighting up with a smile when he saw me. I couldn't bring myself to return it. Castro's call still echoed in my mind, and the run had done nothing to quell the anger inside me.

"What's wrong?" Ty asked.

"Have you been keeping anything from me?" My words were sharper than I intended, but I couldn't help it. The rage I'd been suppressing threatened to spill over.

Ty's eyes widened, and guilt flickered through them. It was there for only a second, but it was enough to fuel my fury. He had promised me no more secrets, but that had been a goddamn lie.

"Castro called," I spat, hands on my hips. "He told me about Maximus Langston offering me up on some kind of shifter black market auction site. Why the fuck didn't you tell me? Why was Castro the one to tell me?"

"Castro?" Ty's confusion quickly morphed into shock. "I didn't want to worry you, Liza. You already have so much going on."

"Who the fuck are you to judge what I should and shouldn't know? I wasn't aware I'd made you some kind of information gatekeeper. How dare you?" I'd never been an angry person before, but lately it felt like it was getting worse and worse. My blood was lava.

"I'm sorry. I was doing the best thing for you. When was the last time you slept all night? You've lost weight. You don't have bags under your eyes, you have fucking suitcases." Ty's words did little to put out the fire I'd started.

"You promised me, Ty. You swore no more fucking lies, no more secrets. You keep telling me we are in this together, but how can we be in it together if I don't know all the fucking details?" The rage had taken control, and I was just along for the ride. "Do you know what really hurts? What really makes this worse? To be told my mate was lying to me by anyone would have hurt, but for it to come from Castro..." I wiped angry tears from my face. All I could think about was the betrayal.

"Look at yourself," Ty finally snapped. "You're not sleeping, and that makes it easier for you to expose yourself. Go look in the mirror, Liza."

I stubbornly refused, folding my arms beneath my chest. Ty wasn't having it. He grabbed my arm, pulling me toward the mirror in my parents' living room, and when I finally looked, my heart stopped. My eyes were glowing red like an alpha's.

"Liza?" My parents' cautious voices appeared behind me. "Is everything all right?"

"Everything's fine," I said, not taking my gaze off the mirror.

"Fine?" Ty scoffed. "Liza, you're a danger to yourself when you don't have control. You have so much going on, and it's making it harder for you."

My parents stood behind me, mirroring my worried expression. The truth was, I looked exhausted and downright scary. But more than that, I felt betrayed and vulnerable.

"Ty's right," Mom said softly. "We've never seen you like this."

"Look at the state you're in, Liza," Ty continued. "I didn't tell you about Maximus because I was trying to protect you."

And as much as I hated to admit it, he had a point. My anger simmered down slightly, replaced by a bone-deep weariness. I stared at my reflection, red eyes glaring back at me. How had everything spiraled so far out of control? Losing control was terrifying, and now there were these voices in my head. It couldn't be normal.

"Why is this happening? You claimed me, and things were supposed to get better, not worse." My frustration built with each word until I could no longer contain it. "I never showed signs of being an alpha before. Why now?" The question tore from my throat as a desperate scream, rattling the room around us.

I watched Ty's face closely for some fucking semblance of understanding, but all I saw was concern. We stood there, suspended in time, waiting for answers that refused to come.

The silence that followed my outburst was deafening. I cautiously looked around the room, my heart pounding like a damn drum. Books lay scattered on the floor, their pages splayed open. A lamp had tipped over, its base cracked and the lightbulb shattered.

"Wh-what just happened?" I stammered as tremors coursed through my body. My eyes flicked to Ty, searching for an answer. All I found was fear. "Ty... what's wrong with me?" I said, my voice cracking.

His eyes softened, and he stepped forward, pulling me into his strong, protective embrace. "There's nothing wrong with you. Nothing. We just need to get control of these surges," he said into my hair. "We'll figure it out, I promise."

I clung to him, allowing myself to be consumed by his warmth, but the fear still gnawed away at me like a ravenous beast. How much more of this could I take? Everything in my life was spiraling out of control, and I didn't know how to make it stop.

As if drawn by some invisible force, my gaze wandered to the window, where the moon hung heavy in the sky, almost full and shining with a silvery glow. For a moment, I was eight years old again, staring out at that same celestial orb and desperately asking it why I couldn't just be normal.

# Chapter 23 - Ty

The soft glow of the moonlight filtered through the curtains, casting a gentle radiance over Liza's face. She'd been sleeping fitfully, but for the first time in hours, she looked peaceful. Carefully, I covered her with a warm, plush blanket, hoping not to wake her. I'd been by her side for a solid hour, rubbing her back and trying to calm her down.

She hadn't wanted to leave after her meltdown, and it didn't felt right to return to the estate against her wishes—not when she was in such a vulnerable state—so we stayed, and the comfort and familiarity of her childhood home seemed to have helped.

I pressed a tender kiss to her forehead. Everything in me wanted to protect her, to keep her from these external threats as well as the ones inside her, but I was failing.

Turning away, I closed the door behind me with a soft click and walked down the dimly lit hallway toward the living room where Liza's parents were waiting. They turned their worried gazes at me.

"Thank you, Ty," Liza's mom said softly as I took a seat across from them on an old, worn armchair.

"You've been so gentle with her. It's astonishing how you were able to approach her when she was in that trance-like state and bring her out of it."

I sighed, rubbing my temples. "I'm glad I can help her in any way, but I wish it wouldn't happen at all. Unfortunately, no one seems to understand what's going on with her. We went to see a therapist who's working with her on controlling her triggers, but I'm not sure if it's making any difference. It all seems to be escalating."

Scott, Liza's dad, leaned forward and narrowed his eyes on me. "There has to be someone out there who knows about omegas. It can't all be myth and legend. There must be people from other packs who have some experience, even if it's secondhand. We need to find them so they can help our girl."

"I guess it's possible." I nestled into the plush armchair, letting my own body relax after helping Liza recover from her latest flare. "You would think with all the media attention, someone with sound knowledge about their existence and capabilities would have reached out to us by now."

Rory spoke up. "I'm not sure that's necessarily true, Ty. The elders, the old ones in the packs may have heard stories firsthand from their parents or grandparents about the powers of the omega. We know they existed, but can you imagine what it would have been like? Just look at all the attention Liza got. Granted, things are different today with the internet and social media, reports spread so much faster, but if even half the legends are accurate, omegas would have been prized, and a pack would have been made to swear secrecy. If someone wants to buy Liza now in some black-market deal, why not in history, too? It's possible they wouldn't want to come forward for fear of reprisals from the packs they were sworn to."

That was a good point. We spent the next hour discussing potential leads, keeping our voices down so we didn't wake Liza. She needed the sleep more than any of us.

When each idea became more outlandish than the last, I stood and stretched. Exhaustion seeped into my bones, and I excused myself to join Liza in the small bed that had once belonged to her.

Spooning her, I hoped my warmth would provide the comfort she needed to sleep soundly, free from the dreams that haunted her. Somehow, she hardly moved all night, probably from the sheer exhaustion of her powers.

I lay in the dark, with my mate's warm, soft body nestled against me, replaying the events. I'd never seen Liza so pissed. The memory of her standing in the doorway of her parents' living room was frightening—her eyes flashing red, her hair lifting in a white-blonde halo around her, while any object not nailed down hovered three feet in the air. Then the guttural scream ripped through her, and the ground beneath our feet had quaked.

The shock on her parents' faces would remain with me for a long time. I was only grateful Liza couldn't remember the fear on her mom's face. But it was taking longer and longer to bring her out of these episodes. The anger management didn't seem to be working, but then I'd already acknowledged I'd failed my mate there. Anna Anderson had told me to monitor Liza's stressors and keep her calm. More proof, if I needed it, that I was letting her down. Yes, I had been keeping stuff from her, but I truly believed I'd been doing the right thing by not telling her about Maximus's threat to sell her. I had him handled, and we were already dealing with so much.

The whack-job omega fans demanding that she perform, the letter from her birth parents, the missing Liam Russell. She was already spread thin. I'd taken it upon myself and decided she didn't need the added strain of constantly looking over her shoulder, wondering if she'd be grabbed, but I should have told her and been honest. I kept telling her we had to work together, yet I was the one who kept going off on my own.

That fucking bastard Castro. He just had to insert himself, create division. Why couldn't he let my mate go?

The next morning, Liza had risen before me, and I woke to the sound of the shower. I shut her bedroom door and dialed my dad's number with shaking hands.

"Dad," I said, my voice strained. "I'm in way over my head, and I don't know what to do."

"Tyson? What's wrong?"

"Liza had another anger flare last night. The worst one yet," I said, rubbing my forehead. "We're still at Liza's parents' house. She didn't want to leave."

"Stay put," he instructed firmly. He may have given up his position as alpha and become a beta, but his alpha instincts still shone through. "I'm on my way." And before I could protest or worry about Liza's or the Mims' reaction to his unexpected arrival, the call disconnected, leaving me with uncertainty and the hope that Dad might have some answers.

The doorbell rang exactly twenty minutes later, which gave me enough time to give everyone a heads-up. I opened the door to find him standing on the doorstep with his hands shoved in his pants pockets. His brow was furrowed when he stepped inside.

"Thanks for coming, Dad." I led him toward the dining room, where Liza and her parents were already gathered. Liza and her mom had made a quick breakfast of scrambled eggs and bacon.

"Of course, son." Dominic gave me a reassuring pat on the shoulder before taking his seat at the table.

Liza looked paler than usual, her fork moving the eggs on her plate without actually eating them.

Dad glanced at her, taking in her lackluster appearance. "Liza, can you tell me exactly what happened last night? Ty said you had another anger flare."

She bit her lip, focused on the food she wasn't consuming. "One minute, I was mad about Ty keeping information from me, and the next thing I knew, the living room looked like a tornado had run through it. I have no fucking clue how I got from point A to point Z."

I reached out and placed my hand on her leg, offering silent support. "Her eyes were glowing red like an alpha's," I added. "And when she screamed, it shook the entire room, like an earthquake."

Dad's face paled, his jaw tightening. "I've seen many things in my life, some you all wouldn't believe, but never anything like that. I've never heard of anyone having that sort of power, not even an alpha." He shook his head and took a sip of orange juice. "I don't know anybody who could possibly have any insight."

Liza's parents exchanged glances, their expressions mirroring his concern.

I briefly gave Dad and Liza a rundown of the conversation Rory, Scott, and I had the night before, with oral history elderly pack members may have committed to memory but sworn their silence for fear of retribution. Dad didn't discount it, and together, they vowed to do as much research as they could, united in their desire to find someone who might be able to shed some light on Liza's condition.

As the conversation continued, my thoughts shifted to Liza's childhood. Did Liza's biological parents know what she was capable of? Had the Wylde pack kept any records that might help us understand her powers?

"Would Liza's birth parents have kept any records that might help us?" I suggested, looking to Dad for insight, since he'd known Liza's parents personally.

Dominic rubbed the back of his neck. "I honestly have no idea, Ty. Remember, I didn't even know Liza was an omega. If her parents had records of anything, they were burned down with the pack, other than the register I kept."

Frustration coursed through me as I buried my head in my hands. There had to be someone out there who had the knowledge to help Liza, but where would we find them? Then it hit me. The letter from Liza's parents. They'd told her to find her brother Liam, saying he could help her. Could it be possible that Liam knew what Liza was going through and also knew exactly how to help her?

My desperation to find him intensified, but so did my caution. We still didn't know anything about this mystery man or his true intentions, especially after the incident at the warehouse. For now, all we could do was keep searching and hope that the answers lay somewhere within our grasp.

A faint vibration pulled me out of my thoughts, and I took me phone out of my pocket. The warehouse manager's name flashed across the screen, and I frowned as I answered the call.

"Ty, we've completed the investigation," he said in a hushed tone. My stomach twisted into knots.

"Damn it," I muttered under my breath, feeling Liza's presence beside me. The last thing I wanted was to leave her when she needed me most. What kind of mate was I if I hit the damn road every time she had one of these episodes?

"What's wrong, Ty?"

"Someone sabotaged the equipment at the warehouse and it caused a fire," I explained. "Management has been looking into it. They wrapped up the investigation and seem to think it's important I'm there."

"Go," my dad said, his authoritative tone leaving no room for argument.

Liza placed a comforting hand on my arm, her touch soothing my frayed nerves. "It's okay, Ty. I'll stay with my parents, and the guards are right outside. I'll be fine. Honestly, I may just go back to bed."

I hesitated, torn between duty and desire.

"Your pack needs you, son," Dad reassured me, his warm eyes full of understanding. "We'll take care of Liza."

I looked at Liza's pale face, and nodded reluctantly. "Okay. I'll go." I leaned down to press a lingering kiss on her forehead. "I'll be back as soon as I can."

"Be careful." Her fingers curled around mine in a desperate grip.

\*\*\*

When I got to the warehouse, I followed the manager to his office. He seemed uneasy, no doubt anticipating my reaction to whatever evidence he had uncovered, which meant it couldn't be good.

"Here," he said, gesturing to a monitor displaying grainy security footage. My eyes narrowed as I watched the shift manager, a stout man with graying hair, enter the frame. He walked straight ahead, not bothering to glance at his surroundings. He clearly thought he was alone. The building had been empty, so Bryce and I had entered unnoticed. As I continued to watch, he got down on his knees and fiddled with the machine that had caught fire, his face contorted in concentration. The video left no room for doubt. The man had attempted sabotage. By the luck of the gods, we had been there, and we'd been able to prevent significant damage by quickly extinguishing the fire.

"Where is he now?" I wanted to talk to the asshole and see if he'd admit to what he'd done. Of course, the evidence was irrefutable, but still, I wanted to see him fucking squirm as his boss and alpha loomed over him.

"Per your instructions, we're holding him in the conference room." The manager's fingers drummed nervously on his desk.

"Perfect." I strode toward the conference room, putting all my force into pushing the door open. The guy looked up from where he sat, arms crossed, his expression defiant despite the beads of sweat gathering at his brow.

"Talk," I demanded when sat down across from him. I wasn't expecting much. People like him rarely gave up information without a fight. "Why did you tamper with the equipment? Don't try to deny it. We've got you on camera, and I could easily get the police involved."

He stared me down and spat out his words. "Upper management needed to pay. I've spoken to every one of them about the conditions on the factory floor. None of them listened. Even HR doesn't give a damn. I followed every one of their grievance policies, but they shut me down. They pay us like dirt and treat us even worse. I wanted this place to burn to the ground so they'd finally pay for not listening to their employees. We're the ones busting our asses out on the floor every day in this heat, working unpaid overtime. They're in their cushy offices with the air conditioner cranked on high. They don't give a fuck."

His words caught me off guard. This wasn't connected to Liam. I ground my teeth together as my frustration amped up, but I couldn't ignore the concerns this man had brought up, even if he'd gone about it the wrong way.

"Listen." I leaned forward and looked him dead in the eyes. "You're getting off easy this time. Had your plan succeeded, your fellow workers would have been left without work. How would that have helped them? I'll be looking into your allegations about management and HR myself, but don't think you can pull something like this again. I make it clear to everyone who works for Keller Enterprises that my door is always open. Next time you have a grievance, try sending an email or making an appointment with me through my secretary."

The manager's jaw dropped dramatically as if I'd slapped him, but I couldn't find it in myself to care. If I decided to sell the building to Liam, it wouldn't matter, anyway.

Before I left the parking lot, I texted Bryce.

*Take care of the shit show at the warehouse. Employees are so disgruntled they're willing to burn the damn place to the ground. Fix it.*

Moments later, an unlisted number called. Fuck. I didn't have to answer it to know who was calling. He'd just called Liza yesterday, so why not harass me today when I was already at the end of my tether?

"Hello?" I answered cautiously.

Castro's laughter greeted me. "Ty, Ty, Ty," he taunted, his voice dripping with disdain. "Such an incompetent mate, you are."

"Shut your fucking mouth, Castro," I snarled, already at my limit. "You have no idea what you're talking about."

He stopped laughing abruptly, his tone turning icy. "What kind of mate are you for letting Liza's name come up in some underground trafficking ring? If people actually feared you, they'd never dare speak her name. Honestly, you disgust me. You're so fucking weak."

"Listen here, you piece of shit—" I began.

"Your precious Liza may be brainwashed by you, but I won't let your incompetence endanger her," Castro snapped. "Maximus will learn to fear me, and I'll show Liza who's really worthy of protecting her."

The line went dead before I could respond, leaving me cursing and gripping the steering wheel so tightly my knuckles popped.

Still fuming, I grabbed my phone off the dashboard holder and dialed Dad's number.

After a few rings, he answered. "How are things going?"

"Castro called," I said, cutting straight to the point. "He's threatening Maximus now, saying he'll make him fear him more than he fears me."

There was a momentary pause before Dad said, "My advice would be to warn Maximus. Yes, he's a scumbag, but we both know what Castro is capable of. I wouldn't put it past him to murder Maximus or torture his family. No one deserves that."

I hesitated, considering the idea. Maybe letting Castro take him out wouldn't be such a bad thing. It'd be one less problem for me to deal with.

"Tyson, don't even think about it," Dad warned, sensing my thoughts. "You're better than that. And remember, Maximus is still a danger to your mate."

"Which is exactly why I should let Castro do the dirty work," I argued. "Liza would be safer without him around."

"Perhaps, but if you let Castro take him out, he'll feel like he's got something over you. That's something we don't need."

He had a point. Reluctantly, I agreed to warn Maximus. After hanging up, I started the car and made my way back to Maximus's lands. The front gate was already open, being repaired from my previous visit. As I parked my car and stepped out, Maximus appeared at the front door, clearly unhappy to see me.

"Come to your senses, have you?" He shoved his hands into his pockets, trying a little too hard to prove my presence didn't unnerve him. "Ready to discuss backing my casino idea?"

I took a step toward him, and he instinctively retreated a step back. His security guards emerged from the house, surrounding him protectively.

I held up my hands. "I'm not here for trouble." I tried to keep my voice level. I had a message to deliver and then I wanted to get the fuck out of there. I didn't have the mental energy to be peaceful around Maximus for more than a few minutes. "I'm here to warn you."

"Oh, really?" Maximus smirked, gesturing toward the broken gate. "Are you here to warn me before you destroy more property that doesn't belong to you?"

"Listen," I said, gritting my teeth. "Castro is targeting you. You're in danger, whether you believe it or not."

Maximus scoffed. "You expect me to believe that? You're just trying to scare me. It's not going to work."

"Fine," I said, my patience wearing thin. "But if you don't heed my warning, you'll regret it. You don't wanna fuck with Castro. He killed his own parents, and he won't think twice about snapping your neck to make a point."

"Get off my land, Keller," Maximus spat. "And don't bother coming back."

I shook my head at his stubbornness, but there was nothing more I could do. The moment I stepped into my car, my phone buzzed with a text from my dad.

*Brought Liza home with me to the estate.*

Relief surged through me, knowing that she was safe and sound. The tension in my body eased slightly, and I started the engine and drove through the broken gate.

As I pulled up to the house, a sense urgency propelled me out of the car. I needed to see Liza to know that she was truly okay. I burst through the front door and scanned the room. No sign of her downstairs. Without missing a beat, I dashed up the stairs, taking them two at a time.

"Where are you?" I muttered under my breath, my nostrils flaring as I tried to catch her scent.

I found her in my office, standing at my desk, holding the envelope we'd been avoiding for days.

Her eyes met mine, obviously determined to find more answers. "It's time," she said softly, her voice steady and unwavering. "We've put this off long enough."

# Chapter 24 - Liza

The mysterious envelope felt heavier than it should have. It had become a symbol of all the unanswered questions that hovered between us.

Ty took one look at it and sighed heavily. "It'll have to wait a bit longer, Liza."

He plopped down into the large leather chair behind his desk, his shoulders weighed down by some invisible burden. Tension radiated off him. Something was eating him alive.

"What's going on? You seem stressed." What was I saying? Of course, he was fucking stressed. One look around and anyone could see that the world was burning around us. "Well, more stressed than usual."

"Castro called me," he revealed, pinching the bridge of his nose as if trying to ward off an impending headache.

I walked over to his side and gently took a seat in his lap, rubbing his back with one hand, silently showing my support. At least he was telling me. I could only hope he wouldn't keep anything from me. Again. "What did he have to say?"

"Apparently, he's pissed because I allowed Maximus to advertise you to fucking shifter traffickers." Ty growled low, his arms wrapping around my waist in a protective gesture. "As if I had any clue Maximus would stoop so low. If it weren't for Hiram, I'd still be in the dark. I'll never understand how Castro has his finger on the pulse of every damn thing happening not only in our lives, but in the whole of fucking Texas."

I nodded. "You're right. And for the record, I know you would've stopped Maximus had you known what his plans were."

"Of course I would have." Ty stared at me with eyes that pleaded for me to believe him, to know beyond all certainty that he'd never let anything happen to me. "Castro said he's going to take matters into his own hands. He said he'd take care of Maximus."

I bit back my anger. It wasn't directed at Ty, just the whole situation we'd found ourselves in. "So, what are you going to do about it?"

"Nothing more than I have to," Ty said, resting his head on my chest. "Maximus and I aren't allies, so I have no obligation to help him. I warned him, but he chose to ignore it. If anything happens to him, it's because he didn't want to listen."

I couldn't argue with that logic, but it still left me uneasy. Before I could voice my concerns, though, there was a knock on the door.

Ty loosened his hold on me, lifting his head. "Come in."

Dominic walked into the room, his eyes scanning our intertwined forms. "Am I interrupting?"

"Not at all. Join the pity party, Dad." Ty shook his head. "We were just discussing Castro's threats to Maximus."

Dominic took a seat across from us, his eyebrows knitted together.

In my opinion, Ty had done the right thing by warning Maximus, even though I wasn't a fan of the guy for wanting to sell me off to the highest bidder. And yet, I couldn't shake my concerns.

"If Castro is targeting Maximus, it could mean he's finally planning on coming out of the shadows. Wouldn't this be a good opportunity for us to catch him?"

"Good point, Liza," Dominic said, nodding thoughtfully. "How else would Castro get to Maximus?

He'd have to come out of hiding, unless he has someone else working for him, and considering the amount of money he seems to have access to, we can't discount that. Might be a good idea to send someone into Maximus's territory to scope things out and see if they can spot Castro."

Ty cracked his knuckles. "I agree. This would be the type of thing to bring Castro out of hiding, especially since he's obviously still obsessed with Liza. This is his chance to prove to her that he's the superior mate. If he's as cocky as I think he is, he'll want all the glory and praise for taking down the man who didn't give two fucks about selling her. I'll send some guys over to scout the area. If there's any sign of Castro, I'll go and handle the bastard myself."

"Sounds like a plan." Dominic leaned back in his chair.

Some type of scuffle outside caught my attention. "Ty," I said. "Do you hear that?"

His head jerked up, and he turned to face the window. The three of us exchanged a confused glance before hustling over to the wall of windows at the back of Ty's office. We stared out at the scene unfolding below us.

Ty rapped his knuckle against the glass. "What the fuck is going on down there?"

Several guards sprinted toward the front gate. The chaos outside was jarring, especially considering how calmly we'd been talking.

My heart pounded as I tried to comprehend what might be happening. Had Sabrina been wrong about the tourists leaving town? Were they back to try and catch a glimpse of me, to shimmy up the gate and storm the estate? I shook my head as I imagined them with pitchforks and torches, their goal to harm me to see if I can miraculously heal myself.

Ty's phone rang, the piercing tone slicing through the tension in the room. He grabbed it, saw that it was Isaiah calling, and immediately put it on speakerphone. "Isaiah, what's going on out there?"

"Hey, boss. Don't be alarmed. The guards are just following protocol," Isaiah reassured us, his deep voice steady and calming.

"Protocol?" Ty scoffed. "What kind of damn protocol would cause them to go running like fucking chickens with their heads cut off?"

"Look, I can't get into specifics right now, but we've got a situation that needs to be handled. Just stay put, continue your day as normal, and I'll keep you updated."

"Fine," Ty said, clearly unhappy with the lack of information. "Just... keep us informed." He hung up, staring at the phone in confusion.

Dominic scowled and sat down. "Well, that was odd."

"Very," Ty agreed, still watching the guards moving about frantically.

We stood in silence, all of us lost in thought and wondering if everything truly was under control.

"All right," Ty finally said, pulling me out of my thoughts. He turned away from the window, his arms crossed beneath his chest. "Let's not dwell on it for now. There's nothing we can do but trust Isaiah to handle it."

Dominic cleared his throat. "While we're all gathered here, there's something I'd like to discuss about Liza."

I raised an eyebrow at him. This should be interesting.

"Your parents and I have been talking, and we've come up with an idea. Since you are exhibiting signs of an alpha, we think it might be a good idea for you to learn how to handle that power, especially considering how... profound yours seems to be."

"Alpha training?" I asked hesitantly. What would that entail?

Dominic nodded and leaned forward. "Yes. It'll just be the same lessons that young alphas learn when they're coming into their power."

"Ah, yes," Ty interrupted with a grin. "I remember that training very well. So, Dad, does this mean Liza will get to play the same games I got to play during my training?"

Ty's smirk brought a smile to my face, even as I wondered what sort of games he was referring to. It was a relief to see Ty in a better mood, despite the stressful situation we were facing.

Dominic rolled his eyes. "No, Tyson. Liza won't be facing obstacle courses with chocolate at the end. Her training will be more geared toward an adult, not a child with attention and focus issues."

"Hey," Ty protested, feigning offense. But his eyes twinkled with mischief. He wasn't truly upset.

"Anyway." Dominic turned his attention back to me. "Liza, are you up for it?"

"Of course," I said without hesitation. "I don't want another repeat of the night before."

Dominic gave me an approving smile. "Good."

"Thank you, Dominic," I told him sincerely. There was no guarantee it would work, but I appreciated the time and deliberation Dominic had obviously put toward my predicament.

Ty's phone rang again, causing me to jump. He glanced at the screen. "It's Isaiah again." With a sigh, he answered and put the call on speaker.

"Sorry to bother you again, but I'm happy to say it was all just a false alarm."

Ty raised an eyebrow in confusion. "What the hell does that mean?"

"One of the guards at the front gate thought a group of people were heading to the property to try and break in to see Liza."

Ty scoffed, his gray eyes narrowing. "How the fuck could that be mistaken after what we dealt with the other day?"

"He's a new guard still in training. Honestly, he meant well." Isaiah paused. "I'd rather him be too on guard than for him to be lax and allow something, or someone, to slip through the cracks."

"If it was a false alarm, then who were the people walking toward the gate?" Ty asked.

Isaiah hesitated before we heard him chuckle for the first time. I didn't know he was even capable of laughing. I'd always thought of Isaiah as more of a robot than a human.

"It was a group of kids and their parents trying to sell fundraiser discount cards for their soccer team."

Ty burst out laughing, a genuine smile crossing his handsome face. "Those kids probably got the scare of their lives."

Isaiah caught his breath. "We won't have to worry about them coming back, that much is sure."

After Ty hung up, we all exchanged amused glances. The tension in the room dissipated, replaced by a lighthearted atmosphere. It was refreshing. "I'll have to make a donation to their team by way of an apology. Those kids must have been terrified," Ty commented. And that was why I loved him. Even though the people had ignored the warnings and signs not to come near the estate without an appointment, he still felt he should apologize.

"If you guys don't mind, I'm going to get back to it." Ty sat down in his office chair. "I've got some pack business to take care of."

Dominic stood. "That's perfect because I can use the afternoon to train Liza."

I was eager to see if Dominic's training would help me to better control my anger flares. "Sounds good to me." I was determined to make it work, to finally be in charge of my own body.

With that settled, Dominic and I ventured into the clearing in the woods behind the estate. The sun shone brightly through the canopy of fall-colored leaves, casting dappled shadows on the forest floor. Birds sang harmoniously above us, creating a soothing ambiance that was so desperately needed. I was grateful Dominic had chosen the outdoors for my first training session.

He stood in the center of the clearing, his broad shoulders squared back. Even though he'd passed his alpha powers to Ty, his history of dominance was still in his eyes. Without any small talk or further explanations, he began our lesson. "The first step of being able to control an alpha wolf is connecting with your wolf at all times. You have to be fully aware of your wolf at all hours, even when you're sleeping."

"How do I do that?" I failed to understand how someone could consciously connect to their wolf while asleep. It sounded like an impossible task or a riddle.

"It's something you'll slowly learn to do," Dominic said patiently. "We aren't clear about how your balance is, though."

"Balance?" I echoed, not understanding the term.

"Whether you're more omega or more alpha," he clarified. "It's not important right now because the lesson remains the same." He took a step closer, his blue eyes locking onto mine. "You need to learn to recognize where the alpha in you lies." As if to emphasize his point, he patted the center of his chest with his palm. "Find where the alpha is and tap into its presence."

Processing his words, I wondered if he wanted me to try right now. The expectant look on his face told me that he did. I closed my eyes and concentrated on my wolf, trying to imagine the sensations I'd experienced each time my anger flared, when my eyes glowed red and I somehow made the ground shake, and objects levitate.

Minutes passed, and I finally opened my eyes, only to find Dominic standing there with his arms crossed, watching me expectantly. I shrugged helplessly. "It doesn't seem to work."

A pang of disappointment shot through my stomach. I was so hopeful that this training with Dominic would be the answer to controlling my abilities. I bit my lip and tried to fight the tears that threatened to fall. "My wolf is there, but I'm as omega as I've always been. There's no sign of an alpha wolf."

Dominic sighed, rubbing a hand over his stubbled chin. "I guess the theory of you possibly having two wolves inside of you is a bust."

My heart sank. I was utterly defeated and could no longer keep my emotions bottled up inside. Tears spilled, and a sob escaped my throat. I covered my face with my hands, not wanting Dominic to see me crying like a little girl.

"Hey," he said softly, placing a comforting hand on my shoulder, then when it was clear there were more tears, pulling me into his arms for a hug. "We're not giving up. We'll find a way to help you until Isaiah locates your brother. Hopefully, he'll be able to shed some light on things."

I nodded, swallowing the lump in my throat. This wasn't the end, though it sure as hell felt like it.

As we walked back toward the house, my senses suddenly sharpened. My pulse quickened in my ears when I detected another rhythm—faster, more frantic. The scent of malice clung to the air like a heavy fog. I immediately froze in place, my gaze darting around the trees.

"Dominic." I said, grabbing his arm. "Do you feel that? Someone's coming. Is this part of your training? Dominic?"

Dominic frowned, clearly not picking up on what I detected. He stopped in his tracks and looked at me, concern flashing across his face. "I promise, Liza, this is not part of some surprise training. Nobody is supposed to be here unless they somehow got through security, which is highly unlikely."

"Trust me," I said, fear clawing at my chest. "Someone's out there, and it doesn't feel right."

The second the words were out of my mouth, a man burst through the trees, lunging for me with a sinister grin plastered across his face. My instincts kicked in, and the dormant alpha within me roared to life. My vision sharpened as I homed in on my target.

Power surged through my veins, pushing me to protect myself.

"Stay away," I snarled, launching myself at the man, my movements swift and precise.

The attacker seemed taken aback by my sudden ferocity, but he quickly recovered and tried to grab me again. I ducked out of his reach and delivered a powerful kick to his abdomen, sending him stumbling backward.

"Who are you?" I asked with an authority that took even me by surprise. The alpha wolf inside me paced, ready to pounce if needed.

"Doesn't matter," the man spat, recovering from my attack. "You're coming with me!"

"Like hell I am," I retorted, dodging his next attempt to seize me. I landed a solid punch to his jaw, the impact reverberating through my knuckles. What happened next was a blur, my body on autopilot. Fury pulsed through my veins, and the world went black for a moment.

The next moment I was aware of my surroundings, Ty shouted my name and rushed out of the house, followed closely by security guards. His eyes widened when he saw me pinning the man to the ground, hovering over his body like a lion over his prey. One quick glance was all I needed to see that Ty was livid as he stared at the scene.

I glanced over my shoulder at Dominic, who looked more than a little stunned. He pointed at the man and turned to Ty. "He's part of our security team."

# Chapter 25 - Ty

I stared at Liza in disbelief. Her eyes glowed red with fury while she pinned one of our own guards to the ground.

"Restrain him," I barked, my alpha instincts kicking into high gear. I had no fucking clue what had transpired, but there was no reason for Liza to go after someone unless there was trouble. As I moved forward and took her by the arm, her feral gaze met mine, but she slowly softened beneath my touch.

Dad approached, concern and awe evident in his voice when he said, "This guard tried to attack Liza, to take her. And somehow, she heard him coming before I did."

His words settled heavily on my chest. How could this have happened within our own ranks? We'd never, in all my life, had one of our own security guards turn against us. They were our most trusted employees; the ones we depended on to protect our estate and, most importantly, ourselves. This was unchartered territory, and I needed answers.

I was so pissed I was trembling as I turned to face my security team. "Take him inside away from prying eyes. There's no need for anyone else to see this." I gestured toward the house, and Liza slumped against me as her adrenaline left her. Together with Dad, we followed the team into the estate and downstairs to the basement security office.

The guard was unceremoniously shoved into a metal chair, heavy duty handcuffs snapping tightly around his wrists. He grimaced and looked over his shoulder at the guy placing the cuffs, which only pissed me off even more. Did he think that little pinch was anything compared to the hell I was about to inflict on him?

Liza and Dad took seats off to the side while I grabbed another chair, straddling it like I'd seen in countless cop shows. I never thought I'd find myself in such a situation, having to interrogate my own employee. What the hell was going on?

I glared at the guard, suddenly recognizing him. He'd been keeping a close watch on the security cameras, had pointed out the tourists trying to break down the gate to get to Liza. Where did his loyalty lie? Obviously not with the Keller pack.

"Explain yourself," I demanded, struggling to keep my anger in check. "Why did you attack Liza?" I clenched my fists, itching to rip the man's head off but forcing myself to listen instead.

"Check my back pocket," he spat, eyes blazing with defiance.

With a nod from me, one of the security guards cautiously removed a folded sheet of paper, inspecting it for any hidden dangers. Deeming it safe, he handed it over to me.

"What the fuck is this?" I asked, my patience wearing thin.

"It's the price currently on Liza's head for her capture." He sneered, as if he was disgusted by my very presence.

Unfolding the paper, my stomach churned at the sight of Liza's face captured in a screenshot from her televised address, the one where she exposed Castro and discussed her old pack, telling the world that she was an omega. The photo was grainy, but Liza's face was clear enough for anyone to identify her.

So, Hiram hadn't been able to shut down those whispers from the underground after all. If he had, I wouldn't have been staring at a damn traitor who was willing to throw his job away, possibly even his life, depending on my wolf, in order to kidnap Liza.

I focused on the numbers listed beneath Liza's picture. The price on Liza's head was staggering. More than he would make as a member of my security team in five years. Toward the bottom of the page, the call to action was typed in bold face.

**Capture the omega alive, and the reward money is yours, no questions asked.**

My anger boiled over, and without thinking, I lunged at the guard, my hand closing around his throat. The force of my movement sent both him and the chair toppling backward. A guttural growl tore from my lips as the alpha wolf within me took over.

"How dare you have no regard for Liza's safety? How dare you fucking try to kidnap my mate?" I cried, my fingers tightening around his neck. Dad stood but made no attempt to stop me.

The other guards sprang into action, grabbing hold of me. I struggled against them, desperate to break free and exact vengeance on the traitor, but there were too many of them. At least six strong guards held me back, their muscles straining against mine. Through the haze of my fury, I caught sight of Liza slumped in her chair, her energy spent. Her eyes pleaded with me to stop, and for her sake, I forced myself to calm down.

"Fine." I shook off the guards and held up my hands. "I won't touch him." I pointed at the rogue guard, my voice dripping with venom. "But there is no redemption for you. You will rot in jail for betraying your pack, your alpha, and attempting to harm my mate."

The guards dragged the rogue out of the room, leaving Dad, Liza, and me staring at one another in disbelief. I rushed to Liza's side, concern for her replacing the rage that had consumed me just moments before.

"Are you okay? Did he hurt you? I fucking swear if he even laid one finger on you..."

Before she could answer, Dad interjected. "Liza held her own. He didn't get a chance to lay a finger on her."

Relief surged through every muscle in my body, though the threat was far from over. With a bounty that high, there was no telling what people would do to get to Liza. As much as I wanted to expect the best out of people, I'd seen enough in my lifetime to know many would sell their souls for the payment they'd receive from a trafficker.

I paced the room, raking my hands through my hair. "This is a bigger cause for concern. Liza is officially a target. There will be more attempts on her life. It's not a matter of if but when." I stopped, looking at both of them. "We need to send a message, loud and clear, about the severity of punishment that will come down on anyone who tries to harm her."

Liza shook her head weakly. "I think it's pointless. Look at the money being offered." She held up the piece of paper that she'd snatched from the ground at some point. "If you bring public attention to this, it will only put a bug in people's ear, and they'll start questioning if that amount of money is worth the risk. It's too much of an award for some to ignore."

"Fuck." I exhaled. "It just feels like keeping you hidden up at the estate seems like the best plan right now, but I know that's not a long-term solution."

Dad eyed us warily. "Are we sure your team is completely trustworthy? If you have one team member willing to betray you, who else might give it their best shot?"

Liza and I exchanged a worried glance. Greed could make people choose money over loyalty any day. My fist met the wall with a resounding crack, the pain barely registering. Growling, I faced them both, determined.

"Looks like I'll have to do something I've never wanted to do before: use my influence over my team." The heaviness of the decision hung in the air, leaving us all on edge, wondering what would come next and who, if anyone, could be trusted.

I led Liza and Dad up the grand staircase to my office. My mate's life was at stake, and I needed answers. What better way to uncover the truth than going straight to the damn source? Once we entered the office, I gestured for Liza and Dad to sit while I picked up the phone. It was time to call in the staff.

"Send the housekeepers up first," I instructed my assistant before hanging up. I paced back and forth, trying to calm my racing thoughts. The door opened, and the housekeepers filed in, all looking confused.

"Thank you all for coming." I made sure to look each employee in the eye, searching for any hint of dishonesty. "As some of you may know, there's a bounty on Liza's head. I need to know if any of you have heard anything or know someone who might be involved." I paused, letting my words sink in. "I'm not here to punish anyone. I just want to protect Liza."

The housekeepers exchanged glances, but no one spoke up. I could see the fear in their eyes. They were loyal to our family, but this was a dangerous game. Finally, one of the housekeepers, a petite woman named Maria, raised her hand hesitantly.

"Mr. Keller, I... I know someone who's part of the underground," she stammered, tears welling in her eyes. "He knew I worked for your family, and he told me about the bounty. He wanted me to help them get to Liza, but I swear I never agreed. I wanted to tell you, but I was so afraid of putting a target on my own back."

Her confession was like a punch to the gut. I had hoped that none of my employees would be involved, but hearing it confirmed unsettled me. I dismissed the housekeepers, telling them to send in the landscapers next. As they filed out, I knew Maria's tearful expression would haunt me for hours.

"Is there anything we can do?" Liza whispered.

I clenched my jaw but forced a weak smile. "We'll figure this out, Liza. I promise."

The landscapers entered the room, and I repeated my questions. But just like the majority of the housekeepers, no one admitted to knowing anything about the bounty. I thanked them for their time and called in the security detail.

"Listen," I said. "I need to know if any of you have heard anything or been approached by someone from the underground. We already had one person on your team attempt to kidnap Liza. If you have any information, now is the time to come forward."

Silence hung heavily in the air, and my frustration mounted. I needed answers but none were forthcoming.

Finally, I dismissed the security detail and sank into my office chair, resting my head in my hands. "We can't handle this on our own. We need help."

"I agree." Dad shifted in his seat. "Remember, this is why you hired an informant. Sometimes the requirements of alpha stretch beyond our capabilities. You can only do so much, Tyson."

"I know, Dad." I grabbed my phone out of my pocket, my fingers hovering over the buttons. I tried to call Isaiah, but he didn't answer. With a frustrated sigh, I dialed another number. It was time to call in a favor.

"Hello?" Nico's tone was surprised.

"Hey, Nico. It's been a while. Wish I had time for pleasantries, but I'll get straight to the point. There's a bounty on Liza's head, and I need your help. I know you're not our informant anymore, but mine's currently putting out fires all over the damn place. I promise I'll pay you well for this job."

"Give me twenty-four hours, Ty," Nico said. The line went dead before I could thank him, and I set the phone back on the desk.

"Do you think he can make a difference or, at the very least, get to the source of all this?" Liza asked.

"Let's hope so," I said, my heart heavy with worry. It seemed like this was spreading faster than we could keep up with. What if time was running out and I had no way to protect Liza?

I turned my focus to Liza, who was sitting on the couch, her gaze distant and unreadable. I knew she had faced some sort of confrontation before I'd come outside, but I didn't need the details from her. I had the security footage, where I could watch it for myself in full technicolor detail. I walked to the computer and pulled up the camera feed that faced the edge of the woods. Rewinding it a few hours, I pressed play and watched Liza and Dad appear on the screen.

My breath caught in my throat as I watched her movements. She was swift and graceful, like water flowing effortlessly around obstacles. Her body twisted and bent in ways that seemed almost impossible. Even on the grainy video, I could see her powerful alpha nature. It was mesmerizing, and I couldn't tear my eyes away.

"Ty." My father's voice broke through my trance, and I glanced at him. His mouth was turned down in a tight scowl. "I'm concerned about Liza."

My eyes flicked over to the couch, but she wasn't there.

"About what happened out there?" I gestured toward my computer screen.

"It seems she can't grasp how to turn her alpha on and off. It's almost like it comes and goes. That's not normal, Ty. If she can't learn to control this here at home, how can we expect her to handle it in public?"

I stared at him as I tried to come up with an intelligent answer, but I had nothing. "I know, Dad. But what can we do? We're already doing everything we can to protect her and find out who's behind all this. I'm out of ideas."

"I'd hoped the answer would be training her, but she couldn't even find her alpha side, almost like it doesn't even exist."

"Clearly, it does." I closed my eyes and replayed Liza's maneuvers, as she not only protected herself from the guard, but also took him down easily.

Later that evening, I found Liza sitting on the back porch, staring at the woods like she expected someone else to come rushing at her. Her body was tense, her eyes still red from the earlier confrontation. It took a minute before she even noticed I had joined her.

"Oh, I didn't see you." I could barely hear her quiet voice over the gentle rustle of leaves in the wind. "I know you're worried, I can smell it on you."

I looked at her, taking in her stoic expression. But beneath it, fear radiated from her like heat from a fire. My poor mate couldn't even go out in the garden of her own house without being attacked.

"I'm scared. I don't know what's going on," she said, her eyes filling with tears. "It's freaking me out, Ty. I'm trying not to have another fucking meltdown because there's no telling what sort of natural disaster I'll start next."

My heart broke for her, and I pulled her into a tight hug. I wanted to offer her words of comfort, but everything felt hollow on my tongue. I was in over my head and didn't pretend to have answers. One thing was certain, I was failing Liza as her mate, unable to protect her from the danger that was closing in around us.

# Chapter 26 - Liza

The darkness in my bedroom was disorienting when my eyes fluttered open. It seemed late and like I'd slept well past an acceptable time, but the room was darker than I expected it to be. I glanced at the clock on my bedside table and groaned. Already ten thirty in the morning? My body ached from the tension that had settled into my muscles over the last few days. Ever since that rogue guard tried to kidnap me, I hadn't been myself. The overwhelming emotions brewing inside me threatened to tear me apart.

I forced myself out of bed, my limbs stiff and uncooperative. My fingers fumbled with the curtains, and I sighed in relief at the overcast skies. At least now I understood why it was darker than usual. For a split second, I half-expected my omega powers to have worked their magic while I slept, causing an eclipse or some other damn weather phenomenon.

With a heavy sigh, I stretched my arms above my head, trying to coax some life back into my exhausted body.

"Time for a shower," I muttered. The en suite bathroom beckoned, a sanctuary where I could wash away the grime of my emotional turmoil. As the water warmed up, I stared at myself in the mirror, taking in the haggard reflection. My eyes seemed to have sunk deeper into their sockets, the dark circles beneath them a testament to my unrest.

"Son of a bitch," I said quietly, averting my gaze. What a mess I'd become. The energy it took for my anger flares left me drained both mentally and physically. I stripped off my clothes, the fabric sticking to my skin as if even it didn't want to let go. Finally naked, I climbed into the shower, with the hot water cascading over my body and washing away the remnants of sleep. I ran my hands over my body, lathering up with soap and enjoying the pressure on my sore muscles.

My mind drifted to the last time Ty and I had fucked in the shower. His tongue was magical, and the thought of it flicking over my nipples sent a wave of heat to my core. I slid my hands up my stomach and over my breasts, rolling my hard nipples between my fingers. I needed a release. Since my mating with Ty, my hypersexuality had calmed, but if I ignored my body, my needs, it was just as dangerous as a bounty to bring strange men flocking.

A moment focused on my pleasure and no one else's...

cupped my breasts, and then slowly slid my hands down my stomach, my fingertips dancing across my skin. Ty's approval of my body, his words of praise, would be helpful right now. I ran my hands lower, trailing down over my mound. Ah, yes, there was the heat. I slid one finger across my slit, the warmth almost shocking after being in such a deep sleep. The sensation was an immediate relief, a reminder that my body still had the ability to relax with or without Ty's assistance. I slid my hands back up and cupped my breasts again, pulling at my nipples. I closed my eyes and imagined Ty grazing my nipples with his teeth, his tongue dancing around them, his fingers twisting them, and the pain of it sending an arrow of pleasure straight to my clit. I pinched them harder and rolled them between my fingers. The pleasure was growing, the pressure inside me demanding a release.

"Ty," I moaned his name as I slid a hand between my legs, rubbing down the length of my slit. I was already wet, my arousal spiking at the sensation of my fingers on my naked skin.

"Mmm," I groaned, my other hand sliding around my neck as I stroked my clit. The heat of the shower and the teasing of my hands slowly ramped me up, the desire building in my core. My breathing became louder, my chest rising and falling in time with the motions of my hand. I slid my fingers down to my slit, sliding two fingers deep inside me, mimicking the motions of Ty's cock. I pulled them out, swirling them around my clit before plunging back into my pussy.

Pleasure shot through me, each movement amplifying my desire. I massaged my clit with my thumb, rubbing circles around the swollen nub. My other hand slid down to my entrance, pushing two fingers deep inside me, stretching my pussy as much as possible. My moans echoed off the shower walls. I slowly pulled them out, my body begging for a deeper penetration.

I pushed my fingers in again, this time curling them up and stroking my G-spot. The sensation was overwhelming, and my body jerked in reaction to the touch of my fingers. I ran them up and down, rubbing across my clit and sliding deep inside me, then pulling my fingers out to massage my clit again.

"Oh, fuck," I said, my hand a blur between my legs.

I increased the rhythm, my fingers plunging deep inside. Every thrust was accompanied by a moan. I pinched my nipples hard and then let go, the pain-pleasure combination sending a gush of wetness to my soaked center.

I fucked myself with my fingers, sliding in and out, my clit swollen and aching. The pleasure was mounting, my body tightening as I moved faster.

I was close, the orgasm building within me. I pinched my nipples again, this time twisting them as I slid my fingers in and out of my pussy. The pleasure intensified, the tension growing with each thrust.

My body tightened, my pussy clamping down on my fingers as I raced to my orgasm. My breathing was labored, my chest rising and falling as I stroked myself. I pressed my fingers against my clit, rubbing hard as my body spasmed. I let out a cry, my pussy tightening even more as I came. I dropped my head back and let out a scream, then collapsed against the shower wall, my hand still between my legs.

"Fuck," I said, my breathing still harsh.

A smile danced across my lips as my body relaxed, one hand still holding my weight against the wall as the other hand slowly slid out of my core. The water washed over my body, cleaning my thighs of the juices that dripped down them.

After what felt like hours under the soothing spray, my muscles were relaxed, and my breathing eased. I emerged from the shower, wrapped myself in a warm towel, and slowly got dressed. With each layer, I felt a little more put together, but the heaviness in my chest still lingered. I needed food, and maybe someone other than my reflection to talk to.

As I descended the stairs, I was shocked to find Persephone sitting on a bench in the foyer, scrolling through her phone. She wore a light pink jumper with gold accents, and black jeans that made her look like a million bucks. The sight of her momentarily took my breath away, her elegance and grace a stark contrast to my disheveled appearance.

"Didn't expect to see you here," I said, trying to sound casual, but even to my own ears, the words were accusatory.

Persephone looked up, her eyes widening as she took in my weary expression. "You look tired," she observed.

I nodded in agreement, unsure what else I could say. We'd never been close, but part of me longed for her understanding.

"Would you like to have brunch with me?" she asked suddenly, breaking the silence that had settled between us.

I hesitated, not feeling entirely up for company but knowing I couldn't refuse her offer. "Sure." I managed a weak smile.

"Wonderful." Persephone's face lit up. "I was hoping you'd say that. I already asked the chef to prepare a meal for us."

She led me out onto the patio. It was a gray morning, but it wasn't cold. A table with a large bouquet of flowers in its center awaited us. My eyes were drawn to the vibrant colors. They weren't there yesterday.

"Those are for you," Persephone caught my gaze lingering on the blooms. "Dominic told me about the incident with the guard the other day. I thought they might cheer you up."

"Thank you." I was touched by the gesture. It was more kindness than I'd expected from her, seeing as how I was making an utter fucking mess out of my responsibilities as Ty's mate. I appreciated it more than I could express.

We sat in silence for a moment, the air between us thick with unspoken words. Persephone finally spoke up. "I know what's been going on," she said. "I know about your uncontrollable anger flares, and I've been trying to keep my distance to give you time to step into your new role, but it seems you need a bit of guidance."

"Guidance?" I laughed bitterly, the sound hollow even to my own ears. "That's an understatement. Being lady of the pack is one thing, but I'm dealing with a shitload of other stressors all at once."

"Believe me, I can relate in ways others can't," Persephone assured me, her gaze empathetic.

"Really?" I asked, genuinely intrigued. Persephone had always seemed so composed, so untouchable. It was hard to imagine her ever being anything like the wreck I felt like right now.

"Absolutely," she said, a hint of amusement in her eyes. "In fact, there were more stressful moments than I can count. But that's part of the process. Learning to navigate the challenges and come out stronger on the other side."

The chef arrived, balancing a lavish tray laden with an assortment of sumptuous brunch items. My stomach growled when he set it down on the table, revealing delicate pastries filled with rich, melted cheese and ham, a colorful fruit salad accentuated by vibrant mint leaves, and stacks of fluffy pancakes drizzled with maple syrup. The scent of coffee mingled with the sweet aroma of warm cinnamon rolls, beckoning me to indulge. I didn't hesitate.

"Wow." My mouth watered at the sight of the feast before us. "This looks incredible."

"Doesn't it?" Persephone said, her eyes twinkling as we both filled our plates. "Now, while we enjoy this amazing spread, I thought I'd share some stories with you."

I raised an eyebrow, my appetite momentarily forgotten as I braced myself for what was sure to be a series of fairytales. "I'm not sure I have the brainpower for that right now."

Persephone smirked, her eyes dancing with delight. "Oh, I think you might find these particular tales quite enlightening. You see, I didn't always have my 'shit together', as you so eloquently put it. In fact, there were more stressful moments than I can count during my time as lady of the pack... especially at the beginning."

That piqued my curiosity. I was intrigued, despite my initial reluctance. "Please, do share," I said, hoping to glean some insight from her experiences so I didn't feel like such a damn loser. "Maybe I can learn something from your mistakes."

"Very well." A soft laugh escaped her lips as she picked up her fork. "One of the most difficult aspects I faced in my position was the sense of isolation."

"Isolation?" I echoed, surprised. "But you were surrounded by pack members, weren't you?"

There was no judgment in her smile. "A polite way of saying many of the women in the pack would freeze me out. Others were jealous fate had chosen me for Dominic, not unlike Cecily..."

She lowered her voice, as if we were at risk of being overheard. "I've come to realize she was a superficial piece of work. I'm embarrassed to admit she had me fooled. I hate to think of the damage she'd have caused the pack as the alpha's mate. Still, nobody deserves to be used and killed in such a horrific way." Cecily's betrayal was a bitter pill to swallow, and as we ate the chef's amazing spread, we sat in silence for a moment, lost in our own thoughts.

Persephone sipped her coffee, wiping her lips elegantly with her napkin, then resumed our conversation. "There's a certain loneliness that comes with leadership, as I'm sure you've noticed. Although, I had many associates and fair-weather friends. Unlike you, I didn't have a Sabrina in my life—an unwavering female support. Don't take her for granted. It will be important for you to have people you trust. For me, the responsibility of making difficult decisions while projecting an unwavering exterior often led to times of quiet solitude." As Persephone spoke, her voice softened, and I detected a hint of wistfulness in her expression. "I found solace in those rare times of reflection, as well as in Dominic's unwavering support."

"Really?" I asked. The idea of Dominic providing comfort was almost foreign to me, given his intimidating demeanor. Although, he had tried to cheer me up when his alpha training failed the other day. Maybe he had a soft interior he only showed to those he cared for.

"Indeed." Persephone waved her hand dismissively. "Don't get me wrong, it wasn't all sunshine and rainbows between the two of us. Sometimes we fought viciously, but any bad feeling between us had to be put aside to show a united front to the pack."

"Sounds familiar," I muttered under my breath, recalling the heated arguments Ty and I had already engaged in during our short time together.

Persephone's face turned serious. "Then there were all the times I missed out on birthday parties or Sunday family gatherings due to pack duties. It was a lot to adjust to. My marriage wasn't just Dominic and me, the pack had to be taken into consideration in every decision, and how it would affect them."

I never imagined I'd have anything in common with Persephone, never mind a relationship—at least not anything more than formal discussions and pack events. This strange connection bridged a gap between us, and I caught myself looking at her through a new set of eyes. She was much more than the bitch I'd deemed her long ago.

We ate in companionable silence for a few minutes, the delicious flavors of the meal melting away some of my lingering tension. What was Persephone's purpose in sharing those stories with me? Was she simply trying to offer encouragement, or was there something more at play?

"Listen." She set down her fork and fixed me with a serious gaze. "I know it's been difficult for you, adjusting to this life and all it entails, but I also believe that you possess the strength and resilience necessary to not only survive but thrive in your new role."

"Is that so?" I scoffed, my insecurities heavy on my chest. "Because right now, all I feel is overwhelmed and out of control."

"Trust me, Liza." Persephone took me by surprise by reaching for my hand and giving it a reassuring squeeze. "You are capable of more than you realize. And with time, patience, and the support of those who love you, I have no doubt that you'll rise to meet every challenge that comes your way."

The clouds hung low in the sky, casting a somber mood over the patio where I sat with my new mother-in-law. A soft breeze tickled the leaves of the surrounding trees, the gentle rustling providing a calming background noise while I struggled to hold my tongue to keep from sounding like a bitch.

Against my better judgment, I narrowed my eyes at Persephone, my voice laced with annoyance. "I doubt you ever had a group of underground traffickers trying to capture you."

Persephone's smile was kind, almost pitying. "No, and I can't pretend to know what you're going through." She sat back in the chair and folded her hands in her lap. A flicker of sadness crossed her face as she continued. "It was hard for me to adjust during a time when everything was changing within the pack. Dominic was trying to steer the pack into what it is now, to rid the Keller pack of some of the unscrupulous business dealings. There were many things we disagreed on, and we fought viciously on how the pack should be run, but he was my mate, he was the alpha, and I had to trust he was doing the best thing for us and the pack."

I studied her, taking in the vulnerability in her eyes. "It's not an easy role to have, is it?"

Her gaze met mine, earnest and sincere. "I'll be the first to admit that you don't have any direct power over the pack but have to trust that your mate will confide in you and respect your opinions." She looked at me, understanding in her gaze. "As the alpha's mate, you always have eyes on you, so there is no room to slip up. I know it's a lot to take on, and you have more eyes on you than you probably ever imagined. So I can understand why you're melting down."

My cheeks burned with embarrassment, but Persephone waved me off. "I can't imagine what it's like being an omega. Especially an omega with your pack's history. But I know enough about you to know that you can overcome anything if you put your mind to it. You overcame my hesitancy to accept you. You overcame Dominic's betrayal and what he did to your family. You're a fighter, Liza."

Her words were a shock to my system. After all this time of feeling alone and unnoticed by Persephone, she'd been on the sidelines, watching and paying attention to it all. She recognized my pain and was willing to remind me of what I'd overcome. Few people could say that about their mother-in-law. I was surprisingly lucky.

She finished her coffee and winked at me. "Remember, you're not alone. You have a team at your side, ready and willing to hold you up when you feel like crumbling."

I nodded, some of the weight lifting from my chest. The patio suddenly seemed less oppressive, the clouds overhead less suffocating.

"Thank you, Persephone." I smiled as one of the staff members cleared the table. "You've really helped me today. Just having someone to talk to who somewhat understands the pressure I'm under is a relief."

"Of course, Liza." She laughed and gestured to the lavish surroundings. "I'm always here if you need to chat. I have all the time in the world for you."

Just then, my phone buzzed in my pocket. I pulled it out to see a text from Sabrina.

*Are you busy tonight? As the omega fans have gone, how about an evening on the town with your bestie?*

My heart yearned for a night out and a brief escape from everything, but it was a bad idea. After the attempt to kidnap me, there was no way in hell Ty would let me out of his sight. It was worth mentioning to him, though. I looked up at Persephone. Hadn't we just been discussing the importance of maintaining close friendships?

"Please excuse me, Persephone," I said, standing up from the table. I crossed the patio and stepped back into the house, heading upstairs to Ty's office.

I found him hunched over his desk, intently focused on the paperwork scattered across his desk.

He glanced up and smiled when I entered. "Hey, what's up?" His gray eyes searched mine, no doubt hoping I hadn't created more fires for him to put out.

"Sabrina texted me. She wants to go out tonight." I tried not to sound too needy, but I didn't have the energy to pretend I hadn't considered her offer.

Ty dropped his pen onto the desk and leaned back in his chair, crossing his arms. His expression was pensive, his eyes clouded with concern. "I don't think that's a good idea."

"Neither do I." My shoulders slumped in defeat. I was an idiot for even considering Sabrina's offer.

His gaze softened as he studied my face. "What if we put a large security detail on you and you go hang out at Sabrina's place?"

A small smile tugged at my lips, and I nodded. "That's a fantastic compromise."

Ty was still on edge after the kidnapping attempt, but I knew he understood how much I was dealing with. "I don't want you out of my sight," he said. "But I also don't want you locked away like a prisoner. I just want you safe."

I crossed the room and kissed him gently on the cheek. "Thanks, babe. I promise I won't be gone long."

The moment I agreed to go to Sabrina's house, Ty wasted no time in assembling a team of guards to escort me. Four of them, to be exact. As they led me down the front steps of the estate, I tried not to laugh. It felt like overkill, but considering recent events, I wasn't about to complain.

"Try not to worry too much, Liza." Ty's hand was warm on my lower back as we approached a blacked-out SUV.

I shot him a reassuring smile. "I'm not the one worried."

"Have a fantastic time with Sabrina, and tell her I said hello. Also, please make sure she's not being too hard on Bryce." He chuckled and opened the door for me to help me inside, his touch lingering just a little longer than necessary. It was a small gesture, but one that spoke volumes about his concern for my safety.

Once settled into the leather seat, I watched as one of the guards slid into the passenger seat while another took up position beside me. The last guard climbed into the third row, and I gave a wry smile.

"Sure we can't fit a few more of you in here?" I joked, attempting to lighten the mood. My comment was met with stony silence, and I found myself scowling as I turned to look out the window.

Fucking hard asses.

The SUV glided smoothly through the front gates and onto the main road with no issues. There weren't any tourists standing on the side of the road hoping to get a glimpse of me as if I was some fucking movie star.

I leaned my head against the seat and closed my eyes, the hum of the engine lulling me into a peaceful trance.

"Shit!" The security guard's panic jerked me awake.

We hadn't been driving for long when a car suddenly cut us off, swerving in front of the SUV and causing our driver to slam on the brakes. Before I could even process what was happening, two more vehicles skidded to a halt on either side of us. We were trapped.

My heart thundered in my ears as men dressed head-to-toe in black, with masks hiding their faces, leaped from the cars. They wrenched open the doors, and I screamed for help as they grabbed me. I sniffed the air but didn't recognize their scents. They weren't pack members, just a bunch of fucking thugs who wanted to kidnap me and collect their reward.

My guards tried to fight them off, but the attackers were fast and furious, utilizing taser guns and other weapons before my guards had a chance to pull their guns. I watched helplessly as my protectors were quickly overwhelmed.

I struggled against the masked men, kicking and biting in a desperate attempt to break free, but it was no use. Their grip on me was unyielding. As they dragged me from the SUV, I tried to run through my options. Ty had no idea I was in trouble, and my guards were knocked out, if not worse, in the middle of the road.

My anger flared, feeding the omega power that coursed through my veins. "Let me go!" I growled, unable to contain the rage that consumed me. In an explosive release of energy, I sent the men flying through the air, their bodies crashing into trees on the other side of the street.

"Control yourself," a voice whispered inside my head. "Don't let them see your true power."

# Chapter 27 - Ty

I was poring over yet another stack of papers that needed my attention when my phone rang. My instincts were suddenly on high alert, and I felt a strong sense of urgency.

I snatched it up. "What?" I snarled vigorously.

"Ty, it's Rick," the voice on the other end was panicked, and my stomach immediately sank. "Liza's SUV was hijacked, and the guards who were accompanying her were attacked by several masked men."

My blood ran cold. "What the fuck happened? Tell me," I roared, fear and anger threatening to choke me.

"Sir, they came out of nowhere. We're twenty-four clicks northeast of the estate. They boxed in the vehicles. We tried to fight them off, but..." His words caught in his throat.

"Enough. I'm on my way." I didn't wait for him to finish, slamming the phone down and grabbing my keys with trembling hands. My chest was tight, I couldn't breathe, so upset and pissed at myself because I should have said no when Liza asked to see Sabrina. I shouldn't have let her go, no matter how pitiful she looked or how much she needed a break from the mundane life within the estate. Yet again, I'd failed my mate. This was my fucking fault. I'd never forgive myself if something happened to her.

Racing down the steps, my mind swirled with images of what I might find when I reached her. My wolf paced and huffed inside me, just as frantic as I was. The drive to Sabrina's house was one I knew well, but now it seemed like the longest, most arduous journey of my life. I sped out of the gates, barely registering the raindrops beginning to pelt against the windshield.

I pressed my foot down hard on the throttle, the engine screaming, and pushed the car to its limits. The heavens suddenly opened up, and the rain began to pour down, beating against the roof of my car with such intensity that it was impossible to see more than a few feet in front of me.

It had been threatening all day, and only now it decided to start?

"Son of a bitch."

The large amount of surface water meant the roads were dangerously slick, and I had to slow down if I didn't want to risk hydroplaning. I'd be no use to Liza dead.

Traffic slowed to an almost complete stop as visibility worsened. With the windshield wipers rendered useless by the deluge, drivers were left to strain their eyes and peer through their windshields to make out the road ahead. My fury surged, and I considered driving over the middle of the road. Just as that thought crossed my mind, an ambulance raced by in the median, its siren cutting through the sound of the pounding rain. I prayed to the gods that the ambulance wasn't heading to Liza.

My hands tightened on the wheel. The minutes ticked by like hours, each second a painful reminder of my helplessness. "Fuck!" I navigated the congested road, my rage only growing as the traffic refused to let up.

I blamed myself for whatever trouble Liza had found herself in. If I had insisted she stay home, none of this would have happened. The weight of that guilt threatened to crush me. All I wanted was to keep her safe, to protect her at all costs. But now, because of my mistake, she was in danger.

"Come on, come on!" I yelled, willing the car in front to move faster. My wolf snarled inside me, just as desperate to reach our mate. With the rain still pouring down and making visibility difficult, there was nothing else I could do but inch forward painfully slowly, and hope that I would make it to her in time.

Finally, after what felt like an eternity, the traffic cleared, and I raced ahead, my heart pounding against my ribcage. The rain lightened to a drizzle. It was like the heavens themselves were granting me a small reprieve. It wouldn't last long, but it allowed me to increase my speed.

The closer I got to the location Rick had given me, the more my stomach churned with a mounting sense of apprehension and fear. What if I was too late? What if those bastards had already taken her, or worse?

But as much as fear gripped my very soul, I couldn't. No, I wouldn't allow myself to think like that. Liza was strong, and I had to believe that she was still fighting. I'd watched the security feed. I'd seen the way she'd fought that traitorous asshole. If she could just hold on, I was on my way, if she just kept fighting...

"Please let her be okay," I muttered into the damp air, my eyes darting along the wooded road, scouring for any sign of her or the attackers. My wolf echoed my plea, our bond with Liza pulling us forward like a magnet.

Suddenly, the scene came into view, and my heart stopped. The rain had slowed to a drizzle, but it did nothing to lessen the impact of what lay before me.

"Damn it," I cursed under my breath as I slammed the brakes and skidded to a stop. The chaotic scene before me was like something out of a nightmare. Multiple black SUVs were parked haphazardly on either side of the road, their headlights casting eerie shadows. Four men lay on the ground, tied up and writhing in pain.

"Alpha Keller!" one of my team members shouted, running toward me.

"What the hell happened?" I demanded, not waiting for them to reach me. I sprinted over to the nearest SUV, searching for some sign of Liza. Where the fuck was she? If they'd taken her...

It was only when I walked around the car and saw a familiar figure huddled in the backseat that the iron band squeezing my chest loosened. She was wrapped up in a blanket to shield her from the cold. Her gaze was unfocused as she stared off into some unseen void. She looked like she was in shock.

"Liza," I called to her, checking her over for injuries and trying to keep the panic from my voice. But she didn't respond, just continued to stare blankly ahead.

"Boss," one of the guards said, moving to my side. I turned to look at him and recognized fear in his eyes, which wasn't exactly comforting. "You won't believe what happened."

"Spit it out." My patience wore thin. I needed answers, and I needed them now.

"Delta team tried to intercept, but they boxed us in from all sides and we were overwhelmed when the aggressors used tasers to incapacitate. They were just about to make a grab for Mrs. Keller when, according to Jamie, who was still in the SUV with Liza, he said they grabbed her and pulled her out of the vehicle. Her powers went into overdrive. She threw the aggressors high into the air, and they crashed into the trees. They're all pretty banged up, a few of them have injuries that probably require medical attention."

I glanced around at the rest of my security team, noting the way they all seemed to be avoiding looking at Liza. Their expressions were mixtures of fear and uncertainty. We'd tried to keep her abilities under wraps, but it was becoming harder to hide. And now my security team had witnessed just how powerful Liza truly was.

"Listen up!" I barked, calling them all to attention, using my dominance over them. "I want every single one of you to understand something. You are not to whisper a word about what happened here this afternoon to anyone. Not a damn soul. Do I make myself clear?"

They all nodded quickly in agreement, and I turned my attention back to Liza. She still hadn't moved, her eyes glassy. I couldn't stand it any longer. I needed her to snap out of this stupor.

"Get these men to the holding cells," I ordered the guards, gesturing toward the battered kidnappers. They hurried to comply, and I gently lifted Liza up, carrying her from the guard's truck and into my car. I touched her face, trying to coax her back to reality, and I whispered soothing words into her ear.

"It's over now, baby," I told her softly. "I'm here now. You don't have to do anything, just lean on me, okay?"

I fastened her seatbelt and knelt on the pavement, looking deeply into her eyes. Desperate for a connection, I leaned in and kissed her softly on the mouth. It appeared to work because she finally snapped out of her daze.

"Ty?" she groaned, her voice strained as if she'd been screaming, and looked around her as if she didn't know where she was. "What... what happened?"

"You really don't remember?" My stomach twisted.

She shook her head, clearly disoriented, which only added another layer of worry. I needed to get her home where she could rest and recover.

"Let's get you back to the house," I said, starting the engine and pulling away from the scene.

While I drove, I tried to piece together the events of the day, my mind racing with questions. Who were those men? Had Maximus sent them, or were they simply trying to earn a buck? And what would this mean for Liza's safety moving forward?

I couldn't get us home fast enough. The rain had stopped, but I ran red lights and blew through stop signs with my emergency lights on. Each second felt like an eternity, and I silently dared anybody to try and get in my way. Liza needed to be somewhere safe where we could figure out what the fuck had happened.

When I sped down our driveway, I felt a fleeting sense of relief. We were almost there. I parked in front of the main entrance, turned off the engine, and unbuckled my seatbelt before carefully lifting Liza into my arms. She was still so fragile and disoriented, and it killed me to see her like that.

My parents waited for us just inside the door, their worry oozing off them. The moment we entered, Mother stopped pacing and rushed to Liza's side.

She took in Liza's pale face and distant expression, and immediately held her arms out. "Ty, give her to me." There was a gentle authority in her command.

"Mother, I..." I hesitated, unsure of what to do. My instincts screamed at me to keep Liza close, to protect her with everything I had, but my mother's unwavering gaze told me to trust her.

"Trust me with this," she said softly.

Reluctantly, I placed Liza into my mother's care, watching as she cradled her gently and helped her walk up the steps.

Satisfied that Liza was in good hands, I turned to Dad and his grim expression.

"Let's talk," he said, motioning for me to follow him into the library. I trailed behind him, my mind racing as I tried to organize my thoughts and explain what had happened.

Once we were alone, I recounted the events, the ambush, the attempted kidnapping, and Liza's display of power in front of the guards. Dad listened intently, his eyes narrowing.

"None of the men looked familiar." I let out a frustrated growl. "But whoever they were, they knew about Liza, and they wanted her."

Dad crossed his arms and lowered his voice. "This is bad, Ty. We need to figure out who's behind this, and fast."

"You think I don't know that?" I snapped, my fists clenching at my sides. "Liza really can't leave the house again. It's too risky."

"Agreed." My father nodded solemnly. "She won't like it, but after tonight... She'll understand it's a sacrifice that has to be made."

"Fuck," I cursed under my breath. Liza valued her independence. "I want Maximus's head on a spike, if Castro hasn't gotten to him first."

Before either of us could say anything else, my phone rang, piercing the tense silence that had settled throughout the house. I glanced at the screen as Nico's name flashed across it.

"About fucking time," I muttered, swiping to answer the call and putting it on speaker so Dad could listen in.

"You're just the man I need to talk to." I forced my damn tongue to stop wagging so Nico could fill me in.

"Ty, I'm calling to make you aware there was an attempt made on Maximus's life." Nico sounded breathless from whatever had just transpired. "I was at his property in time to save him."

"Shit." I was torn between relief and frustration. "I don't know if you've heard, but there was an attempted kidnapping today. Some assholes tried to grab Liza out of the secure SUV. They were equipped to fight my security team. I want Maximus questioned about this latest attempt. Find out if he knows anything."

"Understood. I'll report back soon." Nico hung up and left me staring at the phone, not knowing what to do next.

The call only added to the weight on my shoulders. As much as I hated to admit it, I needed answers from Maximus. If he was involved in the attack on Liza, I wanted to know. And if not, I needed to find out who else was targeting her before it was too late. This attempt was too organized for it to be civilians out for a bounty.

I paced the floor, cracking my knuckles as the pressure threatened to consume me. The bounty on Liza's head was a problem, and we needed to figure out how to solve it before it got any worse.

"Ty..." My mother's hushed whisper reached my ears, pulling me from my thoughts. She had come downstairs and now stood near the doorway. "You can breathe easy. Liza is in bed. She was clearly spooked, but she just needed a maternal touch."

"Thank you, Mom," I said, pressing a gentle kiss to her forehead. The softness of her hair brushed against my lips when I pulled away. I was more than thankful for the woman who had always been there for me and who had accepted Liza as if she were her own.

I strode upstairs and toward our bedroom, my lungs tightening with each step. My mind raced with images of what I might find when I opened that door. Would she be curled up in the bed, still shaken from her ordeal? Or would she be sitting up, her eyes full of questions and confusion?

As I listened for any indication of Liza being awake, my hand gripped the doorknob. I was surprised to see the opposite. The bed was empty; the sheets rumpled and abandoned. Panic clawed at my insides, my pulse quickening as I scanned the room for any sign of Liza.

"Where the hell is she?" I muttered under my breath, my stomach churning with dread. Just as I was about to call out her name, movement caught my eye, a flash of something on the terrace beyond the glass doors. I stepped closer, squinting through the dim light until I made out Liza's slender silhouette.

She must've realized I was behind her because she turned to face me. "It's fine, Ty. You don't have to tiptoe around me. I won't toss you in the air like the others."

A heavy sigh escaped my lips. She remembered. That was one less thing to discuss.

"Hey," I said, wrapping my arms around her from behind and pulling her close, breathing in her scent. She tensed at first but gradually relaxed into my embrace as I cradled her against my chest. "You won't hurt me, Liza. I know you won't. And we'll find a way to help you, I promise. Just trust me, all right?"

"Okay," she said, nodding as she buried her face in my shoulder. I could feel her tears seeping through the fabric of my shirt, and it only fueled my determination to make everything right for her again.

"Come on," I said finally, giving her a gentle squeeze before releasing her from my embrace. "Let's get you back to bed. You need some rest."

I led her back to the empty bed, sorting the sheets and gesturing for her to climb in. She hesitated for a moment before complying, settling down beneath the sheets with a weary sigh. I noticed the lingering tremble in her limbs, the haunted look in her eyes as she gazed up at me.

"Try to get some sleep," I said, brushing a stray lock of hair away from her forehead. "I'll be right here if you need me."

"Thank you," she said as her eyelids fluttered closed. I watched her for a moment longer before turning off the lights.

Now, more than ever, I needed to figure out some way to help Liza. But what if it was already too late?

# Chapter 28 - Liza

Hunger gnawed at my insides as I stood in the kitchen, fridge doors wide open, staring mindlessly at the array of food. My stomach growled, reminding me that it desperately needed something more than a few swigs of water. But for some reason, I just couldn't focus on what to eat. All I could think about was the conversation I'd had with Ty earlier that morning.

He said I was officially on lockdown. No leaving the house, not even to step outside on the back porch for fresh air. It simply wasn't safe. I studied his face closely and there was a hint of remorse, but mostly his eyes were set and his voice firm.

In Ty's defense, he'd gone out of his way to say how sorry he was and how he recognized it would be difficult since I valued my independence so much. His words went in one ear and out the other, though. I was numb. This would be my new reality.

The irony of my life hit me like a slap in the face as a humorless laugh escaped my throat. I glanced around to see if anyone was around, but I was alone in the massive kitchen.

Not that I was completely surprised. Honestly, given everything that had happened, I didn't even have the energy to care. After almost being kidnapped twice in a matter of days, leaving the house seemed like the least of my priorities.

A throat cleared behind me, making me jump. I turned to see a staff member staring at me and blinking rapidly. She seemed nervous about interrupting me. "Ms. Sabrina is here to see you. She's waiting for you in the library, Mrs. Keller."

"Thanks." I forced a smile and tried to sound calm and completely in control of my life. Who was I fucking kidding? You'd have to blind not to see what a mess I was.

As I walked toward the library, I thought about the call I'd made to Sabrina, explaining why I never showed up at her house last night. She was in tears while I explained the situation, so I wasn't surprised she'd decided to come see me.

Rounding the corner, I found Sabrina pacing the floor of the library, her anger palpable.

"Hey, you didn't have to come over." I spoke gently, hoping she'd react calmly. "I promise, I'm fine."

She spun and ran to me, throwing her arms around my neck and squeezing all the air out of my lungs. I let out a little laugh and peeled her off me. The moment our eyes met, it was obvious Sabrina was more than a little pissed.

"Oh shit," I mumbled quietly, my heart sinking.

"Oh shit is right," Sabrina said, glaring over my shoulder.

I turned to see Ty standing in the doorway of the library, his expression unreadable.

"Tyson Keller," Sabrina spat out as she tore off in his direction, pointing her finger at him accusingly. "You better explain what the fuck is going on and why my best friend was almost kidnapped."

Ty opened his mouth to speak, but I interjected, putting my hands on Sabrina's shoulders, trying to calm her down. "Hey, hey. Take it easy, Sabrina. This isn't Ty's fault. Truly. It's not."

But Sabrina was livid, and when she got this wound up, there was no stopping her. She glared at Ty, each word dropping like a bomb between them. "None of this insanity started happening until your wolf moon magic shit put Liza in your path. Now your enemies are targeting her." She wiped her tears on the back of her arm as her breath caught in her throat. At that point, she was full-blown sobbing, and I couldn't remember the last time I'd seen my best friend that upset.

I wanted to say something to defend Ty, but Sabrina was right—all my troubles had started after Ty and I realized we were fated mates, and that hurt more than I cared to admit. I clenched my jaw and tried to keep my composure, but all I felt like doing was screaming and running out of the room like a toddler throwing a temper tantrum. Was it acceptable for the alpha's mate to completely lose her fucking mind and curl up in the fetal position of her bedroom?

"Look." Ty was obviously frustrated but determined to convince Sabrina of his innocence. "I never meant for any of this to happen, but we're in this together now, and I'm going to do everything in my power to protect Liza. You know more than anyone how much I love Liza. I'd never intentionally put her safety at risk."

"Words are cheap, Ty," Sabrina shot back, her eyes never leaving his. "Actions speak louder."

Ty's expression hardened as he took a step closer to Sabrina, now pointing his finger at her. There was no way he would stand by and let anyone, even my best friend, portray him as a lousy mate.

Just then, the front door opened with a loud bang, and all three of us bolted out of the library to see what the hell was happening. A roughed-up man stumbled through the entrance, with Nico right behind him, followed by another man I also didn't recognize. The guy in the center had his hands tied in front of him as Nico and the other guy gripped his upper arms to keep him from bolting.

Before Ty could ask questions, Nico gestured to his assistant. "This is one of Isaiah's guys."

Ty studied the man for a second before exploding in rage. "Who the fuck are you? And where is Isaiah? He's been MIA for days."

The man stared at Ty with wide, terrified eyes, obviously not used to being in the presence of an alpha. "Sorry, Mr. Keller, sir. I'm Graeme North. Isaiah sent me in his place. He told me to pass along a message. He's neck deep in his investigation but will follow up with you shortly."

Ty scowled. "He sure as fuck better follow up with me shortly. What kind of informant disappears for days on end and doesn't even show up when the alpha's mate is almost kidnapped in the middle of town for every damn person to see?"

I studied the man who was restrained, his wild hair sticking out in all directions and clothes covered with dirt. There was something about his expression, desperation and cunning, that made me uneasy. I glanced at Ty, trying to gauge his reaction. Who the hell was he?

I watched Ty step closer to the stranger.

"Maximus," he spat, his voice dripping with disdain. The tension in the room built as Ty narrowed his eyes at him. He moved even closer and lowered his head so that he was eye to eye with Maximus. "You've gone too far. Did you think I wouldn't know immediately that it was you?"

"Ty, what the hell are you talking about? Why the fuck are your goons pulling me out of my place and dragging me here?" Maximus sputtered, his face contorting with confusion and fear.

"Cut the crap, Maximus." Ty growled. Though I couldn't see his face, I imagined it must have been twisted into a snarl.

I took a step back, suddenly worried Ty might lose control and attack the poor bastard.

"I'm fully aware that you're to blame for the kidnapping attempts." Ty turned and gestured in my direction. "You know what I'm fucking talking about... the ambush on Liza's SUV yesterday."

"Look, I didn't send anyone to kidnap your mate. I swear." Maximus's voice cracked as he shook his head violently.

"Maybe not, but you're the one who planted the seed. You stirred up everyone's interest in Liza's omega powers and how much she'd be worth. Your efforts to gain power and build your fucking casino brought about this mess. Liza's innocent in all this, yet she's trapped like a damn rat in her own home because of *you*."

My breath hitched. So, this was the piece of shit responsible for putting the bounty on my head. This was the person who had set off a chain reaction of events that had nearly cost me my life. I stared at Maximus, with his hands tied in front of him, while Nico and Isaiah's assistant held him in a submissive position. My hands balled into fists as my anger resurfaced. That bastard had caused me so much pain and anguish. Now, what would Ty do about it?

"Ty, please," Maximus pleaded, his eyes wide with terror. "I didn't mean for any of this to happen."

"Save your fucking breath." Ty turned to Nico. "Lock him up. I'll deal with him later. We've got more important things to discuss."

Nico and Graeme dragged Maximus away, and his frantic pleas for mercy echoed through the halls.

Ty took a deep breath and turned to face Sabrina. "I'm sorry, but this is pack business. You'll have to excuse us."

Sabrina's face twisted, clearly unhappy at being dismissed so abruptly. "Fine," she huffed, shooting Ty a glare that would've made anyone else quiver in their boots. "But I'll be waiting for Liza in the entertainment room. And if you think you can keep me away from her when she needs me, you're very much mistaken. You may be the alpha of the pack, Tyson Keller, but I'm not pack. She so much as sighs the wrong way and I'll come running."

"Understood." Ty rubbed his forehead and shut his eyes, staving off a headache.

Sabrina spun on her heel and stalked out of the room, leaving us to stare at each other in silence.

As we stood there, trying to process everything that had just happened, my anger simmered barely below the surface. It wasn't raging to the point I'd pick Isaiah's assistant up and chuck him across the damn house, but it was there, and it was palpable. How dare Maximus put my life and the lives of those I cared about in danger for his own gain? What kind of alpha did that? He was a fucking monster and deserved whatever punishment Ty deemed fit, and if Ty couldn't think of one, I was certain I could think of two or three.

"We need to ensure he never does anything like this again. We can't let him hurt anyone else."

Ty moved to my side and wrapped his arms around me. "I promise you I'll handle Maximus and make sure he pays for what he's done."

"Good." A sharp pain shot through my jaw as I gritted my teeth a little too hard. We watched the security detail open the basement door to take Maximus down to the cells. "Because if he thinks he can get away with this, he'll just keep taking advantage of others for his own advantage."

In a split second, Maximus twisted and lunged forward, breaking his hands free and escaping Nico and Graeme's grasp with unnerving ferocity and speed. He was on Ty before anyone had time to react, his nails slashing across Ty's face. I gasped and covered my mouth, pressing my back against the wall to avoid being caught in the crossfire of their brutal struggle.

"Get off me, you bastard," Ty snarled as Maximus thrashed and scratched at him.

Ty's growl cut through the chaos, his primal instincts taking over. He swiftly retaliated, flipping Maximus onto his back and straddling him with so much force I wondered how Maximus's ribs couldn't be broken. The rapid fire of Ty's punches rained down on Maximus, each strike carrying a visceral intensity. My stomach churned as I watched the brutal exchange.

Blood spurted with each hard punch, and Maximus's pained moans echoed in the air. My hands shook as I wiped away tears that had escaped without my notice. The sight of Ty's unbridled rage shocked me to my core, his every blow laced with a raw fury I'd never seen before.

"Stop! Ty, stop!" I cried out, but my voice was barely audible over the sounds of the brawl.

Nico and Isaiah's assistant rushed to Ty's side, attempting to intervene, but it was too chaotic. Ty's punches came in quick succession. His words were incoherent, alternating between enraged shouts and curses. He growled with each strike, his rage consuming him.

"Ty, that's enough! You're going to kill him," Nico's voice rose above the chaos, his words desperate and urgent, warning Ty that he was on the brink of crossing a line he couldn't come back from. He kept moving toward Ty, wanting to stop him, but he couldn't. Ty's swings were so wild and unpredictable, Nico would surely get knocked out if he tried to intervene.

Sabrina came to the door, and I saw her face pale. Her eyes caught mine. I shook my head and held up a hand. She needed to stay back.

Nico made one final plea, yelling above the chaotic screams. "If you kill him, you'll never get to the bottom of everything and save Liza from those who want to kidnap her! You're about to murder your key witness!"

Nico's plea seemed to penetrate Ty's uncontrolled anger. His blows gradually slowed, the momentum of his assault weakening. He stared down at Maximus's battered face, his chest heaving with exertion, and the realization seemed to dawn on him.

Nico and Isaiah's assistant lunged forward, separating Ty from Maximus's broken form. The aftermath was a chaotic scene of gasping breaths and the harsh rasp of Ty's labored breathing. My cheeks were wet with tears, my body trembling.

Maximus was alive, but the floor looked like a fucking murder scene.

A knock at the door came so suddenly that it startled us all. Ty let out a frustrated laugh. He threw his bloodied hands in the air. "What the hell else could be going on?"

Nico and Isaiah's assistant scooped Maximus from the floor and ran at superhuman speed to the basement door, disappearing into the dark and closing the door behind them.

"Police. Open up!"

Ty's eyes widened as we both surveyed the blood. There was no time to hide it, so Ty motioned for me to stand in front of it. "We'll try to block their view. It's the best we can do."

He flung the door open to reveal two stern-faced police officers on the other side. They both stood with their hands on their hips and looked far too official for us to imagine they were simply making rounds in the neighborhood.

They took in Ty's appearance, obviously stunned to see the alpha of the Keller pack opening his own door and looking like he'd just been run over by a Mack truck.

One of them raised an eyebrow. "Are you okay, sir?"

Ty faked a laugh. "I guess you're wondering why I look like this." Ty gestured up and down his body. "I had a bit of a mishap in the woods this afternoon. Let's just say I'm too old to climb trees and assist our gardener. I'm not as nimble as I once was."

The police officers shared a glance and then turned their attention back to Ty. They didn't ask any questions, obviously suspicious and allowing Ty to lead the conversation.

"Thank you both for taking the time to swing by. We don't need any help with the kidnapping attempt. We've got it under control. But if I think of a way you can be of assistance, I'll contact you." Ty gripped the door handle, ready to close it in their faces.

One of the cops looked Ty up and down as if he had two heads. "Kidnappings?" The officer glanced at his partner again before continuing. "Sorry, Mr. Keller, that's not why we're here. We've come to discuss a situation at one of your factories. We executed a search and found a substantial quantity of drugs."

My mouth dropped open in disbelief. The Keller pack didn't deal in drugs—Ty and his father assured me they didn't.

"Drugs?" Ty cocked his head to the side, clearly shocked by the accusation. "That has to be a mistake."

"A building inspector attended the Keller Enterprises factory located at 223 Poplar Street earlier today, regarding a sale of the property," the other officer explained, his tone serious. "During his inspection, he found a significant amount of illegal substances on the property."

Ty's face darkened, and I watched as the anger boiled beneath the surface. "You've clearly made a mistake," he spat through gritted teeth.

"Regardless," the first officer said, unfazed by Ty's growing agitation, "we need you to come down to the station for questioning."

"Fine," Ty relented. "I give you my word as alpha of the Keller pack that I'll comply. I'll present myself to the police station in town under my own recognizance." He glanced down at his bloodied, disheveled appearance and back at the officer. "I'm sure you understand?"

The officers exchanged glances before nodding and departing, leaving the door wide open in their wake.

I hesitated to speak up, afraid I'd break the delicate balance between Ty keeping his cool and completely losing his shit. "What's going on?"

He shook his head. "I have no fucking clue. But I intend to find out." He touched his bleeding lip and scowled. "Guess I'll get cleaned up before driving to the warehouse to get some answers."

When Ty ran upstairs to take a quick shower, I slumped into a chair in the corner, staring at the remnants of Ty's fury on the floor. Drugs? I tried to wrap my head around the accusation.

There was no way the Keller pack was involved in that kind of thing. Right?

# Chapter 29 - Ty

Steam filled the bathroom, and I stepped out of the shower, the hot water having done little to calm my nerves. Grabbing a towel, I wiped the foggy mirror and looked closely at my reflection. My face bore the marks of a brawl, bruised and battered, but alive. Maximus was in much worse shape, his pathetic life spared only by Nico's intervention. If it weren't for him, I'd have ended that bastard without a second thought.

"Yet another fucker I should have killed when I had the chance," I muttered, pulling on jeans and a sweatshirt. The familiar weight of my wallet, keys, and watch reassured me as I checked the time. There should be enough of it to run by the warehouse and get some answers before dealing with the police at the station.

Drugs in my factory? What the hell?

Descending the stairs two at a time, I found Liza where I'd left her, sitting in the same spot, looking fragile and pale. Two housekeepers were on their hands and knees, scrubbing away the bloodstains from the hardwood floor. I scowled. "Sorry about the mess. I promise you'll receive a bonus with your next paycheck. Just be sure to keep this to yourselves."

They smiled hesitantly, scrubbing harder and faster, clearly eager to erase all traces of the violence that had occurred.

"Hey," I said softly, sitting down next to Liza. "I... uh, have to go deal with this warehouse situation. I have to clear my name before this reaches the news. If the media catches wind of drugs at a Keller business, we'll never bounce back. It will completely destroy our family name and make the pack look like drug handlers."

Liza glanced at me, her eyes clouded with worry. I cupped her head gently, turning her face toward mine. "I don't want to leave you, babe, but I have to handle this. I'll be back soon and then we'll talk."

"I get it. It's fine. Just go," she said as she stared off into space.

"Look, Nico will be here, and the security guards are on high alert. Try to get some rest, okay?" I knew that was easier said than done.

She grunted in response, not meeting my gaze. I couldn't blame her—she had a lot on her mind.

"Nothing's changed, Liza. We'll deal with all of this, I promise. We're a team, and before we know it, this entire nightmare will be a distant memory." I gave her a lingering kiss before standing to leave.

The engine roared to life, and I headed toward the warehouse, my mind racing almost as fast as the car. I needed answers, and quickly. Grabbing my phone, I dialed Bryce.

A groggy voice answered. "Hey, man. What time is it?"

"Are you fucking kidding me, Bryce? Did I wake you?"

"Ah... yeah, late-night rendezvous. You know how it is." I could practically hear him smirking through the phone.

"Of course. Why did I even ask? Listen, you won't believe what's happening. Looks like you missed some calls from our factory manager."

He sounded fully awake now. "Really? What the fuck's going on?"

"Police came by the estate this afternoon and said they found drugs at the factory on Poplar Street."

"Shit. That's serious."

"Tell me about it. Get your ass out of bed and meet me there."

"All right, on my way."

I pulled into the factory parking lot for the third time in a week. The lack of cars struck me as odd. It was midafternoon, the lunchtime shutdown was long past. This place should have been bustling with activity, but now it seemed abandoned. I got out of the car and walked toward the entrance as I caught sight of the manager just inside the door. He looked flustered, his face white as a sheet as he sprinted toward me.

"Mr. Keller, I'm so sorry. I tried calling you several times." He stammered over his words and looked like a kid who'd been caught with his hand in the cookie jar.

"Save it. What's going on?" I held up my hand, silencing him as I surveyed the eerily quiet warehouse. The machines were silent, and there were hardly any employees in sight. "Why is no one working?"

"Uh, well, after the incident, we sent everyone home," he explained nervously.

"The police filled me in on the drugs. Why didn't you call me as soon as they were found?"

"I did try, sir. Several times, actually."

I realized that amidst the chaos with Liza's kidnap, then Maximus, I hadn't even noticed the missed calls. "Fine, let's talk in your office."

He led me to the same cramped office where we'd reviewed the security footage after the fire, and offered me a seat, which I declined. Instead, I paced the floor, my anger mounting with every step.

"A building inspector came in this morning," he began, fiddling with some paperwork on his desk. "He said he was here to inspect the building and equipment because a client was interested in purchasing the factory. But now... I'm not sure if he was who he said he was."

"Get to the point," I snapped. "Why do you think that?"

"Because he's the one who found the drugs taped underneath some of the production lines," he stammered, hands shaking, "And after he left, I realized he never left his name."

Rage bubbled up inside me as I clenched my fists tightly. "We don't deal in drugs. How could this have fucking happened?" I roared.

Just then, Bryce knocked on the office door. Instead of motioning for him to come in, I stormed past him without a word. My rage was threatening to consume me, but I couldn't let it. There was too much at stake. Who the fuck was this inspector?

"Ty, wait up!" Bryce called, running to catch up with me. "What the hell is going on?"

"Get in my car," I barked, jaw clenched. "I'll explain on the way to the police station."

Bryce followed me without another word, and we both got into my black SUV. The engine roared to life as I hit the gas, speeding down the road toward our destination. I kept one hand on the steering wheel and raked the other through my hair as I filled Bryce in.

"Drugs, huh?" he said, trying to lighten the mood with a smirk. It took every ounce of my self-control not to punch him right then. He was just making an attempt at joking around, but this wasn't the time for humor.

"This isn't a fucking joke, Bryce," I growled through gritted teeth. "If we can't clear our name, we're all in a ton of shit. There were drugs strapped to the assembly lines."

"Shit," he muttered, his playful demeanor dropping instantly. The severity of the circumstance dawned on him as he ran his hand down his face. "We're fucked."

"Not if I can help it. I have to answer the police's questions and try to explain the situation." I cleared my throat and turned onto the street that housed the police station. "The question is, will they believe me?"

We skidded into the station parking lot, tires screeching against the pavement. I didn't bother waiting for Bryce as I marched past the front desk receptionist and straight to the lead detective—the same one I'd given Cecily's phone to just weeks before.

I simmered with unbridled anger and stormed through the building, no one daring to approach me. I entered the detective's office unannounced.

The man rose up from behind his desk. "Mr. Keller, I've been expecting you." If I wasn't mistaken, a smirk flashed across his face as if he'd been waiting for this moment. It was unusual for a human to throw his authority over an alpha shifter. This was one of the first times my position meant nothing, and there was

537

not a damn thing I could do about it other than hope my reputation stood for something and beg for understanding.

"Detective," I said with a curt nod.

Bryce followed me in, closing the door behind him. He took a seat next to me, staying silent and letting me take the lead. When the detective opened his mouth to speak, I held up a hand, stopping him mid-sentence.

"Surely you know the reputation my family has here in Presley Acres," I began. "None of my companies have ever had drugs on their premises. All potential employees undergo a thorough background check before they are hired, and we also conduct random drug tests."

The detective straightened his back and regarded me with narrowed eyes. "We'll need an official statement from you, Mr. Keller. Please, follow me." He led us down the hall to a small room containing only a table and a couple of chairs. "Would you like an attorney present?" His gaze flickered between Bryce and me.

I considered his offer for a moment before shaking my head. "No, my answers will be the same regardless, and I'm confident that you'll see my company's innocence in all this."

Hours passed as they questioned me relentlessly. Why had I been to the factory earlier in the week? Was that when I had hidden the drugs there for later distribution? They enquired about my involvement with the day-to-day running of the factory. The company's drug policies, how they were enforced. They wanted to know details about the business and my employees. I answered every single question.

I was furious at this latest development—I needed to get back to the estate. I was worried about Liza, so was my wolf, who was pushing me to return home to my mate. The memory of her sitting on the floor with her head in her hands was killing me inside. She'd looked so lost.

Then there was Maximus. I was itching to spend some more time with that fucking bastard. The beating I had given him was just the tip of the iceberg—there was much more to come. I needed to know exactly with whom he'd shared information about Liza.

The room was hot and stuffy, and the detective was being a jerk. They kept drilling me with the same questions, trying to catch me in a lie or a contradiction. I felt like I was being put through a test of endurance and mental strength.

I told them I believed someone had deliberately sabotaged our warehouse in an attempt to incriminate me. "What about the building inspector who visited this morning? Have you questioned him?"

Their faces remained impassive. "We don't know who he is, and we have no way of tracking him down, as the manager at your factory didn't ask for his name or ID."

Fucking manager. The disgruntled employee had a point. The management at that factory sucked. I'd deal with him later. "Look through our security camera footage from the factory." I was desperate to clear our name, and surely the police could identify the fucker if he was caught on tape.

"We've already done that." There was a slight hint of impatience in his voice, obviously tired of going round and round in damn circles and getting nowhere with me. "The guy kept his head at an angle so the cameras didn't pick up on his face."

"Fuck," I muttered under my breath. "He knew exactly what he was doing. Can't you see how obvious this is? Someone posed as a building inspector and planted drugs in my facility. What might look like him retrieving the drugs could have very well been him pretending to take the tape of them. Please tell me you're going to look into this." I squeezed the bridge of my nose, hoping to the gods that they'd take my words into consideration without automatically placing the blame on the Keller name.

When they finally dismissed me, I left the station with my head held high. I had done everything in my power to clear my name, and the detective said he'd be in touch. Surely, if he thought I was guilty, he wouldn't just let me walk free. If they believed me, I would have succeeded in clearing our name.

When Bryce and I walked out of the police station, a car screeched into the parking lot. To my shock, Isaiah emerged from the vehicle, sprinting toward us. My initial surprise quickly turned to anger.

"Where the fuck have you been?" I demanded, my fists clenching at my sides.

"Ty, I'm so sorry," Isaiah panted heavily, trying to catch his breath. "I swear I'm going to explain everything. I called my assistant to arrange a meeting with you. He told me about Maximus going after Liza, and the police coming to the estate, and he told me where to find you. When the warehouse parking lot was empty, I assumed you'd come here. Thank fuck I found you. I have some important information that needs to be delivered in person. I couldn't risk calling you in case someone's tapping into your cell phone."

"Start talking. Explain yourself, and do it fast." I crossed my arms and glared at my informant, who had been gone for days with no word. He'd forced me to reach out to Nico. It made me look like I had no control over my employees. It didn't make me look good, and I wasn't happy about it. Whatever information Isaiah had, it had better be fucking well worth it. I was not in the mood for this shit,

Isaiah took a deep breath before dropping the bombshell. "Liam is not a man to be fucked with. Liam Russell could not be found because Liam Russell no longer exists. At some point, he legally changed his name from Liam Russel to Mika Liam Petrov. Petrov is his biological mother's maiden name. He buried it deep. When I started to uncover the link to Petrov, I had to go blackout. That's why I couldn't risk contacting you."

The moment the name Petrov left Isaiah's lips, alarm bells went off in my head. I was very aware of the Petrov empire and their dirty dealings.

"Holy fucking shit." I tried to wrap my mind around this new information. Suddenly, the drugs in the factory made sense. Liam Russell, as the prospective buyer, had a right to send in a commercial inspector to assess the property before purchasing, which meant he could set me up by using the inspector to plant the drugs for the inspector to 'find'—if the fucker had even been a true inspector.

My body vibrated with rage as the truth washed over me. Liza's brother had set me up.

"Fucking hell."

"I read the file you gave me on the Wylde pack, and it appears Liam is following in his biological father's footsteps." Isaiah rested his hands on his hips. "This is much more serious than we ever imagined."

"I know the types of deals Petrov is involved with. He's not a man I'm interested in getting involved with. Any business transactions with him could only lead to trouble... much like Dad did with Liam and Liza's father.

"Let's move." I quietly motioned for Isaiah and Bryce to step aside as a few police officers exited the station. We required privacy to continue our conversation. The last thing I needed right now was an officer overhearing the dark shit we were discussing. So we walked down from the station to the far corner of the parking lot.

"All right, Isaiah. Tell me everything you've been doing, and it better be damn good."

Isaiah glanced around to ensure no one was within earshot. "Getting information on Mika Petrov wasn't easy. It was clear he didn't want anyone to find the connection between him and Liam Russell."

My wolf growled in frustration at the situation we found ourselves in. I clenched my fists, struggling to maintain control. "Go on."

"Essentially, the paper trails don't connect. The Russell empire is being run by a man named Deacon Wallace who's never even met Liam. It's Deacon who sends Isabel her yearly dividends, but this was all set up as a trust before Wallace started. He's been left to run the company with no input from Russell. When Liam disappeared, he left the bank account in his name open. It's been unused, until Liza made her appearance on TV, and we can only assume Petrov saw the report and discovered she was alive, because..." Isaiah paused, his expression grave. "Just after Liza's appearance, Deacon got a call from Liam. It was short and to the point. Deposit money into the old account, which belonged to his father. The one Liza now has control of."

"Other than that?" I prompted, my mind racing with the implications of this information.

"Other than that, Liam was a ghost. But Mika... Mika was making a name for himself in the world." Isaiah's eyes filled with concern. "He's dangerous, Ty."

I stared at Isaiah, my thoughts swirling like a tornado. How had we gotten ourselves tangled up in this mess? And how the hell were we going to get out of it?

"Thank you, Isaiah. I appreciate your hard work. Now we need to figure out our next move."

Isaiah nodded, his expression full of sympathy. "I just wanted to make sure you knew what you're dealing with, Ty. This won't be an easy fight."

"Thanks for the heads-up," I said. While Isaiah and Bryce continued discussing the situation, I pulled out my phone, desperately trying to reach Liza, but she didn't answer. I tried Robin, the head of Liza's security detail, but still no response.

Panic clawed at my throat, and I moved farther away from the police station without a word, leaving Isaiah and Bryce behind. I had to get to Liza. I had to make sure she was safe.

"Damn it," I muttered under my breath, feeling the hairs on the back of my neck stand on end. Surely she was safe at the estate. Nico was there, along with a veritable army of guards. I tried calling her again, my heart hammering in my chest when the phone went unanswered once more.

"What's wrong?" Bryce moved closer, his eyes narrowed as he watched me intently.

"Something doesn't feel right. I can't get a hold of Liza."

"Maybe she's just busy," Isaiah suggested, though I could hear the uncertainty in his voice.

"I hope that's it." I knew better than to ignore my instincts, especially when it came to Liza's safety. I dialed the number for the guard's office at the estate, praying that one of them would pick up. "Come on, come on," I muttered, my unease growing when the call went unanswered. My anxiety was a living, breathing being.

"Fuck!" I snarled, feeling my control slipping away as my wolf threatened to surface. "No one's answering."

In a last-ditch effort, I tried calling Dad, hoping he'd be at home and could run over to the estate to check on everyone. No answer. I ran to my car and jumped in, speeding out of the parking lot, leaving Bryce and Isaiah behind with no explanation.

# Chapter 30 - Liza

After Ty left, I trudged to the entertainment room where Sabrina had been instructed to stay. With each tentative step, my eyes darted back and forth between the contrast of the pristine walls and the wet floor that the staff diligently scrubbed to get rid of the blood. My nose wrinkled at the lingering metallic scent in the air, a reminder of the fact my husband had almost murdered a man before my fucking eyes.

Maximus's faint screams echoed from the direction of the basement, or maybe it was just my imagination playing tricks on me, just like the mysterious voice that haunted my thoughts. My life had been turned upside down in the past few days, and I was struggling to process everything. It was as if my brain was kicking into survival mode, almost like autopilot. I didn't want to think about any of it.

When I finally reached the entertainment room, I found Sabrina curled up on the couch next to the fireplace. Her petite frame was dwarfed by the plush cushions, and she rubbed her arms like she was cold, despite being only a few feet from the blazing fire. I sat next to my best friend and reached for her hand.

Our fingers intertwined, and we sat in companionable silence, staring into the dancing flames.

"I guess you're staying here tonight," I said at last, breaking the quiet. "There are probably a hundred men standing guard, so it's safe." As the words left my lips, I realized I was trying to convince myself as much as Sabrina.

She scoffed, her blue eyes narrowing skeptically. "Safe? Am I truly safe from the animal being held hostage in your basement?"

"Maximus is locked up behind bars until Ty and his council can deal with him." I hoped she could hear the conviction in my voice.

Sabrina shifted on the couch to face me, her expression incredulous. "This is all so weird, Liza. Your life has turned into some sort of basic cable drama shit. You know the type—bad acting, lots of fake blood, and a plot that thickens with each episode."

I sighed. I couldn't argue with her. The scene outside the door could've been taken straight out of a horror movie. "I know." A pang of guilt speared into my stomach. I had inadvertently dragged her into this mess.

"Did you ever think your life would turn out like this?" she asked.

"Never in my wildest dreams." I shook my head. "But I can't change what's happened, Sabrina. All I can do is try to protect the people I care about."

"Like Ty?" she probed gently, raising an eyebrow.

"Ty has his own share of burdens," I said defensively, feeling a sudden need to protect him as well. "He's trying to do what's best for everyone, even if it means locking up a fellow alpha."

"Does that include you, too, Liza?" Sabrina pressed, her eyes searching mine for answers. "Is he doing what's best for his mate?"

"Of course, he is. You might not see it, but I'm with Ty all the time. He wants nothing more than to protect me, even if that looks like something else to you."

"Promise me something." Sabrina gripped my hand tightly. "Promise me that you won't let this change who you are. You're strong, independent, and you don't need some wolf shifter to protect you."

"I'm not going to change," I promised her, although a part of me wondered if that was even possible anymore. My life had been irrevocably altered, and there was no going back.

My phone buzzed, startling me out of my thoughts, and I reluctantly pulled away from Sabrina to fish it out of my pocket.

"Who is it?" Sabrina asked, concern etched on her face as she sat up straighter.

I scanned the text quickly, feeling my stomach plummet like an anchor thrown overboard. "It's my mom," I said, barely able to get the words out. "She says I need to come home now. It's urgent."

Sabrina's eyes widened with fear, and she gripped my arm tightly. "Liza, you can't leave. It's not safe."

"Look, I don't know what's going on, but if my mom needs me, I have to go." My stomach clenched as I imagined what might be wrong. I was going, come hell or high water.

"Call Dominic. Maybe he can help," Sabrina suggested, her grip on my arm unrelenting.

"Fine." My fingers fumbled with the screen as I nervously dialed Dominic's number. He wasn't exactly someone I'd automatically think of when I needed help, but he lived on the same property and was still the beta of our pack.

He picked up after just two rings. "Hey, Liza. What's going on?"

"Something's wrong at my parents' house," I blurted, trying not to sound as panicked as I felt. "My mom just texted me saying I need to come home right away. It's urgent."

Dominic exhaled sharply, clearly conflicted. "I know Ty doesn't want you leaving the house..."

"Damn it, Dominic," I said, my patience wearing thin. "My mother is telling me to come home, and I'll be damned if I ignore her."

Dominic's silence lasted only a moment before he finally relented. "Fine. But you're not going alone. I'll escort you myself, along with some of your guards." Relief flooded through me, and I thanked him before ending the call.

Sabrina's worried expression made my heart clench. I pulled her into a tight hug. "Stay put, okay? You can help yourself to food in the kitchen or take a long shower upstairs in my room."

She smiled slyly, her eyes twinkling with mischief. "I know what happens in that shower, Liza. I think I'll pass."

I rolled my eyes but was happy to see my friend smiling again. With a final squeeze, I pulled away from Sabrina and made my way to the front door, where Dominic and a group of guards were already waiting.

"Are you sure about this?" Dominic asked as we climbed into a blacked-out SUV.

There was no room for doubt in my mind.

"More than anything. My mom needs me, and that's all there is to it."

"Okay, then. Let's go." Dominic nodded, and the vehicle sped off toward town.

The scenery outside blurred together as we raced to my parents' house. My hands curled into fists, my nails nearly breaking the skin of my palms.

When we finally arrived, I leaped out of the SUV and sprinted up the walkway, barely registering the concerned calls of Dominic and my guards behind me.

An overwhelming dread clawed at my heart as I burst through the front doors. "Mom?" My voice cracked as I called out for her, but there was no reply.

Shaking with fear, I tiptoed through the dimly lit rooms, my pulse beating loudly in my ears.

"Mom!" My hands shook as I tiptoed through the familiar rooms. The eerie quiet that filled the house sent shivers down my spine, my wolf pacing restlessly within me.

And then I found her, my innocent mom, lying on the kitchen floor, blood pooling around her head. I screamed, my heart shattering into a million pieces as I rushed to her side. With dread like I'd never felt before, I placed two fingers on her neck. There was a pulse. She was alive. I shouted for Dominic to call an ambulance.

Gently, I took one of my mom's hands in mine. It seemed so small and frail. A montage played through my mind's eye of all the things she'd done for me: kissing my booboos when I fell, standing beside her in the kitchen covered in flour as we made cookies, helping me get medication to hide the truth of what I was when we discovered I was an omega, her face on my wedding day when she looked on so proud. When I lost my biological mother, I'd been blessed to be given another. A mother of the heart. I didn't think I could survive if I lost her.

I knelt on the floor in her blood and called her name over and over until she finally stirred.

"Liza. Run…" she mumbled weakly, her eyes barely open.

"Mom, what happened?" I begged, tears streaming down my face.

"Run, Liza," she said again. The urgency in her words confused me.

Panic surged within me, but before I could question her, a strange sensation crept over my skin, and my wolf howled inside me, urging me to run. I couldn't leave Mom behind, so I ignored the overwhelming instinct.

"Mom, we've got to get out of here," I said, my voice trembling as I tried to maintain control. My wolf's instincts were screaming at me to protect her, but the human part of me was struggling to understand the seriousness of the situation. I glanced toward the door, expecting to see Dominic charging in to help, but he was nowhere in sight.

"Please, Mom, you need to stand up. We have to leave now." I wrapped an arm around her waist, careful not to hurt her with my strength. With a strained grunt, I managed to pull her up, her legs wobbling beneath her.

"Okay... okay," she said, her face pale and her eyes clouded with pain. She leaned heavily on me as we made our way toward the back door, every step feeling like an eternity.

"Wait, where's Dominic?" I asked, suddenly realizing he hadn't followed me inside. Bile seared my throat as I helped Mom, desperation clawing at me.

When we finally reached the back door, my worst fears were realized. Dominic lay sprawled face-first on the ground, his large frame unnaturally still. My panic surged to an entirely different level.

"Oh, gods!" I cried out. Who in the hell had taken out an ex-alpha?

"Gotcha!" someone sneered from behind me, making me spin around. A man—no, a monster— stood before us, holding a bloody steel bar. His rotten teeth flashed in a sinister grin as he approached, and I instinctively stepped between him and Mom.

"Let's make a deal," he hissed, his eyes gleaming with malice. "You come with me, and I won't hurt anyone else."

"Stay away from her," Mom growled, but her strength was waning, I could see it in her eyes.

"Or what?" Before I could react, he grabbed Mom, pinning her against him with his claws at her throat.

"Please," I begged, clenching my fists at my sides, my wolf snarling within me. "Let her go."

"Come with me, and I promise not to hurt her." A wicked smile played on his lips. "Or anyone else, for that matter."

"Let her go!" I shouted, barely able to contain my fury, but even as I tried to hold back my transformation, my instincts screamed that I had to do something, anything, to protect my mother. At the same time, I didn't want to lose all control and inadvertently harm her.

"Give me one good reason why I should," the man taunted, smirking cruelly as he tightened his grip on Mom.

"Because if you don't, I swear I'll rip your throat out," I warned. It took every ounce of self-control I possessed not to shift right then and there.

"Big words for someone who can't even control her own beast," he sneered, his disgusting breath washing over me like a toxic cloud.

"Let her go," a new voice ordered the man holding my mom hostage. "She's not going to be any trouble. Look at her, she's half-dead already."

"Fine." The man smirked and released her.

"Mom!" I cried out, rushing to catch her before she hit the ground. I was too late. Her limp body hit the ground with a thud.

"See?" the second voice taunted. "No fight left in her. Pathetic."

"Shut up!" I roared. My wolf snarled just beneath the surface of my skin. At that moment, all my restraint vanished. I couldn't hold back any longer. I was going to make them pay for what they'd done. The fucking kidnappers wanted proof that I was different? I'd give them what they wanted.

My fury unleashed as my body shook from unadulterated rage. Before I could transform, a sharp pain lanced through my neck.

A burning sensation coursed through my veins, and the world around me faded into darkness.

# Chapter 31 - Liza

My eyes slowly fluttered open as I tried to make sense of my surroundings. Trying to roll over proved to be much harder than it should have. I shifted from my side to my back, my body unnaturally heavy. What the fuck? Had someone tied weights to my limbs?

I opened my mouth to yell for help, but it was dry and felt like cotton. I pushed myself upright, grunting from the effort. Slowly, I looked around the room. Fuck. The memory of the kidnappers came rushing back. Dominic lying in the grass outside my parents' home, my mom falling to the ground, the fury running through my body like lava erupting from a volcano, and the sharp pain in my neck...

At the thought of it, the delicate skin a few inches below my ear twinged. I reached up and touched the spot, which had formed into a tiny bump. I'd been drugged.

With every ounce of effort, I pushed myself out of the bed and glanced around the room. It didn't look anything like a cell or holding room for a prisoner. The walls were painted a light gray, the ceilings were tall, and a beautiful chandelier hung in the center of the room. The bed was a four-poster, and every bit of fabric was a bright white. There was even framed artwork on the walls.

Where the fuck was I?

I had no memory of someone taking me, and had no clue how long I'd been asleep. My stomach growled, but was that because I'd missed one meal or five?

Rushing to the door, I took hold of the golden knob and tried to turn it. Locked. Why wouldn't it be? I was a fucking prisoner, after all, just in a gilded cage. Staring at the door, I weighed my options. On the one hand, I could shout and scream for help... but who had taken me? And were they the type of person I wanted rushing in the room? Would they torture me in some way? Maybe it was best to stay quiet. It wasn't like they'd forget I was in there, but at least I could let them think I was still unconscious.

Fuck. Wait. Had I already been sold? The room certainly looked like it belonged to someone rich enough to pay the bounty on an omega's head.

My hands clenched into fists as a million scenarios ran through my head. I reached into my back pocket, but they'd taken my cell phone. I closed my eyes, trying to calm myself, but it was too late. I'd already reached the tipping point.

Adrenaline rushed through my body as my emotions got the best of me. I grabbed the dresser and held on as the room shook beneath my feet. I was losing control quickly, and once that train started, there was no stopping it.

A voice in my head said my name. My eyes snapped open. Was I imagining it again?

*"Liza? Liza? Liza?"*

The voice just kept repeating my name over and over again, looking for confirmation that I could hear them.

"Who the fuck are you? What do you want?" My voice came out as a growl, and I glanced in the mirror only to confirm exactly what I'd suspected. My eyes glowed red. My control was slipping away with every passing second.

*"Liza? Listen to me. I need you to calm down."*

I was so far past the tipping point, I'd toppled and gone over. I lost all control over my body. The room shook violently as the black consumed me again.

Printed in Great Britain
by Amazon

40109117R00311